WOLF OF THE NORTHERN STAR

SJ HIMES WRITING AS
SHEENA JOLIE

WOLF OF THE NORTHERN STAR

SJ HIMES WRITING AS
SHEENA JOLIE

Edited by Miranda Vescio
Cover design & interior formatting by Kelley York of Sleepy Fox Studio

Content Advisory: On page recovery from abuse, rape. Mentions of child abuse.

AUTHOR'S NOTE

Any dialogue that appears between two asterisks is telepathic speech.

To my friends, near and far. I miss you.

For Mom. She waited the longest.

This book is also dedicated to everyone looking for a place to belong.

May you find the home of which you dream.

PROLOGUE

A Memory

"THERE IS A LEGEND, MY CUBS, THAT IS OLDER THAN THE WOLFKIN. AT the dawn of mankind, before men learned to build walls with mud and straw, before the first metals were scorched into shape, there was a Power amongst us all. This Power existed within all creation, from the lowliest blade of grass to the mightiest mammoth.

This Power was an entity, what the world would come to call a deity. Before the word goddess was even conceived, She roamed the forests and steppes of the far north, Life and Death walking at her heels, the most devoted of companions. Fierce and deadly as the high winter blizzards and immovable as the glaciers that choked the mountain ranges, She encompassed all that mankind sought to survive.

She watched as humans learned to stand tall, to cover their frail selves with the pelts of their prey, as they conquered fire and chipped away at the ice and snow that covered the world. Always hidden, always observing, she was charmed by the tenacity of this intrepid species. They grew in numbers and spread across the land.

She followed a collection of tribes over time, a group of three clans combined under the leadership of Red Fang Clan. They ignored the warnings of their kin, trekking north, the brightest star in the fiery heavens their guide and new, fertile hunting grounds their hope. The tribe journeyed further than they had intended, to a place unfit for mankind, for even with their fire and stone-shard tipped spears, it was too much for their thin furless skin, blunt nails and teeth. Yet temptation was too great for these hunters, for in the far north, roamed the mighty mammoths, capable of feeding dozens of people from one kill.

And in the north, were the beasts who hunted the mammoths.

Dire wolves, pack hunters that flowed over the steppes in waves of single-minded, predatory determination, relished the incursion into their hunting lands. For these wolves did not see mankind as predators, but as prey. Humans were small and weak, their senses dull, their fires and stone spears easy to avoid. The clans, besieged by these great hunters, fell in ever increasing numbers, until grief affected every family, and the clans were left on the edge of ruin.

A wise man, heavy with the weight of scars and long years, walked one night out into the steppes with hunters from each of the clans. He was the canniest and most experienced hunter of Red Fang, and he walked with the men who would one day lead Red Claw and Bright Moon clans. Three men in total, convinced they had no other option but sacrifice. They went with weary steps, their blood and flesh chilled by the deep winter; they were to die. They were a sacrifice to the Wandering One, the One Who Walked the Trails, the Woman. Only glimpses of this Power had been caught by humans over time, yet they knew, as surely as the sun melted ice and that winter meant Death, that She was out there, and watching.

They went to the steppes alone, expecting to die in a last helpless plea to the Power.

She Who Was watched, curious. Never had humans appealed to Her directly, and that this young species would even be aware of Her in such a manner drew Her near, her curiosity roused.

'Great Mother,' the Red Fang hunter cried into the cold winds, 'spare our kin. The last of our people. Take our flesh, drink our blood, and give our children the strength to survive.'

She came to them, cloaked in starlight and a coat of mist-gray fur. She took the form of those who hunted the humans, and they fell back, certain they were to die. As vast as the sky, tall as the glaciers that swallowed the mountains, Her breath the icy winds that scoured the earth, She eclipsed the night.

'You would die for your people?' She asked them, Her words shaking the ground beneath their feet as the men shook with terror. The oldest hunter met the eyes of the celestial wolf, eyes that blazed brighter than the steadfast star overhead in the night sky.

'Yes,' the Red Fang hunter replied, baring his neck, falling to his knees, his companions following. 'For our children, our mates, we would die. Take our flesh, and spare them. Give them the strength to survive.'

Such bravery was a new concept to Her. She could see fear in the old hunter's heart, but it did not stifle his desire to see his people safe. Selfless and brave, devoted to one another and willing to die for each other, the humans were far more than even She had seen.

It was then, in that moment, my little wolves, that the wolfkin were born. Stirred by the novel idea of sacrifice, She gave to the men instead of taking their lives. In their hearts She saw their greatest fear, and gave it form and flesh.

Pelts and spears became fur coats and fangs; limbs trembling from the arctic chill grew sturdy and sure; claws gripped the frozen tundra and muzzles lifted to the sky, songs spilling from thickly muscled throats. She poured Her will into the men and they became more—they became our forebears, the First Wolves.

The First Wolf, the greatest hunter of Red Fang, grew strong again in body, his spirit matched in flesh. He walked at Her side, listening to Her words on the wind, the songs She sang among the stars and forests. Her words, Her will, his duty and honor to obey. He sought Her guidance, and our people flourished.

The early years of our people are shrouded in mystery and ancient legend—but one thing is certain. Our Great Mother, our Goddess—she walked with us, as one of us, guiding our path and teaching us the ways of our new forms. Her First Wolf lay the foundation for our society. And in those ancient days, the First Wolf became known as the Wolf of the Northern Star. She was a constant, as faithful and static as the unmoving star in the infinite sky. He followed Her as he had once led his people north looking for life and hope.

Wolf of the Northern Star was an honor given to the wolf who walked at Her side, to denote his place, that his words were Hers. As eons passed, and the First Wolf left this mortal coil and his spirit ran free among the stars, his true name long forgotten, the title was eventually returned to the Great Mother, our Goddess. As surely as the northern star burns in the sky above us even now, our Goddess is with us.

She is both the Star that led us to our birth as a people, and the Wolf who guides the clans."

—*From the teachings of Shaman Gray Shadow*

PART ONE

I

THE YOUNG WOLF

HE WOKE QUICKLY, HEART THUMPING, A SHOUT DYING IN HIS THROAT. The room was dark, curtains deepening the already murky shadows that crawled across the bed. He rolled to his feet, the sheets falling away. He shivered, sweat chilling his skin.

The house was quiet. He didn't know why he was awake, or what woke him. A nightmare, perhaps. He recalled a darkness, a deep moonless night, and a whisper in the shadows. Eyes glowing from the dark, and a harsh whisper woke him, the words indistinct but the urgency enough to make him wake, terrified.

The house had been empty since his father disappeared one day, not coming back from work. A few days missing, and nothing. His repeated calls to the labs where his father worked went unanswered, and eventually, the phone calls stopped going through at all. The police came up empty handed. Since he was eighteen, there was nothing they could do for him. He didn't have access to his dad's accounts, the car was gone, and his after-school job was in downtown Augusta. While taking the bus was an option, there was no route nearby where he lived in the suburbs. He couldn't handle the cold very well; he wouldn't survive getting sick if he walked to the nearest bus stop. If the police didn't find his father soon, he didn't know what he was going to do.

He walked out of his room, flicking on the hall light on his way to the bathroom. He paused at a framed paper on the wall.

Dr. Mitchell Harmon graduated with honors with several degrees in genetics and biology, and had a medical degree from some big-name school in Boston. The diplomas lined the wall. There were no family portraits, no smiling faces and cheesy birthday photos. From the sparsity of personal touches, even he had trouble believing anyone lived in this house at all.

He continued down the hall, doing his best to ignore the quiet and solitude. Even if he called Mitchell Harmon his father, he was not all that close to the man who adopted him when he was a toddler, but the emptiness was enough to make him miss the remote and sometimes callous man. He was ill, had been all his life, and having a doctor for an adoptive father was probably why he was still alive. Dr. Harmon was infinitely better than the cold and insidious man he worked for. Just thinking about Simon Remus was enough to make him walk faster.

He reached the bathroom and took care of his needs, washing his hands and then flicking off the light. He paused, thinking he heard something. A thin sound, a whisper of wind? He stepped out into the hall, and took a few steps towards the front door. There it was again, something, a rustle. The wind, it had to be, otherwise there was someone whispering to him through the door.

The door slammed inwards, bright light flared in his eyes, and he screamed, covering his face. Shouts and thuds from many feet assaulted the quiet as he was knocked off his feet. Rough, gloved hands twisted his arms behind his back, and plastic ties went around his wrists. He tried screaming, but a fist knocked into the side of his head, stunning him.

THE WAREHOUSE ECHOED with a ragged scream that escaped from the steel crate when it was jostled, the large metal box raking along the inside of the moving van. The cry was shrill and piercing, and made Simon's head hurt. This was the last van, several others carrying out the rest of the specimens earlier in the night.

Simon winced, wishing the sedative could be stronger to silence the occupant, but a higher concentration would leave the specimen comatose, not to mention the silver poisoning degrading blood samples. Simon moved away, watching as the warehouse was systematically emptied, his soldiers removing all traces of the experiments and test subjects. The scientists and doctors were already moved to the new secret location, and he would start over. With Dr. Harmon now an unwilling guest of the werewolves, he had no doubt Harmon would spill the truth about the locations of his labs. And Roman McLennan was by no means a loyal beast.

His heart raced thinking about the monster that, for the last twenty years, had conspired with the Remus family to exploit the werewolves' abilities. The last time he saw Roman was when the beast was fresh from forcing himself on Simon, leaving him naked, bloody, and fueled by rage and shame.

And lust.

His body thrummed, the bite mark on his neck sore and throbbing, and Simon remembered the weight of the werewolf on top of him, spreading his legs wide, fucking him like his bitch, making Simon whine and whimper for mercy...and for more. His body wanted Roman, ached for him, despite the humiliation and damage to his physical self. His mind was left in shambles.

Every night he dreamed of that beast. Heard him whispering in his ear, his malicious laugh and savage growls, felt his hard body holding him down. He woke hard and leaking, and it took only a few strokes before he blew, shuddering in a climax unlike anything he'd ever felt.

"Mr. Remus?" Simon turned to the head of security, the man was in tactical gear and carrying a weapon across his chest. Simon banished the visions of Roman's body and the blood smeared sheets, focusing on the guard. "Sir, the specimens have been evacuated. The remaining werewolves loyal to McLennan have been sent forward to the new site. The compound is scrubbed."

"How many of Roman's wolves returned?" Simon asked, eyeing the shadows warily. He had never been on the best of terms with the rough and vile creatures that Roman combed from the clans over the years, and without Roman around to keep the survivors in check, he had no trust in them at all.

"Three came back from the aborted mission in Baxter, sir," the security chief replied, hands tightening around his weapon. Simon wasn't the only one who distrusted the werewolves. "I don't think they're going to be much use, scraggly, whipped runts that they are."

"If they give you any trouble, shoot them," Simon ordered.

"Understood, sir."

Simon forgot what he wanted to say next, an image of Roman pushing into his thoughts, distracting him, making his heart race.

"Bring my car around, after I've left, do one last sweep," Simon said, voice hoarse and words short of breath. He coughed, then spoke louder. "Once the premises are clear, detonate the charges."

"Yes, sir." The other man nodded, and Simon snorted, practically seeing the man's desire to salute him. Military men had habits of a lifetime drilled into them, adjusting to civilian trappings was difficult, even for men with dishonorable discharges…which is why so many of them took the chance to work for him.

The soldier left, Simon walked out of the building, heading for his limo as it pulled up in front of him. Another soldier got out and held the door for him, and he slid in the back.

Simon sent a glance at the huddled figure on the far rear-facing seat, covered in thick wool blankets and silver chains. Not even a rattle to distinguish if the creature was even alive, but Simon wasn't worried. Dr. Harmon's one pathetic success was still unconscious. Simon smirked. The silver chains were unnecessary, but his guards insisted.

"Take me to the new site," Simon ordered as the limo pulled away.

His experiments would continue. He would fulfill his government contracts, harness the power of alpha and shaman, and mankind would finally have the weapons needed to eradicate the werewolf abomination from their world. Part of the puzzle lay quietly a few feet away, and one day he would learn how to unlock the secrets of the wolfkin.

The company his brother started, and Simon took over, would eventually be able to name its price in all endeavors. And no one would tell him no.

Snow fell, the quiet streets of Augusta empty at this hour. Tomorrow the news would report a gas leak and the explosion of an empty warehouse in the industrial district with zero casualties.

PAIN WOKE HIM. That and the cold, damp floor under his cheek. He tried moving his arms, they stung as if he'd lost circulation. He groaned when he pushed them under his chest, sitting upright slowly. He blinked, and sat back against cold metal bars that glimmered in the low light.

Metal shackles clinked from each wrist. A metal chain connected his wrists, the links a smooth, heavy metal that shined like the bars.

He was in a cage. A cage, and he was naked and wearing chains. His heart pounded, cold sweat clammy across his body, terror filling every shallow breath.

"Don't get worked up, human." A whisper from his left. He turned his head, and there was another cage. A shadow hunkered down in the dark, he thought he saw the glow from a pair of eyes that flickered. "You cannot withstand the cold as we can. Save your energy for staying warm."

"What...what's going on? Why..." He gasped, a whole-body shudder rolling through him. He grabbed the bars next to him, holding on.

"I can't tell you why," the shadow growled. "Far as I can tell, you're human. You don't smell like wolfkin. The bars and chains are silver, and they aren't burning your skin. What Remus wants with a human, and measly, scrawny, sick one at that, is anyone's guess. Did you piss the monster off?"

His mind was spinning. He didn't understand anything, least of which was why his father's boss would kidnap him and throw him into a cage naked. He grasped onto what he could, and stammered out, "Wolfkin?"

The shadow leaned forward. Eyes glowing with a fierce inner light, and elongated, sharp teeth peeked over the man's thin, wide lips; his mouth oddly shaped. Thick brown fur grew along his cheekbones and down his neck to his shoulders. "Aye, little human. Wolfkin. Your kind might call us werewolves."

He screamed, the sound thin and full of terror. His eyes rolled back in his head as he fainted.

2

WHAT THE GREAT MOTHER DECREES

CAIUS OPENED THE DOOR, THE WIND HOWLING AND SHARP AS IT TORE through his clothes. The evening sun was long hidden behind the deep gray clouds, twilight losing its grip as the hour sped toward full darkness. He could see, the gifts of his kind allowing him to navigate where humans would be handicapped by the deepening shadows.

He walked down the path, the White Wolf's cabin soon disappearing at his back as he wound his way along the mountainside, taking the route to the visitors' cabins further back among the trees. Ice crackled under his feet, his boots snapping the thin layers covering the gravel and stones. Any wolfkin in the area would hear him coming. Hiding his approach to where his new-found grandson and Caius' Heir were staying was impossible once he took the final bend in the path to the cabins. There were several cabins along this path, some as old as the park itself, some far older than even that. He reached the blown out and blackened shell of one cabin, and he paused for a second, taking in the scent of sulfur and soot. This was the place bombed last week by one of the traitors at his son's insistence. Claire, daughter of Andromeda, nearly killed Caius' son, Heir, grandson, his Clan's Speaker, and his Heir's First Beta. All for the unrequited love of another of Caius's worthless sons.

Caius snorted in displeasure, and took the path deeper into the snow-covered trees. Spring was only a few weeks away, but winter in Maine was unrelenting, the temperatures hovering below freezing and snow coming at least once a day. The last heavy storm happened just hours before

Caius and his fellow Greater Clan Leader, Heromindes, arrived in Baxter last week. It was that same storm that covered the attack of Roman's misfit band of traitors and Simon Remus' group of mercenaries. Luckily Kane, his Heir, had his tactical team already in place in Baxter, and they defeated the humans at the park gates. Andromeda easily and quickly took out Roman, Caius' son and the great traitor they'd been searching for for twenty years, and Luca… Ghost…took care of the exiled traitors, deep in the woods.

Caius and Heromindes, along with Hero's cousin Gabriel, under the watchful eye of Andromeda, had gone the evening after the battles to see the killing ground in the woods. Gabriel recounted, in halting words and averted eyes, the tale of how they'd been ambushed by unknown wolves, and Luca, who now went by Ghost, killed the ambushers in a storm of lightning that came from the air around them. Gabe told them all, disbelief and some fear building in their expressions, how the lightning *avoided* touching Gabe and Gerald, instead dancing around and through the attackers. Burnt and decimated corpses littering the ground gave credence to Gabe's tale, the scorched earth and fire-damaged trees were an indicator of just how much power was unleashed. An astronomical amount of shamanic magic had left several wolfkin nothing but ashes, charred flesh and bones, in a matter of seconds.

Caius stopped, just in view now of the cabin where Kane and Ghost had been holed up the last few days. Ghost flat-out refused to allow Kane to remain under guard in the cellars of Andromeda's cabin where Roman was currently being held, and Caius privately agreed. Whatever discontent lay in his heart towards his oh-so-perfect heir, Caius did not believe that Kane forced a bonding upon Ghost. Their gift, the one they shared, did not work on shamans. And regardless of what Heromindes thought, no matter of proper training or technique was responsible for the shamans' immunity to the Voice; that was a gift they were born with, that flowered when they came into their roles as keepers of the faith and the magics of their kind. Kane was innocent of using the Voice to force Ghost into a bonding, and Caius had seen a few soulbonds in his long life. He knew the difference between a regular mating bond, a forced bond, and the even rarer soulbond.

The most recent soulbond he saw was that between his late daughter, Marla, and the long-missing son of Gray Shadow, Josiah.

Just thinking about Marla and Gray Shadow in the same thought was enough to make his heart pound painfully, his eyes shutting as he clenched his fists and fought back the tears. His daughter was dead. And Gray Shadow…. his heart was long dead, too, no matter how strongly it beat in his chest.

He blinked back tears, refusing to give into the pain, but what he saw when he looked again at the cabin was enough to stagger him.

The pair silhouetted in the big window in front of the cabin made his heart pound even harder. The large alpha was curled around the smaller shaman protectively, care and affection in every long line of Kane's body. Pain tore at Caius, the image enough to pull up long-denied memories of another place and time, of a hidden glen in the Old World, where two young male wolfkin first found love of their own.

A love that back then meant death. And it was a similar love that now threatened the life of his Heir and his grandson.

"WHAT IS IT, little wolf?" Kane asked, powerful hands coming around his naked waist and a pair of soft, warm lips kissing his bare shoulder. Ghost leaned back into Kane's heat, enjoying the warmth of his mate's smooth skin on his back.

"Grandpa Caius is outside, and he's just staring at us," Ghost replied, not really caring what his grandfather was doing in that moment, since Kane's hands were wandering south and finding interesting places to stroke and squeeze.

Well, they had been.

Kane straightened and put his hands back on Ghost's waist, and Ghost sighed in frustration. Hiding away with Kane in their cabin while they waited for something called the Tribunal to happen was, to Ghost at least, a respite from the stares and whispers from Red Fern wolves. The cloying worry from the Black Pine members who tried their best not to let Kane or Ghost go anywhere alone, as if they would be attacked, was equally frustrating. And perhaps they might be, if Roman weren't locked up, Claire under guard, and Simon Remus confirmed to be living very publicly in a faraway place called Augusta. The human doctor Kane knocked unconscious at the gates was under guard as well, and Ghost would stay far away from that man, considering the only time they'd met Ghost was nearly incapacitated by drugs and his human packmates were almost murdered.

The Red Fern patrols had caught the scents of several wolves that came a short distance into the park. They were unable to find traces after the storm swept through, erasing any signs of where the strangers may have gone, or their identity. Andromeda was of the opinion they were the remnants of Roman's wolves, and Ghost agreed. He caught sight of them occasionally when he lay in bed at night using his Spiritsight, seeing how far he could reach with his ability. Little stars, sickly in muted shades of color and light, flickered here and there amongst the slumbering pines, but they quickly faded away, lost in the subtle glow of life in Baxter.

"Get dressed, Ghost," Kane said, stepping back, reaching for his sweats that lay across the couch where they had been thrown earlier when Kane was teaching him what he meant exactly by rimming. "I think he wants to talk to us, and doesn't want to see his grandson naked with another man."

Ghost peered back at the lonely figure standing silently in the shadows while random snowflakes fell around it. Impatience was not what Ghost saw in the Clan Leader's body. That was pain, but not the kind caused by physical injury. It was a pain Ghost saw in the older wolves, a pain that seemed as old and original as the mysterious lilts in their voices. For some reason, Ghost knew that Caius carried that pain with him every day of his life, and from his own memories, the Alpha's pain was there for longer than Ghost had been alive. Kane's few words over the last few days about Caius and his demeanor was enough to cement Ghost's suspicion that Caius carried an old wound in his heart.

What pain predated the loss of his grandfather's best friend, daughter, and grandchildren?

"Pants, now," Kane said with a grin as he smacked Ghost's ass. Ghost jumped, mock snarling at his mate, catching one-handed the cotton pants tossed his way.

Caius was walking up the path now, and Ghost pulled on pants just as the greater alpha reached the door. Kane opened it before the clan leader knocked, the Heir stepping back with a respectful nod as Caius entered. Caius gave Kane the barest flicker of his dark eyes, taking in

Kane's half-naked state before zeroing in on Ghost. His grandfather's regard was searching, seeming to miss nothing, but he let the inspection slide off him, as impacting on his nerves as leaves falling over his furred back in autumn. Caius was at times stern and remote, then he would see moments of pain in his dark eyes. Eyes, now that Ghost was looking at them directly, that were much like Kane's. Wondering at that for a moment, Ghost gave his grandfather a small smile in welcome.

"Hello, Grandpa Caius," Ghost said, and Caius gave a him a slight twitch of his lips, as if being called grandpa was unusual in some way for the older wolf. Perhaps it was, since from what his Uncle Gerald told him of his family, none of Caius' other grandchildren were left in Black Pine, the rest choosing to leave after the tragedy almost fifteen years prior. Gerald, Kane, and now Ghost, were the only kin Caius had left in Black Pine territory.

"Hello, Luca, Kane," Caius said, tone quiet, but power rumbled under the surface of his words. Ghost arched a brow and smiled when Kane huffed in small irritation at Caius' use of his old name. Caius frowned, but stepped further inside, letting Kane shut the door. Caius was wearing nothing but boots, a thin shirt, and dark blue denim pants, snow had collected on his lower legs from the blowing drifts. Their kind were rarely bothered by the elements. Older, more powerful wolfkin like Andromeda could withstand arctic temperatures in nothing but thin layers.

"Have a seat, please," Kane gestured to the small kitchen table, and Caius nodded, somehow now at a loss for words. He sat in one of the two chairs at the table, while Kane took the other. Ghost prowled around the outside of the room, the kitchen area and the living room one open space in the front section of the cabin. Caius watched him, as did his mate, but Ghost was more interested in the shifting dynamic between the two greater alphas.

Caius was exhausted, worn down by that old injury on his soul that Ghost could sense. Yet the Clan Leader was powerful; his sorrow and grief didn't diminish his strength at all. The way he moved, the play of muscles under his shirt and across his tall frame, communicated quite clearly that Caius was still a wolfkin male in his prime.

Ghost turned his attention to his mate. Kane was as tall and powerfully built as Caius, and the vitality and subconscious confidence that poured from him was both unsettling and reassuring. Lesser wolves moved around Kane like a river would a mountain; in some few, he drew them in as a moth to flame. He'd asked Kane about it, and all his mate would say was that it was the charm of an alpha—they either frightened or appealed to the wolves under their care. Ghost remembered as a child how he was drawn to Kane, wanting the older male's eyes on him, smiling at him in approval and affection, and a part of him understood what Kane meant.

Side by side, the two alphas were similar yet vastly different, dark haired, dark colored eyes, golden skin. Caius spoke with an accent, and the longer he spoke, the more obvious it grew. Kane had no accent, aside from something Cat, his human beta packmate, said was a New England drawl. Ghost had no idea what that meant at all, and just nodded at his human, while Glen, his human alpha, laughed fondly at his mate.

Kane was young by wolfkin standards, forty-four years of age, and from what he'd picked up in the last week or so from the betas of Red Fern, Kane was one of the youngest Clan Heirs in the world. Burke, another greater alpha and Kane's lieutenant and the Black Pine Speaker, wasn't much older at forty-nine years of age. Caius was old—so old that he'd come over from the Old World, leading the Great Exodus of wolfkin clans over two hundred years before. Ghost knew, from the thrumming power in the older wolfkin's soulstar, that his grandfather was far older than even that historical marker. Caius was ancient, though Ghost had a feeling he was not as old as the formidable leader of Red Fern, the only female Clan Leader in the world, the female beta known as the White Wolf. Andromeda was an old friend of Caius'—she, Caius and Gray Shadow, Ghost's other grandfather, had long been a triad of superior strength, bound by iron-clad ties of friendship and a mysterious history.

One that was now strained by the loss of Gray Shadow in an act of betrayal nearly fifteen years prior. Ghost could see, could sense, the ache and the horrific loss of the venerated shaman in Caius—it was a loss of love and companionship that Caius carried with him still. And it had warped his emotions to such a degree that Ghost was learning to hear past the words he spoke, listening instead to the true emotions underneath. Caius was a wounded animal in so many ways, and he was in denial in regard to what that pain was doing to him.

Caius was on the edge of ruin, his future clouded by grief and pain.

"What can we do for you, Sir?" Kane asked, and Ghost pulled himself from his observations. Kane and Caius faced each other across the table, both males' expressions closed off, thoughts hidden. Ghost sensed wary curiosity from Kane, and from Caius, that same tired pain, but now it was layered beneath the stony resolve of what Ghost reasoned was the mantle of leadership.

"Decisions need to be made," Caius began, fingers of his right hand idly scratching the table top. "About many things. Some are more urgent than others, but we are out of time, so choices must be made now."

"Out of time?" Ghost asked, tilting his head to one side, eyes locked on his grandfather. He paused, seeing the minute tension around Caius' eyes, the way he held his shoulders. A faint whisper threaded through the air in the silence between them, and Ghost listened. Wordless, yet still conveying a sense of urgency. Kane reacted, though he hid it well, and Caius showed no sign of having heard the whisperer. "Someone is coming. Someone or something is coming, and you wish to act before you can't anymore."

"Damn shamans," Caius grumbled, exasperated, but without malice. Caius gave him a narrow-eyed glare, and Ghost grinned in response. He was not intimidated in the least by his grandfather, though everyone else treated him with caution.

"Who is coming, Sir?" Kane asked, maintaining his respectful composure. Caius gave Ghost one more glance, then returned his attention to his heir.

"The first members of the Tribunal are arriving soon. I just got word that Greater Clan Leaders from Dread Claw, Birch Grove, and Red Wraith Clans are arriving, as early as tomorrow. They will be bringing honor guards and some of their advisors." Caius' words were calm, but the tension around his frame was telling.

"You mean they're bringing in greater alphas," Kane said, mouth in a grim line. "An honor guard is easily six greater alphas, and that's per Clan Leader."

"Yes."

"Why not the Clan Leaders alone? Why honor guards? What were they told when notified of Heromindes' request for a Tribunal?" Kane was angry, each word layered in frustration. "These clans are our allies, and they've never traveled across borders in such numbers outside of a gathering!"

"If they are allies, why are you angry?" Ghost asked, interrupting before Caius could speak. He paced forward, yet skirted around the table, eyes locked on Caius. His grandfather, for all their blood connection, was still an alpha. Ghost respected his power, yet was not afraid of it—but he would also stay out of reach. Older wolves in the wild would snarl and snap at younger, impetuous younglings. Not that he expected such from Caius, but caution was wise.

Kane made a noise in his throat, half-strangled snort and half a sigh. Ghost gave his mate a quick grin but went back to watching Caius. "Why are you angry at those you would call friend?"

"Luca—," Caius began, Ghost quirked a brow at his grandfather, who shook his head and corrected himself when he spoke again. "Ghost, they are bringing honor guards. Almost twenty greater alphas who do not answer to me, in the company of my peers. In a gathering, there are many greater alphas, but also a hundred times more betas to temper the imbalance of power that results when greater alphas congregate in too large of a group."

"What he means, little wolf, is that there is potential for aggression, fighting, frayed tempers, and extreme violence. Red Fern is all betas, but they are not enough to even out the rough nature of so many dominant personalities in one space, especially if the situation is tense already," Kane said, reaching out for Ghost, taking his hand. "I don't think the clan leaders would bring wolfkin guards with control issues, but we see problems like this during gatherings, too. Better to be prepared."

"Andromeda reigns in Baxter," Ghost stated, squeezing Kane's hand but still watching Caius. "She will allow no violence to spill out amongst her clan." Of that, Ghost was certain. She would never allow her people, her family, to be in danger. Andromeda was power and authority personified—she was the White Wolf, clan leader to the core. For a female, unheard of—for a beta, even more so. Though Ghost had his doubts about her beta status. "And why tense—because Kane is charged with blasphemy?"

Caius blanched at the word, and Kane's hand tightened on his, almost painfully. Andromeda came to them the day before, warning Kane of the pending charges of blasphemy. Apparently, the clan leaders, Heromindes leading the way, discussed the bond between Ghost and Kane and decided Kane was guilty of two violations of Law in one occurrence—using the

Voice to force a mating bond on a shaman.

"Yes, because of the charge of blasphemy," Caius said, a subtle growl in his voice. "It is almost unheard of for that charge to be levied against any wolfkin, much less an heir to a clan. We have so few religious Laws."

"I don't understand," Ghost said, brows lowered, biting his lip. He sent Kane a searching glance, then looked back to Caius. "Kane's thoughts give me the meaning of the word, but the…concept? The concept is hard for me to understand. We are soulbonded, and She made it so. That has always been a sacred gift. Always."

"They doubt that we share a soulbond, my love," Kane told him, tugging on his hand and making him look down. Kane gave him a half-smile, a twist to his full lips that spoke of anger and some odd pain. "Heromindes, whether through bruised pride and fear, or ignorance, believes I have forced my gift upon you. I used the Voice against him in Worcester, and he cannot fathom how an untrained whelp of nineteen could withstand me. He leads the others in their mindset—there cannot be a soulbond between us, because I am alpha and you are shaman."

"I see our bond with every glance of my Spiritsight," Ghost replied, leaning on Kane's shoulder, speaking now to his mate, his grandfather forgotten for the moment. "Every touch we share, every time we have sex, it grows stronger. We're almost one soul now. How can they not see it?"

Ghost knew other wolfkin could sense the bond between them. They may not be able to see it, as he could, but their mental abilities gave them the ability to recognize a mated wolfkin. Some were better at it than others, and surely a clan leader would have the experience and skills to understand the bond between he and Kane.

"A soulbond is incredibly rare, Ghost," Caius said, leaning back in his seat, the chair creaking. "Last count, there was only a dozen soulbonds scattered between the clans. There's just over two hundred clans across the whole world. Hundreds of thousands of wolfkin, and only twelve pairs. Well, thirteen, now. There is only one other wholly male pairing, but those two wolfkin are a beta and an alpha, not alpha and shaman."

"So, because our Great Mother has only gifted twelve pairs before us, that rarity makes our bond less likely?" Ghost was fed up. He growled, a soft rumble in his chest. This was not the welcome home he'd dreamed of when he was trapped in his wolf-form lost in the North. Though then, he'd been worried his people wouldn't want him because he was defective and Gray Shadow died saving his life, but now it seemed they did want him, just not bonded to Kane.

How was their pairing wrong?

"Ghost, it'll be alright," Kane said, his free hand rubbing over Ghost's stomach in soothing circles. Ghost rarely felt his temper slip free from his usual calm, but it was escaping his control now. Last time he got this vexed he tore apart an ugly couch back at the sanctuary, but he was a man now, he didn't think his mate or the White Wolf would appreciate him destroying furniture.

"Then we prove we are bonded," Ghost said decisively. "Show them the truth, and they must leave us be."

Caius sighed and shook his head, and Kane hugged him even as he frowned. Ghost could see the doubt and the underlying worry that weighed down both alphas' shoulders, but he had an unshakeable faith in his soulbond with Kane and the support of the deity who created it. They would be fine.

3

CAGED

Ghost left the cabin, leaping from the front stoop. Paws sank in the fresh snow cover when he landed, puffs of flakes kicking up behind him as he ran through the trees. The sun was bright, the sky cloudless, the mountain air was harsh, clean, and searing, and his blood felt electrified.

Kane was back in the cabin, still talking to Caius. All night long, and for most of the morning, the alphas bickered, plotted, and conjectured, driving Ghost to lose what tolerance he had for endless what-ifs and maybes. He'd given up trying to follow along. He was still not used to having conversations and talking to others, no matter the species, and his habit of getting up and leaving when he was bored was rude, or so said Cat and Glen. Having manners was another thing he wasn't used to at all.

Being a wolfkin man was harder than he thought it would be…being a wolf was easy. Hunt, run, play, sleep, repeat. No arguments and veiled frustrations, no seething resentments and fractured trust. There was dominance to determine in packs, but such events were about willpower and strength, and wolves settled in naturally and with no resentments once the hierarchy was determined. Laws did not exist; religion did not exist. There was a type of faith, but it was less defined, with no rules attached except that all creatures must eat, and some will be eaten. Some will lead, and some will follow. Each creature to its own nature, and none to say, or even think, that one way was not the right way, or that another was wrong. Such concepts did not exist. Barring illness, animals truly did not care.

Ghost headed up the mountain, away from the cabins and park center. The scents of other wolfkin faded away and the trees thinned out the higher he climbed. *Little wolf?*

I am well, my mate, Ghost whispered to Kane, his alpha's worry a slight sting upon his conscience. He had left without a word, stripping his human clothing and running for the door, shredding frustrations as he shed his human form in a rush of silver-white energy. Kane had called after him, but thankfully his mate did not follow him. He needed some time alone.

Kane sent back a wordless mental caress of affection, receding from Ghost's higher mind, their bond still intact in the recesses of his brain. Kane was an anchor, a touchstone, and was always with him.

Ghost continued to run, his body flowing over rocks and snow, the wind cutting through his thick gray coat in random gusts. His heart thudded with his race, blood roared through his ears, the sunny sky blinding him as he reached the scraggy peak.

Ghost took in the world once his eyes adjusted. Mountains dipped and swelled in all directions, black pines blocking out great swaths on steep inclines, the valleys dark even in the daylight, and he could see the mirror bright surface of the river as it wound through Baxter. Below him was the park center, and the wolves of Red Fern who kept the park. Red Fern maintained the illusion that only human caretakers for the state park resided in Baxter. Ghost had been here before, as a child, though he had never seen Baxter like this—a wilderness, a rare, almost untouched sanctuary for his kind. Humans came here only during the summer months, and every step they took was watched.

He was no longer alone. He was surrounded by hundreds of his kind, with more to come any day now, and his humans, Glen and Cat, were down there in the valley, too. Ghost was soulbonded and mated to a fine alpha, and he knew happiness. He wasn't alone—so why did he feel like he was?

Ghost threw himself down on a wind-cleared boulder, head on his paws, and tried his best to let it all go—worry, doubt, frustration. Such emotions clouded his thoughts. They were stronger now that he could find his human form, every day he spent as a man instead of wolf changed him and the way he thought. He was thankful, yet part of him didn't want to change. Such a short time with his kith and kin and Ghost was coming to believe the wolfkin were closer to humans than even they believed. While Cat and Glen were kind, smart, and accepting, Ghost knew most humans were not as special as his packmates. His humans went from believing him to be a rather strange and unusual wolf to accepting him as a sentient being that could use magic with very little trouble. Ghost was thankful for this—his humans were explorers of knowledge, and spent more time amongst wolves than their own species; Ghost had a feeling that was part of their ability to accept him and his kind as easily as they had. Other humans would not be so accepting—from his memories as a child of being hunted and his family being attacked by mercenaries to the times Ghost could accompany Cat into town and his exposure to humans that way, Ghost was sure most humans would react badly were they to ever meet a wolfkin and learn their nature.

The wolfkin he'd met since his return were either the paramount example of their kind—Kane and Andromeda—or were all too human in their faults, like Claire and Roman. He had a feeling most of the wolfkin fell in the middle, and a part of him mourned the loss of his naïve opinions of his own people. He was happy to be home, but he was also grieving.

Where were the wolfkin of myth and legend, the selfless hunters and guardians who held the wellbeing of their people above all things?

The sun warmed him despite the wind, and his eyes began to drift, heavy. He curled up tighter, tucked his nose under his bushy tail, giving into the desire to sleep. He dozed.

In his dream, he was no longer on the mountain. Darkness clouded his thoughts, indistinct figures moved in the shadows, voices were familiar but the names of those who spoke were just out of reach. There was a figure huddled, misery etched in every muscle and across his shadowed face, but Ghost thought he was young. His view changed, twisted, and in the darkness a small black and red mass glimmered, as if floating in water, bobbing gently in an unseen current. He tried to get closer, to see what the mysterious thing was, but all he could hear was a beating heart and the sound of crying. His heart ached, and he wished for the mountainside with its clean, cold wind.

The dream changed, and he settled, the disturbing images receding.

He lost track of time, the sun moving in the sky, and the angle was lower when he blinked himself awake. Fingers drifted through the fur on the top of his head, down his neck into the thick ridge that covered his shoulders, digging deep, scratching. Ghost shook his head, ears flapping, and stretched out under the kind fingers that chased nascent itches down his spine and back up. He grumbled, rolling to his back, clever fingers scratching his tummy. He almost fell off the boulder, flipping himself back to his stomach to regain his balance.

A deep, throaty chuckle made him lift his head to see Kane smiling down at him. "Enjoy your nap, little wolf?"

The wind lifted Kane's long dark hair from his shoulders; his mate wore only a thin t-shirt and dark jeans with heavy boots at the end of long, thickly muscled legs. The sun gilded Kane's features, darkening his already golden skin tone. His mate's beauty stirred his heart and body, waking him completely. Ghost whimpered happily, and jumped up, licking Kane across the nose. "Hey, now! Watch it!"

Kane laughed, pushing him away. Ghost jumped from the rock, yipping in excitement. He could sense a darkening on the distant horizon, change was coming, but now, in this instant, he would banish worry with joy. Kane chased him through the snow, with the wind having scoured most of it away at this height they were well matched. Ghost was fast, whipping about in the smallest of margins, nipping at Kane's heels then running away. Kane's reach was long, and his fingers tugged on Ghost's tail as he ran around his mate in a mad dash. Kane lobbed snowballs at him, Ghost caught them in his teeth, smashing the clumps to bits before running again.

Kane tackled him when he dared get too close, and they tumbled head over tail into a deep drift on the leeward side of a tall boulder, cut off from the wind. Ghost shivered in happiness when Kane wrapped his long arms around his neck and shoulders, squeezing him tight to his chest.

"You are glorious, little wolf," Kane murmured in his ear, breath making his ear twitch. Ghost heaved a great sigh, and snuggled deeper into his mate's embrace.

He sent back a wordless burst of emotion, full of every shred of happiness and joy he could muster at how it felt to be held and adored by his wonderful alpha mate. Kane was perfect. Surely, he knew that.

"Not so perfect," Kane chuckled, sensing his thoughts. Kane kissed the top of his head. "I wish we could stay here all day, the world at our feet, but the Clan Leaders are going to be here soon. Caius wants us back at Andromeda's."

Ghost sat up and Changed, his form dissolving into a small storm of silver-white energy, rearranging his body at the barest of thoughts before reforming. He sat as a man on Kane's lap, the cold air chilling his naked skin. Kane smiled, and cuddled him closer.

"I would yell at you for Changing without clothes on if I thought the cold bothered you at all," Kane said with a small smile, dark eyes twinkling. "But watching you do that leaves me in awe."

Ghost tilted his head curiously at his mate, thoughts divided between the approaching arrival of the wolfkin who would determine his mate's fate and the stray thought that the way he Changed was unusual. "Does no other shaman Change as I do? I managed it when I was five—I can't be the only one."

"Not everyone had the great Shaman Gray Shadow show them to their wolf-form in such a manner either, little wolf," Kane replied, brushing the back of his fingers along Ghost's cheek. "Per Shaman River, the First Wolves Changed as you do, but until now, that was only considered legend. But enough history—we need to get back."

Kane stood, even with Ghost on his lap, and Ghost let himself drop away landing on all fours in the snow, Kane laughing at his instantaneous Change back to wolf.

Kane took off at an easy lope, his long legs devouring the ground at a fast clip. Ghost ran at his mate's side, content to match the speed Kane set in his human form. His mate was a big man, though more lean than bulky, his body one long line of carved muscle and predatory grace.

Instead of heading back to the cabin they shared, Kane diverted their path toward Andromeda's cabin, the huge wooden structure on a small plateau that overlooked the majority of the park center. It was a good distance away from the other cabins, the closest building being the stone council house. Memories haunted the mountainside, Gray Shadow a near constant in Ghost's recollections.

Kane knocked snow from his boots before opening the front door of Andromeda's cabin and striding inside, holding the door for Ghost. He Changed as soon as he entered, grabbing a set of sweats from the short bench next to the door. Spare clothing was left beside doorways for wolfkin to use. Nudity wasn't an issue for Ghost, though his mate didn't like other wolfkin seeing his bare form, so he tugged on the pants, leaving off the top. He still disliked wearing a shirt, the sensation of anything around his neck making him twitch.

A gasp just down the hall made Ghost look up, and the elastic waistband of the pants snapped across his hip bones as a small beta female blushed and looked down at the floor. She was young, a girl on the cusp of adulthood, and she snuck a glance at Kane before darting off down the hall, her giggles echoing off the walls. Ghost laughed, enjoying the ruddy hue on his mate's cheeks.

"I warned you about making Helen fall in love with you, Kane, though I may need to extend that warning to our young shaman," a husky voice said, and Ghost smiled at Andromeda as she joined them in the foyer. The elegant female clan leader was dressed in her customary cotton sheath that covered her shoulders and fell to her knees, this time a soft dove gray that accentuated her glacial-blue eyes and blonde hair. Golden highlights shimmered in the light from the large front windows. "Nursing a youngling through a broken heart is difficult, no matter how many times I've done it."

Her smile put aside any worries he might have that Andromeda was upset, and Ghost walked alongside Kane as she gestured them into the kitchen and attached dining room. Caius was there, sitting not at the head of the table but to the left, letting the White Wolf retain that honor. Ghost sat beside Kane across from his grandfather as others came into the room. Gerald, Ghost's uncle and Caius' only son remaining in Black Pine territory, came in with Sophia, Kane's First Beta and Burke, Black Pine's Speaker.

Sophia was short and trim, leanly muscled and one of the older wolves in the room. Shoulder length black hair and dark green-brown eyes complimented her golden skin, and she moved like the predator she was. From listening to the male wolfkin of Red Fern and the assorted wolves from Black Pine, Sophia was very attractive, though Ghost was confused by the measure applied to the females that determined beauty. He saw strength and capability, and admired the female beta, though his blood was not roused by her. Many of the male wolfkin present responded to Sophia to some degree, blood heating at an appreciative level. All but Caius, Burke, and Kane sent Sophia heated glances, though no one said anything to her at all. Sophia was a dangerous creature, her gender was in no way a handicap. In fact, his Uncle Gerald watched her even now, though his eyes darted away from her face before she noticed. His uncle often stared at Sophia with an awed expression, his scent giving away his fascination.

Burke winked at Ghost when he sat down, and Ghost grinned back at the bigger alpha. Burke was Kane's lieutenant, best friend, and served as the Speaker for Black Pine. When the day came that Kane was clan leader, Burke would be his second. Burke was built much like Kane, the two alphas alike enough to be mistaken as siblings. Burke smiled more often than Kane, and his emotions were easily discerned in his expressions and eyes. Burke was phenomenally powerful, his gift of command—what Ghost had heard Cat call telepathy—was so strong he could mentally communicate simultaneously with dozens of wolves, maintaining mind links to so many wolves that, if another alpha were to try, their mind would collapse under the strain. Burke's ability made him Black Pine's Speaker, a role that was rare, even among greater alphas. Only a handful of clans on the continent could boast having a wolfkin they could call a Speaker; Kane had admitted with a rueful smile that Burke was courted by other clan leaders on a regular basis at gatherings.

Gerald gave Ghost a tight, small smile, but the warmth in the dour alpha's eyes made Ghost smile in return. The heavy cloud of depression and bitter anger than hovered over his uncle was dissipating, slowly but surely, Ghost knew it was due to Kane's influence. Gerald had been given to Kane under his authority as a greater alpha and Black Pine's tactical team leader, and the change in Gerald was obvious. Even as the lesser alpha scowled and grumbled, his step was lighter and he tried to talk instead of growl. The way he followed Kane's lead, without hesitation or petulance, showed his change of allegiance quite clearly. Caius had said little to his own son, instead watching how his heir and his son interacted, a small frown furrowing his brow.

Andromeda's children, some older than Sophia and some as young as Ghost, helped carry in food from the adjoining kitchen. Platters of meat, sandwich bread, and other assorted foods made up their midday meal, and Ghost watched happily as Kane set a roast beef sandwich on his plate before making another sandwich for himself. Kane did small things like that for him, while Ghost had learned in the last several days how to make a sandwich, it tasted better when Kane made it for him and it made his mate happy. The powerful greater alpha was tender and caring, treating Ghost like he was precious. Ghost gave Kane a sweet smile and dug into his sandwich, happy growls escaping as red juices dripped down his chin from the succulent meat.

Caius spoke softly with Andromeda, two clan leaders, one fair, the other dark, heads close together as they ate. Everyone at the table could hear them, it was apparently rude to listen in, but Ghost ate his sandwich and stared at his grandfather and the Red Fern clan leader.

Caius was very like Burke, Kane, and Gerald in appearance, that Ghost wondered at the family ties. Kane was the only child of a distant cousin of Caius, and Ghost didn't know about Burke's family history. Kane and Burke were former lovers, so presumably if they were related, it was distant and far enough back not to be prohibitive. Sophia was dark as well, her eyes green and brown, whereas Burke's were a subtle chocolate brown that lightened to gold when his wilder nature grew closer to the surface.

Thinking about family ties distracted him until a sound came at the door to the hall, and a tall, young alpha slunk into the dining room. Gabriel Suarez was young, only a year or so older than Ghost, and still recovering from the trauma of being held hostage, tortured, and sexually assaulted by his captors. The slavers who purchased Gabe and his relatives were dead, and Kane and Caius had made some noise about finding out if any other wolfkin had been sold to humans in the last twenty years by Roman and Remus Acquisitions.

Ghost jumped up, and went to Gabe, enfolding the newly affirmed greater alpha in a hug, Gabe hugging him back with a tight embrace. Ghost pulled back and smiled up at Gabe, "I thought Heromindes sent you and your family back to Worcester?"

"He did, but I decided to stay. My mother and siblings are already gone, under guard. The other Clan Leaders are coming, and I wanted to be here for the Tribunal," Gabe replied with a half-shrug, cheeks red. "You saved me, and Kane and Clan Leader Caius can teach me to use…. my gift before I hurt someone."

Ghost tilted his head, searching Gabe's features. His friend still carried pain and fear in the depths of his eyes, in the tension around his mouth. Yet he had the courage to stay, and defy his clan leader and kinsman. "Come eat."

Ghost tugged Gabe to the table, a chair was pulled up from a space along the wall. Gabe sat between Ghost and Andromeda as Caius gave him a long, searching glance, Gabe shifting nervously in his seat. Ghost glared at his grandfather, and nudged the plate of sandwich fixings closer to the young alpha.

Kane gave Gabe a short but welcoming nod, and put a big hand on the back of Ghost's neck, as if placing a claim upon him. Ghost gave a mental snort of amusement. Everyone knew they were bonded, no one was going to poach, least of all Gabe. The young alpha felt safe with Ghost, and Ghost wanted him to get better. Pain hovered over Gabe, in his eyes and soul. Ghost had no idea how to help, his training as a shaman nonexistent, but he still wanted to help. Needed to help.

"Will Heromindes be joining us for lunch?" Caius asked Gabe. Gabe quickly swallowed a bite of sandwich before nervously replying.

"No, sir. He and his honor guard are eating in the mess hall."

Red Fern wasn't a large clan, but there were enough members that they typically ate in the park's mess hall. There was a cafeteria setup that could hold a few hundred wolves. Andromeda's immediate family ate in here with her in the cabin, though she made regular appearances during the week at community meals. Family packs in Red Fern either ate in their own cabins or joined the community at the mess hall.

Caius frowned at Gabe's reply, and Ghost wondered. The tribunal would happen once the summoned Greater Clan Leaders assembled in Baxter, and that would be any day now. They were close, and Kane had said they would be here soon. Ghost wasn't nervous, and he wasn't afraid. He was confused and frustrated, almost annoyed, by the traditions and Laws that claimed Kane was guilty and that their bond was anathema. How could something created and blessed by the Great Mother, their Goddess, be anathema?

SIMON ENTERED THE new facility, guards surrounding him. The lab was beneath an abandoned chemical storage facility used by the Science Department at the University of Maine Augusta, and it still stank of sulfur and ozone. A hefty donation to the university guaranteed no questions and kept the curious away.

Shadows moved in the dark as they went down a level, water dripping from exposed pipes in the ceiling. Roman's few wolves were still around, and while they showed no sign of flipping and revealing the location of the new lab, they were also worthless nasty brutes who snapped and growled at the humans and the werewolves restrained in the silver cages. If they didn't get too bothersome Simon was fine with them staying—he never knew when the doctors might need new specimens.

He reached the far side of the structure, where it opened to bare support beams and electrical conduits. Medical equipment and machines he had no name for cluttered the space, some still covered in clear shipping plastic wrap. His lead scientists fussed about the machinery, directing technicians to arrange it all to their satisfaction. Armed guards stood off to the side, overlooking the cages that held the living specimens. They were drugged and restrained by silver bars and chains, but Simon didn't believe in taking chances.

"Dr. Walsh!" Simon barked out, the man in question jumped. He was as rabbitty as Harmon had been, but he was marginally more cooperative and didn't require hand-holding when it came to the specimens.

"Mr. Remus! You're…early," Dr. Walsh stammered, gingerly approaching a few steps before his courage failed him. He eyed the armed guards around Simon with trepidation, but managed to talk. "What can I do for you?"

"How soon until we're operational again?"

"Soon, sir, very soon. The incubation unit we found in Dr. Harmon's laboratory made the trip over successfully on the battery backup, and was the first thing we got online and running. The rest will be online by this evening. I can have a progress report for you by tomorrow."

"Where is this unit now?" Simon demanded. Dr Walsh gulped, but pointed to the corner. The unit was a tank full of a cloudy gel-like substance, and there was dark, indistinct blob the size of a football floating in the slime. The whole thing was lit up from within, highlighting the grotesque contents. He sneered, stomach twisting at the sight of the growing organs and bones. He hastily looked away, and glared at Dr Walsh. "And the data from Harmon's lab?"

"We've been examining the information thoroughly, sir. I believe I have a firm grasp of his procedures and we should be caught up once the rest of the equipment is in place."

"Good. No more delays. Begin as soon as you can."

Without waiting for a reply, Simon turned and left, walking past the cages. Soft growls and whimpers came from the specimens, Simon chuckled, unaffected by their anger or fear. One small form darted back from the bars as he passed, a frightened gasp making him smile.

CAIUS LEFT THE cabin, his wolves and Andromeda's at his back. The Greater Clan Leaders for Dread Claw, Birch Grove, and Red Wraith had arrived, their convoys having just cleared the park gates. They would be there in less than ten minutes. Evening had fallen, the temperatures dropping with the sun, and Caius waited ahead of the crowd. Ghost and Kane stood with Kane's tactical team, the Black Pine wolves shoulder to shoulder in a show of support. How the other clan leaders would react to Kane not being in custody was unclear—though Kane's reputation for being a good man and a fair alpha may be enough to temper any complaints. Roman and Claire were still locked away in the cellars, the doors guarded by greater alphas loyal to Caius.

The human doctor was under guard as well, and had spent quite some time crying and wailing through the door, alternating between demanding to be set free and begging for a chance to tell them everything he knew. The human was ill-suited to stress, the stench of fear permeated the hall outside the room he was kept in. The only interaction he had was with his guards, wolves who brought him food twice a day and took him to the restroom when needed, not once talking to the human Caius was certain was behind many atrocities. Caius was waiting for the Tribunal to convene, hopefully his attempt at courtesy would shed some favorable light on Black Pine and his Heir from the other clan leaders.

Black Pine was powerful, but on shaky ground. Roman's betrayal, the killings and abductions, along with the remaining missing wolves, were all black marks on Caius' leadership. Having solved the mystery as to who was responsible for the ambush at Baxter fifteen years prior was useless since Simon Remus was still free—the human was very publicly known in New England, a rich man who spent enough time on the front page of tabloids to be recognizable, he surely would be missed if Caius had him kidnapped and killed like his older brother Sebastien. Getting retribution for his slain wolves would require patience, but not having anything to show for his restraint would make him, and Black Pine, look weaker than they were—and that left them open to challenges. Whether political or physical, it didn't matter, any move against Black Pine by another Greater Clan Leader could lead to a blood feud.

The rumble of tires over ice and gravel heralded the arrival of the clan leaders. Caius straightened his back, wiping any emotion off his face. Andromeda silently came to his side, her face just as cold, her formidable strength hidden beneath the willowy lithe grace of her slim frame. They may not be as close as they once were, but Andromeda was his most powerful ally, and they would both need each other if they were to keep Black Pine and their wolves intact once the Tribunal convened. Kane was as much a liability now as he ever was as an asset—his very gift was the source of contention.

The increasing rumble became a long line of vehicles, several black SUVs, and near the end, a long black luxury limousine. The engines shut off, ticking in the cold, the clearing in front of Andromeda's cabin was silent for a long moment before the lead vehicle's doors opened. As if a signal, greater alphas all stepped out of the vehicles down the convoy. They all radiated power, that aura alphas carried as a mantle that signaled their rank and strength to any wolfkin.

Caius lifted his chin, his instincts rising to the fore. This may be Andromeda's land, but Red Fern was part of Black Pine, and having this many greater alphas in his territory that did not answer to him made his hackles rise. His heart thumped with adrenaline, and Caius bit back a growl that threatened to escape. Andromeda's small hand settled on his shoulder, out of sight, Caius breathed in, trying to settle his more aggressive tendencies.

He was no cub. It was time to show his peers that Black Pine was stronger than ever.

GHOST BREATHED IN, his mate's scent filling his nose, settling his desire to shift. He was unaccustomed to his human form; living life as a wolf made him suited to handling tense and potentially dangerous situations differently, with fang and claw. Though chasing off a hungry brown bear that wanted to eat wolf puppies was a far different situation than the legion of greater alphas that were exiting the black vehicles.

They were built much like Kane and Caius—big, broad shoulders and chests, heavily muscled, they moved with a grace that was purely predatory. Many of them were dark, from hair to eyes and golden skin, but a few were lighter, hair blond and one a deep auburn. The golden complexion seemed to be very common, with the Red Fern wolves and himself as exceptions. Even Kane, Burke, and Gabe shared the same golden hues to their skin as these foreign wolves.

Ghost breathed in again, catching the scent on the wind of the new wolves. He summoned his Spiritsight, and blinked in surprise. These alphas all glowed to his inner vision, their soul-stars vibrant and pulsing with power. Many of them were the same shades, reddish hues that ran thick with orange and yellow, some even red and deep blues, some shades of purple. Red was a common color then for alphas; Ghost looked at Caius, and even his grandfather's soul-star burned a deep crimson laced with a smoke gray.

Three of the greater alphas burned with an intensity that matched Caius and Kane; only Andromeda burned brighter to Ghost's Spiritsight. He smiled at that discovery, and looked back to the three greater alphas that burned the brightest. These three came from separate vehicles, one of them from the rear of the long limo.

That alpha, presumably a clan leader, glowed with a silky rose red and silver—his star was similar in hue to the shade made by the bond shared between Ghost and Kane. He was lanky, and blond, hair the color of wheat and straight. Ghost met that alpha's eyes across the span, and the greater alpha's forest-green eyes latched onto his, and Ghost felt a slight mental nudge. He pushed back, not appreciating the attempted intrusion into his mind, and the greater alpha's eyes widened briefly before he grinned, a feral flash of white teeth that Ghost took as a promise and challenge in one. Ghost curled his lip in response, and the clan leader chuckled before walking up the path towards Caius and Andromeda.

The clan leader at the head of the convoy was shorter than most of the greater alphas Ghost had seen in the last several days, but he was thick with muscle, his suit jacket fitting tightly to his broad chest. He was built more like a bear than a wolf; while the others moved with a loping stride, this alpha lumbered ahead, and Ghost found himself wondering if perhaps a bear cub had been raised by wolves in some distant past, since this wolfkin male was the least wolf-like he'd seen so far. That was until Ghost got a brief glimpse of his inner star, and it burned with an orange and red flame, like fire devouring seasoned wood. An overlay of a great hulking wolf flashed in Ghost's inner vision, a beast garbed in dark brown fur and gray eyes that stalked prey from the shadows. The vision of the wolf left, and the human form of the clan leader returned. Bear-like as a man, this one was all wolf inside where it counted, his size would rival even Kane's black beast.

The third clan leader was the auburn-haired male. His hair glinted with fiery highlights in the cabin's exterior lights, his eyes flashing green and gold as he turned his head. This alpha looked straight at Ghost, unerring and deliberate—he stared back, and this alpha carried a sense of menace about him, a dangerous hint of violence that made Ghost stiffen. Kane growled beside him, but the clan leader spared Kane not a single glance—his regard was for Ghost alone, and even though Ghost felt no mental appraisal, his gaze had a heavy sense of being weighed and measured. This male's inner star was odd—it was red, bright as berries on the vine that grew even in winter and was poisonous to every living creature in the deep wood. Tendrils of leaf green twirled through the red, and Ghost pondered the disturbing combination. Something inside told him such a blend was unusual, though he had little experience to tell him why. The clan leader looked away, and joined his peers as they greeted Caius and Andromeda.

The crowd parted as the clan leaders finished their greetings, the four greater alphas and the lone female clan leader all leading the way into the cabin. Caius sent Kane a quick glance, and while his grandfather did not use the mental communication of their kind, Ghost and Kane felt their alpha's desire for them to not follow. Caius looked away, and led the others inside. The door shut, and Ghost could see the assembled leaders through the tall windows entering the living room, the hearth lit with a cheerful fire.

"I feel slighted," Burke whispered loudly, bumping Kane with his shoulder. "We weren't even introduced. Ghost got a ton of attention though. Feeling jealous, Kane?"

"Jealous? No. Protective? Yes," Kane responded, holding Ghost to his side under his big arm. "Julian was looking especially hostile."

"Which one was Julian?" Ghost asked, though he thought he might know.

"The redhead. Clan Leader for Birch Grove. He rules New York City, Manhattan, all New Jersey and parts of Pennsylvania and Delaware. Has a smaller number of wolves in his territory, but his clan is wealthy and has connections to human governments."

"He carries violence in his spirit," Ghost mused, and Kane gripped him tighter.

"I don't think he would try and hurt you, little wolf, but stay away from him. Don't be alone with Julian at any point. He's killed several of his own wolves over the years, for various reasons; if he were human I'd call him a psychopath."

"Why is he a clan leader, then?" Ghost asked, the rueful glances his packmates shared leaving him even more confused. "Why haven't the shamans stopped him?"

"He's the strongest in his clan, boy," Gerald grumbled. "The strongest rule, and whether they are decent beings is irrelevant. And Birch Grove doesn't have any shamans. If they have need of them, the shamans from neighboring clans travel into Birch Grove territory, then leave when no longer needed."

Ghost frowned, not liking the connotations he sensed in Kane's mind when his mate thought of the word psychopath. An animal that was sick like that would be ostracized by its own kind or killed, chased off—not allowed to lead. The humanity wolfkin eschewed had more influence than even they thought, if a madman could lead a clan. And for there to be no shamans in Birch Grove spoke of a sickness on a deeper level, one that left Ghost even more unsettled by the redheaded clan leader.

"Who are the others?" Ghost asked, and Sophia answered. The female beta stood next to Gerald, not quite touching, but closer than she usually was when it came to the lesser alpha.

"The blond is Royrick, clan leader of Red Wraith, one of the three clans directly descended from the First Wolves. He rules over all upper New York State, the northern half of Pennsylvania and up into Canada. His territory is as large as Black Pine's, but maybe half of the same number of wolves. Royrick is also obscenely rich, and spoiled, too," Sophia stated, glaring over her shoulder. Her expression was fierce, but there was a soft glow in her eyes that spoke of a deeper emotion. "He's a brat, but not cruel. He's likely to be the only one aside from Caius on the Tribunal who'll actually listen to testimony without bias, though I'm not sure how his judgment may go."

Burke coughed, and Kane smacked his shoulder.

"What?" Ghost asked, brows furrowed.

Sophia growled, punching Burke in the side, making the Speaker stumble back a step. Kane laughed and Burke sent Sophia an irritated snarl without any heat behind it. Sophia smiled innocently before she answered. "For a very brief interlude when I was young and foolish, I had a...relationship with Royrick. It was just after he became clan leader."

"If you want to call a twenty-year affair brief, sure." Burke snorted out a laugh. "You damn near mated with him. You broke up with him and went lone wolf for decades before landing in Black Pine."

"Thankfully I came to my senses before that happened," Sophia snapped, crossing her arms and growling under her breath. "It was several decades ago. I was not a lone wolf—I had a standing invitation from many clan leaders to join their clans, I just took my time deciding which one to choose. You weren't even born yet, Burke, so shut it."

Burke chuckled, Sophia narrowed her eyes at him, and he moved until he was hidden halfway behind Kane and Ghost. Gerald frowned at the cabin, then looked back to Sophia. He shuffled a bit closer to the short beta, his whole body radiating displeasure. Sophia gave Gerald a quick glance, letting him shuffle closer until he stood right at her shoulder. Sophia wrapped a small hand around Gerald's elbow, her grip tight, and the lesser alpha relaxed, his frown falling away.

"And the last one?" Ghost asked, thinking of the stocky brute.

"Mercuriel, clan leader of Dread Claw, who rules over Vermont and New Hampshire, up over the border into Canada. Smaller territory than most, but his clan has almost as many wolves as Black Pine, far more than the other two clans. He is a brutal fighter—his wolf-form is almost as large as Kane's, and probably heavier. Man's built like a tank, and is one of the longest ruling clan leaders in the New World. He took control of Dread Claw the winter of the Great Exodus from the Old World. Fierce and ruthless, though he is a solid leader, respected by his people." It was Gerald who answered this time, his brow lowered as he remembered. "I was a youngling back then, but the upheaval in leadership was severe enough to send ripples through all the other clans. Things settled down quickly though. He was brutal in assuming control from the former clan leader."

"He reminds me of a brown bear," Ghost murmured, and Kane chuckled.

"That he does, little wolf."

"Will they judge us fairly?" Ghost asked the group, and the silence that answered him was clear enough in its meaning. "How could they not? Can't they see the truth?"

"When it comes to politics, the truth is irrelevant," Kane said calmly, rubbing Ghost's arm. "Black Pine is vulnerable for the first time in centuries. They may be our allies, but we cannot count on them acting impartially."

"We are threatened by greed?" Ghost growled, fed up. "We are not humans! Greed has no place in our nature. They would threaten our bond, blessed by our goddess, for a chance to topple Black Pine?"

"Most wolfkin play token service to our faith, buddy. Only the shamans hold true to the old ways, though even among the shamans the younger generations are less devout. The few older shamans remain faithful as ever, but our Goddess hasn't moved amongst the larger population in a very long time." Burke told him, chocolate brown eyes flashing gold for a heartbeat. "Faith is something many are lacking."

"She is here, with us, every second," Ghost disagreed. "Can't you hear Her?"

"We aren't shamans, little wolf," Kane murmured, kissing the top of his head. "I can hear Her when She speaks to you, but it's hard for me to hear Her on my own."

The others looked at Kane like he'd just announced he was on fire. Sophia blinked at him, Burke made a gurgle and coughed, and Gerald appeared to be choking. Sophia recovered first, whispering, "You've heard Her?"

Kane nodded, then pressed his chin to the top of Ghost's head, breath ruffling his hair. "She's been speaking to Ghost since he came home."

"Longer, I think," Ghost said, recalling when his gifts started to manifest when his memories of being more than a wolf began to surface. "The wind carries a woman's voice, sometimes clear, sometimes clouded, but She's guided me every day. She spoke to me in a meadow of snow and ice, and gave me the way back to myself. She helped me find the courage to return to my human form."

Kane stilled, his mate frozen. The others stared at Ghost, shifting nervously. Kane eventually thawed, and hugged Ghost to his chest, squeezing until he squeaked. Kane loosened his embrace and kissed him, deep and thorough, until his mind lost its ability to process thought and his cock wanted out to play.

Kane let him go, but kept him close. The milling crowd in front of the cabin was dissipating, the Black Pine wolves remaining behind as the Red Fern wolves returned to their homes. Ghost pressed his nose to Kane's shirt, breathing in the scent of his mate. Kane was warmth and strength and affection, and Ghost felt an aching *want* in his bones, a want that demanded Kane. Ghost was riding a wave of desire when Kane and Burke both shifted, bracketing him between their bigger bodies.

Ghost tore his attention away from his mate, and looked up to see Heromindes, Clan Leader of Ashland, and his young kinsman Gabe walking from the shadows. The last Tribunal member was already here in Baxter, and Ghost had yet to speak directly to the greater alpha since he laid the charges against Kane.

Heromindes swept up the path, Gabe at his heels, the younger alpha's head down and gaze averted. Heromindes appeared displeased, strides aggressive and quick, forcing Gabe to almost run to keep up. Ghost worried for his friend, though he was certain Heromindes wouldn't hurt Gabe. The clan leader was Gabe's cousin, and fiercely protective of his people. Gabe's defiance in not returning to Worcester was surely one of the reasons why Heromindes was upset— the glare Heromindes sent towards Ghost and his group made it obvious what else angered the Ashland Clan Leader. Kane had accidentally used the Voice against Heromindes in Worcester during the raid that rescued Gabe and his family. Kane kept Heromindes from slaying the human slavers captured during the raid, and then returned the other alpha's will to him as quickly as he stripped it. Kane tried to apologize, but Heromindes rebuffed his attempts.

Heromindes swept into the cabin. Gabe sent Ghost an anxious glance before following his kinsman through the entranceway, carefully shutting the front door with a soft click.

"Things are getting pretty heated in there, and fast," Burke murmured, shifting so he could keep an eye on Kane and Ghost and the cabin. The Speaker tilted his head, obviously listening to the clan leaders inside the cabin. Ghost thought about trying to listen, but his attention kept drifting away.

Something…someone was coming. More than one.

Ghost took a step away from Kane, his focus set upon the gravel drive. He tilted his head, ears picking up the sound of tires. A vehicle broke through the darkness, headlights flashing across the front yard, and it parked behind the last vehicle of the clan leaders' convoy. The silver SUV went silent as the engine died, and Ghost's heart jumped in anticipation.

A whisper rose in the chill wind, coiling around his head and shoulders, caressing his face before it peeled away, leaving him with his heart in his throat and his hands curling to fists.

Kane and Burke were talking, unashamedly eavesdropping on the clan leaders, as were the others in their group, discussing amongst themselves what they were hearing from the Tribunal members.

Ghost took another step away, the occupants of the new SUV opening their doors, stepping out.

It was as if the heavens dripped stars to earth, each soul-star within the shamans before him glowing and pulsing with their heartbeats. Golden yellows, gentle robin's egg blues, vibrant moss greens and even a subtle purple and silver star flashed, nearly blinding him. Ghost blinked and dropped his Spiritsight, and he saw the four shamans that exited the vehicle and waited in the drive. All four of the strange men were staring back at him, and the one in front, the driver, took a couple steps forward and stopped. Ghost took a slow, even breath, and banished his nerves.

The shaman in front was a tall, lean brunet with pale skin and warm brown eyes, and his smile was kind. Ghost smiled back, certain he knew this shaman. The wolfkin male's hesitant smile grew into a wide grin, and he jogged forward, arms open, and Ghost had a flash of insight that brought joy to his heart.

Michael.

In his memories of Gray Shadow, there was always Michael—his grandfather's last apprentice. Gray Shadow taught Michael for years before Ghost was born—he learnt from sitting in on Michael's lessons. His first memories ever were listening to Gray Shadow teach Michael about his gifts, while little Luca yearned to be a shaman, too. Michael was old enough to be Luca's father, but he'd counted the young shaman as his very first friend.

"Michael!" Ghost cried out, sprinting across the snow. Kane shouted behind him, and his mate followed him.

Ghost threw himself into Michael's embrace, the taller shaman hugging him close and laughing. Ghost buried his nose in Michael's hair and breathed him in, memories welling up in his mind. Countless days spent learning together, Michael patiently letting him sit in his lap, reading wolfkin histories and the Law, evenings when Michael would babysit Luca and his littermates when Marla and Josiah would go out.

"You're alive, you're alive!" Michael crowed, swinging him around like he had when Ghost was a cub. Ghost laughed, so happy tears ran down his cheeks, face hurting from smiling so wide. Michael put him down and hugged him so tightly Ghost squeaked as air was forced from his lungs, and Michael chuckled before easing his embrace.

"Little wolf?" Kane asked, and a big hand gripped his shoulder. Kane didn't pull him away, but the alpha's disquiet and wariness at his affectionate greeting came across their bond.

Michael chuckled, and gently eased back, though he still held Ghost close. Kane gave Michael a tight smile and a short nod, his hand on Ghost all but screaming his claim.

"Shaman Michael," Kane said, words cool but polite. "It's good to see you again."

"Alpha Kane," Michael replied with a grin, nodding. "It's good to see you again as well. I wish the circumstances were better, but I'm glad to be here regardless."

"What do you mean?" Ghost asked, tipping his head back to see Michael's face better. Michael bit his lip, brows furrowing, and he sighed. Face clearing, Michael looked over his shoulder at his companions before turning back to Ghost and Kane.

"We were asked to attend a Tribunal by our respective clan leaders," Michael said, meeting Kane's regard. Knowledge lit his mate's dark eyes as Ghost tensed in realization, and Michael nodded, confirming his fears. "Yours. We are to stand as witnesses, to attest to the validity of your bond with Luca, and to sever it if it's been determined to be a forced union. The alphas will handle Kane's punishment if he's found guilty."

Angry, Ghost opened his mouth to demand the shamans test their soulbond now to stop this foolish Tribunal, but a shout from the front of the cabin interrupted him and drew his attention. The greater alphas that made up the clan leaders' honor guard surrounded the Black Pine wolves. Sophia looked ready to kill, Gerald was on the ground with a boot in the middle of his back holding him down, and Burke had his arms restrained by two big wolfkin males.

Kane pulled on Ghost, but Michael held him tighter and spun away, yanking Kane's hand from Ghost's shoulder. Ghost growled, and tried to get free, kicking. Kane roared, and leapt for Michael, but Kane disappeared under the weight of several bodies. Ghost cried out, shocked immobile, and Michael dragged him away as half a dozen greater alphas restrained Kane, forcing his mate to his knees in the snow.

"Kane!" Ghost cried, reaching out for his mate. Electricity hissed and spat around his fingers, Ghost's anger and fear spurring his gifts. "Let him go!"

"No!" Michael restrained Ghost, and left him dumbfounded when the older shaman grabbed Ghost's hand, and snuffed the bolts of energy curling around his fingers. Ghost gaped, beyond startled, and found himself picked up off his feet and carried away.

Ghost snarled, his wilder side rising, fury at his mate's treatment bringing his feral nature to the fore. Michael said something, shouting, trying to keep Ghost restrained as he fought. Hands came to rest on his face and shoulders, avoiding his elongated fangs and curled claws.

"Kane!" Ghost screamed, and he lost sight of his mate as the shamans surrounded him, separating him from the chaos.

4

UNCERTAIN FUTURES

KANE CURSED AS HIS ARMS WERE YANKED BEHIND HIS BACK. ROUGH hands put shackles on his wrists, and his feet were restrained with steel and silver bands. He spat out a mouthful of dirty snow, growling as his attackers backed away. He searched for Ghost, but the shamans had quickly taken his little wolf away, Ghost's enraged snarls and screams leaving Kane afraid for his mate.

"Move out of my way!" Caius snapped, the crowd around Kane cleared out, letting his clan leader through. Kane bit his tongue is surprise when Caius knelt in the snow next to him, brushing his long hair back from his face. Caius was angry, so angry Kane could feel his alpha's fingers shaking before Caius regained himself.

Growls and harsh whispers rose from the pack of greater alphas around Kane, but no one stopped Caius as his clan leader helped him to sit up out of the snow, legs under him. He was already soaking wet, though the cold wasn't bothersome. Wet jeans were annoying, and his arms ached from being yanked behind his back.

Kane looked up when a shadow moved in his periphery. Andromeda stood over them, hair raised on the wind, eyes glowing a brilliant blue. She took a few more steps until she was right next to Kane, and put a slim hand on his shoulder. The greater alphas who ambushed him took a few steps back, warily eyeing the formidable beta.

"The Tribunal members decided the charges warrant incarceration until your trial, youngling," she said, and her fingers tightened on his shoulder until he wanted to wince. She was cautioning him to be quiet. Just past her, Kane saw the other Tribunal members, the clan leaders watching impassively from the front porch of her cabin.

Say nothing, not even in your defense, Caius told him, so soft in his mind that the others about them wouldn't be able to overhear. Kane nodded discreetly, and breathed in and out a couple times to ease his racing pulse.

Ghost? Is he okay? Kane was worried for his mate. Ghost's presence in the back of his mind was a riot of anger and fear. There was no blast of lightning and scent of burning flesh, so the surge of energy Kane had sensed in Ghost was stopped before his mate's fears overrode common sense. He sent a burst of calm and affection, and hoped Ghost was in a state to feel him through their bond.

Ghost is unharmed. The shamans could have done that better, that was poorly thought out. They are attempting to calm him now, Caius replied, one big hand going under Kane's upper arm. His clan leader lifted Kane to his feet, and when he was steady, Caius knelt down and unshackled his feet so he could walk. Growls came from the crowd, but none contradicted the clan leader's actions.

"The accused is to be locked away until his Trial," Julian declared, loudly enough to be heard over the wind. "The afflicted youngling is to be kept separated until the shamans' testimony to his mental state and the nature of the bond."

Gerald and Burke snarled, and Kane met Burke's eyes across the distance between them. He shook his head once, a short motion, and Burke settled back, though he shook off the stranger's holding his arms. Sophia went to Gerald, and helped him to his feet, brushing snow off his shirt and pants.

"I will see him to the accused's cell," Andromeda said calmly, gloriously indifferent to the brittle and hostile tension. Caius nodded, and squeezed Kane's arm once before stepping back. Andromeda stepped to Kane's side, and gestured for him to follow. "Come along, youngling. It's not far."

Burke took a step, as if to follow them, but Sophia reached out and took his arm, yanking him back. *Burke—take care of Ghost!* Kane held his best friend's gaze until the crowd got in the way. He had no doubt that Burke heard his thought, and his best friend gave him a tight smile and a short nod, reassuring him. Kane took a deep breath and followed the

White Wolf into the woods.

THE WOODS WERE dark, little light from the rising moon and stars breaking through the boughs, the crunch of snow under their feet loud. The pines hung heavy with snow and ice, the recent storm having dropped a significant amount. The pines grew taller and denser as they walked on, Andromeda leading the way through the woods. An old path was cut through the dormant undergrowth, easier to see with the flush of green receded in the depth of winter.

Kane had explored very little of the park around Andromeda's cabin; her territory was, while not off limits, clearly defined by her scent and it left most wolfkin wary of encroaching on her land. She held sway over all of Baxter, but the woods around her cabin were private space, so Kane had never been to this part of the plateau.

Figures rose out of the darkness, his wolfkin eyes able to discern the tall monoliths of stone sentinels nestled amongst the trees. Pines and oak curled around carved stone, the trees adapting to the foreign objects placed by wolfkin hands hundreds of years prior. The ancient pictographs of wolves as big as men and the vaguely female outline of a radiant moon peeked out past lichen and dirt. The air grew colder, though less oppressive—it felt as if the sky opened above him, and he was about to fall into the abyss. Andromeda's hand on his arm tightened, anchoring him, reminding him he was walking, feet firm on the ground.

"There are places, even here in the New World, that are touched by the Great Mother," she murmured. "Places that She has appeared, or blessed for reasons unknown to mortals. This is one such place. Humans knew it as sacred long before wolfkin migrated to this continent. We found it not long after Black Pine and her lesser clans took over this land."

The darkness receded. They stood at the edge of a wide clearing, a deep bowl cut into the earth with high sides reinforced by large blocks of stone and clay. At least a hundred feet across, and maybe twenty feet deep, the space at the bottom was filled with gravel and sand, coated in a windswept swath of ice and snow. The pines towered high overhead, blocking out the sky and most of the wind, though stray, thin breezes cut through the night air. Silence echoed, their misty breaths loud in the night.

It was a pit, an old stadium reminiscent of coliseums in the Old World. Seating was tiered around the edge of the lowest part of the pit, covered in moss and roots from the trees, the forest reclaiming the efforts of man and wolfkin. Two breaks were built into the pit on opposite sides, black holes that presumably lead out from somewhere nearby, allowing combatants to enter separately. A breathless quality held sway, and not even the creaking of boughs laden with ice or the heavy beat of Kane's heart disturbed the atmosphere of expectancy and infinite patience.

"Come, this way," Andromeda motioned, tugging gently. Heart in his throat, Kane followed, nerves tingling along his spine and shoulders. Instinct told him they were being watched, but his senses said they were alone but for some small rodents and a pair of ravens in the trees.

Andromeda led him away from the pit, around a monolith and into a grove of pines, the space beneath the giant trees free of snow, thick with spent needles in hues of pale gold and deep red. The darkness was nearly total, but the iron cage wedged between boulders and tree trunks made his heart skip a beat.

"I'm not an animal," Kane gasped out, for the first time feeling a trickle of concern. He was rarely worried for himself, his strength and regard saved for those under his protection, and he was left adrift for a moment before he felt Ghost reaching out to him. Wordless affection and concern from his little wolf gave him pause; his emotions were causing Ghost to be afraid, and Kane yanked himself back under control. His mate's well being was paramount—Kane could handle a little rough treatment.

"We are all of us more animal than many are comfortable admitting," Andromeda said, their steps muffled by the pine needles underfoot. "It is the suppression of one side of our nature that leads to the conflict with the other. Prejudice is a human failing, and the wolfkin have made it their own. The bias against shaman and alpha pairings has led to more than one pair being slain. Our Great Mother meant for the gifts to be sundered, not the wolves."

"What?" Kane said, shocked.

"Surely you didn't think, that out of the thousands of years and countless wolfkin born, that you and your little wolf were the first shaman and alpha to fall in love? Love knows no gender, youngling. You are not the first alpha to love a shaman, and you and Ghost will not be the last pair bound by love. I have never heard of a pair bound by love and Goddess, but even in my long life I have missed many things." Andromeda chided him, and Kane shut his mouth, pressing his lips together. "I am old, youngling. I was born in the shadow of the Sundering, a generation past the sweeping genocides perpetrated by the War Wolves, the omnipotent alphas of old. My father was one of the First Shamans."

Kane stared at Andromeda, left speechless. If her father was one of the First Shamans, then the White Wolf, this small and beautiful female beta, was the oldest living creature on the planet. Her age would rival the years of redwoods and the hidden leviathans that slumbered in the depths of the deepest oceans. Stormcloud, her father, had been one of the oldest wolfkin in their recorded history, and his daughter was nearly as ancient.

"Has a pair survived?" Kane asked, afraid of her answer. "A shaman and an alpha that loved each other. Has any pair survived?"

"History would tell you that no such pair has existed. But memory tells me you should have hope, youngling. Sacrifice, some greater than others was required, but some pairs have escaped prejudice and the retributions of the clans. Just as some have died or been broken apart by fear and disapproval."

"Ghost is my hope," Kane said as Andromeda opened the cage, hinges screeching, rust flakes falling from the thick bars. "Goddess bound or not, I'd do anything for him."

"Hold onto that hope, Kane of Black Pine," she replied, unlocking the restraints on his wrists. "It may yet see you through. Now strip and Change—you'll bear the elements better in wolf form. Your guards approach, and they won't care for your comfort as I do."

Kane stripped, Andromeda putting his boots and clothes under a rocky overhang out of the elements. Kane Changed, his massive wolf form coming over him in one smooth wave. It was effortless to him as breathing; he shook out his fur, his long tail sweeping through the air. Andromeda smiled down at him, though by not much. He was nearly eye to eye with the clan leader in this form; he had yet to meet another wolfkin who matched him in size. The clan leader from Dread Clan might match him, though Kane hadn't the occasion to see for himself.

His ears swiveled as the padding of wolfkin paws through snow reached him. Kane entered the cage, turning around in time for Andromeda to close the door and lock it, the antique lock dropping more dark rust flakes to the pine needles when she forced it shut. Several wolfkin all in their wilder forms loped into the small clearing, growling in aggression and satisfaction when they saw him locked away. These were greater alphas all—and he knew none of them. It made sense though—it would hardly be wise for the Heir of Black Pine to be guarded by his own wolves.

Fingers scratched behind his ear, and Kane leaned into Andromeda's hand. A few wolves growled at the sign of affection, but Kane was thankful for it. Andromeda's support may mean the difference between life and death. Her fingers found a sensitive spot behind his ear, and he sighed, relaxing despite the tense situation.

I'll see how your mate fairs, youngling. Keep your communication to him minimal—we don't want anyone in the honor guard or Tribunal to listen in, the White Wolf advised, and Kane nodded, a single dip of his muzzle. She scratched his head once more, then walked away, the wolfkin males parting with alacrity.

Not a one dared to make eye contact with the Red Fern Clan Leader—they may feel safe enough to growl and snap at Kane with him behind bars, but Andromeda was flat out scary. Back straight and steps effortless, Andromeda left him alone in the clearing, and his guards turned their regard to him, teeth bared, ears flat.

Kane dropped his head, hackles rising, and let out a deep, low rumble, so deep a human ear would miss it completely. Several of the greater alphas around his cage stepped back, wariness entering their eyes. A few braved his ire, and snapped at him, though such a show of bravado was meaningless several feet away with iron bars between them.

He sniffed at them in disdain, dismissing them completely, turning in a circle several times before settling down in the soft pines needles that covered the floor of his cell. Kane ignored their grumbling, and closed his eyes, mind centered inwards, where Ghost burned silver-white and pure.

5

FINDING HIS FEET

"LET ME GO!" GHOST SNAPPED, SWINGING WIDE, HIS FIST MISSING Michael's face by an inch when the older shaman ducked. Ghost scurried away, his back to the wall of the kitchen in Andromeda's cabin.

Michael put his hands up, fingers open, and tried to calm him. "Luca, please, relax. No one is going to hurt you."

"What have they done to my mate?" Ghost snarled, lips pulled back, his teeth gritted. He growled, his chest rumbling, and Ghost curled his claws into his palms. His wilder side was close, so very close to erupting, though every time he tried to Change, Michael snuffed out his attempts with a quick touch of his hand. "Where is Kane?"

"Alpha Kane is where all criminals should be when charged with blasphemy," Heromindes declared, stepping into the kitchen from the hall, the other Tribunal members behind him. Caius stood at his shoulder, looking as displeased as Ghost was feeling. "He hasn't been harmed, though the same cannot be said for you."

"He has never harmed me!" Ghost shouted, and the walls shook, vibrating from the force of his words. Michael moved towards him, hand up, and Ghost dodged his former friend's touch, not wanting his abilities to be extinguished again. Whatever Michael was doing was siphoning his power away, leaving him weaponless unless he Changed, and Michael seemed to know exactly when Ghost was about to attempt it. Ghost snapped his jaws, fangs elongated, and crouched against the stove and cabinets, wishing he wasn't cornered.

"He has no control over his abilities. He is too young—he's gone feral away from our kind! Restrain him!" Heromindes ordered, gesturing to Michael. The older shaman looked surprised by such a command, hands clenching for a second before looking at Ghost again.

"Touch me and I'll take your hand off," Ghost growled past his fangs, and his eyes glowed silver and white.

"He's an untrained whelp! Restrain him!" Heromindes shouted, pointing at Ghost, and a few guards moved past him and came at Ghost. Michael was pushed out of the way, and Caius yelled at Heromindes to stop, but no one listened.

An alpha loomed over him, blocking out the light. A big hand took his upper arm in a harsh grip, trying to yank him to his feet. Ghost roared again, the walls and floor shivering, and his free hand came up in a fist, punching the alpha in the chest. There was a snap and flash, the air stunk of ozone. The alpha flew back, barreling into his comrades, and shouts came from everyone as chaos erupted.

Caius pushed Heromindes back into the hall, and alpha guards boiled into the room. Michael tried to shout over them all, yelling at them to stop. There was a moment where the way to the other door in the dining room was clear, and Ghost took his chance, leaping up and over the counter. He cleared the table, kicking off his shoes as he sprinted out into the hall, voices raised behind him. He found his wolf form in the swiftest of thoughts, his reality changing in a swath of silver and white energy. He skittered to a halt on the hardwood floors before he slammed into the wall, and made to run down the hall, deeper into the cabin. There must be a back door out of the large home. If there wasn't, he would make one.

There were shouts and cries of shock and anger, Caius was calling for him by his old name, Ghost ignored them all. Claws tearing into the smooth floors, Ghost ran, far enough ahead of his aggressors that he knew he could escape. He would find his mate, and they would leave. The idiocy of his people left him disillusioned and angry—their soulbond was Goddess blessed and sacred, any wolfkin who refused to see the truth suffered from a condition no shaman could cure. Even Ghost knew stupidity was impossible to treat unless the afflicted made the choice to open their mind and learn.

A figure moved in front of him, he was about to swerve around whoever it was when a flash of golden white light winked and glowed for a second. He leaned back, sitting in his haunches to avoid slamming into Andromeda. She stood tall in hallway, River at her side, the siblings well-matched in physical attributes and steely miens. Ghost scrambled to a halt at her feet, and she moved him behind her. She hissed at him to be still and Ghost pressed himself to the back of her legs, peering around her at the group thundering down the hall in pursuit.

"Enough," she whispered, but the strength behind her voice echoed through the house. Ghost's ears itched, and he shook his head. The pack of alphas halted a few feet away, their angry and excited state evaporating at the sight of the clan leader's deathly glare.

"Enough," she said again, just as low, but her words reached every pair of ears in the hall. "This is my home. My children live here, my grandcubs live here. This is my den! Mine! I may owe allegiance to Black Pine, but this is my den. I rule within these walls! Enough!"

Ghost dropped to his belly, whining. Caius stood to the side, his back to the wall, chagrin on his face and the way he held his shoulders. Heromindes stood shocked, mouth working but no sound emerging, the other Tribunal members were backing away, caution in their eyes and wary nerves in their motions. The alpha guards froze, too close to move away without drawing her eye or ire; they remained unmoving, vibrating with apprehension.

Ghost saw the White Wolf, the soulstar in her core that made her a terror, even among her own kind. There was a very real and dangerous reason why Andromeda hadn't been unseated in her rule over Red Fern—she was Power. The wolfkin world saw an unusually powerful female beta, her wolf-form was immense and lethal, and the moniker of White Wolf was legendary across the globe. Yet Ghost saw the truth, and knew her for what she truly was—why she hid the fact that she was a female alpha, Ghost may never know, but it was not his secret to tell. He was thankful for her strength, for when faced with it, the instincts and temperaments of those in the hall cooled rapidly. Ghost may have been forced to commit more violence to keep himself free, and as his desire to flee faded, his cooler head regained control, he would have regretted hurting those only following orders.

"Ana…" Heromindes began, and her eyes snapped with glacial blue when she looked his way. He dropped the condescending tone, and tried again. "Ana, the youngling needs to be restrained until the shamans can examine him. He is untrained, and we all know how dangerous untrained shamans can be. Let them do their duty."

"Ghost is perfectly in control—his mentor in the shamanic arts exceeds even the combined skills of those here now. His actions have been a direct response to unwarranted attempts to restrict his movements and the foolish actions against his mate. Shaman River has already told you all that Ghost's will is his own, yet you disregard his testimony."

"Ana, River is indeed a formidable shaman, but surely the combined skills of our shamans are more than up to the task of restraining the youngling until he can be taught, and an outside opinion as to the youngling's mental state is prudent," Royrick said, moving up until he was next to Heromindes. Andromeda turned her cool gaze to the new clan leader, and Royrick smiled nervously back at her.

"I wasn't referring to River when I mentioned Ghost's mentor," Andromeda said. She looked past them all to the shamans clustered at the back. "If our spiritual kin would only open their hearts and listen, they would know the truth, and this would all be unnecessary."

Ghost could hear it. He had always heard the wind, the whispers that sifted and flowed through the quiet and peaceful moments of his life. The wind was there when his gifts woke after long years of playing at a mere creature, a simple wolf, and each time he listened, She spoke, and his powers grew. The whisperer was there now, and he watched the faces of those gathered in the hall, wondering if any of them would hear Her.

The alphas wore blank or confused expressions, and Ghost dismissed them quickly. He stared at Michael, the other shamans at his back, and Ghost saw a brief flicker of consternation flash across the older shaman's eyes. Michael was Gray Shadow's last apprentice; one thing Ghost recalled very clearly about his old life was that Gray Shadow never left his students wanting in terms of education—Michael gasped, eyes wide in alarm, and he strode forward, gripping Royrick's arm and whispering in his ear. Ghost shifted on his paws, claws digging into the wood floorboards, ready to run. His eyes darted from face to face, wondering if the chase was to begin again.

A warm and steady wave of affection and support swept through his mind, soothing his spirit. Kane was with him and was unharmed. Unhappy and frustrated, but Kane was not hurt and safe for the moment.

Ghost got a glimpse of where his mate was being kept, but he pulled back from their connection when Andromeda tugged on his ear. Caution was best—many greater alphas could break into any mental connection, even private ones, and overhear the thoughts of the wolves involved.

"We need to talk," Royrick announced, gesturing to his fellow Tribunal members, Michael hovering at his side. Heromindes frowned, but Royrick shook his head firmly, lifting his hand and putting it on Hero's shoulder, moving him back down the hall. Caius stared at Ghost, he felt his grandfather's perusal on his mind as a heavy weight. Ghost growled, pushed past his reserves of patience, hitting back with a mental shove, forcing his grandfather out of his head. Caius glowered at him, and Ghost lifted his lip in a defiant curl.

Caius surprised him, though. His grandfather smiled, and chuckled, breaking the remaining tension in the hall. "Leave my grandson alone. Shaman River and the White Wolf have him well in hand. His mate is in custody, so he won't run."

Caius gestured to the honor guards in the hall, and they grumbled under their breath, but they followed Caius down the hall to the large living room in the front of the cabin.

Ghost released a heavy sigh, relaxing. He sat on his rear, tail thumping on the floor in thanks when Andromeda scratched behind his ears.

"We need to talk as well," River said quietly to his sister, and Andromeda nodded.

"Come along, youngling," Andromeda said. Ghost got up and followed as the two older wolfkin walked down the hall away from the front of the cabin. Ghost's guess about the back door was confirmed when he was led to a small room full of boots and heavy coats with a door that opened out underneath one of the bedroom balconies overlooking the rear of the cabin. The overhang kept the snow and ice off the patio stones, and Andromeda closed the door behind them, the wind quiet and still.

"Change, so that we can speak. There are too many greater alphas about that may overhear our thoughts," Andromeda advised, and Ghost nodded his head once before initiating the Change. Power swept over him in a rush of silver-white, and he stood tall as a man. Andromeda smiled at him, while River's shoulders shook with silent laughter. "You make it effortless and pure. It's a pleasure to see such a feat of magic again after all these years."

Ghost scrunched his face up in confusion, but ignored her statement in favor of figuring out what was going on. "Why won't they leave me alone? What was Michael doing to me? He would touch me and my powers would stop. I didn't like it at all."

"The lot of them have trouble believing that their ways aren't always best. The horrible flaw in living forever is that our kind develop bad habits that time convinces us are prudent." Andromeda gave him a small smile when he tilted his head, confused. River exhaled loudly, getting Ghost's attention.

"What do you remember from growing up with Gray Shadow, Ghost?" River asked him with a small half smile just like his sister's. This was Ghost's first time seeing River since the battle with Roman's wolves. He figured River was trying to handle his own personal feelings of betrayal, since it was his niece who helped Roman kidnap, kill and enslave members of their people. Ghost focused on River's question, and looked down, thinking back.

"I remember sitting in on Michael's lessons with Grandpa Shadow," Ghost answered, memories coming slowly to the surface. His time with his wolfkin family was hard to recall. His clearest memories were of the days he spent with Gray Shadow and Michael. "I remember the tales of our people as he taught them to Michael. I remember Grandpa Shadow teaching Michael how to use his powers, and some days were spent with the two of them meditating for hours. There's bits and pieces I can see in flashes, and sometimes I recall things when I'm dreaming. Mostly Grandpa Shadow talking to me."

"You said you remember Gray Shadow teaching Michael," River said, and Ghost nodded. "Tell me what you remember, exactly."

"Why?" Ghost demanded, then flushed at his own tone. "I'm sorry, that was rude." He might have trouble knowing when he was being rude most of the time, but one thing he did know what that getting upset at a shaman was not acceptable. Though Michael and his friends deserved his anger. River might be reserved and somehow aggrieved by Ghost, but that didn't mean he was deserving of Ghost's anger when it was caused by someone else.

"It's okay. Just tell me what you remember, it'll be clear why I'm asking in a minute," River encouraged, and Ghost frowned, but did as

River asked.

"Grandpa Shadow spent a whole day once making shadow wolves, Michael would reach out and touch them, and they would disappear." Illusions, his mind supplied now. His grandfather would create illusions, one of his greatest abilities, then Michael would reach out and do... something. The shadow wolves disappeared.

"Michael has a singular talent," Andromeda said to him, but she paused and looked to River for a moment, clearly thinking carefully about she was about to say. "Michael can cancel out another wolfkin's gifts. It's a very rare talent, an ability seen only a handful of times in our history as a people. He can heal to some degree, and has a kind, patient nature that makes him well-suited for the life of a shaman. He went to Gray Shadow specifically as an apprentice because of this talent."

"How does he do it?" Ghost asked, afraid now to let his old friend anywhere near him, at least in touching distance. Ghost was not a big man nor a large wolf; his abilities were all he had to give him an edge against most of his brethren. If Michael could render his gifts useless, then Ghost was left defenseless.

"It's an extension of a shaman's immunity to an alpha's influence. Where most shamans are immune to the influence of an alpha in a passive manner, Michael can actively control his immunity, and can focus it against any wolfkin, be they shaman, alpha, or beta. Gray Shadow taught him how to use his ability, since Michael had no active control over it and was using it accidentally on people he came in physical contact with. It's limited to touch only, so he cannot diminish your gifts from any sort of distance," River explained. Ghost nodded, understanding. He learned early on what it meant for a shaman to be immune to the charm of an alpha and the Voice—Gray Shadow made it his most frequent teaching lesson to the cubs of Black Pine. Which now made sense, since both the Clan Leader and his Heir had the Voice, though to varying degrees.

"So, no touching. He can't control me if he doesn't touch me."

"It's not control, Ghost. He can't stop you from using your powers unless he touches you. If he doesn't touch you, then his gift is useless." Ghost nodded to Andromeda, thinking he would have to forego hugs from Michael for the immediate future. Though after what just happened, the ambush in the front yard and Kane's incarceration, Ghost wasn't feeling very charitable towards Michael and the other shamans.

"I'll talk to the shamans. Worst outcome is you'll have a babysitter for the next few days," River murmured, and Ghost tried to find some reassurance in his promise. "The last few hours have cast our people in a bad light. I'd ask how your homecoming has been, but I'm afraid your answer won't be pleasant."

Ghost grumbled, and Andromeda chuckled. River rubbed his shoulder with a warm hand, then slipped past them into the house. Ghost grumbled to himself, muttering about idiot alphas and willful blindness.

"The Tribunal convenes in two days," Andromeda said suddenly, interrupting his angry mutters. "Two days of waiting before we can free Kane and be done with this farce. Until then, mind yourself as best you can, don't give anyone any reason to doubt you're in your right mind."

"I'll try," Ghost said after a moment's thought. "What if Kane and I were to leave? Just run away and never come back?"

Andromeda tipped her chin, her glacier-blue eyes catching the winter light and seeming to glow. "Running away is an option. Many before you have taken that route. And many have died for that choice, alone and vulnerable, without pack or clan to stand with them, to keep them safe. I won't tell you not to take that option, but right now, it's not the best one. Save it for the bitter end, if reason and logic cannot clear the foolishness from the hearts and minds of others."

Ghost gave her a nod, for he could see her reasoning. He was aware he was more handicapped than the average wolfkin, as his years as a mere wolf left him uneducated in the ways of mankind and their laws. Growing up with Cat and Glen helped, but he hadn't lived as a man, learning as a man. Some things were beyond him right now. Kane could survive in the human world, he knew how to live amongst them, but Ghost refused to depend upon Kane's skill for the rest of his life. He needed to learn to live as a man on his own, eventually.

And he knew, in the deepest part of his heart, that Kane wouldn't run. Not unless there was no other option. Kane was built to be a protector, a leader of their people, and he would never abandon them, even as they turned their backs on him.

A part of him yearned for the simplicity of those years he spent as naught but a spoiled wolf in a sanctuary buried in the northern wilds.

"Go for a run," Andromeda gave him a slight nudge with her slim hand, lifting a teasing brow. "Clear your head, find your calm, and come back ready to defend yourself and your mate."

He wasted no time. Quicker than thought, his human body was swallowed by the silver-white storm of magic that answered to his will. He shook out his coat, and leapt from the patio into the snow. He felt the clan leader's regard on his back until he slipped amongst the slumbering black pines, hiding him from view.

"Stay away from Kane!" Her warning was the only thing that made him turn from the temptation of his mate. Ghost pointed his nose down the mountainside, disappearing into the wild forest.

He would spend the night hunting, thinking of the best course of action. Everyone was pulling at him, telling him to do this or that, and his mind was ready to fracture. He needed Kane—the bond between them when fully open steadied Ghost, gave his awakening mind as a thinking man something solid upon which to function.

If he lost Kane…Ghost would be lost, too. Perhaps some measure of his blood father survived in him after all, for he could not see himself remaining in civilization if he lost his soulbonded mate. He would return to the wilds, his human side forever gone.

ANDROMEDA KEPT ONE eye on Julian, the other on Heromindes. Neither of the clan leaders were anyone she would call friend or family—Hero tended to ignore females unless they were useful to him, and Julian was a mad dog. If not for his too convenient ties to the human government of this country, she would have slipped south one summer night and killed the fool. Her dislike of him was well-known, if he were to die mysteriously, it was likely she would draw immediate suspicion. She didn't feel like having a clan blood feud, so he lived. For now.

"Where's the pup? The crazy one?" Julian asked, sneering at the leather and white maple furniture that decorated her study. She gladly gave it over to Caius as was his due as clan leader, she rarely spent time in here but for paying bills for the park's expenses, but she made an effort to use and have the best items in her home. It's where her family lived, after all, and money was nothing in the grand scheme of things, yet Julian sniffed in disdain as if she had garbage lying about. For a wolf who lived in a glass and steel tower in Manhattan, his opinion was warped.

Andromeda lifted a brow when Julian picked a random book of a shelf and then tossed it to a chair with a negligent flick of his wrist, wiping his hand on the chair fabric as if the knowledge in the book burned his skin.

"My grandson is none of your business, Julian." Caius said, leaning back in the chair behind the desk.

"Well, that's not true, is it? The whelp getting stuck by your heir is exactly why we're here. Who gives a fuck if Kane embarrassed Hero? Hero embarrasses himself just getting out of bed in the morning," Julian said. Hero growled from where he stood next to the window.

"Do not provoke violence in my home," Andromeda snapped, and Hero's growls went quiet. Julian dropped his smirk, eyes wary as Andromeda narrowed her own back at both alphas. "There are cubs in this house. Mind yourselves."

"Sorry, Ana," Heromindes said, his anger receding. His temper was frayed, and Julian plucked at the strings of his humiliation with every sidelong glance and sharp comment. Julian said nothing, merely shrugged and sat in the chair, picking up the book he tossed aside earlier and flipping through the pages.

"My grandson is fine," Caius said. "The matter we're back here to discuss is about what to do with the human doctor."

"I don't care what you do with him. None of my wolves are missing," Julian said. Royrick snorted from where he was standing in the back corner of the room by the door. Julian sent Royrick a nasty glare, continuing to flip through the book. "Unlike those in this room, I haven't lost any of my wolves to human corruption and weak bloodlines. Seriously, Caius? Your own son is a traitor and it goes unnoticed for decades?"

"I accept the blindness that let this atrocity continue on for so long," Caius admitted, expression a blank mask, but for the deep glimmer in his eyes. "I will bear the fault to the day I die and Roman will have his moment before the Tribunal."

"I say Simon Remus and the human doctor are your problem, not mine," Julian crossed one leg of the other, and leaned back, matching Caius in posture. "Keep the mess behind your own borders."

"Hero? Your wolves were the last affected by Remus and Roman. Any thoughts?" Caius asked.

Hero shrugged, and Andromeda sighed. This one was too concerned with his pride and injured reputation. Hero would have fared far better if he had kept the incident with Kane to himself—bandying it about did nothing but embarrass him further, and it blinded him to more important things, like stopping the murder and experimentation of their people. Every time it came up, all it did was further drive a spike of discomfort into the Ashland clan leader. He certainly cared about his kin—his own cousin and his family was still torn asunder, half of them missing—but he was fixated on revenge against Kane.

"Hero—will you leave this to Caius to settle, or do you want to participate? This isn't a hard question, laddie." Mercuriel finally spoke up, looking away from the window where he peered out over the valley. "Step up or step aside."

"Fine! If the doctor can reveal where my people are, tell me. We are still searching in my clan territory. Once this Tribunal is over, we can see what to do with Remus." Hero all but spat his words out.

"What did Remus want with them, anyway? Did he really sell your cousins to sex slavers?" Julian asked with casual cruelty, and Hero's golden skin bleached white with rage.

"There is talk of experimentation. Remus wanted to give humans alpha and shamanic powers," Caius said, careful to avoid mention of the horrible conditions in which Kane found Gabriel Suarez and his family.

"Did they manage it?" Julian asked. "I went down to see Roman earlier. Looks wretched. Doesn't look like he managed to feed himself, let alone mastermind a grand scheme twenty years in the making. And he smelled like he's been fucking a human."

"Julian!" Royrick snapped. The red haired clan leader flashed a nasty grin, but he stopped. Caius was stone cold and pale, his eyes locked on Julian like he wanted to rip him to pieces. Andromeda moved just enough to draw her old friend's eyes to her, and it broke his predatory tunnel vision enough for him to find his equilibrium.

"No, I don't think they have. The human has been remarkably close-lipped about everything," Caius answered, no sign of his rage present in his words. He ignored Julian's ruder statements and focused on his question. "Roman has not been forthcoming, either."

Andromeda did not like the gleam in Julian's eyes. That one was too human-like for her comfort—the madness humans carried in their souls sometimes could be found in the wolfkin, rotting them from within. Julian was mad, but he held a leash upon it, and had yet to step too far over bounds.

"I sent out a request for aide in this matter," Royrick spoke up, thankfully changing the subject. "The wolf we need will be here soon."

"Is his gift strong?" Heromindes demanded, and Royrick gave the impatient clan leader a wide grin.

"Strong as Caius' wayward heir, if not stronger," Royrick said, and that seemed to satisfy Heromindes.

"Well, this is boring," Julian said, standing, straightening out his suit cuffs, and heaving an exaggerated sigh. "I'm going to bed. This Tribunal business is going to be so very fun, I can tell."

The Birch Grove clan leader left without another word, not bothering to shut the door as he departed. Andromeda went to close it, and she got a glimpse of Julian as he walked to the front door, scrolling through his smartphone as if he were without a care in the world. His guards fell in behind him, and the tension dropped in the cabin when they left.

Andromeda closed the study door, glad the unstable clan leader was gone. He would be trouble, she knew it, a heavy weight in her gut that spoke of something bad to come.

"That one is broken inside, I tell you," Mercuriel rumbled, and Royrick nodded in agreement.

"So, lassie, anymore cubs since I saw you last?" Mercuriel smiled at her, red on his cheeks, his eyes bright. She gave him a crooked smile, shaking her head.

"None since the last time you asked me, Mercuriel. Though plenty of my daughters have had several in the last few years."

"They all take after their matriarch, I can tell. Lovely and delicate creatures, pretty as the day is long," he flirted. Andromeda chuckled.

"I'm not looking for a mate, so save your flattery for another beta, old wolf," she chided, and Caius and Royrick both made sounds of amusement. Mercuriel ignored them of course—he had been after her for a few hundred years. By this point, it was merely a game to them both. "And if one of my daughters falls for your honeyed words, I wish you all the luck in the world. Most of my cubs came out exactly like me."

She needed a mate like she needed her head chopped off. Hard to keep her secrets if she had a mate bond with which to contend.

THE BARS WERE cold. He shivered, his body desperately trying to keep him warm. He didn't care—he wanted to die. Maybe then the nightmare would be over and he could finally rest.

A familiar sound woke him from a light doze. He pried one eye open. Not far from his cage a man stood, back to him.

Simon Remus lifted his ringing phone to his ear. "Hello?"

He couldn't hear the other side of the conversation, but the way Remus straightened up, shoulders back, and his whole body shivered, told him that whoever it was, he or she was someone Remus was afraid of. Remus acted tough, yet he went nowhere without his guards.

"How do I know you are who you claim to be?" Remus demanded. "This could be a trap for all I know."

Remus turned just enough he could see his face in profile. His jaw was tight, his fingers clenched tight around the phone, the case creaking. "Roman is imprisoned? On trial?"

Remus stiffened, a drop of sweat beading on his temple despite the chill air. "That's a lie. I never slept with...no. I don't know how you know that." Remus hung up, eyeing his phone with something close to terror and horrified fascination.

It rang again. Four times before Remus put it back to his ear, shaking. He said nothing, but the person on the other side must have known he was there. After a minute, he swallowed roughly, voice dropping to a whisper. "You said we'd met before. Where?"

A pause, then Remus dragged in a ragged breath. "In Manhattan. Yes, sir, I remember you now. I did not know you were one of them."

Remus began to walk away as he spoke, and it grew harder for him to hear, but he caught one last bit from Remus. "I'll wait for your call."

Remus left, never once looking down at their cages, never once acknowledging their presence. He shivered, nothing now to distract him from the cold. He was going die in this cage, the last thing he would see or hear would be Remus, and that pained him more than anything.

"Here, cub, take it." A rough voice from the left made him jump. He looked to see a clawed hand reaching out across the space between their cages, a blanket in his grip. "You'll not last much longer without it. I don't need it."

He no longer feared the monster in the cage next to him. How could he, when they were both miserable and locked up like animals? He reached out, and took the blanket. It was warmed by body heat, and he thankfully draped it over his shoulders, sucking up what warmth he could. "Thank you."

"No problem," the monster replied. He frowned, looking down at the blanket. Not a monster, not really.

"What's your name?"

There was such a long pause that he thought perhaps the monster would not answer, but just when he was about to give up waiting, it came. "My name is Enrique Suarez, a greater alpha of Clan Ashland."

He smiled, liking the way Enrique said his name, as if it were magical somehow. "Hi, Enrique. My name is Wren Harmon, adopted son of the bastard who abandoned me to this nightmare."

6

CONFRONTING EXPECTATIONS

GLEN GOT UP FROM THE COUCH AT THE FIRST KNOCK ON THE CABIN door, opening it before their visitor could knock again. Cat was still sleeping, and he didn't want her awakened. He finished chewing his breakfast, glad he swallowed before surprise made him choke.

He certainly wasn't expecting a naked Ghost to walk past him with a smile and a cheerful wave. Glen gaped, then found his wits. "Hey, buddy."

"Hi, Glen." Ghost scampered to the couch and jumped on the cushions, dropping to his knees and flopping over. Glen closed the door, charmed by the odd yet sweet behavior of the young creature he helped raise. Of course, he thought Ghost was an abnormally intelligent animal back then, not an actual paranormal creature who could shape shift with a mere thought.

"Is Cat here?" Ghost asked, lifting his head and sniffing the air.

"She's still sleeping in, she hardly got any sleep. Silly scientist was up all night listening to our neighbors howling at the moon. Cat is convinced she can decipher the howls if given enough time."

"Huh. Why doesn't she just ask them? The Red Fern wolves are nice. They can tell you what they were saying to each other. They like you."

Glen was reaching for a thick quilt on the back of the couch, and he paused a moment, looking down at the young creature sprawled out naked without a care for his state of undress. "They do?"

"Sure they do," Ghost rolled onto his back, giving Glen an eyeful of lean muscles and youthful exuberance. He chuckled, cheeks heating, and tossed the quilt over Ghost's lap.

"I know you're not used to being human yet after all these years, buddy, but maybe you can practice. I'm not used to seeing a naked man lounging about where I plunk down my own ass."

"I hate clothes," the kid grumbled, his plump lower lip coming out in a pout.

"I can tell. It's weird for me though. I raised you, so that's like you're my kid. I don't need to see my grown kid's junk flapping about." Glen shook his head and laughed when Ghost pouted a moment longer, then slumped in defeat.

"Where have you been? With your mate?" Glen asked, and Ghost grumbled.

"Been running around the mountain all night long, thinking. Being a man is hard. How do you do it?"

Glen snorted out a laugh. "Practice." He nodded at the blanket, and Ghost sighed loudly.

Ghost sat up, wrapping the quilt about his hips. He threw himself back down almost immediately, and Glen found himself unable to resist the plaintive whine that came from his pretty lips. Glen was as straight as they came, but even he could acknowledge the sheer beauty of the human form of his wayward wolf. Ghost was beautiful, inside and out, and yet he had a shade of sadness hovering about his expressive silver eyes. He walked around the couch and paused as Ghost scrambled out of the way long enough for him to sit down. A bare second later he had an armful of lean youth and wiggling limbs.

Ghost curled up in his lap like he used to as a pup, though it was different now, as Ghost was not a wolf anymore. Glen heaved out a groan in complaint, but let Ghost hide under his chin and snuggle. He hugged the boy to his chest, and they both relaxed, adjusting easily enough to the new dynamic.

"What's wrong?" Glen asked, and Ghost responded in a tiny voice.

"They put Kane in a cell in the woods yesterday. And they want to destroy our mate bond."

Glen could recall only two times in his entire life he ever got angry enough to kill. Once was back in college when he tore a drunk frat boy off a cussing and furious redhead who then proceeded to wallop her attacker. The other time was when he rescued a malnourished wolf-hybrid from a careless and ignorant suburban family in the outskirts of Toronto, the poor thing starved near to death and skeletal thin. As he did then, he ran his hands over the back of a young wolf's head, and said, "Everything is going to be okay."

Glen managed to hold onto his temper, but it was a battle. The youngling needed a shoulder to cry on, a place to relax his guarded emotions, and Glen would be that safe place for him.

"I wanted to come home more than anything," Ghost whispered, pressing his face into Glen's chest. "But nothing good has come of it. They think me damaged, weak. Vulnerable."

"We both know you are not damaged or weak. I don't think I would have survived fifteen years locked away in the body of a wolf, deprived of any sense of self or family. You're strong. And what do you mean nothing good has come from returning to your people? You have your man now, Kane. He's your mate, no matter what those fools may say or think."

"He's in a cage, Glen. In the woods, alone, surrounded by alphas who wouldn't hesitate to hurt him. I can feel him through our bond. He's frustrated, and misses me. I haven't seen him since they took him away yesterday We can't talk because the alphas might be able to overhear us, but I can still feel him. It hurts not being with him."

"I don't know a thing about what you can do, buddy. They call you a shaman, yeah? It's all magic to me. You're not by any means weak, or vulnerable. You're dangerous, just like any wolf, no matter how tamed or domesticated. Danger is part of your very existence. So, own it."

"Own it?"

"Yes, own it. You may not have all that super-secret training the other shamans seem to have, but that doesn't mean you're not their equal. Make them listen to you. I'm not saying hurt anyone or go power mad—just find a way to make them listen. Prove to them the bond between you and Kane is real."

"There's to be a Tribunal tomorrow, and Kane has to face these charges of something called blasphemy. I'm not allowed near him, and Andromeda told me not to talk to him."

Glen huffed out an exasperated breath. "Ghost, you have never played by the rules. Never. Even as a pup, you flaunted the rules. Why are you following them now?"

Ghost sat up, leaning back in his arms. Silver eyes narrowed, Ghost tightened his jaw and Glen could almost count the thoughts as they raced through Ghost's mind. He grinned, unrepentant, when Ghost slid from his lap without a word and headed for the door, dropping the quilt to pool on the floor. The door magically opened with a weird sigh and rush of cold winter air, and Ghost leapt from the stoop, a brief flash of white and silver before he disappeared.

"What did you just do?" Cat demanded, Glen looked back over his shoulder, still grinning wide. Cat had her hands on her hips, green eyes glaring at him, her expression stern. She was cranky in the morning and gloriously tousled.

"I just pointed out the obvious," Glen said, getting up with a groan, stepping to the door, and shutting it against the wind. "I think he's about to set some tails on fire."

GHOST MADE SHORT work of the miles between Glen and Cat's cabin and the cabin where the shamans resided. Their combined presence shone as a beacon on the mountainside. It was a new day, so perhaps tempers were cooled enough for him to approach his erstwhile peers. His Spiritsight lit up with the brilliant inner stars of the shamans, and from what he could see, they were all there, plus one.

Shaman River.

Ghost paused his headlong run in the field of snow outside the cabin's front door, materializing as a man before taking the stairs in one bound. He opened the door, walking in to be met by startled expressions and exclamations. He huffed, thinking they wouldn't be surprised by his appearance if they opened their senses. How blind were they?

"Ghost, I would say I'm surprised, but you're not one for taking advice," Shaman River sighed, a wry smile on his lips.

"This is all human failings and foolish politics," Ghost declared, sniffing at the combined shock and disgruntled expressions of the assembled shamans. "Test my mate bond now. It will not fail whatever test you put against it."

Michael stood from where he sat near the cold hearth, shoving his hands in his pockets staring back at Ghost. Ghost stood his ground, determined not to show how upset he was at his friend. The Tribunal members did things as most alphas did—bluntly and without grace, it was the role of a shaman to temper the actions of an alpha. Instead, Michael and his peers let the clan leaders ambush Kane like a criminal, throwing him in a cage. Michael held his gaze for only a moment before breaking away.

"Before your impetuous arrival, I was attempting to convince our brethren to do just that," Shaman River gave a sigh, a wry tone in his words that made Ghost twitch. Perhaps he was too impatient.

"Oh." Ghost shrugged, but was too riled up to calm himself. He wanted this matter settled now. Ghost walked over to the coffee table set amongst the couches and chairs where the shamans were gathered, and sat down on the rough wood surface. This was an older cabin, with the dusty scent of an unused space, and the furniture looked like stuff Cat would have kept in the storage shed back at the sanctuary. There was a plate of sweet smelling foodstuffs by his hip, and Ghost snagged one, moaning in quiet joy at the explosion of berries on his tongue. He sniffed at it, licking at some of the filling as it dripped onto his hand.

"He is a wild thing, not even a shaman. He's all beast."

Ghost continued to eat the delicious food, but he sent a sharp glance to the one who spoke. An older shaman sneered back at him, Ghost licked his fingers clean, maintaining the challenge in his gaze. Eventually, like Michael, this shaman looked away, and Ghost huffed in satisfaction. Human insults were just that—meaningless to a wolf. Ghost tried so hard to find his footing as a man, after years as a wolf, but perhaps that was not wise. Why change who he was—She never expressed the desire for him to be like these...tamed wolves.

"Orsen, don't be cruel. The boy has been a man for only a handful of days," Shaman River scolded the older shaman, but Ghost flapped a sticky hand at him to back off. Shaman this one may be, but Ghost had his measure.

"I was a wolf for many years," Ghost said, grabbing another of the bread things and taking a huge bite. This one was apple, and he swallowed with enjoyment before continuing. "I don't care about laws or rules or politics. It all smells of lies. I like the scent of truth far better. So maybe you should say what you really mean. You call me a beast, as if to lessen my words, my voice. A beast gets no say in how it is treated. You call me a beast so you can follow the path of least resistance, and let the Tribunal do to me as they wish."

"How dare you!" The shaman named Orsen spat out, Ghost remained unmoved by his display of temper. Like an old wolf snapping at a younger, stronger male, this Orsen knew his weaknesses and hated that others saw it.

"Correct me then. Prove you are not a pawn of your clan leader. You act like an alpha, all snapping jaws and sharp temper. You say I'm not a shaman? Neither are you."

A whisper broke the silence, an instant before Orsen jumped from his seat to swipe at Ghost. He licked his fingers clean, sparing a flicker of thought and a twitch of his pinky finger. Orsen gave an aborted howl in shock when he was smacked backwards, the couch skidding a few inches. The whisperer became louder, the shouted complaints from the other shamans grew quiet as swiftly as the unseen speaker's voice arose. Ghost spared Orsen not another moment of his concern, the whispers in the room harsh, sharp, and full of disapproval. The words were indistinct, but they weren't for Ghost.

She wasn't displeased with him.

BURKE SNUCK OUT the back of Clan Leader Andromeda's cabin, closing the door silently behind him. It was still early, and the grounds around the cabin were empty and quiet, the shadows long under the trees. He took off for the tree line, disappearing in the deeper shadows. He sprinted in the direction of the old worshipping grounds, and followed the pack links to where his best friend was being held. The noise of his boots crunching the thin ice was absorbed by the thick snow and the heavy branches of the pines, but he slowed his approach. No point in being careless.

He stopped, his gift stretching out through the woods, the minds of the greater alphas lighting up in his awareness like the tiny flares of lightning bugs. There were six of them, only two of them known to him by casual greetings at gatherings past. Burke kept his mental touch light, delicate as gossamer spider silk, and opened his mind. The way he saw minds was different than a shaman's ability to see soulstars—Burke saw mental signatures, the energies created by thought and the organic charges generated within living creatures' nervous systems. Shamans with Spiritsight saw the soul—Burke saw the energies of the mind.

A clan without an alpha should be easy pickings.

Shame that Kane had to fall into such disgrace.

Blasphemous monster! Poor pup must be broken.

A myriad of thoughts and impressions flew by, Burke's mind catching and deciphering every one of them, pinning each thought to the mind that birthed it. Some of the greater alphas burned with anger and righteous indignation, deeply insulted by Kane's presumed indiscretions. Others were entirely indifferent, thoughts focused elsewhere, bored with guard duty. One wolfkin mind was deeply perturbed by the lack of an alpha clan leader for Red Fern, bothered by the thought a mere beta female was considered a clan leader. That wolf had nascent ambitions of rising in the ranks, too young to believe Andromeda a true threat but old enough to be wary of her reputation. Burke expected an unwise challenge issued sometime soon, considering the grumbles. The other wolfkin were quiet, minds on their tasks of guarding Kane.

Burke increased his mental touch, sending out wordless inclinations to sleep, to doze. It was boring here in the woods, nothing to do but stare at the trees and listen to each other breathe. Nothing to do but wonder why they were there, bored out their minds. They had been out here all night long, and their prisoner had been quiet, doing nothing but sleep.

Burke smirked when two of the greater alphas put their heads on their paws and closed their eyes. He may not have the Voice like Kane or Caius, but his gift of command was more than enough to sway a vulnerable mind with suggestion. Burke waited a few moments, then slunk through the woods, coming within line of sight of the old rusted cage stuck beneath the pines.

Kane was curled upon a thick layer of pine needles, bushy tail covering his snout. Kane was as black as the depths of a moonless night, his fur without any hint of brown or sable. Burke hunkered down in the shadow of a wide tree trunk, and mindful of the greater alphas nearby hidden in the woods, sent a thin thread of awareness to Kane.

A bright eye that glowed with the strength of Kane's wilder nature cracked open, a pinpoint of light in the gray haze of early dawn. *Burke.*

Brother.

Can they hear?

No. Their minds are open to me, and they are focused elsewhere.

Can any mind stay closed against you? Kane's usual dry humor came across clearly, and Burke sighed in relief that his best friend was no worse for wear.

I'll let you know when I start hearing humans. His gifts were only useable between himself and other wolfkin—human minds remained closed to Burke, despite his power.

Day that happens you'll take over the world. Kane could quip, but Burke could feel the worry beneath the teasing. *How is Ghost?*

I lost track of him when the shamans took him away, but Andromeda put her foot down when the Tribunal suggested that Ghost be sequestered. I've been tracking him mentally—he spent the night running around the mountain, hunting squirrels and talking himself out of coming to see you, afraid he would bring trouble to your feet if he didn't stay away. Ghost is fine, if a bit of a loose cannon.

Kane's satisfaction and pride in his mate came across clearly. Burke smiled, glad for the shadows he hid within. *I haven't tried to talk to him. Who knows who may be listening.*

Burke splintered his focus, maintaining his link to Kane while part of his mind went back to the greater alphas hidden around them, blissfully unaware of Burke's presence. A swift measure of the minds around them was all he needed. *A pair of them here have the strength to overhear you, so caution is wise. I'm not sure what they would do if they spied upon you and your mate speaking to each other.*

The less trouble for Ghost, the better. Find him and stay with him, Burke.

No problem. He paused, then let some of his concern leak through to his best friend. *Are you well?*

I am fine. The accommodations are a bit small, but that's all.

Burke sighed silently, smiling ruefully at Kane through the darkness. Kane had yet to move, a lurking monster amongst the slumbering trees. The cold night caused Kane little difficulty, but loneliness was something Burke wished he could spare Kane. Were they even feeding him? He would mention it to Andromeda, though he had a feeling she was taking care of it.

If there is trouble, reach out to me, Burke said at last. *I will hear you no matter what happens.*

I will. Find Ghost. Tell him I...tell him I miss him.

Burke suspected Kane was going to say something else, but those words were best said for the first time in person. He gave Kane a short nod and a grim smile. Burke moved quietly through the shadows, leaving behind his alpha and the oblivious guards. Dawn was coming quickly, and he had a wayward shaman to find.

GHOST LIFTED HIS chin and squared off with Michael. "Test the soulbond. All of you. Whatever is done in proving such things, do it now."

Michael blinked at him, before turning to Shaman River in appeal. River sighed loudly, shaking his blond head, and spoke to Ghost. "Youngling, the test of a mate bond by a shaman is a deeply intimate process and can be…intrusive."

"Intimate? What does that mean?" Ghost frowned, sending a suspicious glare at Michael and the watching shamans, the other male wolfkin all looking uncomfortable.

"The shaman testing the bond will enter into a trance, allowing him to See into the soul of the mated wolfkin. During this time, the shaman will be privy to memories, feelings, and will be able to feel the bond of the mated wolfkin as he were a part of the pairing."

River was decidedly uncomfortable, and Ghost glowered. How was this a hindrance? It made sense to him—all stronger wolfkin could apparently sense a bonded pair, but sensing the bond and proving it was entered without coercion were a matter of degrees. Ghost shrugged, and turned back to Michael. "This is the reason you came, isn't it? One of you would be doing this regardless. Do it now. I am not afraid. Witness what our Mother has wrought. I have a mate to free."

"If he was compelled by the Voice, surely the cub wouldn't be so eager," a nameless shaman said from his seat on a nearby chair. "The process is uncomfortable, but he is right—one of us would be doing this anyway."

"Youngling, wouldn't you rather Shaman River perform the procedure? He is familiar to you. Having a relative stranger perform such a spell may be too much." This from another shaman, one yet to speak. Ghost shrugged, impatient.

"Would Shaman River's word count amongst the Tribunal?" Ghost asked, and the scent of guilt was acrid in the room. "I thought not. Michael can do it. He counts as a stranger, since I have not seen him since the day Gray Shadow died."

Michael flinched, Ghost almost regretted the words, but he did not apologize. Michael had erred, one choice after another, since appearing back in his life. Let Michael see the truth. Prejudiced the other shamans may be against the validity of his mating, Ghost had no doubt they would believe Michael. And if they didn't? Then Ghost would tolerate all of them performing the mysterious spells themselves.

He had nothing to hide.

7

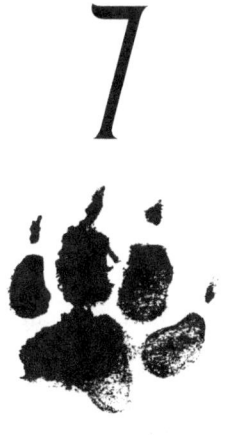

A VERDICT

THE FIRST TOUCH OF MICHAEL'S MIND ON HIS WAS STARTLING. GHOST gripped his knees tighter, and fought to open his mind to the other shaman. The touch of another's mind on his was still new, a mind he'd yet to communicate with made it even worse.

They were both sitting on the floor in front of the fireplace, cross-legged with hands on knees. Michael was still clothed, Ghost had abstained when offered a pair of sweatpants that smelled of one of the shamans. The thought of another male's scent on him made his skin crawl.

Relax as best you can, Michael whispered, and Ghost glared back at him. Michael's lips twitched, but he made no reply. *Don't think of anything.*

Ghost closed his eyes, and waited. His breathing slowed, his heart calmed, while Ghost did his best to remember that this was what needed to happen. He wasn't afraid.

The cabin and the wolfkin watching fell away. How could he not think? He'd just learned how to become a man again, his mind was somehow freer and yet burdened by the new reality he found himself living. Ghost waited, and in his impatience, he spun his awareness out.

Life glowed to his Spiritsight, colored stars in infinite hues across an endless field. The edges were blurred, beyond his range, but the weight of this reality echoed back to him where he stood in the center.

He sensed someone watching, and figured it was Michael. He had nothing to hide, so he sought out the star that shone in tandem with his own. The other presence followed, Ghost leading the way past spectral trees that slumbered, dormant earth covered in otherworldly ice and snow. Tiny bursts of light for the hidden creatures in the woods lit his way. He had no body, no limitations. Bright stars for wolfkin foreign to him surrounded his goal, and he cast their light aside as irrelevant to his purpose. His will became action, and soon Ghost hovered above the brightest star of them all.

The bars were inconsequential, the cage nothing compared to the red, fiery star of Kane. Vibrant, pure in strength and purpose, the lines of energy between them coalesced into a seamless river. Ghost's own energy, silver and white light merged with Kane's, a depthless crimson and unfathomable black. Where they joined was a maelstrom of rose and silver, the energies twirling in an endless knot before cycling into the other and being absorbed by the primary colors of the soulstars.

Kane must have sensed him through their bond, as a rush of relief and a sweet, nearly painful yearning echoed over their bond. Wordless, which was only right, for there were no words or thoughts that could encompass the boundaries and whole of their union. Their souls, the brilliant stars that glimmered in this formless place, were closer than they had been just the day before.

Ghost welcomed the rush of emotions from Kane, echoing them back. He missed Kane's strong arms, the weight of his body, the charming lift of his lush lips when he smiled. Kane was a beacon of power, resolve, and safety. The healing warmth of a den in winter, the sweet tang of fresh blood from a kill. Kane was home.

This is not what I expected. Michael's voice intruded upon Ghost's quiet longing, and he struggled to withhold his impulse to expel the shaman from his mind. Michael needed to see. See the truth, in its most basic form. Forget looking for proof of coercion or abuse—the soulbond was evidence enough.

Their souls were joined. In mating bonds that were chosen by the wolfkin involved, the bond joined their minds and emotions, and employed some limited power exchange. Those ties were chosen, put in place by willpower and intent. With concentrated power and focus, any one of the pair or a shaman could break those bonds. Here though—in this place of souls and stars and the wellspring of life, there existed a bond made not by mortals. Their souls were joining, beyond the first brush of connection and surface contact. As the days became months and then into years that morphed into lifetimes, Kane and Ghost would become one soul, their star an endless fusion of energy and power. A soulbond was forever, even past the reach of death and mortality.

How? Michael asked, and Ghost finally snapped. He sent Kane a wave of yearning, and pulled away, heart aching at leaving Kane's presence. Regardless of his lack of hands or form, Ghost 'grabbed' Michael's star with his own, and pulled the shaman behind him. *What are you doing?* The other shaman's alarm was sharp and disbelieving. Ghost ignored him in favor of finding the starlit path back to their bodies.

With a sharp gasp and a hand over his heart, Michael came back to himself. Ghost blinked, settling back into his body, stretching his spirit to fit his within his physical self again. "Tell them what you saw."

River and Orsen knelt beside Michael as he coughed, his face leached of color, eyes wild. "How? I have never…"

Ghost leaned forward, gritting out between sharpened fangs, "Tell them!"

Everyone in the room waited, inching closer. Michael struggled to stand, and plenty of hands helped. Ghost followed, standing smoothly without a hitch. Michael had yet to tear his eyes away from Ghost, hand still pressed over his heart.

"It's true," Michael gasped out, sucking in a deep breath before speaking again, control returning to his voice. "I didn't need to examine his memories at all—somehow we went beneath that, into the Spirit realms. The souls of the Black Pine Heir and Ghost are joined in a soulbond."

Orsen spun to stare at Ghost, the stares of the other shamans followed. River nodded to Ghost, tension dropping away from the older shaman. "How?" Orsen demanded.

"How else?" Ghost all but shouted back through his dropped fangs. He growled, fingers grown to claws, and he pointed at the shamans squared off against him. "You all heard Her before when She spoke to you yesterday at the clan leader's cabin. Michael has seen the bond in person, with his own abilities. This is no lie or illusion. All of you are shamans through Her grace and will, bloodlines be damned. Do you dishonor your purpose and our Great Mother by denying what you can all sense? Or will you embrace your duty and admit the truth?"

"Michael?" One of the unknown shamans sent a quiet query to the still shaken Michael, who nodded before answering. "Luca…Ghost is right. The bond is true, Goddess-forged. No wolfkin, even the most powerful alpha, could fabricate a soulbond. It's all true. A shaman and an alpha have been joined by the Wolf of the Northern Star."

Ghost watched as one by one the shamans turned from Michael and looked to him. Even the dour Orsen wore an expression of wary belief, and confusion was prominent across all their expressions.

He turned for the door, opening it to the cold evening air. With naught but a thought, Ghost took his wolf form, and looked back at the shamans. *Are you coming?*

BURKE STUMBLED TO a halt on the icy road when Ghost came running around the bend in his wolf form. Burke stepped in front of the young shaman, hands up. "Hey, cub. Where have you been?"

Ghost stopped, tongue lolling out of his mouth, tilting his head. *Convincing the shamans that my bond with Kane is true and real.*

"Did you do it?" Burke asked, but he guessed he got an answer when an SUV rumbled around the corner from which Ghost came. It was the shamans' vehicle, and Burke moved to the snowbank to let it pass, Ghost following him out of the way. "I guess you did!"

We go to the alphas now, for the shamans to testify Kane is innocent of blasphemy. Will you come?

I wouldn't miss this for the world. Burke replied to the small shaman at his feet, and Ghost wagged his bushy tail before taking off up the hill at a gallop. Burke ran after Ghost, his boots crunching loudly in the otherwise quiet morning. Ghost was gone in seconds, disappearing after the SUV. Burke grumbled before throwing himself into the chase. Watching after Ghost was harder than it sounded.

By the time he made it back to the cabin on the mountaintop, the shamans and Ghost were gathered in the living room. Burke pushed through a crowd of blonde wolves and excused himself past the shamans, coming up behind a naked Ghost, the smaller male scowling with his arms crossed. Burke shrugged out his coat and dropped it over Ghost's shoulders. Ghost spared him a quizzical glance, the large garment all but swallowing him whole. Ghost took a sniff of the collar and went to take it off, but Burke moved his hands away and buttoned it up instead.

Loud voices came pouring down the hall from Andromeda's study, and Burke took the distraction to whisper to Ghost, "You'll appear less feral and more believable with clothing on. Trust me."

Ghost glared at him, but the little shaman finally bit his lip and gave a short nod in understanding. He might look like a toddler playing dress up, bare legs visible beneath the coat's bottom hem, but at least he wasn't naked and oblivious to the impression he frequently made of being less than civilized.

"What is going on?" Caius demanded as he entered, the other Clan Leaders following him. Andromeda cut her eyes to Ghost and Burke before looking to the shamans and her brother River. Royrick, Julian, Mercuriel and Heromindes arranged themselves behind Caius, their backs to the cool hearth. Andromeda looked miniscule beside the hulking greater alphas, the powerful wolfkin males towering over the smaller female beta.

Black Pine wolves appeared next, standing in the foyer, the wolves of Kane's tactical team bigger than the smaller Red Fern wolves. Burke saw Sophia and Gerald with Kane's tactical team, the lesser alpha looking everywhere but at his own father. Sophia hopped up a few steps on the stairs, getting a clear view. She caught Burke's eyes and winked at him, a hopeful smile on her face.

"Brother? Speak, for I can see that you have all come to say something." Andromeda stood beside Caius, everyone's attention turning to River.

Shaman River took single step forward, and spoke to the assembled Tribunal. "Alphas, we have examined the mate bond between the youngling Ghost and Black Pine's Heir, Alpha Kane. It is indeed a soulbond. Goddess-forged and real."

"Is this true, Michael?" Clan Leader Royrick asked, speaking past Caius to address his clan's shaman. Andromeda frowned at the doubt cast in her brother's direction, but held her peace, her steely regard landing on the younger shaman.

"Yes, Alpha. I was the one to determine the bond's validity. The soulbond is real." Michael replied, his answer ringing clearly over the gathered witnesses. "I can swear this upon my gifts and duties as a shaman—the bond cannot be broken, and to try would be an insult to our Great Mother."

"This has to be a mistake," Heromindes blurted out, outrage and doubt warring across his face. He turned to Ghost, and pointed. "This feral creature cannot be a shaman then. The joining of a shaman and alpha is anathema! Something is not what it seems here, this will not stand."

"Enough, Hero," Andromeda said, cutting him off. "The youngling is as much as shaman as you are an alpha. The bond has been tested. Your own shamans are here for the very purpose for which you brought them, Alphas. Nothing forged by our Great Mother can be anathema— nothing She does is blasphemous. Do now as you are charged, and decide. Is Kane, Heir of Black Pine, guilty of blasphemy?"

Her challenge rang out in the suddenly silent room, not even a stray breath to break the tension. All eyes fell to the clan leaders, and the five alphas who held Kane's fate in their hands.

"We should really do this in an official manner…" Julian said, brushing at his sleeve, a sneer on his lips.

"Shut it, whelp," Mercuriel snarled. Julian lifted his lip but held his tongue. The clan leader for Dread Claw was an imposing figure, even if he was shorter than the other alphas. "I'll not waste my time away from my clan with foolish officious bullshit. I say Nay to blasphemy. I don't understand, but then I'm not meant to. Caius?"

"Not guilty to the charge of blasphemy," Caius replied without hesitation. The few Black Pine wolves at the rear of the crowd smiled in relief, and a few Red Fern wolves gave some quiet cheers. "Royrick?"

"I trust Michael," Royrick said slowly, green eyes on his shaman. "It was why we brought them, after all. It is their duty to dissolve forced and coerced mate bonds, regardless of the ranks of those involved, and if they have not done so in this case, it must be true that the bond is Goddess-forged. I say not guilty to the charge of blasphemy."

"A simple Nay would have worked, laddie." Mercuriel grumbled and Royrick sent the glowering alpha a wink. "Julian, what say you?"

"I think the Nays have a majority at three, so I'll abstain." Julian sniffed, and walked out of the room, heading for the kitchen. Burke inwardly snarled at the rude alpha's back, but the male had the count right—Not Guilty held the majority at three votes.

"Runt's a coward," Mercuriel growled, then slapped Heromindes on the shoulder. The taller alpha staggered a step then regained his balance, glaring at Mercuriel, who shrugged it off like it was nothing. "Cast your vote, Hero, or abstain as the designer-dressed gutter rat did."

Heromindes' glare was hot, and it landed on Ghost. Burke stiffened, and put a hand on Ghost's shoulder, making his protection clear. Hero's gaze fell to Burke, and he held the stare almost too long before dropping his eyes. He offered no challenge to the Ashland clan leader, but he would make his stance clear. Ghost was off limits.

Heromindes growled. It was Orsen, an older shaman, who sighed loudly and broke the tension. "Hero, enough."

"Fine! Not guilty of blasphemy. But my charges against him for illegal use of the Voice shall stand!" Heromindes said loudly, and then left the room, scattering wolves before him as he went for the front door. It slammed behind him as he left.

Ghost's shoulder sagged beneath his hand, the young shaman turned and looked up at him, silver eyes glimmering. "Burke? Is he free? Is Kane free now?"

"Not yet, but the worst is off the table. A guilty verdict for blasphemy is an automatic death sentence," Burke replied, he sighed in relief himself, letting go of the bitter tang of worry and fear he'd carried for the last day. "Alpha Caius? Can Kane be freed until the Tribunal decides the last charges?"

Alpha Caius broke off his conversation with Mercuriel and Andromeda, his clan leader's jaw tightening before looking to Mercuriel. The clan leader of Dread Claw thought for a moment, then shook his head. "Best not push it. Heromindes is ready to snap. Last thing we need is a blood feud. All of our clans are too close together for casualties not to spill over borders."

"Kane can survive another night in the darkness. He wouldn't be my Heir if a little cold could hurt him," Caius answered, sending Ghost a knowing look. "You'll not go bust him out, either. Understood? Leave your…mate where he is until the tribunal says otherwise."

"Yes, Grandpa," Ghost obeyed quietly, but Burke could already see devious little plans being birthed behind his guileless silver eyes.

Caius humphed, obviously doubting as well, but made no mention of Ghost's intent to circumvent his orders. Caius might be an ass, but he wasn't stupid.

"But I think he can have visitors," Andromeda stated, and neither alpha gainsaid her as she walked to Burke and Ghost. She took their hands, towing them behind her as she headed for the kitchen. "I think our lonesome alpha needs something to eat. I'll take Kane some breakfast, and some company. You two can carry his food for me."

"Yes, ma'am." Burke knew when it was best to agree.

8

THE DAY BEFORE

IT TOOK ANDROMEDA'S PRESENCE TO KEEP GHOST FROM RUNNING ahead. Laden with several pounds of raw steak, Ghost and Burke trudged through the snow behind the lithe clan leader. Burke toted a gallon of fresh water and a clean dinner bowl, and Ghost was reminded strongly of his years spent as a wolf.

A large shadow peeled off from the trees, stepping in their path. Andromeda didn't even pause, just swept past the greater alpha standing guard as if he were part of the scenery. A hulking brute with dark gray and brown markings, he growled low in his chest at the effrontery, though made no move to intercept the Red Fern clan leader as she led the way to Kane's prison.

Ghost's control broke the second the cage came into view, and he ran for his mate. Kane surged to his feet, pushing his muzzle through the bars as best he could, a sharp, short whine escaping. Ghost threw himself to his knees in the snow, arms winding through the bars to wrap around Kane's thick neck. Hot breath frosted the air and blew across his neck, Kane scenting him and licking his skin, wet nose snuffling. Ghost tipped his head and let Kane have his way, his larger mate examining every inch he could reach through the bars. Ghost pressed as close as he could, laughing in delight when Kane lowered his nose and breathed deep against his lower abdomen. It tickled, and Kane did it again.

My little wolf, Kane whispered in his mind, the words so soft they were closer to sensations than anything else. A yearning so intense that tears came too his eyes rose in Ghost, and he pressed his forehead to Kane's, indifferent to the rust and dirt that fell from the ancient bars.

Kane! Ghost cried out, fingers clutching his mate's thick black fur. Kane smelled of musk, sex, and blood, and his body stirred despite the circumstances. *Miss you, need you.*

Missed you too, my mate, Kane replied, and Ghost kneaded at the firm muscles under his fingers, making Kane rumble at his ministrations.

A smoke-smooth chuckle came from behind them, and a bare toe nudged Ghost's thigh. Ghost pulled back, and hurriedly scrambled for the plastic container piled high with meat. He pried off the top and lifted high a choice cut of venison, presenting it to his mate. Kane gave him a fond glance from one large eye, before snapping his jaws and devouring the hunk of meat in one swift bite. Ghost took a quick, appreciative lick of the blood his fingers before reaching for another steak, feeding Kane by hand. It was intimate, and somehow it felt like just the two of them, wolves wild and free under the sun.

Thank you, Ghost, Kane said as he licked Ghost's fingers, his long, hot agile tongue cleaning every drop of fluid left behind. Ghost's body burned—he needed, he ached, and he wanted to howl his frustrations to the moon, tear the bars from the earth and burrow beneath Kane's large and powerful frame, safe from friend and foe alike.

Burke knelt beside him, and Ghost regretfully pulled his arm away and sat back on his heels. Burke gave Kane a small, rueful smile, and slid the dinner bowl into the cage sideways before pouring fresh water through the bars. "Sorry it has to be this way, brother. But we have news."

"I am sorry—I was so excited to see you I forgot! Kane, you're not guilty!" Ghost declared eagerly, earning him chuckles from both Andromeda and Burke. Kane tilted his head in confusion, poking his nose at the bars of his cage, and Andromeda clarified.

"The Tribunal was given testimony by the shamans that your bond to Ghost is indeed Goddess-forged, and therefore you are innocent of blasphemy. Heromindes has not dropped his charge against you for improper use of the Voice. For that, the Tribunal will still meet tomorrow as planned."

Kane growled low in throat, Ghost echoing the sentiment. His relief at the blasphemy charge being dropped was so strong that he felt extreme aggravation at the remaining charge against his mate. Kane spoke to them all next, his own frustrations heavy in his mental touch. *That was faster than I expected. Why am I still caged?*

"Better you are behind bars than free to be Challenged by an angry and embarrassed Clan Leader. Hero is no match for you, but Black Pine needs you as Heir, not as Ashland's new alpha. Bid your time for another night—they decide tomorrow in regards to the last charge. It helps that Mercuriel is eager to return home, and that Julian is as impatient and self-centered as always. Their impatience will spur the other three into action."

"What is the punishment for illegal use of the Voice?" Burke asked next, nudging the bowl towards his alpha to drink. Kane grumbled but lowered his head and sated his thirst. "I don't think I've ever heard of it being levied against an alpha with the Voice before."

"It's an old Law, one meant to prevent the usurpation of one clan by another, causing upheaval. A Challenge between a Clan Leader to another, or one of comparable rank, such as an Heir, are the only times it is sanctioned to be used on a Clan Leader. There are Clan Leaders out there in the world without the Voice—and they are suited to their places, whereas a greater alpha with the Voice but no moral compass would be devastating as Clan Leader. The Voice, as you know, can be used by any alpha or clan leader upon their own wolves, but never on an out-Clan wolf. When Kane used it on Heromindes, it was both accidental and necessary—but outside of a Challenge, Kane broke the Law. The punishment is not death—but he can still die."

"What?" Ghost demanded, sick of the explanations and needing a direct answer. His hands buried themselves in the thick scruff of Kane's neck and clung. Andromeda stood over him, a white wraith in the long shadows, her blonde tresses lifting in a faint breeze.

"I have seen the punishments range from a whipping, docking, and banishment. Even a turn in the Pit." Andromeda's words sank into Ghost's heart, and he curled his fingers tighter. Kane gave him a lick across his cheek, trying to reassure him, but Ghost was appalled.

"What is docking! Whipping! And they call me a feral creature!" Ghost was at a loss, his stomach roiling. "Tell me what docking is!"

They would make me take wolf form, then cut off my tail. Sometimes, a paw or even an eye is taken. Kane told him, calm and cold, as if the act wasn't a possibility to be faced. Ghost caught an image from his mate of what that would look like, and stumbled away a step, vomiting onto the frozen earth.

"I will destroy them all if they tried it! That's far more evil than whatever crime it could be punishing!" Ghost sobbed as he threw up again, nothing but bile left in his belly. Burke knelt behind him and rubbed his back, Kane watching him worriedly from behind the bars of his cage. "How could our people do something like that?"

Andromeda shrugged, her features expressionless, but her eyes glowed an eerie blue in the darkness under the trees. "We are both human and wolf—the ruthlessness of one is fueled by the imagination of the other. Atrocities are not owned purely by the humans, regardless of what our younglings are taught today."

"Will they…are they…" Ghost tried to crawl back to Kane's side, his body shaking. Burke picked him up, then sat them both beside the bars. Ghost huddled on Burke's lap while Kane nuzzled his face. Burke was warm, and despite his immunity to the cold, Ghost was thankful for the support and comfort of shared body heat.

"I will do my best to advise them away from such an act, youngling. And you have Caius and Royrick on your side—neither of them has condoned such barbarity in the past, and have spoken out against it many times. But—the Tribunal is likely to find Kane guilty."

Ghost buried his face in Kane's scruff, breathing his mate in, trying to fill his whole body with Kane. His warmth, his strength, the feel of his fur, the thrumming of his heart.

Burke hugged him close, curling around him, and Kane gave him kisses across his cheeks. Ghost refused to believe such horror would fall upon his mate. *I won't let them harm you. I will not.*

Not even I am above the Law, Kane answered, and he seemed resigned. Ghost smacked his nose, then went back to snuggling as best he could.

"I'll come fetch you in a while, younglings. Take your time," Andromeda murmured. She then addressed the witnesses in the trees. "And no one will bother you, or face me."

Not a growl or displeased rumble to be heard, only the wind. Andromeda melted away into forest, leaving them alone. Ghost felt a measure of hope, sandwiched as he was between the two alphas.

9

THE TRIBUNAL

Dawn broke cold and brittle, fragile as a last breath. He watched the sun rise high over the mountains, burning so brightly it stole his vision before the soothing warmth of piled wolves lulled him into dozing.

He woke when Sophia, in her wilder form, slipped from beneath his head and changed back into a woman, picking her way over the jumbled Black Pine wolves. She went around the corner, and Ghost went back to watching the sun move over Baxter. Noon was soon approaching, and the wolves around him were awake, but none made to leave. Burke was at his back, Gerald at his side, and Sophia had served as his pillow most of the night.

Andromeda had returned for them late the previous evening. Ghost cringed, whining quietly when he remembered clawing at Burke's arms, determined to stay with his mate, terrified the next time he would see Kane it would be to find him cruelly mutilated. Burke carried him from the woods, making no mention of when Ghost fell limp in his embrace, his human body learning again how to sob uncontrollably, his composure fractured at last. With every step from Kane, Ghost felt his mental foundation crumble, shatter, and he was a mess of emotions and tangled thoughts.

His memory was foggy after shifting, the change rolling over him faster than thought, his instinct to return to the form he knew best. Soon after, he found himself covered in Black Pine wolves, those wolfkin who followed Kane with love and devotion, bolstering his faith and mental reserves.

Ghost sensed that Kane was still sleeping, his mate reserving his strength for whatever may come when the sun reached its zenith.

"Burke." Sophia was back at the doorway to the living room looking anxious, hands fisted at her sides. Burke, in his wilder form a large wolf with a dark chocolate coat, lifted from Ghost's side and stepped around them, claws clicking on the hardwood floor. Gerald grumbled and pushed closer to Ghost, and they both watched as Burke changed back to his human form and spoke quietly to Sophia. A moment, no more, but the stiffening of Burke's shoulders and the way he looked back at them told Ghost it was time.

He stood, staying as a wolf, and Gerald rose at his side. The remaining Black Pine wolves stood and changed back, reaching for clothes discarded in the night. Burke came back, digging through the tangled clothing on the couch, pulling his out a piece at a time. Burke sat to tug on his boots. "The Tribunal is convening. It's time."

HE STOOD IN a pair of borrowed jeans and a V-neck tee, barefoot and feeling small, surrounded by Black Pine wolves and Andromeda's family. The vast place carved from the mountainside smelled of moss, mud, and wet fur. Ghost looked up through the trees, the midday sky covered in white clouds that moved briskly across the small opening in the high treetops. The tops of the trees moved in the high wind, but here beneath the boughs, the sounds of winter were muffled.

Ghost shivered, but not from the cold. A weight, a pressure made itself known, his awareness of a hovering presence prickling the longer he stood amongst the growing crowd. There was something here, something watching, as if they were the center of the everything and the universe was spinning around them. He breathed, in and out, steadying himself. He struggled for calm, for peace, his fears were sneaking past his faith that everything would be all right. He did his best not to become distracted, and focused on what was happening around him.

Wolves climbed the tiers, settling in small family groups, friends and packmates sitting close together. The old ruin was filled with wolfkin,

Red Fern wolves unmistakable with their bright blonde tresses. Ghost and his entourage stood on the lowest tier, directly overlooking the snow and ice filled pit, the bottom a mix of forest debris, mud, and frozen stretches that the sun couldn't reach. His heart ached, thinking that his mate may end up fighting for his life.

The Tribunal gathered across from Ghost on the other side of the pit. The five alphas who were to decide Kane's punishment sat upon a stone slab that left them situated above most of the crowd. Andromeda was in front of Ghost, standing on the ledge overlooking the pit. She was dressed as she always was, in a slip of fabric from shoulders to just above her knees, this time a brilliant white that rivaled the snow, long blonde hair lifting in the subtle breeze. The many voices eventually feel silent, eyes drawn to the White Wolf as she waited. Ghost reluctantly sat, Burke on his right, his uncle Gerald on his left, with Sophia and Gabe behind them on the next tier up.

Ghost searched the pit and surrounding the seats, but there was no sign of Kane, and about half of the greater alphas brought by the clan leaders weren't present. Ghost tried to reach out to Kane, but his mate's mind was closed off, a trickle of aggression and frustration slipping through. No pain, so whatever was happening, Kane wasn't hurt yet.

Michael and the other shamans sat near the Tribunal, except for River, who was with Andromeda's brood, the shaman looking tense and wan. Ghost shifted impatiently, wondering what they were waiting for.

Andromeda slowly moved, turning to face most of the witnesses who sat above and behind Ghost. Her voice rang out over the crowd, carried on the wind.

"I am Andromeda, the White Wolf of Red Fern, vassal of Black Pine. Here, in this sacred wellspring of our Mother's blessing, I call forth the presence of our ancestors. May they guide us on our journey for truth and justice, and may the light of the Northern Star shine down upon us. I invoke the grace of our Great Mother. May all of Her children feel Her presence, and let us be worthy of Her Gifts."

The world dropped out from beneath Ghost. He gasped, grabbing a Burke and Gerald, scrambling for an anchor. The unseen presence rose, almost suffocating, pressing down upon him until he was immersed. He swayed where he sat, slamming his eyes shut, whimpering. Burke gripped his shoulder, concern filling the breeze around them, and Gerald growled under his breath, looking around for a threat.

Breathe, my shaman. Ghost sucked in a deep breath and slowly let it out, his heart easing its wild gallop within his chest. He gently patted both Burke and Gerald on their knees, settling the protective alphas. There was no danger from their Goddess.

She was here. Her voice was beyond language, beyond words, far past thought and emotion. She *was*. She was *everything*. And nothing. Here, in his heart, as She was in the air around them, the stone and earth beneath his feet.

"I call the forth the Tribunal," Andromeda continued, and Ghost pried his watery eyes open, blinking until she came into focus. "May their judgments be wise. Let us begin."

Silence, as Andromeda stepped down from the ledge and moved to the side, standing over one of the open voids carved in the stone walls of the pit.

Royrick, blond hair brushed back from his face and his forest-green eyes somehow even more brilliant beneath the dark green pine boughs, spoke above them. "I am Royrick, leader of Red Wraith. I speak for the Tribunal. We call to judgment Claire, daughter of Andromeda, beta of Black Pine."

From one of the dark tunnels in the Pit came a single greater alpha, dragging a small blonde beta by her upper arm. Claire, sometime-lover to Roman McLennan and admitted traitor. Ghost saw again in his mind Gabe standing over a sobbing Claire as his newborn gift of the Voice compelled from her the truth about her misdeeds, and Roman's treachery. Gabe growled low in his throat behind him, and Sophia whispered to the young alpha, asking for calm.

Now Claire was dressed in a dirty shift that reached her knees, barefoot and shivering, hair a tangled mess and her features wan, terror etched beside her wide eyes and trembling lips. She was a lesser version of her powerful mother; Claire was a shadow of that great line, and it showed in her blatant terror and the stench of nervous sweat that drenched her clothing. The greater alpha holding her arm was immune to her whimpers, though he wasn't rough with her, almost oblivious to her presence beside him as he brought Claire to the center of the Pit.

"Claire, you are charged with many crimes, first among them is accessory to countless murders and treason to your people. You will be questioned by an alpha with the Voice, for all the gathered wolfkin here to witness your words. You will not be afforded the luxury of lying." Royrick's handsome face was stern and closed off, nothing of mercy in his tone or body language. Claire shuddered on shaking legs, the grip of the guard all but keeping her upright. Royrick gestured, and from behind the Tribunal came another greater alpha from the shadows under the pines.

This alpha was like all the others who came as honor guards to the clan leaders—tall, thick with muscles, and imbued with a natural arrogance that spoke of supreme confidence. He wore nothing but a pair of dark jeans and boots, bare-chested and long reddish-brown hair twisted into a braid that hung over one shoulder. Same golden skin and the grace of an apex predator, this alpha stalked as if hunting even in human form. Ghost's attention was drawn to this strange alpha, sensing an odd, almost tangible force emanating from him.

His skin crawled and his heart thumped hard when he made the connection. This stranger, this greater alpha, felt like Kane. The same dominating presence, with an undercurrent of impenetrable strength.

The same Gift. This alpha bore the Voice in its full measure, same as Black Pine's beleaguered Heir.

"To remain impartial, those of us on the Tribunal will not exercise our gifts upon the prisoners. We have called for aid in this matter, and the clan of Sorrowfields from the West has answered." Royrick gestured to the strange alpha, who gazed back at the Clan Leader with a remote, nearly emotionless expression. "Roan of Sorrowfields. Begin."

Claire shrank back, shivering with fear. The greater alpha holding her yanked her upright, forcing her to look up at the one named Roan. He strode to the edge of the pit, towering above Claire as she trembled, panting harshly with increasing panic.

Ghost had not been aware that the Tribunal called for an out-Clan alpha with the Voice. He guessed it made sense, in a cold-blooded way—most of those present in the Clans were either related to the victims, the perpetrators, or the Tribunal members. Ghost was glad Caius was on the Tribunal—for all his grandfather callously shunned his sons, he still had a care for his clan and wanted justice. Caius was a contradictory mix of loyalty, vengeance, and vicious disregard. He would see justice for the injured and deceased, even at the cost of his son. Where the Tribunal was without mercy or compassion for those accused, Caius was there to provide a balance—Kane was his Heir, and Ghost hoped his grandfather felt something for the mate of his wayward grandson aside from duty.

"Look at me," Roan spoke, low and firm. The reaction from those present was extreme; betas and alphas without the Voice found themselves looking to the new alpha, drawn in by his voice, his Gift. It spread over the crowd, a grip on minds and eyes and ears that allowed for no refusal.

Except for the shamans, Ghost, and the few present with the Voice. Ghost turned in his seat briefly, to see Gabe immune from Roan's compulsion, while Sophia was under its sway. Ghost looked next to Andromeda, and it was without any surprise, he saw that she was immune as well. She caught his eyes, and gave him a small, swift dip of her chin when he cocked a brow at her. Roan speaking again drew his attention back the trial.

"Speak, beta. Tell me your name, your lineage."

Claire gasped, arching up on her toes, as if speared by his words and yanked upright. She spoke in ragged breaths, her words rising in the deepening silence. "I am Claire…daughter of Andromeda, born to the line of Shaman Stormcloud of Red Fern."

Roan's face was absolutely void of emotion, stony and cold. "Tell me your sins, beta. Spill your hidden truths, reveal the blood upon your hands. Did you assist, in any fashion, in the capture, kidnapping, and murder of wolfkin with Roman McLennan?"

"Ye…ss." Claire shuddered as the word was dragged from her, and even Ghost could feel the wave of power rising and ebbing around him. It didn't touch him at all, though, just broke like rushing water around a boulder in the rapids. He could feel the current, but he was unaffected.

"When did your involvement begin?"

"Over…over twenty years ago." Where Roan remained impassive, Claire was breaking under the questioning. The greater alpha holding her arm let go and stepped away, leaving Claire alone under Roan's regard. The small beta whimpered, sweat running down her temples, her hair matted and stringy. "I told Roman when wolves would be alone, when families in Red Fern and Black Pine were vulnerable."

"Tell me how it began." His words slipped through the air, most of those present leaning forward as one, drawn in by his voice. Every question Claire stumbled to answer, hesitant and spooked. When she didn't know an answer, she shook like a leaf on a branch in autumn, chilled and dying.

Ghost looked at the wolves around him. Burke wasn't deeply affected, able to look away but not for long—Gerald was lost, and Sophia was as absorbed as the rest of Red Fern and the Black Pine wolves sitting around them. Even without being the center of Roan's focus, those present were deeply affected by the Gift Roan wielded. If not tempered by restraint and conscience, the Voice was a mighty weapon.

He understood now the rules behind when the Voice could be used, and the severity of punishments when it was broken. If not for steep consequences, there would be mayhem in the clans. Ghost drew in a deep breath; ever thankful he was a shaman and immune to the Voice.

You begin to see, to know. Her words came quietly, spoken to him alone, and he nodded to the invisible witness. She gave him a gentle touch of warmth, reassurance he was safe, and he could focus better. His distraction meant he missed a good portion of Claire's testimony.

"You attempted to murder wolves of Black Pine, using a bomb made by another. Tell me his name, and why."

"Roman...gave me the bomb. Told me to kill the Black Pine wolves closest to Kane. He wanted Kane weak, and he thought killing his favorite wolves would destroy Kane. He hates Kane."

She left a bomb on the front step of the cabin where Kane and Ghost used to stay. Only the whispered warnings of the Goddess gave Ghost the time to raise a shield, deflecting most of the blast and sparing the lives of his mate and friends. Claire went from passing information to Roman, to trying to kill for him. Terror at how close she came to ending all he held dear swamped him at once, and Ghost quaked down to his soul. Burke put an arm around his shoulders, squeezing hard once before letting him go.

Claire was speaking, and Ghost went back to paying attention to the trial. Ghost growled to himself quietly, annoyed he missed so much.

"Roman colluded with the Remus brothers, first Sebastien, then Simon," Roan stated, tilting his head slightly, the only reaction he'd yet to show. "The humans who are aware of our existence have long coveted our powers, so their motivations are easy to discern. But what did Roman desire?"

Claire shook her head, biting her lip. Ghost smelled blood a second before it dripped down her chin.

"He wanted the strength to be Heir! He hated his weakness. He hated Kane!"

"Why did you help him?" Roan asked, and Claire shook her head, trying to resist. "Speak! Why did you betray your people?"

Claire screamed as Roan's power swamped her, and she was lifted from her feet and thrown backwards. She crashed to the muddy ground of the pit, crying, but Roan was without mercy. "I wanted…"

"Louder!"

"I wanted an alpha!" Claire shrieked from the ground, clawing at the muddy earth. "I wanted him to love me!"

The tension in her body snapped, and Claire went limp. For her desire to claim Roman McLennan as her own, she betrayed her people, her family, and wolfkin by the dozens were dead.

Gray Shadow was dead. Marla, his mother. His brothers and sisters. Dead, one and all, lost to them forever. Claire betrayed them to Roman and his broken, bitter wolves, and Ghost's family was shattered. Ghost's eyes stung, he sucked in a deep breath, hoping the cold winter air would clear the ache from his chest.

Claire was still breathing, but unmoving. Ghost stood and leaned forward, sniffing. He could smell the stench of fear and urine. The Voice left her broken. A beta had no defenses whatsoever against the power of a greater alpha with the Voice. Andromeda was a monolith, immobile, not a twitch of an eyelash or stray scent betraying her feelings after watching her own daughter be tortured by Roan. Burke tugged Ghost's elbow, and he reluctantly sat.

The greater alpha in the pit grabbed Claire and slung her over his shoulder, walking to the opposite tunnel, disappearing into the blackness. There was no movement, everyone who witnessed the questioning subdued in some way. Roan stood motionless and silent gazing down into the pit, as if willing to wait forever until bid to start anew.

Caius stood, breaking the silence, all eyes drawn to the clan leader.

He walked to the edge of the pit and addressed the clans. "I am Caius McLennan, Clan Leader of Black Pine. I call forth Roman McLennan to stand in judgment."

Murmurs rose in harsh waves, wolfkin leaning forward to catch a glimpse of the traitor. Where Claire's testimony left them silent and distressed, the mere mention of Roman's name sent a flurry of excited whispers through the assembled clans. Growls came from one of the openings in the pit, and Roman McLennan, Ghost's other uncle and mass murderer, was dragged from the shadows.

Bound in chains made from silver and steel, Roman was covered in restraints—feet hobbled, arms wrapped around his chest and wrists in shackles with a collar about his neck. Roman was bound as tightly as could be managed while allowing him to walk with short steps. Three greater alphas held his chains, and two alphas in their wilder forms prowled at his heels.

Roman snapped his teeth at the wolfkin holding his chains, though he could do nothing to them, bound as he was. Barefoot in the snow and mud, wearing nothing but a dirty pair of sweatpants, Roman was a pitiful sight. His dark brown hair was pulled back behind his ears, and his face streaked with dirt. His time in the cellar of Andromeda's cabin hadn't been easy.

Insults, growls, and even some flung debris rained down over Roman as he growled back up at the crowd. Ghost sat still, not partaking in the heckling, and those acting up quickly settled when Andromeda sent a frown in the direction of the Red Fern wolves.

"Begin," Caius told Roan, who responded with the slightest of nods. Caius returned to his seat with the Tribunal, expressionless, and Ghost could not smell or sense a single emotion from his grandfather.

Gerald tensed at his side, and Ghost leaned hard on the lesser alpha's shoulder. His brother was in that pit, about to be questioned for treason and murder. Ghost had no memory he could trust concerning Roman— the time elapsed too great a distance in his mind. He remembered Gerald from his days as Luca in vague, shadowy impressions, but for Roman there was almost nothing. A glimpse or two of his mother laughing, Roman standing over her with a smile, and yet that was it. No emotion, no recollections that lent Ghost to sympathy or compassion for the shackled monster in the pit.

"Tell me your name," Roan said, eyes locked on Roman. He growled back, teeth fanged out, that undefinable power rose again, sharp and pointed, and Roman screamed.

He dropped to his knees, mud splattering, blood running from his nose. Gerald shivered, and Ghost gripped his uncle's hand tightly in both of his.

"Roman…" He gasped out, spitting a globule of blood out, red ruining the snow in front of him. "I am Roman McLennan, son of the cold-hearted bastard known as Caius McLennan."

"You are charged with murder, treason, assault, conspiracy with humans, and numerous counts of abuse. You were caught by Clan Leader Andromeda in an attack on Red Fern. A witness has testified to providing you information leading to the kidnappings, torture, abuse, and eventual sale of wolfkin clan members to humans who further abused them. Did you collude with the humans Sebastien and Simon Remus?"

Roman spit out more blood, and the pressure around him rose. Wolves in the seats behind Ghost whimpered as Roan increased the weight of his Gift, bearing down without mercy on Roman. Yet Roman spared not a glance for Roan—he only had eyes for his father.

"Yes, I *colluded* with the Remus brothers," Roman spat out, eyes glowing, his fingers changed enough for claws to grow long, the tips sharp against his ribs where his arms were strapped to his torso. His rage, a foul stink that made Ghost's nose curl in distaste, pushed him to shift. "I sent them wolves I snatched from their beds, the streets. I gave them the locations of families with strong alphas for the taking. I gave Simon Remus my blood and seed, and told him how a wolfkin bitch could control her breeding cycles. I even told Sebastien Remus—," and he screamed the rest to his father sitting above him, still as the stone upon which he sat, "I even told them where and when to grab your beloved Gray Shadow! They wanted the strongest shaman, his blood and body, and I gave them what they needed to take him!"

His last words were spoken at a roar as Roman lurched to his feet trying against all odds to break free. His guards yanked him back into the mud, those in wolf-form snapping at his face. Cries of shock and horror came from the clans, even the Tribunal members looked disturbed.

"Where is Simon Remus now?" Roan asked, the only one seemingly unaffected by the madness spewing forth from Roman.

"I don't know. Your precious Kane took the human doctor, and most of my wolves are dead or run off like the cowards they are—I doubt Remus has stayed in the places I knew him to frequent," Roman answered, some sanity returning to his voice, though his eyes glowed with an intense shine.

"Do you know where he has labs?"

"Yes…" Roman had blood dripping from his nose, and he didn't seem to notice. "But it was standard for all labs to be scrubbed and moved if someone with knowledge of their locations was taken. Good luck finding them now. Remus has already moved them."

Royrick leaned forward in his seat, one hand up to stall Roan from asking another question. "Why was the human doctor here? What use was he?"

Roman growled, his bare feet changing, claws popping free to dig into the slush in which he stood. Roan did something, and the pressure in the pit rose, making several wolves whine quietly and Roman to let out a sharp exhale, shoulders shaking.

"The human doctor was here to take blood and tissue samples from Gray Shadow's beloved whelp." Roman's answer made the Tribunal raise their eyes, one after another searching out Ghost where he sat amongst the clans. Gerald grumbled softly next to him and Burke put a protective hand on the back on his neck.

"Gray Shadow's whelp? You mean the feral youngling returned from the northern wilds is the center of this travesty?" Mercuriel spoke up for the first time, his deep, booming voice carrying across the wide space beneath the trees, echoing. Roman bared his fangs, acting far more feral than Ghost could ever claim. "Answer!"

"We wanted Gray Shadow for his powers. He died and we got nothing but a degraded blood sample tainted by silver. We needed more." Roman's voice was strangled, perhaps by the Voice the same way his body was forcing the change, his emotional and mental state eroding his human form from within. "The pretty little bitch could be the great Gray Shadow, reborn. Looks just like your dead lover, doesn't he, Father?"

Shocked gasps came from everywhere, but none present were more shocked than the Tribunal. Heromindes and Royrick turned to Caius, who was like stone, staring at his son as if he were a whole new entity. Caius said nothing, did nothing, acting as if oblivious to the regard of his fellow tribunal members, his eyes locked on Roman and barren of emotion. Ghost ached for his grandfather. His own heart hurt. Eventually the Tribunal members dragged their shocked and curious attention away from Caius, and Royrick took a deep breath before continuing.

"You mentioned the humans wanted the youngling known as Luca.

Were his powers the focus?"

"Remus wanted the powers of the wolfkin for humans. I wanted the powers of the shamans."

"That's impossible. Humans and wolfkin cannot even breed, we are too different. Remus sought an impossible goal." That was Mercuriel, his doubt and confusion echoing what most of those watching seemed to feel. "Science cannot bend magic to its will. You and Remus sought power that can never be yours. All for what? Jealousy and impotence stole your sanity?"

"Not entirely impossible. Remus used Harmon to create hybrids. Some lived only hours, some days. Each new wave of wolfkin I brought him took him closer to his goal." Roman spat out more blood, grinning. "He's got labs all over New England. I haven't even been to them all. Dr. Harmon said that hybrids were a step closer to giving wolfkin abilities to humans. I didn't bother with that side of the operation—I hunted the wolves Remus needed and threw away the trimmings afterwards."

"Abomination!" Mercuriel thundered, echoing Ghost's feelings perfectly. "Why would you help him do such things?"

Roman snapped and snarled, blood and spit and spraying from his lips. "I wanted to be like the old War Wolves from the oh-so-perfect Gray Shadow's lessons. Pathetic fairy tales that watered down the gods we alphas once were. Shamans crippled the wolfkin. They have powers that once belonged to alphas, and I wanted them back! We aren't meant to hide, our strength leashed! We are conquerors and god-kings, reduced to neutered half-life and mewling, simpering magicians who suck the strength from our clan leaders with a stern frown and wagging finger. How many times did Gray Shadow suck your dick, Father? How many times did he let you bend him over like the bitch he was to get what he wanted? He castrated you, made you weak! You exiled me for trying to claim what is mine, when all along Gray Shadow took it from you with a shake of his ass!"

Ghost could not take his eyes from Caius, his grandfather at last showing emotion. Pain, so clear and poignant and devastating filled Caius' eyes, his expression a rictus of grief. It was there for but a second before control unlike anything Ghost had ever seen before schooled his features back into stony calm.

Roman was still ranting, and Roan let his power fade away. Madness blurred Roman's features, a horrific glimpse at the splintered mind that orchestrated such despair and death. Even without Roan's compulsion to speak, Roman now seemed incapable of remaining quiet, his raving inescapable.

"I killed wolves for the humans. I sold them, I cut them and bled them, I ripped them apart! I raped the bitches and defiled the upstart whelps who dared to laugh at me for my own father casting me aside for another. I gladly and without remorse told Sebastien Remus how to capture Gray Shadow, and I did it because it would destroy you, Father! How mighty was your beautiful Shadow that he died a failure? Did he live up to your expectations, your version of perfection? He's dead! How perfect can a dead wolf be, *Father?*"

It was Heromindes who finally gestured to the guards around Roman. One in human form punched Roman in the back of the head, and he fell face first into the mud and snow.

Ghost felt horror and sadness, his heart breaking for Caius and his family. Her Presence echoed his sorrow, and She faded from the pit, the pressure in the atmosphere changing once She was gone.

Gerald was swearing under his breath. Red Fern and Black Pine wolves alike exploded in a flurry of exclamations and distraught whispers. Mercuriel, Julian, and Royrick spoke quietly to each other, and Roan stepped back into the shadows under the trees. Heromindes turned to Caius as if to speak to him, but he said nothing, shutting his mouth and frowning down at the unconscious Roman in the pit.

Caius held himself stiffly, frame taut, and Ghost thought something terrible might happen. He dreaded what Caius would do if his control were to break. Caius stood, then climbed the stone tiers behind him and jumped out of sight into the woods. A blur of white and gold followed, Andromeda on his heels.

"What now?" Ghost asked Burke, who shook his head, frowning.

"I'm not sure," Burke said after a long moment, brow furrowed. "Kane's testimony is next."

HE WAS ALONE, head down, hand upon a stone monolith that rose from the tumbled roots of ancient trees.

Andromeda stepped lightly, bare feet silent over the dry needles that covered the forest floor like a thick soft rug. She was soundless, but Caius knew she was there.

"I have lost many friends, family members." Caius said, lifting his head and staring out into the quiet woods. "I have lost mates, a daughter, my own brothers and sisters. My parents, grandparents. All dead and gone."

"As have we all," Andromeda agreed, coming to stand at her Clan Leader and friend's side. "We live a very long time, my friend. Death hunts us slowly but steadily. It is one predator that not even our Goddess can defeat."

He was nearly unchanged from the day she first met him centuries before. His eyes were shadowed by grief, his jaw tightened by sadness and strife. The hint of joy he once carried in his youth was gone, to be replaced by a hardened exterior and an empty heart. Caius, the greatest of Clan Leaders within the New World, was a hollow shell of a man.

"I thought that losing Marla and Gray Shadow was the deepest I could be cut by grief," he spoke quietly, his eyes glowing faintly. "But to hear my own son admit to conspiring to capture his own family, that his actions led to their deaths...I haven't hurt like this is very long time."

"I know," Andromeda said. "But we both know what pains you the most."

The stone monolith, easily five feet taller than Caius and several thousand pounds heavy, covered in lichen from standing tall and unmolested by time, shuddered and groaned in protest when Caius made a fist and pushed. Anger showed in the tense frame of his shoulders and the claws that grew from his fingertips. Dirt and snow cracked, frozen roots creaked, the monolith tumbled to its side, rumbling the ground beneath her feet. The crash reverberated through the slumbering trees, and blue jays called out sharp warnings in the distance.

"I...we...Ana," Caius shuddered, teeth pointed and no longer quite human. "No matter how much time passes, I can't forget how deeply I loved him."

"Don't forget, my brother. That love is the only thing saving you. Shadow's love for you was deep and true. Yours for him was, is, just as powerful and everlasting. You may not have been more than friends at the very end, but how he loved you never diminished, despite the centuries and the few mates you tried to love in place of each other."

"Shadow, my Shadow," Caius whispered. "By the Goddess, Ana, I love him still." He spared a glance for the toppled monolith, shaking his head. He spoke again, voice firmer. "My own son, Ana. I knew he was conspiring to depose Kane as my heir. He kept dragging Gerald along with him in his foolish schemes. I just wanted peace in my clan. I may not have been the best father, but I had to be a clan leader first. That meant the strongest heir, and Kane was that wolf. He still is that wolf. Roman has always been weak, in character and ability. Could I have prevented this, if I paid more attention? Gerald seems redeemable—he scarcely reminds me of the sullen and bitter wolf I ordered out into the world weeks ago. He changed. Did I make a mistake—was Roman salvageable at one point? Did I make my own son into a murderer?"

Andromeda put a hand on Caius' shoulder, noting the tense muscles beneath her fingers. "A perfect father you have not been, but even a difficult childhood is no excuse for murder and rape. Roman is over two hundred years old—he knew what he was doing. He let his heart decay, his soul blacken. He made his own decisions. Not even the most loving of parents can prevent their children from making the wrong choices. My own daughter is proof of that."

Caius finally met her gaze, his eyes back to normal. A crooked, pained grin twisted his lips, and he chuckled. "We are a pair, are we not? Our children are traitors and killers."

"And that is their shame to bear, not ours," Andromeda said firmly, holding his gaze until he gave her a small nod in return. "Come, my brother. We must return. Let the shamans testify to the validity of the mate bond between your Heir and your grandson—and then we shall see how much groveling Kane must do to Heromindes to soothe that stubborn beast."

IO

THE LOST WOLF

THE WAREHOUSE STANK, AN ACRID MIASMA OF FEAR, PAIN, AND DEATH that filled his nose and made his teeth hurt. Wren pulled his blankets higher around his shoulders, wishing he had clothing to wear, but the guards took his clothes from him the night he was thrown in his cage. He couldn't remember when that was, or how long ago. He had no concept of time—the nights and days were all cold and dark, damp seeping into his bones. He shivered, curling in tighter.

Footsteps came down the long aisle between the cages. His was at the very end, next to the area where the surgeons did their bloody work, only a thin plastic curtain blocking off most of the gruesome activity. Boots rang out on the concrete floor, and he hid his face and eyes, doing all he could not to draw attention to himself.

There was no sky to see and nothing but shadows, echoing corners, and the sound of water dripping.

And screams.

The screaming never really stopped. It came and went in waves, but there was always some sound of pain and fear that reached his ears. Sometimes he thought he would carry the sound for the rest of his miserable life, ever present and haunting. Even now an unfortunate soul somewhere down the line of cages was crying softly, begging to a deity he had never heard of— someone called the Great Mother. He didn't know what religion that was, but like every god he'd ever heard of, there was no answer to desperate prayers.

He risked taking a quick peek out from beneath his arm, and quickly hid again when he saw a pair of shiny leather shoes walking past his cage.

"Any progress? You've had weeks now to correct the procedure." That was the voice that haunted his nightmares. It was the voice he heard when he was first dragged into the dark and stripped of his identity. The voice that called him an experiment and a failure and yet never got around to throwing him away. Maybe that was the point. He was here for amusement, for them to hurt, and was still trash.

He had a name once. A place he called home. A mother he never remembered, but he remembered his father. Or the man who adopted him, gave him a name, a place to stay. A toddler with no one to love him, he'd clung to the man he came to call father. Even if he was learning that Dr. Harmon was never really his father, but the man who made him in a lab. He was something impossible.

A monster. Child of wolf and man.

The longer he spent in his cage, the more certain he was that he had been here before, or a place very like it. When memories and nightmares collided, fitting together like two separate puzzle pieces, he was struck by a sickening sense of familiarity and déjà vu. It was hard to tell what was real and what wasn't. He couldn't tell if his very first memory of a lab similar to this one was real or not. The brief experiment that was his life began in a cage and was going to end in a cage.

The butchers who call themselves surgeons and scientists were speaking with the man who walked in his nightmares. They discussed what they did like they were normal everyday things, like budget meetings and chatting around a water cooler. Instead they discussed dissecting living creatures and splicing genes.

"Mr. Remus, with the combined resources between our lab and what you brought us from Dr. Harmon, we've made some progress. The original specimen you brought us hasn't shown any changes in behavior or physiology since it has been kept here on the main floor with the other specimens." He winced, the thought he wasn't considered a person painful to hear. "We hoped it might show some similar traits, but so far nothing has happened. We're using it right now as a control specimen in case we succeed with another hybrid. The current clone is at 94% vitality and can be freed from the incubator in a few days. From the progress we've seen, Dr. Harmon decided not to go the humanoid route with this attempt. We hypothesize that growing it in animal form will force it to present the werewolves' natural abilities. Once it's at 100% vitality, we should be able to see whether Dr. Harmon's hypothesis was correct."

There was a glowing tank of weird fluid and a dark mass in the far corner, two guards stationed next to it like they were afraid whatever was in there would burst free and start killing. Whatever it was in there, it didn't move on its own, just floated, oblivious to the horror of its creation.

The horrible man with the cruel voice was talking again, he wished he was unconscious so he didn't need to hear it anymore. "Dr. Harmon was only ever able to make one viable hybrid that actually had a functioning brain, but the tossup was no abilities whatsoever. All he did was make a prettier version of a person. This idea better work. You will figure out how to take those damn animals' abilities and give them to humans—don't need to keep making more of the damn monsters! This experiment doesn't work, take all the samples you need from the hybrid and this clone, and then destroy them."

"Yes, sir. We'll do our best. Going back and growing the specimen itself and using Dr. Harmon's cloning techniques may be the key to what we've been missing. Cloning a werewolf is the first step in identifying which genes can be cut out from their DNA and grafted onto human DNA."

The men, the surgeons and doctors and scientists, their voices and words all blended together, a nameless group of evil men who caused nothing but pain and suffering. They didn't even see him as a person—he was an 'it.'

"I let Dr. Harmon get taken by these monsters for his repeated failures. If I see the same failure in you, I won't hesitate to toss you into these cages and watch them tear you apart." The man sounded as vicious as always, disdain and arrogance dripping from every threat he tossed out with impunity.

Wren huddled quietly in his cage, only a few feet away from where Simon Remus threatened the doctors and scientists who were doing their best to destroy every shred of his humanity and sanity. He hated Simon Remus with all his heart and soul, and if the chance ever came, he would feed Remus to the giant wolves in the cages next to him.

II

KANE

"It's time," a guard growled, and Kane left his cell without a word.

It was just after noon, the testimonies of Claire and Roman had caused a stir even Kane could sense across the pack bonds. Ghost's presence in his mind alternated between chaotic worry and a reserved quiet that disturbed Kane more than anything.

His paws dug into snow and ice as he was led toward the pit. Four guards surrounded him, and he was thankful he was spared the chains in which Roman had been bound. One of his guards was in his human form and he opened a rusty, moss-laden metal gate that was attached to a rock wall. It must be the bottom of the pit, Kane could hear echoes of growls and voices coming from the dark void.

There was little he could see, even with his eyesight better as a wolf than a man. A growl from behind him betrayed his guards' nervousness at being in the dark with him, and he grunted, satisfied he wouldn't be jumped. He was larger than his peers by a great deal—these may be greater alphas, but none were comparable to him in size or power.

A short walk and a sharp bend brought him out into the light. Inundated by sunlight, scents, and the sounds of a few hundred wolfkin bombarding his senses, Kane shook his head in annoyance, ears flapping against his skull. He blew out a deep snort, and that drew the attention of the combined wolves of Red Fern and his tactical team from Black Pine. Kane wasted no time in searching out Ghost—there his mate sat between Gerald and Burke, surrounded by Black Pine wolves.

Ghost leaned forward, one hand on the ledge above the pit, his silver eyes wide, bright, and glorious. His guards prodded at him, but Kane shook off their attempts to drive him to the center of the pit, and shifted. His change was not as seamless as Ghost's would be—but it was noticeably swifter than even he was accustomed to, startled gasps came from those watching in the seats. Ghost was about twenty feet above him, a distance he could jump with ease, even in his human form. He reminded himself that was not the best idea, given he had yet to give his testimony and face judgement. If things went horribly wrong, he would risk escaping, and Goddess help anyone who stood between him and his mate. Never mind what he was capable of –Ghost had no notion of Laws or propriety, his control over his shamanic gifts wasn't hindered by inhibitions or tradition. Ghost could cut a swath through any force who sought to control him.

"Little wolf," Kane murmured, and the smile that erupted on Ghost's face was bright enough to rival the dawn. "Are you well?"

He remembered how Ghost fought to remain with him through the previous night and he was worried for his mate. Kane was not afraid of what might happen to him—his mate bond with Ghost was no longer under contest, and he would accept whatever punishment the council saw fit to dispense in regards to the other charges. Unless they sought his life or to keep Ghost from him, Kane would bow to the Tribunal.

"I'm okay," Ghost said, his sweet voice making Kane smile despite being naked, dirty, and surrounded by angry alphas. Ghost always spoke as if words were unnecessary, his body language conveying as much meaning as the words he chose. He leaned forward so far Burke grabbed the back of Ghost's waistband to keep the youngling from toppling over the ledge. "Are you well, my alpha?"

"I am, little wolf," Kane assured. "This will be over soon, I promise. Sit back with Burke now." Impatient growls and the snapping of teeth next to his heels told him his guards were working up the courage to force him to the center of the pit. Ghost gave an impatient sigh and sat back in his seat, Burke shaking his head in amusement.

Kane turned and strode through his guards, the wolves yelping and backing away. He stopped right in front of the Tribunal, eyeing the clan leaders arrayed in judgement before him. He kept his chin up, and made eye contact with each. Caius was reserved and disturbed, though Kane had a feeling none could tell but for those who knew him well. Royrick gave him a small nod, and Mercuriel met his eyes without hesitation, giving nothing away. Heromindes and Julian alternated between sneering and trying to meet his eyes—Hero glared at him before breaking eye contact, and Julian failed after a few seconds.

Andromeda walked from the shadows to stand over the pit. "Before Kane of Black Pine gives his testimony in regards to breaking the Laws governing proper usage of the Voice, the shamans are asked to testify to the nature of the mate bond between Ghost and Kane." She gestured to the shamans, and Michael stood from their number and walked to the edge of the pit.

"I am Shaman Michael of Red Wraith," he said, speaking loudly, the assembled wolfkin quieting to listen. "As we were summoned by our collective clan leaders to ascertain the nature of the mate bond between Kane and Ghost of Black Pine, we examined the bond yesterday. I can attest that the bond between Ghost, a shaman, and Kane, a greater alpha, is indeed Goddess-forged. It is a soulbond and immutable—the Clan Laws have no bearing in this matter."

"So say your fellow shamans?" Andromeda asked, and a soft chorus of agreement came from the gathered shamans. Andromeda turned to the Tribunal next. "Clan Leaders of the Tribunal, you have heard testimony by the shamans in regards to the nature of the mate bond between Kane and Ghost. Are the charges of blasphemy dropped?"

Royrick stood, and declared, "As the mate bond is Goddess-forged, our Laws have no bearing. Soulbonds are not held to Clan Laws. All charges of blasphemy and coercion laid against Kane of Black Pine are dropped."

A rush of excited whispers surged through the crowd, and it took everything Kane had not to jump up and grab Ghost in a hug. He could hear Sophia and Burke cheering behind him, and the mate bond with Ghost opened wider. He felt his mate's happiness and relief as if they were his own.

Royrick lifted his hand, and the crowd settled. "There is still the charge laid against Kane for improper use of the Voice. The Law is clear—the Voice shall not be used against a Clan Leader or Heir outside of an official challenge for rank. Kane has willfully admitted that he used the Voice against Heromindes of Ashland. We already have testimony of Heromindes as the victim of this crime. What say you, Kane of Black Pine?"

Kane took a moment, thinking of his options. He did indeed use the Voice on Heromindes. He broke the Law. "I am guilty. I used the Voice on Clan Leader Heromindes to prevent him from losing control. He was going to kill two human witnesses before they could be questioned. Those witnesses later gave information that helped in the apprehension of Roman and gave us information on Remus and his activities. Clan Leaders Caius and Heromindes both questioned the humans responsible for assault, torture, and trafficking of wolfkin. I used the Voice to halt Clan Leader Heromindes, and I immediately returned to him his free will after I used the Voice. It was unintentional; I reacted instinctively, to the urgency of the moment, and I apologized afterwards. I am deeply sorry for the affront and wish to make amends as Clan Leader Heromindes sees fit."

The pit was quiet, and Royrick sat down slowly. Caius bore an odd expression, halfway between pride and worry. The other members of the Tribunal were either shocked, thoughtful, or angry, as was the case for Heromindes.

"Was there a witness aside from the involved parties?" Andromeda asked, making several wolfkin jump in surprise. Before Kane could offer a response, Burke rose from his seat.

"I am Burke, Speaker of Black Pine, and I was present. May I testify?" Burke spoke loudly, his words reaching every pair of ears in the surrounding seats.

Andromeda nodded, and waved a hand at Burke for him to continue.

"Kane's use of the Voice was indeed unintentional and instinctive. I was in Kane's mind, and Heromindes' as well, orchestrating the raid on the humans' complex. I could see every thought , decision, and action as it happened. Kane did so without malice or forethought, and returned to Heromindes his free will immediately. Heromindes suffered no permanent damage to his mind or free will." Burke stood at the edge of the pit, one hand behind him keeping Ghost in his seat. Kane gave his best friend a nod in thanks, relieved and grateful that Burke stood up for him.

"He is a Speaker, and one which the members of the Tribunal know to be an honest and forthright wolf. Do you accept Burke of Black Pine's testimony?" Andromeda asked, and Kane was never more thankful that Andromeda oversaw the trials. It was fast, to the point, and free of angry grandstanding.

The clan leaders spoke quietly to each other, Heromindes shooting glares at both Kane and Burke, while Caius remained stoic and remote. He gave a short answer and nod, and eventually Royrick stood again. "Speaker Burke's testimony has been accepted by the Tribunal. We will adjourn for the rest of the day—all verdicts will be given by sunset tonight."

The clan leaders got up and left quickly, Heromindes glaring at Kane for a long moment before Mercuriel blocked his view. Kane's guards crowded in and started ushering him back to the tunnel.

"Kane!"

He looked back over his shoulder, and gave Ghost a small smile, trying to reassure his mate.

Burke took his hand from his shoulder, and Ghost melted into the milling crowd. "Ghost!" Burke called after him, but he couldn't contain himself any longer. He ran, on four paws faster than thought, and ducked through the Red Fern wolves, soon finding his way into the woods.

Sophia and Burke called for him, but he refused to wait. He wanted this whole thing to be over with, done, and he had to wait to get his mate back? What was there to decide? He sat through the long, drawn out misery of a trial—whatever that really was—and thought he was surrounded by humans. Testimony, verdicts, guilt or innocence? The Laws, rules made by wolves long dead and gone—where were the wild dire wolves in their nature? The Tribunal were naught but old wolves playing at being human men. If not for the odd alpha named Roan and the presence of his Goddess, he would have thought he was fully in the human world. He'd watched enough television with Cat when he was stuck in his wolf form to recognize plenty of human customs, and the oddness of the wolfkin adhering to such things as Laws and trials left him frustrated.

He soon lost the desire to run, and found a tree to sit against, staring out at the forest. It was quiet, though he could hear the tiny sounds of life and motion. His ears flicked when a bird fluttered between branches, a rodent dug beneath the snow for its hoard. The wind rustled the tops of the trees, and trunks frozen in the deep cold on the mountain creaked in response. Clumps of snow fell from boughs, soft plops that came and went in waves as the wind blew.

A small scuffle to his right heralded the approach of a rabbit, and Ghost watched the critter curiously hop about, the wind blowing in the wrong direction keeping it oblivious to his presence. He was hungry. He hadn't been eating enough, he knew that, too stressed out over Kane's incarceration and the charges levied against him. He reached out with his mind, and could see that Kane was again back in his prison.

The greater alphas acting as his guards snapped and growled, and his mate ignored them all, indifferent to their attempts to rile him. Ghost huffed, pleased with his mate. Kane was a powerful alpha, and the wolves around him now were nothing compared to the might of Kane in his wilder form.

The rabbit got too close and realized its folly as Ghost leapt. He caught it in his jaws and shook hard, snapping its neck. He returned to the tree and lay down, eating the rabbit slowly. Steam rose from the kill as he licked the hot blood. He wanted to see his mate. Bring him a rabbit or two, share the kill, and run together beneath a bright moon.

EVENING FELL. HE watched the sun set through the trees, the sky awash with fiery oranges and reds, the deep blue of twilight. The rabbit was long gone, his fur coated with ice, and Ghost felt alone despite the mental nudges he got from Burke and Kane. He wanted to reach out to Kane, but he didn't want to cling, to fall apart. He was on the very edge of madness, the wait too much to bear. He found it all easier to endure as a wolf, and so stayed in the woods, avoiding the curious who tracked his trail through the woods. Eventually they left him alone, returning to their cabins.

The Tribunal would be casting their verdicts now, but when Ghost sent a wordless query to Burke, he learned the Tribunal would not be sharing the verdicts publicly with the whole clan at the pit. Burke told him the news quietly before Ghost could ask. He was both terrified and exhilarated. Claire and Roman's fate was decided, but the Tribunal was still arguing Kane's fate.

Claire would be punished and then banished from the combined territories of those on the Tribunal, all other clans informed of her transgressions. Ghost figured she wouldn't last long—even in the wild, an exiled wolf, injured and weak, would fall to the fangs of other packs. She would find no welcome.

For Roman—death. The how and why of it Ghost did not care.

Ghost ran for the place his mate was locked away. The greater alphas guarding him were hunkered down around a fire, in their human forms and clothed. They were eating and talking quietly amongst themselves, Ghost snuck by them without being noticed.

Ghost crept forward, the flickering light from the fires camouflaging his approach to the cage where his mate paced. Kane was in his wolf-form, the great and beautiful beast almost too big for his prison. Ghost could see him with his Spirit-sight, Kane's powerful crimson red star in his core a writhing storm of strength and resolute determination.

Ghost was within a yard or so when Kane's head turned in his direction, his dark eyes glowing in the shadows, only the hint of his outline in the darkness.

Little wolf, you must leave, Kane said, the frantic concern he felt for Ghost's safety coming through clearly along their link. *The guards might try to hurt you if they catch you here.*

No! Ghost retorted, stepping through dead pine needles and sticks without a sound. He pressed his head through the bars, only able to get his nose and muzzle inside. He was not afraid of wolves who went against the Great Mother's will, wolves who wanted Kane punished for having too much power—power they couldn't control or exploit. Kane licked his nose, whining deep in his throat. *I cannot stay away anymore. I need you.*

Little wolf, Kane said softly, pressing his head to Ghost's, the bars keeping them from getting closer. *I am Heir and Alpha, and I cannot disobey the Law. I must see this through unless they give me no other option.*

Law made by wolves who hold their will above the will of our Goddess, Ghost whimpered, thinking he should just use his abilities to destroy his mate's prison and free them both. Let them leave, live in the wilds, wolves unfettered by foolish Law and pettiness. *She gave you the Voice as surely as she made me a shaman.*

No, Ghost, Kane told him, reading his thoughts about escaping into the woods. *We will wait and see what happens. Do you know of Claire and Roman's fate?*

Ghost was about to answer, when the scent of a new wolf nearby interrupted them. Ghost swallowed his snarl, instantly recognizing Andromeda's true-gold star, shining intensely in her heart. The White Wolf padded silently into the small space around the cage, and sat beside Ghost, her wolf-form terrifying in its beauty and grace. Pure white, glacial blue eyes, and fangs sharper than the final cut of Death, Andromeda was the epitome of the wolfkin.

My daughter is to be exiled, she said gently to them both. *Roman is sentenced to death. He will fight Heromindes in the pit tomorrow. The Tribunal agreed that was best, as they will not ask Caius to kill his own son, and Hero's kin and clan suffered last at Roman's hands. No one doubts that Roman will die against Heromindes.*

And Kane? Ghost demanded, paws restless in the pine needles under his toes. Kane was breathing slow and sure next to him. The great white wolf gave a sigh, her shoulders dropping as she exhaled. She gave Ghost a nudge with her nose, almost knocking him over. Ghost was small compared to Kane, and Andromeda was easily a head taller than even his mate.

Kane is to fight in the pit as well, she answered at last, ears back, nose down, unhappiness disturbing her usually inscrutable expression. *Heromindes was given the choice—justice for his wolves by taking Roman's life, or face Kane in the pit. Maiming as a punishment was tossed aside in favor of combat. Only Julian and Hero pushed for maiming, and they were outvoted. Heromindes chose not to risk facing Kane in the pit—Roman was a wiser choice.*

So who is Kane to face then? Ghost asked. He was afraid he knew.

"The alpha from out-clan. Roan of Sorrowfields has been chosen to face Kane in the pit. If Kane loses, Roan may choose to take his life or banish Kane. If Kane wins, he is exonerated from further punishment and the matter is closed.*

12

TOOTH AND CLAW

Morning came too slowly for Ghost's liking. The guards discovered him in the night, but a sharp snap of his teeth and a deep warning rumble from his mate made them back off. Ghost ignored the glares sent his way all night long, and he snuggled as best he could with Kane despite the bars between them.

This morning three would meet their fates in the pit.

A growl from the edge of the small space beneath the trees made Ghost lift his head, ears pricking forward. A large chocolate brown wolf padded from the shadows. Burke's eyes were gold, glowing brighter than the metal humans prized. He was shaggier than Ghost, a burly beast who moved with an easy lope. Burke came to a stop at the cell, sniffing at Ghost before touching noses with Kane through the bars.

The Tribunal has called the clans to attend the punishments. Andromeda has warned that families may want to keep their youngest cubs at home, Burke said, somber. He sat on his haunches and quirked his head to the side, as if listening. Burke was a Speaker, his mental abilities staggering to comprehend, so it was likely he was listening to many minds at once. *Usually in situations like this all would be required to attend, but Andromeda went against the tribunal and warned her wolves it was going to be brutal. No one argued against her after that. Claire is to be punished first.*

Ghost stood and shook out his fur. Cubs were accustomed to violence. Parents hunted with their younglings, fights were common, and bloodshed was easily dismissed as normal. For Andromeda to warn her wolves to keep the younglings away, the coming morning would likely be deeply disturbing. Ghost whined low in his throat, pawing at the cage bars. Burke gave a soft huff, the bigger alpha worried too.

It is our way, to punish with blood and death. We are not humans. We have no prisons. We keep prisoners for a short time before their fates are settled. This is our way. Kane was calm, unperturbed he would be soon facing the mysterious out-Clan alpha in the pit.

A guard in human form came up and opened the gate, Ghost and Burke moving back so Kane could exit. Kane was huge. Burke was almost twice Ghost's size, typical for a greater alpha—Kane was easily another half again bigger than Burke. Ghost was dwarfed by his massive mate, who stood over him as a giant.

Kane stepped up to Ghost, reaching down with his great head and gripping Ghost at the back of his neck. Kane rumbled, pleased, and Ghost went limp in happiness when Kane loped a paw over his back and moved Ghost underneath him. Ghost pulled his tail in and settled down, letting Kane smother him in his scent and body. Kane smelled like the forest and earth, but with a wild tang that hinted of heat, blood, and wild chases through the night. Everyone politely ignored the behavior but Burke sneaked a swift peek before darting his eyes away.

"Move it," one of the guards said after a few minutes, a sneer on his lips. Kane merely looked in his direction and the other alpha went pale and took a small step back. He found some courage and managed to speak without sounding too terrified. "We need to go now."

Ghost wormed his way from under Kane, licking his mate's nose when he got free. Kane indulged him before nudging at his flank. Ghost moved out of the way, and Kane took off at a gentle jog through the trees. The guards complained, hurrying to keep up. Ghost and Burke stayed right on Kane's heels. The guards brought up the rear, their scents confused as they tried to understand Kane heading willingly to his fate, not away from it.

Ghost could not wait for when they were done with Tribunals and fighting. He wanted only his mate, the mountains, and the wind carrying the sweet smell of prey.

HER GRANDDAUGHTER MANY times over darted in amongst the clan leaders, pouring tea for Julian. The alpha gazed at the young beta far longer than Andromeda cared for, and when he finally looked away, she caught his eye. He tried to play it off, but his face tightened and the faint stink of unease wafted across the table.

A tip of her head, Andromeda directed her younglings from the room. Caius frowned at Julian, having seen the same thing she did. Helen and her siblings left, and Andromeda waited until the younglings were out of hearing range.

"Julian," Andromeda said, lifting her tea cup and taking a sip. Julian looked her way, the alpha discomfited. She didn't care. "My family is entirely off limits. Look at Helen, or any of my wolves like that again, I will castrate you and feed you your balls."

"I…" He started, but with a lift of a single brow, she silenced him. Anger seething under the surface, Julian gave a brief nod and growled at the other clan leaders who dared to enjoy his set down.

He won't take kindly to your warning, Caius whispered in her mind, and Andromeda agreed.

He will mind me or suffer for it, Andromeda replied. *I know what he does in his own territory. He will not lay a hand on my wolves.*

Agreed. Caius paused, his mind briefly focused elsewhere. *I have tasked First Beta Sophia with keeping an eye on him. My wolves will intercede if necessary.*

Thank you, brother.

Breakfast done, the clan leaders eventually dispersed. Andromeda touched Caius on his wrist, keeping him in his seat. They nodded to the others as they left to make their way to the pit. The door shut in the front of the cabin, and aside from the guards and the prisoners in the cellar and the subtle heartbeat of the youngling Gabe upstairs, they were alone.

"Ana?" Caius said, sitting back in his chair. Caius had only taken coffee that morning, eschewing food. Likely for the very same reason as Andromeda.

"You asked me once, many years ago, to trust my family into your keeping," she said, then paused. She gripped his wrist, tighter now, crushing the sleeve of his cotton sweater beneath her fingers. "My family grew over the centuries. I have many children. I have lost some, but many of them live still, and I am thankful to the Goddess every day for her blessings. I am thankful for one of my dearest friends, pigheaded and harsh he may be," Caius' lips twitched at that, and she smiled. "I am thankful for you allowing me my ways, and aside from some small squabbles over the years, you have never let me down. So I ask now, my brother, for a small favor yet again."

Caius pulled his arm back just enough to grip her smaller hand in his, holding tight. She thought of the wayward child waiting in the cold cellar, and asked for what she could not do herself. "I cannot bear to punish her. I brought her into this world. I carried her beneath my heart. I taught her to talk, walk, hunt. She was one of the first children I birthed here in the New World, and I cannot find the strength to punish her. Not as the Law demands."

Caius squeezed her hand tightly. "Let me take this burden from you. Red Fern holds vassal to Black Pine—I will see no other do this."

Andromeda nodded, thankful. "Please." She thought of the clan leaders heading now to the pit, and shook her head once. "Julian would kill her in his glee; he knows no restraint. Mercuriel would do his duty, but his strength would do more harm than the punishment calls for. Neither Royrick nor Hero are of the temperament to harm a female beta, even for a banishment. And I...I cannot."

Andromeda looked back to Caius. He was somber, and she knew his heart was already heavy. His own son was to die, and she asked this horrible task of him. He had done worse, in the many years since he became clan leader, but their time here in the New World softened the harsher edges of their lives during the last fifty years.

"I will handle Claire's punishment and exile. She will receive her due, and no more."

Andromeda sighed, clutching Caius' hand.

SOPHIA FOLLOWED THE tribunal members as they made their way towards the pit. Julian was in the front, walking fast to put distance between himself and Andromeda. She laughed quietly, the word of caution her clan leader gave her regarding the volatile alpha from Birch Grove fitting perfectly with what she knew of him. If he made a move toward any of the youngsters of Red Fern while she was around, there wouldn't be anything left of him for Andromeda to kill.

She lost sight of them at a bend in the path, and jogged ahead. She all but ran head first into a solid, thick chest, and came to an abrupt halt.

"Stalking now a hobby, Sophie?" Royrick asked, a wicked grin on his lush lips, green eyes sparkling with mischief. He was alone on the path, the other clan leaders on their way to the pit. She huffed, and tried to get around her former lover. "Sophia, come on."

"What can I do for you, Clan Leader Royrick?" She kept her face blank, her tone dull and respectful. She didn't have time for his typical, bratty banter.

"Ouch," Royrick rubbed a hand over his chest. "Can one old friend not say hello to another? This is the first time I've been able to see you in forever, Sophia."

She sighed, a long exhale, full of exasperation. She was fond of him, and he surely knew that, but what he wanted from her was something she couldn't give. She couldn't be what he wanted. His refusal to bend his pride and buck tradition all those long years ago is what ended their affair. "You see me every gathering, Royrick."

"Once every five years. I asked you to be Alpha Mate, and we were together for two decades. Surely that warrants more than a flat hello and a brush off."

"Your idea of the perfect Alpha Mate was different than mine. Different enough that we broke up because of it. I refuse to be a simpering beta maiden dependent upon her alpha for all things." She crossed her arms and glared. "I can do more than have cubs and cook supper."

"I know you can, Sophia," Royrick started, but she snorted in disbelief. A noise came from the path at her back, and she turned to see Andromeda and Caius approaching, the two clan leaders talking quietly to themselves, and behind them, the prisoners and their greater alpha guards. She darted around Royrick before he could say another word, and headed for the pit.

She heard a frustrated growl from Royrick, but he refrained from continuing his case, following behind.

GHOST FOUND HIMSELF herded away from Kane's side just outside the pit. Burke led him around and up, while Kane went again for the tunnel in the side of hill. They stayed in their wilder forms, and snaked through the gathering clan. There were less clanmates present, and the lack of cubs was apparent. Even the younger adults weren't there in the full numbers Red Fern could boast.

There was no sign of Gabriel Suarez—and Ghost had no idea where the younger alpha may be. Roman was about to be punished, and as it was Roman who was directly responsible for Gabe's abduction and subsequent assault, Ghost was sure Gabe would want to be present for the last hour of Roman's life.

And there was another notable absence—the shamans were not present at all. Ghost thought that an odd thing, but since everything that was about to occur was punishment, perhaps healing the condemned afterwards, if they still lived, wasn't allowed. Or maybe the shamans could not stomach what was about to happen and Ghost found himself again exasperated with those who were supposed to be his kindred. He had yet to encounter a shaman who could live up to the example set by his grandfather and that left him bitter. He shoved that feeling aside as best he could and focused on what was about to happen.

Sophia was looking over her shoulder, a worried expression on her face until she saw them coming. Ghost leapt past her to the ledge, peering downwards. Kane was almost right below him, still in his wilder form and sitting back on his haunches, unconcerned with the growing tension in the guards. They were arranged around him in a semi-circle, as if to keep him from bolting. Ghost huffed, thinking these greater alphas were all brawn and had not a single intelligent thought among them.

Commotion at the tunnel to the left drew his attention. Screams and pleas for mercy came from the dark seconds before a naked Claire was dragged from the shadows. An alpha held her arm while another held a long metal spike and shackles. Ghost crouched down, ears flat to his skull when he realized what was about to happen. Claire was guilty of so much evil, regardless of the fact that she never took a life with her own hands, yet watching her now, Ghost only saw a frightened beta.

The greater alpha who held the spike reached over his head and slammed the point into the stone wall just below where the tribunal sat. The point dug deep into the wall, making a dreadful screech. Ghost flinched, ears flat his head. The alpha then swung the shackles over the spike while Claire was dragged to the wall. She screamed in protest, pleading for mercy. Sounds of dismay from the crowd came from all around Ghost. He looked down at his mate. Kane showed no sign of distress, immobile and unmoved. Ghost dropped to his belly, tucking his tail to his back legs. Burke and Sophia were behind him still, the scent of distress rising from his friends.

Claire's arms were raised over her head, her wrists shackled in the chains. Her guards backed away, leaving her to stand alone on her toes. Andromeda was nowhere to be seen. Ghost checked the surrounding edge of the forest, and he saw no sign of the female clan leader. The Tribunal appeared from the trees, except for Caius. They took their seats, all of them bearing serious expressions but for Julian, the redheaded male appearing to be eagerly awaiting the coming punishments. There was a manic gleam in his eyes that Ghost could see even across the pit.

Movement from the right-hand tunnel drew his attention. Caius, came out from the shadows, bare to the waist, in his hand was a long length of leather and silver. He wore shiny, smooth leather pants and was barefoot. The metal glimmered in the weak sunlight that cut through the clouds, and Ghost could smell the acrid scent of the poisonous alloy. It was a whip, coiled like a deadly snake in his grandfather's hand. Claire saw Caius approaching, and she started to cry and plead with her clan leader. Caius went to the center of the pit, not responding to her cries, his face blank and remote. Ghost could not sense anything from his grandfather, not even a hint of remorse or regret for what was about to happen. Claire must have realized that she would receive no mercy, as she fell to quiet sobbing, her face buried in her arms.

There was a subtle movement at the tunnel Caius had come from, and Ghost could just see the faintest of light from glowing glacial-blue eyes. Andromeda was watching, and Ghost felt sympathy for the female clan leader. She was about to watch her daughter be punished, and Ghost had no idea how Andromeda must be feeling. To be a clan leader meant that Andromeda had to be both ruthless and compassionate, such contrary states must be tearing her part.

Royrick stood and addressed the gathered clan. "Claire of Black Pine has been found guilty of all charges. She is to receive one hundred lashes, then she will be banished from all clans represented by the tribunal. Clan Leader Caius will carry out her punishment."

The whip uncoiled from Caius's hand, falling to the ground with a hiss. Ghost could see a thin metal chain intertwined with the dark smooth leather of the whip, one smooth braid that must be longer than Caius was tall. "Caius, you may begin when ready."

The greater alphas in the pit all moved away until their backs were to the wall, out of reach of the whip. It snaked through the air with a sharp hiss, and the snap as it went forward was loud, echoing across the pit. It happened so fast that Ghost didn't even see the blow land. Claire screamed and arched her back, head thrown back as a stripe of red bloomed on her pale skin. The red was vibrant for a short second then her natural healing abilities soothed the injury. The next blow fell before her scream faded away.

Caius set a brutal rhythm with the whip. Soon her back was a horrific mesh of crisscrossing lines, some of them bleeding from the edges. Blood dripped down her sides, thin lines that smeared as she screamed and fought against the shackles. The silver of the whip soon overcame her ability to heal, even stalling her body's instinctive reaction to Change in response to the pain.

Everyone present was silent, the only sounds to be heard the whip flying and Claire's muted cries. The scent of blood was strong, filling his nose and blinding his senses to anything else. Ghost sneezed, trying to clear his nose. He had no idea how many lashes Claire had already taken—he couldn't count that high—yet he was certain that Caius knew how many lashes remained. There was no hesitation or missing— each blow landed exactly where he meant. Claire collapsed against the wall just as Ghost grew concerned she may not last much longer.

The sound of the whip stopped as what must be the last blow fell, Caius stepping away and coiling the now bloody leather and silver length into his hand. He was still expressionless, but sweat ran down his back and his hair was damp from exertion. Caius nodded to the tribunal, and said, "That is one hundred lashes. Her punishment is done."

Caius nodded to the greater alphas acting as Claire's guards, who went to the unmoving beta. One of them unshackled her, the other caught her as she fell. She was slung over his shoulder, limp and unresponsive. She did not smell of death so Ghost knew she still lived. She was carried to the tunnel where her mother waited for her in the shadows. The guards and their burden disappeared.

Caius took a few running steps and then leapt, landing on the far edge of the pit. He tossed aside the whip and took his seat among the Tribunal. Royrick gave him a concerned glance, but Caius paid him no attention, his eyes on the floor of the pit. Royrick took a second then stood, addressing those present. "Remove Kane from the pit—Roman McLennan is to be punished next."

Kane huffed in annoyance but stood anyway when his guards motioned for him to follow. Instead of returning to the tunnel, Kane leapt up the wall and landed next to Ghost. His guards growled and there were frowns from the tribunal, but when Kane settled beside Ghost and made no further movement, Royrick waved off his guards. They left the pit themselves, retreating into the darkness of the left-hand tunnel.

Ghost took his chance and snuggled with his mate. Kane gave him a lick across his muzzle before looking back to the pit. Growling came from the left-hand tunnel as Roman was dragged into the pit like a dog. Roman was naked, like Claire had been, with a chain around his neck. Ghost flattened his ears and a low growl escaped from him before he could stop it. Roman may be his uncle, but the wolfkin before him had cast aside all bonds of family and blood with his actions. Where he had felt compassion and regret for what was done to Claire despite her crimes, he felt no such things for Roman. Caius was unmoving still, once again an emotionless statue.

Heromindes stood and prowled to the edge overlooking the pit. Roman was forced to the center and pushed to his knees by his guards. Heromindes, without a word, began to remove his clothing, tossing the pieces aside. The guards left the pit, the last one to leave removing the chain from Roman's neck. The guard shoved Roman down and walked away. Roman fell to his face in the mud, then sent a nasty glare at the retreating guard's back.

Heromindes was naked at last, his long dark hair free from its braid, the ends catching in the wind. Roman slowly pushed himself up to his knees, wiping mud from his face. Royrick looked like he was going to say something, but Heromindes sent his fellow tribunal member a stifling glare, and Royrick retook his seat without a word.

"You will face me for what you have done," Heromindes shouted at Roman. "I will snap your neck after I have feasted on your blood. The lives of all the wolfkin you have taken over these long years will be avenged, and justice will be had for my slain kin."

"They were weak and useless wolves," Roman snarled in response. "None of them served their purpose. And your kin are lost to you still. My death will not save them. You can try to kill me and you may be able to do it, but your family will still die screaming for you to save them."

Heromindes roared and jumped into the pit. He landed a few feet away from Roman, who quickly backpedaled to get some distance. Heromindes was changing, his wilder nature taking control. His human form melted away as dark fur sprouted from his twisting limbs. Heromindes took his wilder form in a matter of moments, though not as fast as Ghost had seen Kane transform.

Heromindes was a large beast. His coat was a mix of dark brown and gray with random swirls of white. He was shaggy and brawny, with large paws and a big head, his mouth full of long white teeth that shined with sharp points. He clawed at the ground, throwing mud behind him.

Roman bared his teeth and growled. He was changing too, but far slower than Heromindes. The clan leader of Ashland prowled back and forth as he waited for Roman to complete his change, saliva dripping from his jowls, hackles raised, and hair up along his spine. His great claws dug into the earth, leaving furrows in his wake. Roman shuddered and flopped down on all fours, presumably the silver from his chains prolonging the transformation. It looked painful and difficult.

At last Roman stood as a wolf. He shook his head as if to shake off the trauma of his slow change. His ears flattened back and he dropped his head, lips pulling back from his teeth. He was not as large Heromindes, but he was still a big beast.

They were dire wolves, great predators of the ancient past, despite the modern personalities within their minds, and as the two wolves circled around each other there was nothing civilized about what was to happen. Ghost shivered, pressing to Kane's side as the tension rose and finally snapped.

They came together with a crash, jaws snapping and claws rending flesh. Roman dug in with his back feet and pushed forward, throwing Heromindes head over tail. Mud splashed in all directions. Roman charged, attempting to take advantage, but Heromindes was on his feet and met his rush with open jaws. Roman tried to dodge but slipped in the mud, skidding with a yelp, landing on top of Heromindes in a tangle of limbs. Roman was quickly flipped off of the clan leader and onto his back several feet away.

The fight was messy and loud. Heromindes charged Roman, snapping at his heels and tail, chasing the disgraced lesser alpha around the pit. Blood dripped from wounds hidden by long fur. Roman would try to turn and snap at Heromindes only to be bulldozed down and bitten. What used to be growls of anger and challenge soon changed into screams of pain and whimpers.

Ghost could not watch anymore. Heromindes was enraged, a mindless creature hell-bent on tearing apart his prey. Ghost turned his head and pressed his face into Kane's side. The scent of blood was inescapable, joining the spoor left over from Claire's whipping. He wished he could close his ears to the noises coming from the pit. He could not turn off his mind which supplied images to accompany the sounds of ripping flesh and bones snapping.

He knew when it was over. Heromindes gave a great roar of triumph. The cry cut through the air and trees, startling some nearby crows into flight.

KANE RESTED HIS head upon Ghost's back. His little mate was shaking, face buried in his flank. Ghost was a wild thing, feral and changeable, alternating between a grown man's mind and that of an untamed wolf. Ghost could fight tooth and claw to defend himself and those he loved, but it was not in his heart to watch such a mismatched and forgone fight to the death.

Roman was dead. Heromindes stood over the mangled remains of the great traitor, blood in his fur and dripping from his fangs. Roman's head was twisted back, neck sliced open down to the bone, blood still running in rivers into the mud and snow. He had died with an expression of resigned fear, his once glowing eyes dim and void.

Kane looked to Caius where he sat among the Tribunal. His clan leader was staring at the body of his son, and it was only due to long years of serving as Heir that he could see pain and grief in Caius' eyes. Heromindes was snorting and tossing his head, ears flapping against his skull, tail flagging high as he gave in to his wilder instincts and celebrated his win. Greater alphas waited at the edge of the pit to remove the body but made no move to approach while Heromindes was in such a state. He would be violent and would react viciously to any attempt to remove his prey.

Ghost remained hidden, though his shivering ceased. Kane gave a heaving sigh, exhaling roughly through his nose to expel the too sweet scent of Roman's blood. The Red Fern wolves seated behind him were quiet and subdued. At last Heromindes turned away from the corpse, and he left the pit with one last insulting swipe at the mud, sending damp earth over the body.

Little wolf, lift your head. Look at me, Kane whispered to his mate quietly in his mind. *Can you continue? Soon it will be me in that pit. I will not have you suffer.*

Ghost lifted his head, bright silver eyes glowing. Kane could feel worry and fear coming along their soulbond but also determination. It would pain his mate to watch what was to come, but he would watch regardless. *I will watch and you will win.*

Movement on the other side of the pit drew his attention. Roan, the mysterious alpha from Sorrowfields, came out from the trees and stood just below the tribunal. He was already naked and stood tall as he watched the body being removed from the pit.

As a greater alpha with the Voice, Kane had occasionally, in the last twenty years or so, come across other alphas with the same gift. Caius had the Voice, and young Gabe had it in even stronger measure, and there were a few wolves spread out amongst Black Pine who had a measurable form of the Voice— yet none were as strong as Kane and the gift he carried.

Except perhaps for this strange alpha from Sorrowfields.

Sometimes Kane could sense it in another wolf. It gave off a faint metallic and oppressive atmosphere if the greater alpha who bore it did not bother to hide it or keep it contained. Some greater alphas with the Voice wore it like a badge of honor and used its presence to intimidate and coerce without using the gift. Kane strove always to keep the gift contained and out of his daily interactions with his fellow wolfkin. But for the few moments when he was in error, like when he reacted instinctively with Heromindes, Kane was the least willing amongst all greater alphas with the Voice to use the Gift. Looking now at this strange alpha, Kane could not actively sense the Voice, but it was the fact that this alpha held such tight control over his gift that told Kane that it was immense indeed. Listening to his guards speaking to each other at night gossiping about Roman and Claire's forced testimonies gave him the impression that Roan's gift was a terrible and mighty weapon.

Kane had been unmatched for many long years— in fact, for his whole life. Even as a youngling he had never lost a fight or challenge with his peers. When he became Caius's Heir, Caius encouraged him to fight every challenger who disagreed with the clan leader's decision. Kane won every fight. Some opponents he left alive, as he had with Roman and Gerald a decade before, and a small handful Kane was forced to kill because they would not yield. A part of him was sorry for their deaths, but it was their nature and their culture that made such deaths both necessary and vital for their society to function and keep their wilder natures from overwhelming their humanity. He knew Ghost would disagree, and in fact he could feel his mate's derision at such a concept through their bond. Violence for the sake of violence was what Ghost could not comprehend nor accept. Kane understood the necessity, even if he didn't agree with it all the time.

The body was at last removed from the pit, nothing remaining but some tufts of fur and blood that pooled and froze along the edges. The greater alphas who had been acting as guards withdrew from the pit and disappeared. Royrick stood and gestured to Kane, "It is time, Kane of Black Pine."

Ghost gave him a small lick across his muzzle, a small shiver racing through his slender frame. Ghost backed away until he could lay between Burke and Sophia who put their hands on his shoulders in support. Kane looked away from his mate after one long look and met the eyes of the foreign alpha. There was no emotion in those eyes, only calm acceptance for what was to come.

Kane wanted his words to be heard by all and did not want to waste the energy casting his mind to all those present, so he reached for his human form and changed swiftly. He stood as a man, naked and bare as Roan. "I have no quarrel with you, Roan of Sorrowfields. I will not take your life unless I am forced to do so. This fight can end with either one of us yielding to the other. Agreed?"

"Kane of Black Pine, I accepted the tribunal's request to fight on one condition. If you die or if you yield, I take your place as heir, and all that you own and all that you treasure will be mine. If you do not yield, I will kill you."

Growls and angry muttering came from the Black Pine wolves at his back. Kane tightened his jaw and let the anger wash over him and he let it go as best he could. "Same conditions as a traditional challenge, then?"

Roan gave a decisive nod, his eyes and hands already giving in to his wilder nature. His gaze landed on Ghost and it took Kane a moment to realize; never in any challenge had Kane had a mate to lose if he lost the fight. "Ghost and I are soulbonded—if I die Ghost may die with me. If I yield, he will still be my mate until the day we both die. I do not know what lies or misconceptions you may have believed, but Ghost is not someone you can win. You can take my place as heir and win all that I possess, but you will never win my mate."

"I have my doubts that what you share is a soulbond. When I win, we shall see just what the nature of your bond is when I have the little gray wolf in my bed."

"He can't be that dumb. Roan heard the shamans' testimony. He's goading you, don't believe a word he's saying," Burke whispered urgently behind him. "Don't get angry."

Kane looked over his shoulder at his best friend and gave him a wide grin. "I'm not that worried. Stay with Ghost—I'll see you all in a few minutes."

With that Kane took a flying leap over the pit, and faster than he had ever changed before he landed on all fours in the mud and snow as a great black wolf. He lifted his head and howled to the sky above, a deep resonating call that urged replies from all that heard him. Answering cries came from Red Fern and Black Pine wolves in attendance and a few smattering responses out amongst the trees. He dropped his head and set his feet, eyes locked on his opponent.

Roan gave a slight tilt of his head and cracked a tiny smile. He was changing into his wilder form before he even left the ledge, transforming in the air to land opposite of Kane as a vibrant red wolf. His eyes glowed bright blue as if ice had been set on fire. His fur was longer than Kane's but his teeth were just as white and his claws dug deep into the earth.

Kane dropped his head further and spread his front legs to give himself better balance, eyes tracking his opponent. Roan mirrored his actions. This alpha was accustomed to fighting. Most of them were— a greater alpha fought more than a lesser alpha or even a beta. The shamans didn't fight at all except for self-defense or the defense of those they protected.

He watched Roan's eyes waiting for the attack to come— and it came, but not as he was expecting. A swell of power rose from the red wolf, sweeping across the dozen or so feet between them and Kane had but a second to bolster his mental defenses when Roan's gift crashed over him. He had never fought with the Voice before— but he had been a devoted student of Gray Shadow and knew his history. Greater alphas of the past had fought first with the Voice and then with fang if equally matched.

Kane grinned wolfishly and pushed back with his own gift. He unleashed it with a single target—Roan. Those watching could see nothing but two wolves snarling at each other, but they could surely sense the roiling power that crashed like two rivers joining. It was all mental though; his body felt the strain, muscles quivering as he held his ground, pushing outward against the invading mental presence that was attempting to stifle his free will. He had never felt such an overwhelming and oppressive sensation before, not even when he was a youngster and Caius was teaching him how to use the Voice.

He had never faced an equal.

He refused to buckle under the intense mental pressure. It came at him like a storm, powerful winds pulling at his willpower and trying to shred his determination. It was an assault he almost did not know how to counter— a weaponized version of the Voice. He used his gift to protect, to heal, to lead—no part of him ever wanted to use it to cause harm.

Yet he must.

Roan of Sorrowfields snarled with victory, thinking he had Kane outclassed. He took a small step forward to match the mental push at Kane's defenses, and Kane took the cue and made a small matching step backwards. Gasps came from those watching in the seats above, and there was a deep satisfied laugh that came from the direction of the tribunal. Kane ignored all of it, and laid his trap.

Kane stopped pushing back with the Voice. He pulled it back in, letting it coil within his mind like a snake hidden in the grass, ready to strike. Roan took the bait, pushing forward with his mind even as he took several steps in Kane's direction. Kane made himself small, hunkering down to the ground until his belly touch the mud and the underside of his chin grew wet from bloody snow. He withdrew himself mentally, until not even a hint of the Voice or his gift dwelled outside of his personal boundaries.

Ghost was concerned—he could feel intense worry along their bond. Yet he could not spare a moment to reassure his mate. He would not die nor yield in this pit.

Roan was now standing over him, premature victory and triumph cut in every line of his muscular form. The red wolf made the mistake of lifting his head, his ears pricked forward, and his throat exposed. Roan did not increase the weight of his gift but kept it steady, convinced he had already used it to the point of forcing Kane to capitulate.

Bait taken, and Kane struck.

He unleashed his gift at the same instant that he leapt upwards, his head tilted to the side with his jaws wide. The shock of their minds meeting, hitting like two boulders toiling in the white waters of a raging river, was enough to startle Roan. Kane's jaws closed around the vulnerable underside of Roan's neck, and Kane continued his leap all the way through. The pressure of Roan's mental attack dissipated almost instantly as they flew together through the air, Roan landing on his back with Kane atop him. Kane dug his claws into the red wolf's underbelly deeply enough to draw blood, even as he tightened his jaws on Roan's throat.

Roan gave a choked gasp when Kane closed his jaws further. His teeth just broke the skin, warm blood pooling on his tongue, but he went no further. Roan tried to buck him off, but all it took was the tiniest shakes of his head for Roan to still. The red wolf froze, his head thrown back, face obscured by snow and mud.

YIELD. He shouted it mentally. His mental voice reached the minds of all those present and watching, a wave of surprise and nervous fear rippling across the crowd.

There was no response from Roan. The red wolf was in shock, both his mind and body confused. He went from eminent victory to utter loss so quickly that he couldn't fathom what had happened.

Kane let his fangs dig in just a little bit more, determined to make Roan yield. Despite the red wolf's rude taunting, he had no quarrel with Roan.

"Do you yield, Roan of Sorrowfields?" It was Caius who spoke at long last. Kane twitched an ear in the direction of his clan leader but kept his focus on the wolf beneath him. Roan tried to scramble away; Kane sliced in deeper with tooth and claw. Roan stilled, and finally went limp.

I yield, he whispered, though Kane had no doubt all could hear. He waited, but Roan said nothing more, submissive in his loss.

Kane dropped Roan's neck and stepped away, leaving Roan where he lay. It was over in a matter of minutes.

"No! That's it? A few snarls and then Roan gives in? I refuse to accept this!" Heromindes shouted, gesturing wildly from where he stood next to the tribunal. He was human again, covered in mud and blood.

"He yielded, Hero! Silence! It's over!" Royrick chimed in, and Julian started laughing, enraging Heromindes even more.

"Utter bullshit! He must pay for his crimes. Kane must pay for what he did to me!"

Heromindes jumped into the pit, people were shouting. Caius and Mercuriel chased after him, but rage and frustration made Heromindes faster, and he took his wilder form with a thought, charging at Kane before he even finished transforming. Hero slammed into Kane, and they tumbled head over tail through the slush.

Their tumble halted when they crashed into the stone wall, and they broke apart for a second before Hero came at him with snapping, foaming jaws. All higher thoughts were gone from the clan leader—he was a frustrated animal ready to kill.

Heromindes' claws raked down his shoulder, separating flesh. Kane roared and snapped at the offending limb, catching Hero's paw in his teeth. Bone crunched as he crushed and yanked hard. Hero pulled away, causing even more damage to his paw. Kane charged Hero and slammed his uninjured shoulder into the other alpha, trying to knock him off his feet. Even down a paw, Hero was still deadly and withstood Kane's momentum.

Kane didn't want to kill Hero. If he could disable the other wolf enough, then even if Hero wanted to keep fighting, he would be incapable.

No matter how hard he tried Hero could not topple Kane. With one of his front paws useless, Hero's ability to maneuver was reduced. Hero resorted to lunging as best he could, trying to rend and tear whatever he could reach. Kane danced out of range and avoided the worst of it.

Heromindes' frustration grew to be too much and he suddenly broke away, leaping upon the nearby Roan, who yelped with surprise and pain. Kane chased after Hero just as Caius and Mercuriel joined the fray. The three of them converged on Hero as he tore at Roan, who was in no position to defend himself or fight back. Mercuriel was still in his human form. He reached down with clawed hands and grabbed Hero around his muzzle and twisted enough to make the Ashland clan leader release Roan.

Mercuriel might be shorter than any of the other clan leaders but he was by far the strongest in his human form. He wrestled Heromindes into submission, all but sitting on him and smashing his muzzle into the mud.

"Stop fussing, laddie. I'm not letting you make a fool of yourself anymore. Be quiet before I knock you out." Mercuriel growled down to Hero, who wisely refrained from answering. Hero struggled for a moment but went limp when Mercuriel refused to let him up.

Kane quickly regained his human form and went to see how badly Roan was hurt. Caius had reversed his change as well and knelt as a human beside Roan, who in the few short seconds Hero had been attacking him, bore a multitude of deep lacerations along his side and belly. One gash in his stomach was deep enough to show internal organs. Kane was sickened, and he put a gentle hand on the red wolf's ribs to keep him from moving.

The pit and the surrounding arena had devolved into chaos. Julian still sat in his seat, laughing like a madman. Royrick clocked him upside the head and Julian shut up with a yelp. Red Fern wolves were disappearing quickly while the Black Pine tactical team hovered at the edge of the pit, worried.

"Don't move—we'll get a shaman down here to help you." As if Ghost read his mind, his little mate appeared like magic at his side, changing swiftly from wolf to young man in a rush of silver and white glittering smoke. Caius and Kane were gently nudged to the side while Ghost leaned over the injured alpha.

"Please hold still." Ghost, without any hesitation, placed his glowing hands over the worst of the injuries, and as he had not even a couple weeks before, healed Roan like he healed Burke. The wolf glowed to match the young shaman's hands, and Kane was forced to look away when the light grew too bright.

13

FURY OF THE WHITE WOLF

GHOST HEALED THE RED WOLF, WHO STARED HIM THE WHOLE TIME with bright blue eyes full of surprise and wonder. The one they called Roan was not his enemy, despite trying to defeat his mate in combat. Like many greater alphas, they relished a fight they could win. And if they couldn't win, then they would treat the loss like it never happened.

He had trouble understanding his own kind and their motivations for doing the many contradictory things that they did and said. What need did they have to have things, money, and wealth when they had their pack, clans, and families?

Ghost pulled his hands away and let the light fade. Where there were once deep wounds, now was unblemished skin and fur. Ghost sat back on his heels, looking ruefully at the mud in which he knelt. He was soaking wet and stunk like earth and blood. He made a face of disgust and exhaled in annoyance. He got up and took a few steps away, trying to shake off the worst of the mud.

Suddenly he was wrapped up in strong arms. Kane lifted him off his feet and hugged him tightly. Ghost laughed and hugged his mate in return, looping his legs and arms around his mate as tightly as he could. Kane smelled of cold air, mud, and sweat. And home. Home was in his mate's arms. Ghost hoped with everything he had that this long nightmare was over.

Kane tipped his chin back with a finger and smiled at him before lowering his head and kissing Ghost. He opened his mouth for his mate's tongue and enjoyed Kane's taste. It had been too long since he was able to kiss his mate like he wished. Any time not spent in Kane's arms was somehow painful and deeply frustrating. He wound his arms around Kane's neck and tilted his head to the side to let his mate kiss him deeper. He had no need for air nor any thought of anything or anyone aside from his mate, and he whined in need. He didn't care who watched or heard his whimpers— he needed to reconnect with his mate and quickly.

"Thank you."

Ghost broke the kiss at those two quiet words. Kane pressed his face into Ghost's long hair as Ghost looked down at Roan, who was once again a man. He too knelt in the mud, just as dirty as the rest of them in the pit. "You didn't need to heal me. Eventually I might have managed it on my own, but I thank you all the same for the kindness."

"You're welcome. You can repay me by staying away from my mate," Ghost said quietly but with an edge. Roan gave him a smile in return and a soft chuckle. The greater alpha from Sorrowfields carefully got to his feet with the help of Caius gripping his arm.

"I envy Kane what he has— both in rank and the love he has with you. I lost my chance to gain that through violence and I have lived long enough to know not to try that again. Neither of you have anything to worry about from me." Roan gave them both one last nod and turned away, heading carefully for one of the tunnels, skirting around the spot where Mercuriel still sat upon Heromindes.

Caius followed Roan but not before he sent a searching glance over Kane and Ghost both. Kane gave his alpha a nod before they returned their attention to each other.

"Let's get out of here. I've had enough of pits and fights to last me another fifty years." Kane didn't wait for his answer instead taking a running leap at the wall around the pit. There was no sign that Kane was hindered by Ghost's weight as they landed easily amongst their friends and packmates.

Burke enveloped them in a hug, cheering and smiling wide. Sophia was excited to the point of losing her usual decorum and was smiling ecstatically and jumping around them in celebration. Burke reached out and grabbed the small beta yanking her into the hug. Gerald hung back but Ghost could see him past everyone and managed to get an arm out. He grabbed Gerald by the hand and tugged him forward. His uncle reluctantly joined the hug but accepted the affection with some measure of grace.

"Is it really over?" Ghost asked quietly when the hug broke apart. It was Burke who answered. "It was over the second Kane made Roan yield. Heromindes just couldn't accept the result. He should never have returned to the pit while his blood was still boiling with battle rage from killing Roman— his actions afterward towards both Kane and Roan were dishonorable. Heromindes has not salvaged his honor but sacrificed it further."

"I don't care about honor or actions of foolish alphas. I want this entire mess to be over and all of us safe. Besides, we have a much greater task ahead of us now than blaming and the pointing of fingers." Ghost spoke quietly and with conviction. Burke and Sophia gave him confused looks but it was Kane who explained.

"There are still wolves missing and Simon Remus must pay for what he has done to our people. Gabriel Suarez's family has been torn apart. His father and his uncles are still being held hostage somewhere by Simon Remus along with potentially countless other wolves that have been unaccounted for for the last twenty years or more. The fight may be over here, but there is a greater battle we must yet win."

CAT NERVOUSLY APPROACHED the front door of the beautiful log cabin on top of the mountain. Some very beautiful and helpful blonde werewolves had pointed her in the right direction of the mysterious woman known as Andromeda. Glen shuffled from foot to foot behind her, his boots crunching on the thin ice that covered most of the porch. Paw prints from very large wolves and a few random footprints from bare human feet littered the surface, and Cat grinned, delighted.

The door opened before she could knock, her hand raised an inch from the wooden panel. A young woman, perhaps no older than twenty, gave her an inquisitive smile that reminded Cat of the woman she sought. "Is your, um, mother home? Andromeda?"

"She's busy right now but you two are more than welcome to come and wait." The young woman was slim and about Cat's height, yet she had no doubt that the young woman in front of her was a formidable hunter. The werewolves here in Baxter were deceptive— many of them were like their matriarch. Winsome, blonde and all of them striking in a pale alabaster way that spoke of the strong genetic relationship. Not many of them looked like they could put up much of a fight or cause significant damage, but to a one, they were all predators.

The wolfish grin that she was getting from the blonde girl told Cat that her thoughts must be evident on her face, and she blushed, cursing her own fair complexion. She stepped inside as the blonde girl held the door open wider, Glen following her inside. They took off their coats and hung them on the wall next to the door. "Andromeda is upstairs but I can guarantee she knows you're here. You can come into the kitchen if you'd like something to eat or you can wait here in the front. I just started a fire in the living room."

Glen spoke up. "I'd love something to eat, thank you."

With a smile, she gestured for them to follow and she led them in the direction of the kitchen. They had been in here a few times already but not since the tribunal members arrived a few days ago and Andromeda asked them to remain in their cabin for their own safety. With the trials over, Cat was finally ready to get out of her cabin and see some other people aside from Glen. Not to mention that she was surrounded by hundreds of creatures that she would have never imagined existing before, and not interacting with them was driving her scientific curiosity insane.

"Would you like some tea?"

"Yes, please." They took a seat at the long table in the attached dining room. "I'm sorry I didn't ask your name. I'm sure you remember, but I'm Cat and this is Glen. We're Ghost's... Well? People? I'm not sure what to call us, really."

The young woman laughed and said, "My name is Marjorie, and I suppose the best way to describe who you are would be packmates. We use that interchangeably with family. Clan is used for a wider circle, a larger group of our kind. Since the two of you raised Ghost, packmates is the most apt description."

Marjorie busied herself making tea, setting an old-fashioned iron kettle on the stove and lighting the burner. She got mugs down from the cabinets and went hunting through numerous tea boxes on the counter. "Any preference? My mother prefers the older teas, those with black leaves, but we have a variety."

"I'll take a chai tea and Cat will take anything with caffeine," Glen grinned and gently nudged Cat on the wrist. "Cat's affection for caffeine is really an addiction."

"An addiction that keeps you alive," Cat grumbled in response. Marjorie laughed and Glen gave her a quick wink.

"Here is your tea," Marjorie said, setting down their mugs, a small dish full of sweetening packets, and a couple spoons. "Let me go see if Andromeda can see you really quick— can I tell her what you want to talk to her about?"

"It's just a serious case of cabin fever, but we would both like to get out more and interact with your people. If she agrees, of course." Cat said, adding a couple packets of sugar to her mug.

"Cabin fever bothers even us in winter but at least we can get out on the snow and do some hunting. I can't imagine not having the option. Let me go see my mother. I'll be right back." Marjorie left the room on silent feet and Cat noticed that Marjorie was barefoot. Cat shivered thinking that even wood floors would be chilly in the depth of winter.

"Do you think Ghost got his problem resolved with the shamans?" Glen said quietly stirring his tea. "I know everything is over now, but the werewolves we met on the path couldn't tell us much. Other than the bare basics. I know it's none of our business but I still want to know the details of what happened. Ghost has been ours for almost fifteen years. Since he came home, we have rarely seen him. I know I should be happy that he's back with his people and his family, but I can't help but feel like we've been cast aside. I know that it's foolish, since for most of that time, we didn't even know that he was a person. We treated him like a pet. A treasured pet, but a pet all the same."

"Ghost loves us," Cat said firmly. "My curiosity with the wolfkin and Ghost has to take a backseat. Or at least it did while all this Tribunal stuff was happening. Maybe now that Ghost and his family have some breathing room, we can fix that. We can't keep him forever. I think we need to figure out exactly what our relationship is with him now, and we can't do any of that sitting in our cabin."

"Your timing is a bit inconvenient, but the reason for your visit is still welcome." Andromeda spoke from the dining room doorway, and they turned to greet her, but their greetings fell silent at the sight of blood on her usually pristine dress.

"Oh, my God, what happened?" Cat asked, heart in her throat. "Is it Ghost?"

"Ghost is fine. So is his mate. Forgive me for my state, I forgot humans are not accustomed to seeing blood like this. Now that the tribunal is over, your presence here is no longer under any of their potential authority. If any of the clan leaders object to having humans here in Baxter, they can take it up with me or with Caius."

Cat had trouble taking her eyes off the large red stains that covered the front of Andromeda's dress. The thin fabric was soaked through, clinging to Andromeda's skin. She really hoped that wasn't a person's blood— anyone who lost that much blood would be in trouble.

"This is wolfkin blood. And no, no one is dead. At least, not the person whose blood this is," Andromeda said grimly.

Just then footsteps came from the hallway above and then to the stairway. Andromeda looked to the door of the kitchen and Cat recognized Andromeda's brother, River. There was a figure behind him, small and slim, covered head to toe in a dark gray, thick dress and an even thicker jacket with a hood that obscured his or her face.

"I'm taking the silver SUV. I'll be back in a few days. I have my cell phone if you need me. Please tell Clan Leader Caius, if he asks, that I have already left." River said quietly, not even sparing a glance for Cat and Glen at the table.

"Goddess bless you and stay safe, brother." Andromeda said quietly, and she did not say anything to the hidden figure standing behind River. Her brother nodded once, then turned around and guided the mystery person out of the front of the cabin, shutting the door behind him.

Andromeda said nothing more as she stared at the spot where her brother had been standing. She seemed to be lost in thought, though Cat could not tell all that well considering that Andromeda was nearly expressionless. She came back to herself after a long moment and seemed to remember that they were both there at the table. "I must change, forgive me. I'll be right back."

Andromeda left quickly, departing through the rear door of the dining room. Cat couldn't hear her footsteps as she left.

GHOST REFUSED TO let go of Kane. His mate carried him along the path through the woods to the back of Andromeda's cabin. Burke and Sophia followed with Gerald bringing up the rear of their group. Kane had sent the rest of the Black Pine wolves to their respective cabins ordering them to get their gear ready to leave at a moment's notice. Ghost didn't know exactly what Kane was planning, but he knew his mate wanted to be ready for anything.

All Ghost wanted right now though, was time alone with his mate.

Everyone present at the pit in the woods had dispersed already, the individual clan leaders either leaving alone, like Caius had, or in pairs, like Royrick and Mercuriel. The Red Fern wolves all went back to their daily lives quickly and quietly. Ghost felt bad for them— their peaceful existence here in Baxter had been disturbed by death and mayhem.

Kane still carried Ghost in his arms, just as reluctant as Ghost to let go. Their lives the last few weeks had been hectic and stressful and Ghost was tired. He was finally home and hadn't even had a chance to enjoy that fact— let alone celebrate his soulbond with Kane.

Burke moved ahead and opened the rear door of the cabin, holding it open for Kane to walk by with Ghost in his arms. Burke winked at Ghost as they went by. The inside of the cabin was warm and welcoming in a way it hadn't been even just that morning. There was a difference, though, that made Ghost lift his head in alarm until he recognized it— the scent of fresh blood.

Claire's blood.

The scent of blood was lessening even as they went further into the cabin. Claire was no longer in the building and Ghost could smell River and Andromeda. He could also smell his two human packmates.

He lifted his head from Kane's shoulder and looked around excitedly. The scent grew stronger as they headed towards the dining room and kitchen. Ghost pointed towards the kitchen and Kane sighed in exasperation, but went where he directed with a smile.

"Oh dear God he's naked!" Cat said in a startled rush. "I still can't get used to seeing them running around naked. And look, Kane's naked too!"

Glen was taking a sip of tea, which he promptly spat out as he laughed. Kane was chuckling and Ghost rolled his eyes when Cat grew red in the face and made every effort not to look directly at their nakedness.

"Is it safe for you to be out of the cabin?" Kane asked with concern. "I know that Caius and Andromeda are accepting of your presence here but the other clan leaders are still in Baxter."

Glen was wiping down the table with a napkin when he answered. "Andromeda said we were fine but I have a feeling she might have wanted us to wait a couple more days before coming out of hiding. I'm guessing it's because those clan leaders are still here, too."

"No one is going to hurt you. I won't let them," Ghost growled from his spot in Kane's arms. "I'll stop anyone who tries."

Cat gave him a brilliant smile in her typical fashion, all teeth and bright eyes. Ghost smiled back, reassured at the familiar sight. Kane quickly spoke up. "Let's go put on some clothes, after we wash off this blood and grime. We'll be right back."

"Andromeda went to change as well, so take your time. We'll be waiting for you right here." Glen replied. "Considering the hour, maybe we can convince our hostess to feed us."

At the mention of food Ghost's stomach rumbled and he realized that he was starving. He hadn't eaten anything substantial in days. Kane must be even hungrier, since his mate was four times his size in wolfkin form and hadn't received many meals while locked away in the cell.

Kane continued to carry Ghost as they left the kitchen and headed for the staircase. The other three went their own way and Kane took Ghost to the room they had used previously. Once in the room Kane shut it behind him with a solid thump.

Ghost pressed his nose behind Kane's ear and took a long deep breath, savoring the scent of his mate. Kane was alive and warm in his arms. The hectic mess of the last couple of weeks was at last over, and for the first time since Ghost was dragged away from Kane, they were alone together.

Ghost nibbled on Kane's jaw, tiny little nips that he soothed with kisses and quick licks. Kane chuckled and ran a large hand up and down his spine, pressing their chests together. Kane tasted of sweat, earth, and blood. He needed more. His hands scrambled at Kane's shoulders and neck, Ghost whimpering in urgent desire, arching his back and pushing his hips forward, his hard cock twitching along Kane's rippled abdomen. He didn't care that they were dirty or tired or covered in others' blood—he had Kane to himself at last and he wasn't going to waste this chance.

"Easy, little wolf," Kane whispered before taking his mouth in a wet, deep kiss. "Shower first...." Ghost rolled his hips, and Kane grabbed his ass with a muffled curse, his fingers dipping into the crease. "Bed, now."

Kane took a few steps and fell forward. Ghost felt the impact of the bed beneath them, but his mind, mouth and hands were too occupied with the hard, chiseled frame of his alpha to care. Teeth latched onto the side of his neck and bit down, holding him still as large hands spread his legs, lifting his thighs and hips. Kane held him still with his fangs while fingers explored along his crease and pressed inside. It burned, and Ghost whined, but he panted for more. A dark chuckle came from Kane as he released his neck, a long tongue lapping at the deep impressions of his teeth in Ghost's skin. Ghost arched up, every motion of his body demanding more.

That place in his mind where Kane dwelt grew with each touch and taste. The walls between them fell. Ghost could not define the boundaries of their bodies or souls. He was light and fire, heat and desire. Kane growled, a deep rumble that purred through his body and mind. Ghost arched into his mate, crying out in desperate entreaty. His eyes were blinded by the infinite well of stars and light that dwelled in their joined souls.

He fell, and took Kane with him.

A crimson fire engulfed him. Kane's fire. His alpha, his mate, his everything, burned and consumed him, renewing him with every touch. Pressure and a sharp sting made Ghost pull back from the infinite, eyes blinking up at Kane as his mate entered his body with a slow, long thrust. Ghost smiled, overcome with a sense of completion. This is what he needed. He would always need this.

He wrapped his legs around Kane's waist, lifting into each thrust. Dark eyes that held embers glowed above him, wet lips and sharp fangs nipped and licked at his mouth. Ghost opened, accepting everything his alpha had to give him. Kane groaned, and the driving pace of his hips increased, both reaching the peak together. It was far too quick and yet not quick enough. Ghost howled, hot liquid splashing between them as Kane grabbed the back of Ghost's head by the hair and yanked his head back, slamming his hips against his ass until he came with a roar. Teeth marked his neck, holding Ghost still while Kane came within his body, thick, hot spurts searing his insides with welcome heat.

The bed shook, a shiver of wood and creaking boards, metal springs *twanging* softly. Sweat ran down his face, stinging his eyes, and Ghost blinked away the resulting tears, laughing quietly.

Kane lay upon him, limp and hot. Ghost smiled at the sight, inordinately pleased at his alpha mate's exhaustion from fucking him. *Fucking.* Ghost loved that word. It was a singularly human word, full of different meanings and used in almost every way, but this version he loved the most. Fucking with Kane was worth every frustration and worry since his return.

"Not fucking, little wolf," Kane whispered against his neck, tongue lathing the spot he'd bitten. Their thoughts were each other's. Unique, yet the same. "No matter how eager I am for you, what we share is never so simple as fucking."

"What then?" Ghost whispered, running his fingers through Kane's damp hair.

"I live to make love to you," Kane said, pushing himself on his elbows to speak to Ghost face to face. "Bonding with my mate is a blessing I never thought to have, and I will treasure you forever."

"Kane." His mate's name was a choked gasp, tears flowing in earnest joining the sweat on his face. Ghost didn't have the words to return in kind, so he did what he always relied upon—he turned to the bond.

He poured all that he felt in the bond they shared. Joy at being reunited. Vindication and a fierce satisfaction that those who wanted to harm his mate were foiled in their plans. Lust and desire and this sweet, vibrant pain that somehow made his heart race with yearning and something even more indefinable. It was an emotion he had no name for—something he had never felt. It was powerful and made his heart beat faster, his blood sing, and caused his senses to expand making everything sharper, clearer. Everything had more impact, was more real, more immediate, than anything else had ever been in his whole life. His life as an animal left him woefully unprepared to define or apply a name to this feeling. He gave it all to Kane, hoping his mate would understand, would see and feel what he felt.

"Little wolf," Kane breathed out, and Ghost could feel surprise and then an answering joy. The endearment was said with such affection Ghost thrilled to hear it.

"What is this?" Ghost asked softly, meaning the emotion he could feel coming from Kane in answer to what he gave. The bond sang. The cord between them pulsed, red and silver-white light blending. Hearts settled into a rhythm, a beat that became one.

Kane kissed him, soft and sweet. Ghost sighed into the kiss, tilting his head to accept the gentle and thorough claiming from his mate. Kane pulled back, and whispered, "Do you not know? Think, my little wolf. What hurts your heart and soul at the same time it makes you feel alive?"

"Pain and life…" Ghost whispered, reveling in what was happening between them, soul and body. What was this—it was intoxicating and sobering, a contradiction that left him electrified.

Love. A whisper across his mind. Fond exasperation touched his heart before the Presence departed as quietly as it appeared.

"Oh!" Ghost gasped out, delighted. He pushed at Kane's shoulders, urging him to sit up. Their bodies slipped apart, and Ghost winced even as he scrambled to voice his epiphany. Kane sat back on his hip, a slow smile brightening his usually serious face. "Love! I love you!"

Ghost squirmed onto Kane's lap, kissing what he could reach of his mate as Kane chuckled. Big hands cradled him close, and his mate answered him. "Yes, my mate. This is love."

"You love me, too?" Ghost asked, though he was very certain of the answer.

"Yes, Ghost. My little wolf, precious and glorious. I love you."

SEX, SWEAT AND the sweet scent of happiness made Andromeda pause outside the door to the bedroom that Kane and Ghost used while at her cabin. The sounds of whispered confessions gave her the ability to smile despite her own broken heart.

River was taking Claire away. She was likely to never see her daughter again.

Andromeda went to the stairs. She paused at the top, looking down as the front door opened and Julian and Royrick entered the foyer. She gave Royrick a nod in greeting, which he returned cautiously, perhaps expecting her mood to be more…volatile. She bore the Tribunal members no ill will. Claire was guilty, and her daughter paid for her crimes.

It was only those two would had returned so far—Caius was in out in the woods somewhere, and Mercuriel still dealt with Heromindes. Mercuriel was the best suited, in her opinion, to restore some common sense to the humiliated and angry Ashland clan leader—greater alphas had one fault that ran common amongst their class—their pride too often turned to hubris, and when it was damaged, they had poor coping skills. Luckily, Hero had wanted justice against Roman far more than he wanted to revenge himself upon Kane—Heromindes would have died against Kane. The restraint inherent in the Black Pine heir was commendable in a physical fight—he and Roan had been well matched in the pit, and luckily it hadn't devolved into a bloody mess like Roman's execution. At least, at first, she frowned thinking of Heromindes foolish actions after Kane made Roan submit.

Royrick went to the living room, where her senses told her Sophia and Burke were relaxing. Burke and Royrick were much alike, both greater alphas less arrogant than their peers. Burke had the temperament commonly seen in a beta, an outlier in calm personality and kindness. Marjorie, and what sounded like young Helen, were in the kitchen, talking to Ghost's human packmates. Helen giggled, high and sweet, and Andromeda found the sound soothing to her pain.

Julian sniffed loudly, a growl bubbling up from his throat as he caught scent of those in the cabin. He headed for the kitchen, spurring Andromeda from her musing. His long strides took him out of sight, and Andromeda put a hand on the railing, pushing up and flipping over. She landed on the floor of the foyer just as angry growls came from the kitchen. She sighed, thinking it was time to remind a few alphas just who ruled here in Baxter.

GHOST DRIED HIMSELF with the towel, shaking his head, flinging wets strands everywhere.

"Hey! Dammit, Ghost, I just got dry," Kane complained, and Ghost did it again, making his mate yelp and duck out of the bathroom. A pair of sweatpants came flying through the door, and Ghost caught them with a laugh. He tugged on the dark gray pants that smelled of laundry detergent and very faintly of Shaman River. More of the shaman's clothing, then, but it made sense as Ghost had none of his own and he and River were about the same size.

Thinking about human things like clothing reminded him of everything else that came with being human. Baxter was a place for their kind to gather, but only Red Fern Clan lived year-round within the park. This was Andromeda's home, not his. Ghost could not remember where he used to live with his family before their deaths. He stood in the doorway of the bathroom watching as Kane dressed.

"Kane? Where is my home?" Ghost asked. Kane gave him a startled glance, pausing as he pulled a shirt over his head. Ghost gave a quick shake of his head and corrected himself. "I mean before I got lost, and I lived with my mother and father and my siblings, where was my home? Did we have a house? I remember seeing Gray Shadow often when I was Luca. Did we live with my grandfather?"

Kane finished dressing and sat on the bed to pull on his boots. Someone must have brought all their clothing from the cabin they were using before Kane was arrested. Ghost looked around and saw everything Kane had with him in Baxter occupying some space in the room.

"Before the ambush at the gathering where you got lost, you lived with your mother and father and your youngest siblings in Augusta, not far from the clan house where I live with Caius. Gray Shadow had a large farmhouse with acreage that he lived in with Marla and Josiah after they were bonded and Gray Shadow lost his mate."

"Where will we live? I mean, you and I. Will I go with you back to Augusta?" Ghost wasn't used to thinking ahead, to planning his future, and he found himself both scared and excited. If he got to stay with Kane, it didn't really matter where he lived. Thinking of the future reminded him of the past.

"Well, little wolf, since you and I are now mated, I think it's time for me to get my own house. Since I remain Black Pine's Heir, I have to remain close to Caius, but I don't think I need to live there anymore. Would you like to get our own place, make a home with me?"

Ghost smiled wide, enjoying the rush he felt at Kane's question. He jumped and landed on top of Kane, tumbling them both over the bed and almost off the other side. Kane stopped them from falling and pushed them back to the center of the bed. Ghost flopped down on top of Kane, snuggling close. "I would love to live with you. Make a den, just the two of us."

"Yes, my love. A den for just the two of us." Kane paused, then asked quietly, "Will you be okay waiting until after we resolve the matter of our lost wolves? Remus still needs to be stopped."

"I don't mind waiting. I've already waited a lifetime. I can wait a little longer."

Kane kissed the top of his head, his big arms holding Ghost securely to his chest. He nuzzled closer, breathing in the scent of soap and his mate. He loved the musky, fresh smell of his alpha. Made him warm and left him feeling safe.

A crash echoed through the cabin. They both sat up fast, and heard shouting from downstairs. A female voice raised in alarm had Ghost leaping out of bed, running for the door.

"Cat!"

He threw open the door and sprinted down the hall, Kane on his heels. He wasted no time with the stairs; he made it to the railing and leapt over and down, Kane a split second behind him. He hit the floor and ran, entering the kitchen just in time to shout in surprise as he ducked.

Kane swore and dodged to the side, narrowly missed by the body barreling through the air. Ghost spun in a crouch, fangs and claws out.

The red haired clan leader slammed into the wall next to the front door, shaking the whole cabin. Ghost made himself small and pulled back from the frightening creature that blazed past him, following Julian into the foyer.

She was white fire. Power radiated out from Andromeda in bands of light, flares of sunlight and fury, a firestorm edged by white fangs and black claws. She glided over the distance between her and her prey— Julian was lifted into the air by a single slim hand, fingers tipped by claws choking him. He gasped, face red, veins bulging. He bucked and twisted, trying to free himself. Andromeda was somehow larger, taking up more space, yet she looked the same—but for her power, blazing out around her in a supernova. Ghost breathed in a lungful of hot air, half-expecting to taste fire.

Sophia, Burke, and Royrick appeared in the living room doorway, eyes wide. Royrick grabbed Sophia and moved her behind him and Burke darted past the nightmare that was Andromeda, kneeling between Kane and Ghost, looking terrified and protective. Though what anyone could do against the fury of Andromeda was questionable.

Andromeda opened the front door with her free hand, and carried Julian over the threshold. Ghost crawled forward, dodging Kane, who was trying to pull him back. He wanted to see.

A female alpha in her full power and fury wasn't something he wanted to miss.

Andromeda pulled Julian close, his legs dragging along the porch. Andromeda was shorter than the clan leader she tossed about like a toy, but her strength was far more immense. "Take your vile self from my lands," she spoke softly, almost kindly. Julian's eyes were bugging out, tears running down his face, hands clutching at her wrist. "I warned you about going near those under my protection. I don't care for blood-feuds, and that is the only reason I spare your life. Leave before I forget the benefit of restraint, and kill you for the joy of it."

She flicked her arm, a negligent motion that nonetheless sent Julian flying off the porch and across the front yard. He disappeared when he landed in a snow drift next to several parked SUVs. Snow exploded into the air in a fluffy cloud, falling back to the ground with a hiss.

Ghost stood, and carefully stepped outside. Andromeda remained still, the wind picking at her blonde hair.

She diminished. Became less bright. He caught her face in profile, but enough to see her eyes lose their fire, returning to their normal, vibrant blue. The nimbus of light around her pulled back inside, and she was once again a beautiful woman, wearing a simple dress and barefoot in the snow.

Andromeda saw him looking, and turned a bit more, one eye on him, the other on the coughing, red-faced alpha who was stuck in the drift. Ghost smiled at her, awed. She gave him an exasperated glance, but smiled in return. "Don't look at me like I'm our Goddess brought to earth, youngling."

"You're just as scary," Ghost replied, and she laughed.

"Inside, you scamp. Food, then talking, then sleep. We all need it." She tilted her head, and Ghost went first. Andromeda followed behind him, not concerned in the least that Julian was dragging himself from the snowbank.

The door shut with a soft click. Cat and Glen were near the door to the kitchen, and Ghost ran to his packmates. "Cat!"

She hugged him close. She smelled the same—wind and trees and wolf. He snuggled, and she laughed. "Ghost, you're gonna push me over."

He backed away a bit. "Sorry. Did he hurt you?" She appeared unharmed, but if Julian laid a single claw on her or Glen he was going back out there and setting him on fire.

"He came in sniffing after the young ladies," Glen grumbled, glaring at the door, clearly angry. "He saw us almost immediately and went to attack, but our very scary hostess took him to task."

Andromeda walked past them, and gave Glen a tiny pat on the shoulder as she entered the kitchen. Glen smiled, eyes full of awe and wonder.

Ghost was yanked away from Cat and into Kane's arms. Burke glowered at Ghost over Kane's arms, and Ghost tried to smile in reassurance but Kane was smothering him. Burke laughed, shaking his head, and headed for the kitchen, Sophia and Royrick following. Eventually everyone left, and Ghost was left with Kane.

"Your fearlessness is commendable and terrifying," Kane breathed into his hair, rocking them back and forth on their feet.

Ghost put his ear to Kane's chest and listened to the steady thump-thump of his alpha's heart. It was a bit fast, but that was understandable. "Andromeda wasn't going to hurt me. She knew what she was doing."

Kane huffed out a strangled laugh, full of relief and tension. "Still took a few hundred years off my life, little wolf." Kane released Ghost, giving him a swift, sweet kiss. "C'mon, let's get some food, then figure out what we're doing. Caius should be back soon, too."

Kane took his hand and lead them back to the kitchen, where the sounds of the table being set and food cooking waited for them. Ghost tilted his head, his attention drawn momentarily to the roar of a large engine starting, then wheels spinning furiously as a SUV tore away from the cabin. He smiled, satisfied.

14

END AND BEGIN

THE EVENING CAME AND WENT WITHOUT SIGN OF CAIUS OR GERALD. Night fell, and Ghost, Kane, Burke, and Sophia tracked down Gerald. Ghost's remaining uncle had disappeared at some point, slipping away unnoticed.

The lesser alpha was in the woods, standing vigil over the mutilated body of his older brother. He was in a place Ghost had yet to come across, but he knew it for what it was instantly. The stone pedestals were wide and flat, and the scent of frequent fire and ash was present, even with the snow covering everything. It made sense—their kind were burned, his connection with Kane's mind telling him it was something called cremation. No bodies left for humans to find and experiment upon.

Kane and Burke quietly lifted Roman's body to the top of a stone bier—the surface pocked and blackened. There they laid the broken wolf to rest. The alphas had started to gather wood to burn the body, but Ghost stopped them.

A whisper teased his ears, and Ghost motioned them away. He gently pulled Gerald away from the bier, and with the quiet instructions whispered in the depths of his spirit, he called for fire.

His packmates startled and stepped away when the flames erupted, lighting the body aflame instantly. It burned hot and bright, swiftly consuming the corpse to ash in moments. No long fire to burn, to fill the air with the stench of roasting flesh and bone to haunt the senses of those grieving. Fast, hot, and clean.

His uncle shuddered, and Ghost wormed his way under Gerald's arm cuddling close. Grief poured off his uncle, whose bowed head and curled shoulders all but screamed his pain into the quiet woods. Close they might not have been—and evil might have festered in Roman's heart—but Gerald and Roman were brothers, centuries spent together. Several lifetimes could not be forgotten nor expunged by Roman's crimes. Ghost held his uncle, whose arms lifted to hold him in return.

Kane moved close. He put a big hand on Gerald's shoulder, who shuddered at the touch of his alpha, pushing into the comfort offered. Sophia hesitantly approached, and with a cautious shimmy, slid into the embrace and hugged Gerald. He clutched at her, his arms full of both Ghost and Sophia, but he buried his face in her soft hair and whined, pain and grief in every line of his body. Burke was the last to move, but the pain and sympathy on his face was just as poignant as any packmate's would be in the presence of honest grief. Burke put his hand on Gerald's bicep and squeezed, turning to watch the last of the body burn away to a fine gray ash.

CAIUS HAD YET to return. Two days now, and Caius wasn't to be found. He was Black Pine's Clan Leader, if he wished to disappear into the woods, then that was his right.

Kane was less than patient, though. Ghost watched his mate deal with the remaining Tribunal members and their honor guards—with Kane's fate settled and the trials over, Kane was acting in his rightful role as Heir and handling the goodbyes.

Heromindes left sometime in the night, while they were burning Roman's body. He left with no goodbyes, disappearing with his entourage and without word to anyone. They only knew he was gone when the Red Fern guards at the park gates called and informed Andromeda that the Ashland Clan Leader and his wolves drove out in the night.

Julian left before they finished lunch on the day Andromeda tossed him out. The Birch Grove clan leader didn't even wait for his honor guard to pack up and prepare to leave—they scrambled to follow him. No goodbyes there, but Ghost would have been surprised otherwise. He had a feeling that Julian would not be a problem for Red Fern for a good long while, but a psychopath was a dangerous being to dismiss. He might cause other issues sometime in the future.

"I'm glad things worked out," Mercuriel said, his deep rumble traveling across the front yard of the cabin. Hard to miss him—the Dread Claw alpha was a force of nature. "You're young, so you'll mess up again—just mind your manners and don't get caught. I don't fancy seeing another Tribunal anytime soon. I'll tell my people what the shamans determined about your soulbond with the wildling," Mercuriel grinned at Ghost, who rolled his eyes and stayed silent. "I don't envy you the stress that's heading your way."

"I'll do my best, sir. Will we see Dread Claw at the summer gathering?" Kane bowed his head, minding his manners despite the impatience Ghost could sense along their bond.

"We'll be there. I won't miss the fireworks that are sure to happen." With a solid slap on the shoulder, Mercuriel nodded and walked off. His wolves followed, and he got in the lead SUV with his clan shaman.

Royrick was still in the cabin, not planning on leaving anytime soon. Michael was in there with his clan leader, both chatting with Andromeda as if nothing horrible had occurred in the last week. Shaman River was still gone, and from what Ghost could guess, he took Claire south, out of the combined territories of the Tribunal members.

The one known as Roan was gone. He left as stealthy as he had arrived—no one saw him after Caius helped him from the pit after Ghost healed his injuries. Caius knew where Roan went afterwards, but then Caius was not present to share.

Burke leaned in close to Kane, the two friends watching as the line of SUVs departed down the mountainside. They spoke softly to each other, speaking of things Ghost had no interest in. Ghost sighed, and wandered away. He didn't want to go into the cabin, Sophia was patrolling the forest with the Black Pine wolves, Gerald was in the cabin in his room, trying to sleep. The shamans were all gone as well—they left with their clan leaders, or perhaps even earlier, since he hadn't seen most of them at all since they declared the soulbond legitimate. So far only Michael remained.

He took the path that led downhill, into the trees. Kane saw him go, but Ghost waved at him to remain, though he felt his mate's eyes on him until the trees blocked his line of sight. The trees rose high above him, thick with needles and heavy boughs. It was eerily quiet under the trees, dark despite the early afternoon hour. He followed the path as it wound down the mountainside, and after a few minutes, he came across the old stone council house. It featured prominently in his memories as it was here that he last enjoyed a peaceful night with his family before their deaths.

He didn't remember much, just glimpses in flashes of memory. He remembered the shadow magic that his grandfather used to help teach his tales to the youngest of their people. He remembered a tall charming alpha with a swift and kind smile. Kane, his future mate, shined like a beacon amidst the chaotic last day he spent with his people before he got lost and Cat and Glen found him at the river.

It rose out of the earth as if it had been placed there directly by their Goddess. Giant, rough hewn blocks of stone covered in moss and vines, the roof a sloping dome made of thick logs and covered in clay and grass. An ancient chimney rose from the center of the roof. There was a door roughly cut into the side of the building more an absence of an actual door than something made to be sealed by wood and stone. The space around the Council house was free of undergrowth and trees, and if he looked hard enough, he could see hints of the road a few dozen yards away that led to Andromeda's cabin. It felt like he was lost to civilization, but it was only a few steps away. The weight of the past was heavy here and he could almost hear the voices of his people stretching back into history.

He stopped in the middle of the clearing, wondering if his heart could take going inside. The last memory he had of this place was one of love and peace. His grandfather was dead, his family scattered across the entire country. He had siblings left, born of a previous litter, but he didn't even know their names or where to find them. It felt like going into the Council house would be reclaiming the name and life of Luca— and he didn't want to do that. Not really. He may have been alone the last several years, but if he was to reclaim Luca, he was afraid that might mean giving up Ghost.

The concept of wishing was something entirely human. It was something he retained while stuck in his wolf form. He yearned for home, even if he didn't really understand where home was or what it really meant. All these years he didn't think about who or what would be missing were he to ever make it home. He'd known Gray Shadow died— a painful memory impossible to forget. But he did not know that his mother was dead and that his littermates were gone as well. A part of him felt like he let them down by not remembering them. He had a vague recollection of his mother's face, and now that he had access to a mirror and knew what he looked like as a man, he could see that he was his mother's son. He didn't know if there was anything of his father in him at all— he had trouble seeing his father's face and when he thought hard enough about it, it was Glen who filled that role for him now. Despite Glen raising him as a wolf and not as a boy trapped inside an animal, Glen was the closest thing he had to father.

His own father, Josiah, was lost to friend and family. He disappeared after his mate and youngest children were cremated. If it had just been a normal mating bond between him and Marla, Josiah wouldn't have succumbed to his extreme grief and run off into the wild. But because it was a soulbond, like Ghost shared with Kane, it was an unthinkable and incredible matter of chance that Josiah even survived the loss.

A twig snapped behind him and he tilted his head to listen. A familiar scent was carried on the wind and Ghost turned to see Gabe come out of the trees in his wolf form.

"You hid from Heromindes, didn't you? I had a feeling you wouldn't leave. He left so fast I don't think he's noticed you aren't with him. Are you okay?" Ghost asked Gabe quietly.

Gabe padded over to him, loping with easy strides. Ghost was short compared to most of the wolfkin males he'd met since he had come home, and in his wolf form Gabe's shoulders came to Ghost's waist. Gabe sat next to him curling his long bushy tail around his toes and Ghost ran his hand down the back of his head and neck. Gabe was another wolf seeking solace in the forest, as Gerald had the other night and Caius continued to do. He didn't blame any of them, if he didn't have Kane to offer comfort and support, he too would be in the woods hiding from the world.

"I think Andromeda would welcome you here, if you wanted to stay. But I don't think a new home is why you stayed. Once Caius returns from his grieving, Kane plans to find your missing family and put a stop to Remus. I refuse to be left behind, though I don't think Kane is aware of that yet. I won't let them leave you behind either."

Gabe looked up at him, gratitude in his eyes as he leaned his heavy weight on Ghost's hip. Ghost looked back at the Council house, thinking about how the world kept changing, and how more change was yet to come. Yet, this time, when change came, he was no longer alone and he wouldn't leave anyone behind to suffer in loneliness and despair.

"We will fix this, I swear. We still have the human doctor. And our Great Mother has a plan for me and for Kane, I think the soulbond plays a part of that plan." Ghost gave a soft sigh, Gabe echoing with one of his own.

They stood there long enough for the sun to move in the sky causing the shadows to get longer under the trees. Eventually Ghost could sense his mate's unease at his absence, and he gently nudged Gabe with his knee. "No one will make you leave now. Let's go back and see what plans are in motion. I'm hungry too."

Gabe huffed quietly but followed behind him as Ghost left the clearing and the Council house behind, taking the path back to the cabin. Evening was approaching and the sky was a myriad of colors splashing across the horizon, lighting up the mountainside in brilliant hues of red and orange. It was beautiful and Ghost felt new hope for the first time in a long while.

Kane stood with his hands on his hips on the front porch watching and waiting. He saw Gabe walking along at Ghost's side and shook his head ruefully, though he gave Gabe a nod and smile in greeting. They reached the porch and Kane looked down at Gabe. "Did you happen to see Caius while you were hiding in the woods?"

Gabe shook his head no, ears flapping. Kane sighed in exasperation, looking out over their heads towards the woods as if his impatience would be enough to spur Caius out of the trees. Ghost had a feeling his grandfather was just as stubborn as Ghost was and would come out when he was ready and no earlier. Ghost was quite certain that Caius had never taken time to grieve before and it would do him good to embrace it while he had the chance.

Kane opened the door and held it for them, gesturing for Gabe to go in first. Kane leaned down and gave Ghost a soft kiss before they both went inside. Gabe went upstairs without stopping and was soon out of sight. Royrick, Michael, and Andromeda were sitting in the living room deep in conversation. Burke, predictably, was in the kitchen scrounging for food. Ghost had no desire to spend any time with Michael after the confrontation earlier in the week and headed for the kitchen instead. Burke saw him coming and tossed a dinner roll at him which he caught easily. Ghost chewed on it while he went to stand next to Burke in front of the refrigerator, both perusing the contents.

"There's plenty of vegetables and leftovers but I think we've eaten Andromeda out of all of her fresh meat." Burke sighed and closed the door. "We could go hunting. I haven't hunted in weeks."

"I'm not sure that such a good idea. Caius is out there in the woods and may not take our intrusion well." Kane frowned, thinking. "We could go eat supper down at the mess hall."

"Excuse me, alpha," a shy voice intruded and they looked to see Andromeda's great-granddaughter Helen peeking around the corner. "We have plenty of frozen meat downstairs in the root cellar. I would get some but I'm not allowed downstairs."

"Why wouldn't you be allowed...?" Burke started to ask but a significant glance from Kane made him snap his mouth shut.

"What am I missing?" Ghost asked.

"The human doctor is downstairs," Helen whispered, eyes wide. "He doesn't say much and doesn't do anything except sit there, but Grandmother doesn't want us downstairs. He's just a human so I don't know what he could do but I'm not going to disobey Grandmother. I'm sure that you can go downstairs, being grownups and all."

"Well, I'm not too sure about the grown-up part, but I think one of us might count," Burke said with a laugh. Kane rolled his eyes and smacked Burke on the shoulder. Ghost sensed an exasperated glance between the two alphas and Helen giggled. "Who's down there guarding the human doctor anyway?"

Royrick appeared in the doorway, hands in his pockets, rocking back on his heels. "My honor guard has taken over that detail. Red Fern wolves aren't used to standing guard for anyone and many of them had families to get back to, so Andromeda kindly let me take over that duty. I'll have one of my alphas bring some meat from the freezers."

Ghost was about to offer his thanks to the clan leader but then Michael appeared behind him. Ghost crossed his arms and glared. He had yet to forgive Michael for anything, no matter how well-intentioned he might have been in his actions. Michael didn't say anything, just crossed his arms in return and bit his lower lip, looking anywhere but at Ghost.

"Really? I take back the grownup comment. No one is a grownup." Burke was exasperated and not bothering to hide it. "The two of you are shamans and act like you're pups who refuse to play nice."

Ghost couldn't help it, and a snort of laughter escaped. Michael gave him a hesitant smile and tipped his head to the side in the direction of the hallway. Michael walked down the hallway and Ghost reluctantly followed, staying out of arm's reach. They left the others behind but he was certain they could listen in if they wanted to. It was a given Kane was listening. Even though Michael was a shaman, his mate would still worry.

"I haven't had a chance to really apologize for what happened earlier in the week. I listened to other people's assumptions about you. They told us that you were uncontrollable and feral, and that your gifts weren't under your control. I should have known better. Even without any training, you are still Gray Shadow's grandson. And you were my friend. I know you were just a little cub at the time, not even five years old, but you were my friend. I hope we can be friends now. I am sorry."

Ghost was surprised at Michael's apology. He stood there blinking, thoughts jumbled and so he said the first thing that came to mind. "If you zap me again, I'll bite your hand off."

Michael laughed awkwardly and gave him a tentative smile. "I promise not to do that again."

"Then yes, we can try to be friends again." They stood there stiffly for a moment but then Ghost, exasperated with himself, stepped forward and hugged Michael. The older shaman gave a deep exhale and hugged him in return. They stood there in the dark hallway for a few minutes, and Ghost was happy for the solitude. He did look back over his shoulder, and down at the end of the hall was the silhouette of his tall mate in the shadows.

"Kane and I were once on friendly terms, but I think that's another relationship I need to repair. This Tribunal business was messy and handled poorly. None of us talk anymore— shamans rarely counsel alphas aside from clan leaders and their heirs and take themselves more seriously than they should. Since Gray Shadow died, we've stopped acting like wolfkin and have adopted too many bad human habits."

"That was one of many disappointments I've encountered since I came back. Too many bad human habits, and not enough good wolf habits. We were made to be the best of both, but our people tend to only show the worst. She is not happy with us."

"I'm not surprised," Michael said quietly. "I know she is unhappy with me. Gray Shadow would be unhappy with me. I have not done my duty as well as I should, and I can say the same for many of us."

"Will you stay, or do you have to leave?" Ghost asked, pensive. "When Royrick leaves will you go with him?"

"Before this happened I would say that I would follow my clan leader, but now I'm going to leave it up to you and our Goddess. I'll stay if either of you want me to."

It was almost as if She knew that Michael needed Her reassurance. A soft whisper rose in the dark hallway, winding quietly around them where they stood, still hugging each other. Ghost smiled, happy that She made Her Presence known. Michael tensed briefly, and Ghost could hear his heart race when he heard the whisperer. She left as gently as She came, and Michael gradually relaxed. He gave a nervous laugh, "I guess I'm staying then."

"Wise choice."

"STOP LOOMING OVER here in the shadows," Burke teased from the kitchen doorway, his best friend leaning over just enough to peer down the hallway to see the shadows of the two shamans down near the end. "Are they still hugging?"

"Ghost likes hugging. I like that he likes hugging. I just wish he would contain his hugs to me," Kane grumbled. "Why does he have to hug every male wolfkin he knows?"

"You are the only soulbonded pair for a thousand miles in any direction. You and he are the only mated pair that doesn't need to worry about jealousy. For Goddess's sake, pull it together."

Burke was smiling at him, enjoying his discomfort. Kane lifted a lip at him, giving him a glimpse of fang, but that only made Burke smile wider. Kane heaved a great exhale, but finally looked away from his young mate and put his back to the wall, crossing his arms. Burke chuckled, his brown eyes shifting to gold in the shadows. Burke's eyes were pretty, whether their normal deep brown or the wilder gold, and changed with his mood far more often than most wolves' eyes commonly did.

"And how are you, Burke? I know this has been stressful. Thank you for looking after Ghost, even though he didn't make it easy."

"I'm fine. Just glad this mess is over with…until this summer's gathering, at least. And there is literally no one and nothing that can make Ghost do something he doesn't want to do. At least on this plane of existence. I'm sure She has had a few things to tell him. All I had to do was remind him to eat occasionally. When I could find him."

"My mate is stubborn, isn't he? I wouldn't have him any other way. His stubbornness has kept him alive, kept him sane. I don't think I could have stayed sane if I spent fifteen years locked away as a wolf, and treated like an animal. They may have loved him and treated him kindly, but there is a great difference in how a child and a wild animal are raised. I would have done something drastic— and I don't mean destroying furniture, either." Kane took a moment, and spared a glance down the hall at his mate before returning his regard to Burke. "And our goddess speaks to Ghost— I think She speaks to Ghost more than She has spoken to anyone in a very long time. It makes me wonder if the last twenty years of misery and pain could have been avoided or ended sooner if only we remembered that She was there, willing and able to help us. Ghost never had doubt; he accepted Her presence immediately and without any qualms. I wish I had half his certainty."

"You may not need any certainty of your own. You have Ghost now. A soulbond. That's not just a matter of fate or chance—She made the bond between you Herself. It's there for a reason. Ghost came home for a reason. He came home *now*— and brought our Goddess back with him. I don't know for sure what this means, but there is one thing I do know— this mess with Remus and our missing wolves is going to be over soon. Never mind our Goddess won't let it continue on— Ghost won't let it continue."

"I think you're right Burke. Not just about Ghost but all of it." Burke gave him a wide grin and a wink, and Kane rolled his eyes at his best friend.

"I'm not going let you forget that you said I was right."

Kane groaned and wrapped an arm over Burke's shoulder. They shared a brief hug before they went back to watching the shamans.

IT WAS LATE, and he was in the middle of undressing when his phone rang. It lit up the dark room, the number unknown. Curious, yet dreading who it might be, Simon reached out and answered.

"Hello?"

"Since Roman is dead, they're going to come for you next," the low, menacing tones of the Birch Grove clan leader sent shivers down his spine. Julian sounded nothing like the smooth, cold businessman who threatened him days prior.

"What do you want?" Simon asked. "You wouldn't call, not like this, to tell me something I guessed on my own." He did his best to keep his voice level, calm. Roman was dead. The monster who held him down and fucked him until he screamed with pleasure and pain was dead. He didn't know how to feel.

"Come outside," Julian ordered, and the call dropped.

He stood in the dark, phone in one hand, shirt in another, thinking. His guards hadn't set up an alarm. Julian might be out there, or maybe not.

He slid his shirt back on, not bothering with the buttons, and he pocketed his phone. He left his room, noting the lack of guards in the alcove outside his suite. He had long moved out of the house he once shared with his dearly deceased brother Sebastien, preferring the luxury condo in downtown Augusta. It gave him a view of the statehouse, the business district, and the mountains in the distance.

No guards in the top floor lobby. The door to his condo slid shut, his heartbeat loud in his ears. His pulse thrummed. The bite mark on his neck, a parting gift from Roman McLennan the night the monster fucked him, throbbed with the spike in his blood pressure. He winced, and put a hand to the healing bite. The skin around it was hot, the mess Roman's half-transformed jaws made of his flesh sore and aching. His shirt was open and he pushed the collar back, trying to keep it from the partially healed wound. Up until now, it hadn't been a bother, aside from the first couple of days after Roman bit him. Now it throbbed and hurt, the skin felt tight and the heat increased as his blood pressure spiked again.

"I was right," a deep, husky chuckle came from behind him, and Simon spun. The man he knew as Julian Richards, Manhattan businessman and millionaire, grinned at him with fangs dropped and green eyes aglow. Simon sucked in a shocked breath, and tried to back away, but Julian snapped out a hand and grabbed his shoulder. "Roman fucked you good and hard. Bit and claimed his bitch. It's been a few weeks, and I can still smell his scent all over you. Too bad he's dead—can't enjoy his bitch now."

"Fuck you!" Simon tried to twist free, but Julian's grip was impossible to break—it felt like he was fighting a stone statue. He pulled back his free arm and punched Julian in the jaw. He screamed, pain lancing up his wrist, and he shook out hand.

"Now, now, little human," Julian whispered, and any veneer of sanity the werewolf once carried dropping away piece by piece. He pulled Simon in close, and he trembled in the grip of the clan leader. "Is that any way to treat your new partner?"

"Partner? No! Let me go, you monster!" Simon kicked, scratched, punched, but nothing he did affected the monster who dragged him back into his condo.

He landed on the floor in front of his luxurious leather couch, sprawling. He groaned, and before he could get up, he was flipped to his back, an expensive leather shoe on his chest holding him down. The door to his condo hissed shut.

"What did you do to my guards?" Simon gritted out, trying to get out from under Julian's shoe.

"Me? Why do you think I did anything to them?" Julian chuckled, leaning more of his weight on his foot. "Perhaps I killed them. Snapped their necks. Or slashed their throats. Humans, no matter how skilled, are nothing against me." Julian leaned even more, and Simon coughed at the increasing weight on his sternum. "Ah, but have no fear. I bribed the lot of them to leave for the night and come back in the morning. It's just you and me until dawn."

The bite mark on his shoulder burned, and he cried out as Julian leaned down over him, knocking the air from his lungs. Julian tilted his head, and with a casual flick of his wrist, ripped away Simon's unbuttoned dress shirt and tossed aside a long piece. Fingers trailed over the half-healed bite, pressing, claws lightly scratching. He felt one of the scabs crack, and the sting and sudden wet told him it was bleeding. He tried kicking Julian off him, but nothing he did moved the werewolf. Julian smirked, and shifted, knees straddling Simon's chest, letting him suck in a fast gulp of air. He grabbed at Julian's thighs, the werewolf's knees on either side of his chest, just under his arms, but Julian pulled his hands away and restrained his wrists with one hand.

He watched in horror as Julian's face warped, mouth growing wider, fangs protruding from upper and lower jaw, his eyes no longer human. Red fur to match his hair grew down his neck to the collar of his shirt, the once immaculate dress shirt of his suit straining over shifting muscle mass. The werewolf gave off heat in waves, warmth spreading out from Simon's stomach, up his torso, across his chest, and down his hips and thighs.

Fingers tipped with long, slightly curved claws gently skipped over the now seeping bite, and Julian lifted his fingers to his nose, sniffing, nostrils flaring. He growled, a deep rumble, and Julian smiled down at him.

"Did you know wolfkin take humans for lovers? Not often, but it happens enough that most clans ignore the occasional indiscretion. Most of us fuck humans, of course, but a lover is a different beast altogether. It's dangerous—we can't turn humans, not like wolves in those silly stories humans write—but because humans react to us. The animal in us calls to the primitive part of your spirits." Julian leaned down, sniffing at the bite, and Simon cringed when a wet tongue slipped between fangs and licked the wound. Julian sat back up, closing his eyes as if savoring the taste. "Your kind burns for us, hungers for us. Once bitten, once fucked, a human bitch aches for more. No matter if they want it or not—your bodies betray you every time."

"No!" Simon hissed out, bucking his hips, heels digging into the floor. "Get off me!"

Julian chuckled, leaning down again. A slim tongue, too thin and long for a human, teased across Simon's lips, lapping at them, and Simon moved his face away, but Julian followed him. He suffered the gross indignity of the beast's kiss, not daring to bite the tongue slipping past his lips into his mouth.

He shivered, body awash with heat. His mind shut down, his heart hammering in his chest, and the kiss deepened until the heat eclipsed his resistance, and he went limp. His jaw dropped open even more as he yielded to the kiss. Julian tasted like blood, copper, spice and heat, and Simon moaned into the werewolf's mouth as he turned his head into the kiss, suddenly wanting more.

The werewolf's weight was gone almost immediately. Simon yelped, finding himself flung upwards, and he landed with a bounce on the couch. Julian shook out his sleeves, stretching his neck as red fur receded and his face and mouth shrank back down to human proportions. Simon's breathing matched the frantic pace of his heart, and he gaped in confused shock at the werewolf who now stood over him, as normal looking as any human man.

"Such a good boy," Julian said, gazing down at him with an insane amount of boredom on his handsome features. "Now that you know your place, tell me everything."

"I…What?" He'd gone from expecting to be raped to holding a normal conversation and his brain was flatlining.

Julian sighed. He moved to the couch and sat next to Simon, who stared at him with wide eyes. Blood ran down his shoulder from the reopened wound, and his skin pebbled with fear and adrenaline. Julian leaned back, one arm along the back of the couch, his torso turned towards Simon. "Don't make me repeat myself. Tell me everything. Every experiment. Successes, failures, who approached you with contracts, who is funding you. Everything. Tell me what I want to know, and I won't bend you over this couch and show you exactly why humans never last long when wolfkin fuck them."

THE NEXT MORNING dawned cold and intensely bright—not a cloud in the sky. The wind was calm and blew from the southwest, the first hint of spring on the far horizon.

Ghost scampered around Kane's great paws, his big mate taking one step for every four of Ghost's, but Ghost didn't mind. He was faster than Kane, nimbler, and enjoyed teasing his bigger mate. Tongue lolling as he panted, Ghost led the way through the trees, following the trail of a rabbit.

The rabbit he was trailing jumped out from beneath a snow-laden bush and foolishly ran right beneath his nose. He caught it with a quick snap of his jaws and broke its neck with a sharp flip of his head. He trotted back to his mate and offered the rabbit with a wag of his tail. Kane took the rabbit with great solemnity and grace, and lay down with his gift.

Kane wordlessly asked him he wanted to eat it too, but Ghost shook his head and backed away a few feet before lying down. He was a wolf hunting for his mate, and although Kane was bigger and deadlier in his wolf form, Ghost was still a hunter and quite skilled at catching prey. Catching food for his mate made him happy, and watching Kane tear into the fresh kill was satisfying. His poor alpha had been through quite an ordeal the last couple of weeks and Ghost was finding that he was equally as protective of Kane as Kane was of Ghost.

The forest around them was peaceful, and with the skies clear high above, it was warmer this morning than it had been for months. Baxter was farther south than the sanctuary in New Brunswick by a few hundred miles. He wondered if the distance was great enough to affect the weather. He tilted his head back ears pricking forward as he listened to the sounds around him. Kane was chomping on a bone, there was a squirrel sleeping in a tangle of branches at the base of the tree a few yards away, and in the other direction, there was a brace of crows calling to each other, alerting the rest of the forest to the presence of the wolves.

Ghost called to his Spiritsight and it came alive in a rush of color and sensation. Kane glowed with a fiery red trimmed with silver; he could see the soulbond between them as easily as if it was a tangible thing he could touch. The earth beneath their feet was a soft green with hints of blue, still held in the grip of winter. The trees were alive, their cores of vibrant shades of green with hints of yellow and varying shades of brown. He could see the tiny stars of rodents and birds alike that hid beneath the snow and jumped from branch to branch or flew across the sky. He could see farther, almost through the physical forms of everything around him and he could see vibrant light in an unending vista that blurred into a wall of rainbows the farther he looked.

There was another wolfkin not too far away. The soulstar of the wolfkin was very like that of his mate but it was tinged with undertones of gray smoke and black lines that gave him the impression of grief.

Caius.

Ghost stood and carefully headed in his grandfather's direction. He stepped around trees and over fallen branches taking care to not approach too quickly. Caius had been in his wolf form for several days now and Ghost knew how easy it was to lose the human part of themselves. Kane finished the rabbit with a gulp and followed behind him. There was no need to talk— Kane knew, probably before Ghost did, that Caius was nearby. Kane had the gift of command, something that all greater alphas possessed to varying degrees, the mental ability to sense and communicate with multiple wolfkin minds. Ghost could hear and speak to a few wolves while in this form but not to the degree that Kane could, and certainly not to the degree of which Burke was capable—he was a Speaker, after all. And if Kane knew Caius was out here, then Caius was fully aware that they were nearby and approaching.

His heart jumped a little bit but a part of him recognized where they were. Even in the depths of winter the river that wound its way through Baxter never froze all the way through, he could hear rushing water not that far ahead. He came across Caius's footprints in the snow and followed the fresh trail until the trees fell away and the river was before him.

He knew this place. Here was where Luca died and Ghost was born. Here too, was where Gray Shadow took a shotgun blast to the chest while protecting him from the humans. And where Caius stood on a large wide flat stone was where Gray Shadow died.

Caius was large, almost as large as Kane. They were probably separated by no more than a couple of inches and a few pounds. Kane was slightly slimmer while Caius was all bulk. He was dark, a mix of blacks and brown and hints of gray on the tips of his long guard hairs. When he turned his head his eyes glowed with the power of his spirit and his grief.

Kane stopped at the edge of the forest while Ghost continued on. It felt odd to walk this path, to be again in the place where everything changed so drastically. He hopped up onto the boulder that hung out over the rushing water below. The center of the river was free of ice for a few feet, white water frothing and tumbling down the mountainside. He sat next to his grandfather and they both stared at the water for a few minutes.

You look just like him, Caius said quietly. *It makes me happy and hurts my heart at the same time.*

There was nothing Ghost could say to that. He had always looked like this, and his memories of Gray Shadow as a wolf were blurry, but if anyone was to know his resemblance to Gray Shadow it would be Caius.

You need not say anything, Ghost. You know, don't you?

That you loved Gray Shadow? Yes, I know. I've always known. Ghost replied softly, careful of the teeming grief ready to spill over.

We were so careful. Sex was one thing, but to be a pair? I am a coward. I should have fought more to claim him as mine. So many centuries spent denying what we felt, even taking betas as mates to try and turn our hearts away from each other. We pretended to be naught but friends for so long the lie felt like truth.

Ghost could see many lifetimes of frustration and pain, for all wolves involved. Caius had lost a great love to societal pressure, entered into one failed mating after another, and even lost a mate or two to death along the way. Gray Shadow had taken a mate as well, a nameless female beta that Ghost had never met, dying many years before he was even born.

He could not begrudge them their past mistakes, since he was alive. His mother, Marla, had been Caius's daughter, and Josiah, his father, Gray Shadow's son.

It felt like fate. That if Gray Shadow and Caius could not find their way to each other, their bloodlines eventually did.

A whisper rose on the wind, racing over the river and toying with his ears. Ghost tilted his head, listening, though this time there was no words, no soft feminine laughter to tease him and prompt him. It was still very familiar, and not of this world, and Ghost heeded the prompting.

He changed. A rush of silver and white smoke eclipsed his vision and he reclaimed his human form. He grimaced, but sat on the ice-cold boulder. Caius grumbled at him and shuffled closer, blocking some of the wind. The sky was a bright, intense blue, not a cloud to be seen, and he could almost see the river as it was that long ago summer.

"I don't know anything about being a shaman. Or a man," Ghost stated. He leaned over a bit, and peered down at the swift current before sitting back. "I can catch a rabbit easily. I know how to open a door with my teeth. I can find the best snacks in the fridge. And when it comes to grief, I have a pretty good idea how to deal with it, too."

Caius glanced at him from the side of his eye, listening. Ghost went back to gazing out over the river. It was thick here with tall rocks and fallen trees, stripped bare of branches and moss. "I've been grieving my whole life, and it was part of why I couldn't find my way back to my human self. Guilt, too."

Caius gave a small twitch, fur rippling.

Ghost continued, smiling as a bluejay winged its way above them, crying out an alarm at their presence. It flew away, complaining as it went. "I felt guilty because Gray Shadow died saving me." Caius gave up pretense and gave him his full attention. "Grandpa Shadow died saving me. He taught me to Change—and that healed me from the damage caused by the river. The greatest shaman the clans had ever seen died to save a single small wolf, who poorly repaid him for that sacrifice by getting stuck and pretending to be a wild animal because he was too afraid to find his home."

Caius growled at him, displeased. Ghost just shrugged and kept talking. "Guilt eats at us. It weighs us down and lies to us, too. We think there is nothing on the other side of grief. How can there be anything on the other side of such pain? Combine guilt and grief, you're trapped in a never-ending cycle of pain. Guilt creates more grief, and grief fuels our guilt. No matter how long we live, we are still mortals, and we suffer for our mistakes. I can't fathom living for centuries carrying guilt and grief in my heart. To then learn your own son was partly responsible for killing your family, your people, and the wolf you loved above all others…I can't comprehend that pain."

He didn't fight the tears. He let them fall. Caius whined, quietly enough to be swallowed by the noise of the rapids. The whisper rose again, and Ghost smiled past his tears. "He doesn't blame either of us for our choices."

Caius's whole body jerked. He towered over Ghost even as he lay down beside him, a wall of fur and warmth at his side and back. Caius dropped his head to his paws, eyes locked on the river. Ghost continued. "I know he loves us both. I know fate and our Goddess has a purpose and a plan for us all. He wants you to listen. To believe that there is something worth living for, worth fighting for, that every mistake you've made in your long life is redeemable and understandable. He never blamed you for anything. He made mistakes, too." A soft chuckle on the wind. A warm ray of sunshine caressed his cheek and glided along, smoothing down the long guard hairs along Caius's spine. Caius shuddered again, a plaintive whimper slipping free.

The whisper came again, melding with Her voice. Wordless, yet full of promise. It became less feminine, deeper, with warmth in it that banished the chill winter air. Ghost let the voices in, and closed his eyes. He fell away, and Another spoke. "Caius, you led the Great Exodus, escaped Europe with many of the clans and gave us a new life on this continent. You brought Black Pine to prosperity and strength. You denied the greatest wish of your heart and hardened yourself against love and family. You followed that which you believed to be only duty, and suffered for it. Evil is here, among the clans, killing our people. The paths before you are twisted and full of grief and pain. Your son started this evil, and you feel guilt for his part in all of this. You carry a responsibility and blame upon your spirit that is not yours to carry. Our people are still in danger. Caius of Black Pine—you can fade away...or you can fight."

Ghost breathed in, the cold air shocking him back. He looked around, confused for a moment. Caius was in his human form, kneeling beside him. His grandfather gazed at him with a slow, searching regard. "What?"

Caius shook his head and chuckled. "I don't know who that was there at the end, but I got the message loud and clear." Caius leaned over, and cupping the back of Ghost's head, pressed a kiss to his forehead. He pulled back, "Change back, grandcub. We have things to do."

"Yes, Grandpa Caius."

Caius retook his wolfkin form and shook out his coat. Kane stood from where he had been lying on the bank, cautious and curious. Ghost changed back, and ran between his grandfather and his mate back to the center of the park, leaving the river and its memories behind.

PART TWO

15

THREE HEARTS

It was odd. For the last couple of weeks Baxter had been full of tension, frustration, and fear. Most of the strangers were gone, following their respective alphas. Royrick and Caius remained, though for very different reasons.

Royrick leaned against the wall of the kitchen and refused to take his eyes off Sophia. The Black Pine First Beta was in the middle of making a sandwich, one eye on the front of the cabin and the other on what she was doing. She didn't like not having her alphas where she could see them. As First Beta to Kane, it was her responsibility to carry out his orders and maintain discipline within his tactical team. The last couple of weeks had been very difficult, with Kane under suspicion and then behind bars— her usual authority usurped by the tribunal and thrust into limbo. Having Burke free was really the only reason she didn't give into frustration and snap someone's neck. When Kane wasn't around, Burke was in charge. And if Burke wasn't around, then Sophia, as First Beta, was in charge. The younger alphas within Kane's tactical team had trouble adapting to a beta in charge, but the roles and pack structure were reminiscent of war bands that were in use hundreds of years ago, and it was familiar to Sophia and the few older wolfkin on the tactical team.

"I am standing right here, Sophie." She pretended not to hear him, just because she could. He grumbled about stubborn betas and tried again. "I've been here for several days now, and not a word to me that wasn't polite chitchat. Is there nothing you want to say to me?"

"Ham or turkey?" Sophia snapped out, and he sighed loudly. She could damn near hear him rolling his eyes. A chuckle at the door made her look up.

Gerald gave her a small smile as he eyed Royrick warily. Royrick gave Gerald a thorough once-over, making Sophia bristle and Gerald pale. "Roy, leave him alone. Gerry, you want a sandwich?"

Gerald tore his eyes away from the frowning clan leader, and walked over to stand beside her. "Turkey, please. No mustard."

Sophia slapped the sandwich together and handed it to Gerald on a plate. Gerald flushed, taking it from her while watching Royrick from the corner of his eye. "I'll just go," Gerald said quietly, his courage failing him when confronted by Royrick's displeasure. "Thank you for the sandwich."

She snapped out her hand, catching Gerald by the wrist and holding him in place. "Stay right here." He was startled, but all he did was nod, confused. She dropped her hand and marched to Royrick, stopping a foot away. He towered over her, always had, but she never let it get to her. Royrick was a brat, but he never resorted to violence or laid a hand on her she didn't invite. His eyes sparkled at her, a small smile lifting one side of his lush mouth. She resisted the urge to sigh and run her fingers over his chin. They hadn't been a pair for a very long time.

"Leave Gerry alone," she ordered, uncaring she was bossing around a clan leader. She knew where he was ticklish and the fact he was frightened by spiders. No mystery left to intimidate her. "He's part of my pack, my family, and he's mine."

"Yours? Does Kane know you've claimed Caius' castoff?" Royrick frowned.

Sophia growled. She could damn near feel the misery that rolled off Gerald at Royrick's callous words. She lifted a finger, claw extended, poking Royrick hard in the chest. He flinched, and tried to grab her hand, but she slapped his hand away and poked him again. "Gerald is more than people think. He's a decent wolf, unafraid of hard work and willing to sacrifice himself for his family. He loves Ghost like the pup never left, and has devoted himself to Kane completely. All he needed was someone to trust him, to need him, to bring out the best of him. No one is going to disparage Gerald where I can hear, not even you! Apologize!"

"Sophia, it's okay," Gerald interrupted, voice hollow and dulled. She spun on her heel and pointed at him, and he gulped.

"It is not okay! Never say that again. No one speaks to you or about you like you're nothing. I watched your father treat you like shit for your whole life and you took it. You've only just now started to act like a decent person and I'll not see you backslide!" She spun back around, making Royrick jump, alarm spreading across his features. "Apologize or I'll rip your balls off. You're a better man, a better alpha than that petulant attitude you're carrying. Where's the honorable and forthright alpha I nearly mated? Find him again."

Royrick hated to be embarrassed. Really hated it. The one thing he hated more than humiliation was being wrong. He prided himself on being someone his wolves could look up to, depend upon, and calling out his honor left him feeling like a failure. He couldn't stand it, and despite his bratty ways, his honor was his greatest asset and most redeeming quality. She glowered, growling softly, and he straightened from the wall and stepped to the side, facing Gerald.

"Sophia is right. I apologize. That was needlessly rude and cruel of me. I am sorry, Gerald of Black Pine."

She glared at Gerald over his shoulder, and he stood taller. He put the plate down and with some hesitancy, approached Royrick. He halted, just within reach and dared to meet Royrick's eyes for a long moment before his nature made him drop them away. He nodded, and a fine shiver raced over him from head to toes. "Apology accepted, Alpha Royrick."

Gerald was a lesser alpha, almost a beta if not for his size when a wolf and his meager gift of command. His personality wasn't as dominant as Royrick's, and it showed. Royrick sighed quietly, shame and regret coloring his features before he hesitantly reached out to Gerald.

Gerald watched the greater alpha's hand coming from the corner of his eye, and Sophia held her breath. A verbal apology was sufficient—he didn't need to touch Gerald, especially since Gerald belonged to Kane and Black Pine, not Royrick's clan. Royrick cupped the back of Gerald's neck in his big hand, and Gerald whimpered softly, tipping his head to the side, exposing his neck to the stronger wolf. He settled at the touch of the clan leader, eyes fluttering shut. They breathed, at first at odds and then together. Time fell away and every breath, every heartbeat felt more pronounced. More real. Sophia breathed, filling her nose with the twisting scents coming from the two alphas.

Hurt and…heat. Vulnerability laced with pain and aching need.

Sophia blushed, glad neither of the two men were paying attention to her. Royrick was rubbing a thumb along the underside of Gerald's chin, the lesser alpha's eyes shut, mouth parted as he panted softly. He seemed to be in a trance, which she could understand completely—Royrick's touch was something to appreciate. A long time it might have been since they were lovers, but she remembered well the pleasure to be had in his bed and arms. Gerald was lost, neatly pulled under Royrick's sway and the wounded air he carried about him seemed less sharp, soothed by the attention.

"He needs," Royrick whispered. "He feels everything too deeply. He's vulnerable."

Sophia nodded, wordlessly agreeing. She had thought to help Gerald along now that he wasn't trying so hard to be tougher than he really was, but this was a new and interesting development. She liked the fact Gerald didn't want to be in charge, that he didn't need to lead like most alphas—he was content to follow. Royrick was meant to lead, a greater alpha exactly where he was meant to be—clan leader. He needed to lead. He had to lead. He could yield when he must, but his place was at the top.

Sophia smiled, thinking Fate and their Goddess were far wiser than she would ever be—and she wasn't one to ignore a chance to find happiness. She looked up at Royrick, who was staring at Gerald in soft wonderment. Gone was the brat. Gerald appealed to him, and from the way Gerald was reacting to Royrick, the appeal was mutual.

"Why did you come when Caius called?" She asked softly, careful not to break the spell. "There were other alphas Caius approached in the North who would have come to sit on the Tribunal," She had an idea why, but she wanted him to say it.

"You were here," Royrick answered. He tugged gently, and Gerald went willingly, all but melting into Royrick's slightly bigger frame, tucking his face into Royrick's neck. Royrick slipped his arm around Gerald's waist and held him tightly. "I wanted to see you again. I never stopped loving you. Then I get here, and your heart belongs to someone else. I thought it was Burke at first, but it's this sweet pup, isn't it?"

Sophia exhaled, thinking hard, taking in how Gerald clung to Royrick's body. He needed a greater alpha to support him. Sophia was strong, she was dominant—but she was a beta. She could give Gerald some of what he needed, but she would always fall short in other ways. "It hasn't been done, not openly."

"A clan heir is bonded to a shaman," Royrick grinned at her over Gerald's head. "I don't think anyone is going to notice if a clan leader takes two mates."

"Getting ahead of yourself, aren't you?" She stepped closer, and ran a hand down Gerald's back. Gerald sighed happily, snuggling deeper, all but plastered to Royrick's front. She rubbed her hand up and down his spine, and soft grumbles and happy shivers came from the lesser alpha. She grinned, and gentled her touch. It was nice to see Gerald so relaxed and calm.

"I don't think I'm getting ahead of myself at all, Sophie. You see it too, I know you do. We could make this work," Royrick insisted, and he held out his free hand. She stared at it, then up at his eyes. They held warmth and desire, and a fondness she knew would never fade away, no matter how many decades passed.

"I won't be a sweet beta mate who sits in her den and waits for her alpha to remember her," Sophia warned. "I will never be like that. Pups would be nice, but I am more than my ability to breed."

"I know," Royrick assured her, hand still held out. "Caius has nothing but praise for his heir's capable First Beta, and your reputation is known far and wide. I was stupid to assume you would give up your ambitions. I've had decades to regret my mistakes. I have no First Beta—the position is yours, if you want it."

She looked at Gerald, then back to the hand Royrick still held out to her, enticing and patient. "And the position of mate? What about Gerald? He might not want this."

"I want," Gerald sighed out. He sleepily blinked his eyes open, and his dark eyes were full of desire and contentment. He turned just a bit, and held out his hand to her as well.

"Alpha Mates, First Beta, lovers. I say we try," Royrick wiggled his fingers a bit, grinning. "Sophia. You're far too brave not to try."

She glared, but lifted her hands and took both of theirs. They gripped her small hands tightly and she let herself be pulled forward. Gerald shuffled over a bit, and somehow, they both fit under Royrick's arms, secure in his embrace.

Gerald smiled down at her, and she relaxed, leaning on them both.

"I'm glad I came in for a sandwich," Gerald whispered, and Royrick laughed, tossing back his head.

KANE STOOD BESIDE his clan leader, facing an unrepentant Royrick, who grinned from ear to ear. Gerald all but hid behind the bigger alpha, eyes dropped to the floor, one hand tucked into Royrick's like a child. Sophia stood next to Royrick, shoulder to shoulder, and while she wasn't as blissed out as Royrick, the hope and happiness in her eyes made Kane want to smile, too.

"You come with an honor guard, and leave with two of my wolves? I'm inclined to think you had this planned," Caius drawled, sitting back in the chair behind Andromeda's desk in her study. "The best First Beta Black Pine has had since Josiah disappeared, and my remaining son?"

"Let's not bullshit here, Caius. You tossed Gerald aside like trash and Kane caught him. He's Kane's wolf now, and it's him I'm asking to release Gerald." Royrick looked to Kane, who lifted a brow at his boldness. "Kane, Heir of Black Pine, I humbly——," Kane snorted at that and Royrick winked, both ignoring Caius' soft growls, "I humbly request that you release both First Beta Sophia and Gerald McLennan from your pack and clan. I would take them home as honored mates."

"You left Royrick because he wanted you to only be his mate. You wanted more," Kane said, directly addressing Sophia. "You left Red Wraith and bided your time. Josiah's absence gave you the chance you needed. You came to me and asked to be more, to be allowed to have ambition and a place of responsibility and power. Is that what you still want?" She nodded, and flicked her eyes over the two alphas next to her before looking back to Kane.

"I did. I also know I've since proven myself as First Beta. I know my worth, and so does Royrick." Her voice was steady, sure. He could hear no doubt in her tone. "I can be a First Beta still, and Alpha Mate."

"And Gerald? You would share a clan leader's bed and the rank Alpha Mate with him, a lesser alpha?" Caius asked, and Kane saw Gerald flinch.

"Gerald is worth loving," Sophia declared, lifting her chin. "All he has ever needed was for someone to love him, someone worthy of his devotion. He has no desire nor the temperament to lead, and trying to live up to unrealistic expectations soured his personality and left him wounded to the soul. I will treasure him, and Royrick will, too. We know what he needs, and how to care for him. We are both strong enough to welcome more than one wolf into our hearts."

Caius' expression went blank, eyes dark. Gerald shivered, creeping behind Royrick. The reprimand was there in her words and tone—clear as anything, Sophia just called Caius out on his poor treatment of Gerald for the last two hundred years.

"I release you, Sophia of Black Pine, First Beta. May your new mates treat you with respect and care, worthy of your love and devotion," Kane declared, dropping his arms and smiling. Sophia breathed a sigh of relief and Royrick grinned. Gerald lifted his eyes at last, hope burning in his dark gaze brightly enough to make Kane feel it in his chest. "I release you, Gerald McLennan, alpha of Black Pine. May your mates be worthy of your love and devotion, your loyalty and heart." Kane nodded once to Gerald, who smiled at last, eyes wet with unshed tears. Royrick's smile was near blinding. "Treat them well, or I will head South and break you in half before taking them back. They are priceless. Treat them so."

"I swear to our Goddess that I will treasure Sophia and Gerald forever," Royrick vowed, taking Sophia's hand in his and squeezing Gerald's with the other.

Caius remained seated, but Kane walked around the desk and pulled Sophia into a hug. She squeezed him back, and Kane held her for a moment before letting her go. Gerald was next, and Kane surprised him by reaching out and hugging him as well. Gerald was stiff at first, then relaxed, head dropping to Kane's shoulder. "Thank you for everything," Gerald whispered.

"You're welcome. Take care of yourself, and each other. You need anything, call me, okay?" Kane spoke quietly, rubbing Gerald's back. "I am so proud of you."

Gerald broke at his words, and he gratefully turned the alpha over to his new mates. Gerald melted into Royrick's arms and Kane was pleased by how well they seemed to fit. Sophia was teary eyed but smiling, rubbing Gerald's shoulder and murmuring reassurances to him.

Caius sat, unmoving, but unlike before, he wore every emotion on his face for Kane to see. "Sir?"

Caius startled, and sat forward in his chair, coughing. His eyes looked everywhere but at his son, and Kane frowned. *He will never return, Caius. Your children are all gone but for the one here, now, in this room.* Before Ghost, before the last couple of weeks, Kane would not have dared speak directly to Caius in such a way, or say such things. It was true, though—Gerald would never return to Black Pine, not while Caius remained Clan Leader. There was nothing here for him aside from his nephew, and Ghost was far more likely to go to wherever Gerald was than the other way around.

Caius stood, his usually golden complexion waxy and pale. He stared at Gerald, hands fidgeting, restless.

"Father?" Gerald said, tentatively. Caius flinched, as if wounded.

"May I have a moment with my son?" Caius asked quietly. Sophia and Royrick exchanged glances, worried. His tone grew sharp, impatient. "I will return him in one piece."

"I'll be fine," Gerald told Royrick and Sophia. She hesitated, but nodded, pressing a quick kiss to his cheek before leaving the room. Royrick gave Caius a long, weighted stare, then almost defiantly, tipped Gerald's chin back with a finger and kissed him. Gerald jumped, but settled quickly, opening his mouth and letting Royrick have his way. They looked great together, honestly—Royrick's bright blond hair and Gerald's darker hues of brown contrasted nicely. Royrick took his time, staking his claim for all to see.

Kane smirked, rubbing at his mouth, and headed for the door when Sophia held it open. She winked at him, cheeks glowing as Royrick released Gerald with satisfied grin. Gerald was flushed and his lips wet, blinking slowly. They left, Kane shutting the door behind them.

He took a spot along the hallway, and smiled knowingly when Sophia and Royrick did the same, all three of them unashamedly eavesdropping.

"Father?"

Caius had no idea what to say, what to do. Kane's words rang in his mind, and all he could see was the broken and ravaged body of Roman every time he shut his eyes. Roman's corpse shared equal time with the memory of Gray Shadow's damaged wolf-form, limp on the rocks along the river's edge. His daughter's body, warped, stuck between forms, dead of a silver overdose and wounds she could not heal. His grandcubs, tiny bodies unmoving in their seats, Josiah's screams of loss and pain ringing in his ears.

"Father? Are you well?"

"No," Caius replied, unthinking. What dignity did he have left after such failures? Why was he trying so hard not to feel when every time he denied his heart and emotions, someone he loved died? Roman corrupted by ambition, striving to be more than he was, to live up to standards Caius never meant to set. Marla dead and her babies with her, and he never told her he loved her that last day. Never took the time to see her off, to say goodbye, too busy with duties he could have passed on to his Heir.

Shadow, his Shadow. His heart. A chance, many times over, to give in to his heart's demands and claim Gray Shadow as his mate. They might have made it, against all odds. They might have succeeded, been happy. Instead he clung to duty and tradition, too afraid to try, too certain they would fail, and held the greatest love of his life at arm's length, torturing himself by simply being friends.

"I have failed you." Caius looked up, meeting his son's shocked eyes. "I am a failure as a father. I have been so consumed by duty that I felt that anything short of perfection was a waste. I saw a lesser alpha, and forgot to see my son."

"Father."

"Don't, I must say this. Kane is right. Once you leave, you'll never return. The last of my children, gone, and I am such a fool. I have driven away all your older siblings, and the one to remain festered evil in his spirit. I saw greed and ambition foul your brother's heart. Saw his corruption warp you, drive you to the edge, ruin you. It took Kane's willingness to forgive and move on to pull you back. I did nothing. I turned away, too damn unwilling to risk what remained of my heart to save either of you. I failed Roman. I failed you. And I am sorry."

He could not decipher whether it was anger or anguish that twisted Gerald's face in a grimace, but the tears were easy to understand. Gerald had always been so vulnerable, easy to drive to the emotional edge, and Roman used to tease him mercilessly for it. Caius merely disregarded Gerald, to his shame, and he would never redeem himself enough for his failures as a father.

He didn't remember going around the desk. He was in front of his son, and shocked them both by taking him in his arms. It tore at him that the last time he held his child was almost two hundred years prior. Tears escaped, racing down his cheeks as he clutched Gerald to his chest, holding as tightly as he could, refusing to let go. Gerald was stiff in his arms, hands curled to fists, shuddering as he tried to rein in his sobs.

"I am so sorry." Caius repeated it, over and over, quietly, hoping that it would reach some merciful part of his son's heart. He didn't deserve Gerald's forgiveness, but Gerald deserved to be free, from everything, even the resentment he held for his own father.

PERHAPS WAITING JUST outside the door wasn't such a smart idea. Kane put himself between the door and Sophia, who was determined to get past him and into the room. All three of them could hear quite clearly what was going on inside, and Kane was convinced that it needed to happen. For both Gerald and Caius.

"Move out of my way," Sophia ordered. "You can hear him—he needs us."

Royrick grabbed Sophia around the waist and lifted her off her feet. He backed away until he reached the wall, and leaned on it. Kane was impressed and half-certain he was going to see Sophia kick Royrick's ass. To his surprise, she merely hung from his grip with a glower on her face, eyes locked on the door.

"They both need this, Sophie. Gerald will be fine. We'll make sure of it." Royrick put Sophia on her feet, keeping his arms around her, and she gave a reluctant nod.

Kane was going to miss Sophia. She was fearless and strong. Older than him by quite a bit, she brought to her position as First Beta an air of responsibility and capability. He made no secret of the fact he appreciated her skills and loyalty.

Movement at the end of the hall drew his attention. Ghost smiled at him, silver eyes alight with affection. He made a curious motion with his hand and Kane reached out with his mind. *All is well. Caius and Gerald are working out some things before they depart.*

Ghost gave a short nod. *My grandfather is stubborn and my uncle carries armor that is ill-fitting. Caius would do well to yield more often, and Gerald's strength is in supporting those he loves. Change is necessary for both if they wish to thrive. We *live too long to torture ourselves.**

*Says the nineteen-year-old,** Kane teased, and his young mate blushed.

*Am I then too young for you, my alpha? My human father still worries about our age difference. Is he right to worry? Do you take advantage of me and my inexperience?** The coy and sultry tone to Ghost's mental voice sent shivers throughout his body. Kane stiffened, eyes locked on the young shaman at the end of the hall, his silver eyes glowing brightly, lower lip caught in his teeth as he ducked his chin, looking up at Kane from under long, thick lashes.

*When did you learn to flirt, little wolf?** Kane asked, body tightening, the desire to leap after his mate and tackle him to the ground almost overpowering. His nostrils flared and his eyes glowed, claws teasing at his fingertips as he fought back his body's urges.

*Andromeda's teenage granddaughters flirt quite often,** Ghost said primly, lifting his chin and grinning wide. *I watch and listen.**

*Oh, by the Goddess. We're leaving as soon as possible,** Kane groaned mentally, thinking that his already irresistible mate would be devastating with even a hint of seduction skills to his credit.

CAIUS STOOD BY the front door of Andromeda's cabin, watching as his son and his new mates said their goodbyes. Ghost clung to his uncle, the youngling struggling to hold back his upset at Gerald's departure.

"I forgive you, Father," Gerald had whispered, voice heavy with the weight of his tears. "I can't forget. I won't forget being regarded as less, as useless. But I can forgive you. I must. I don't want to be like this anymore. I hate who I became while I tried so hard to be what I thought you wanted."

Gerald had briefly returned his embrace, a swift clench before backing away, eyes wet and skin flushed from crying. His son left him without another word, striding for the door and into the arms of Royrick and Sophia.

He blinked, clearing the images from his mind. It wouldn't do to dwell over much. They lived for a very long time. Maybe one day he would find a way to connect with his children. Maybe.

Sophia hugged Burke, the Speaker teasing her with his customary charm and quick grin. The clan leader in him was saddened to lose Sophia. She was worth three betas. Strong, fierce, a fighter from the Old World. Her experience would now serve Red Wraith and Royrick's position as clan leader.

Royrick was the last of the Tribunal to leave. He had assurances that Red Wraith would be attending the summer gathering that summer. Dread Claw and Red Wraith still counted among their allies. Whether Birch Grove and Ashland could be considered allies at this point, Caius had his doubts. He would wait and see.

The honor guard from Red Wraith were ready to depart, the SUVs packed and all clan members accounted for but for Michael. The shaman was remaining, his intent to assist in locating the wolfkin who were still missing, and stopping Simon Remus. He stayed inside the cabin, speaking with Andromeda and her family. His was a temporary goodbye—he would see Red Wraith again soon, Goddess-willing.

Burke stepped away, and Sophia gave her packmates a nervous smile and a short nod in goodbye. Kane gently disentangled Ghost from Gerald, and they stepped away. Gerald looked his way once, and Caius gave his son a nod, hoping to convey everything he could no longer say. Gerald and Sophia disappeared into the back of Royrick's SUV, the clan leader for Red Wraith waiting for them to settle before getting in as well. The doors shut, engines came alive, and the Red Wraith convoy slowly drove down the gravel road.

Caius breathed in, the cold air bracing. His eyes watered but he ruthlessly beat back the tears that threatened. Kane, Ghost, and Burke stood with the Black Pine tactical team, watching until the vehicles were lost from sight and the sounds of the diesel engines faded away in the wind.

16

SPEAKING HUMAN

THE STENCH OF UNWASHED BODIES DROVE HIM INSANE. SIMON PRESSED his handkerchief to his face, wishing the ventilation was better down in the bowels of the warehouse where his new lab was located. Sweat, piss, and blood made for a disgusting aroma that stuck to his clothing and the inside of his sinuses long after he left the building.

Machines beeped and droned on in an annoying monotone. Wires came out in a confusing jumble from machines he could not identify and really didn't care to. They connected via small pads along the large wolf's torso, the fur underneath shaved away. Simon held up a glossy photograph and compared the image to the wolf on the surgical table. It looked almost identical, except it was easily twice the size of the animal in the picture.

"Dr. Harmon took the DNA from the original sample we got fifteen years ago and replaced the degraded pieces with the DNA from this wolf," Simon shook the picture at the doctor standing on the other side of the table. "DNA sequences that the small wolf inherited from that dead shaman. There were few pieces that survived the coding process from the sample that the crazy redheaded biologist sent him a few months ago." Simon tried not to breathe in too deep, the stench of fear and rancid blood enough to turn his stomach. "Harmon patched together a clone of the dead shaman the raid failed to capture fifteen years ago. Which would be fantastic, a marvelous step forward in our plans—except for one small detail!" Simon thundered, and pointed at the unresponsive body. "It's an empty shell. And now we have—this brain-dead monstrosity that you got hooked up to machines to keep alive. Tell me why I'm not killing you right now."

Dr. Walsh gulped nervously and cast his eyes about as if looking for something to save him. He finally found some courage and said, "The specimen had minimal brain waves while it was in the incubation unit. This was expected, a part of the normal process. We made an error somewhere in the last stages. The specimen should have more brain activity and have some level of awareness. We have some tests we can run, maybe we can wake it up."

"You can't determine if this pile of flesh and fur has any magical powers if it doesn't wake up. A brain-dead dog is useless. If you can't wake this monstrosity up, harvest what you need from it and toss the body in the incinerator. Then dump this stupid idea and go back to trying to make me a functional hybrid." Simon now pointed at the nearby cage and the figure huddled in the shadows. "Make me a human-werewolf hybrid with fucking powers instead of a sickly, sniveling brat. Understood?"

"Yes, sir." Dr. Walsh nodded and clutched at a clipboard like a shield. Simon was about to turn away, when the expression of horror that spread across Dr. Walsh's face made him pause.

The bite where his neck met his shoulder throbbed with heat, pain dull, but enough to make him tense. He turned slowly, and refused to shake when Julian stepped from the shadows, walking down the narrow aisle between the cages. The Birch Grove clan leader idly peered into the cages, and soft, low growls came from within a few of them as the alpha passed. Simon presumed the clan leader was recognizable to some of the specimens in the cages. Julian smirked, and paused at the last cage. He leaned down, and sniffed. "A human, dear Simon? Why ever do you have a human boy in a silver cage?" Julian leaned as close as he could to the bars without touching them, and the small shadow within huddled back as far as it could. "Oh, I see. Not a human, not entirely. There's a hint of someone familiar around his eyes and mouth. How delightful. Is this the hybrid? I'd be interested in how you made it immune to silver, but then it might mean being more human than I'd ever enjoy." Julian chuckled, and stood up, casually meandering away from the cages and stopping inches from Simon.

"I thought you were going to stay at the condo," Simon gritted out, trying his best to ignore the almost instinctual urge to run.

"You suggested an incredibly stupid idea," Julian replied, and looked past Simon to the beast on the table. "Is that the clone? How disgusting." Julian moved around him, knocking Simon with his shoulder. Julian flicked his fingers at Dr. Walsh, who took the dismissal to heart and all but ran from that corner of the lab. Julian reached out, and with one finger, tapped the black nose of the sleeping specimen. No reaction. He did it again, and not even the machines hooked to it chirped out of rhythm or made any new sounds. Julian sighed, and quickly grew bored. "Let's order in from a new place tonight. The sushi from last night was subpar. I'm used to Manhattan—this backwards tiny city in this pit stain of a state is sorely lacking in fine cuisine."

Julian strolled past him, and Simon gritted his teeth in impotent rage when Julian whistled for him like a dog. "Do come along, pet. I'm hungry. Leave your toys for tomorrow, it's suppertime."

WREN LAID HIS head on the bars, facing the monster in the next cage over. The red haired man who came in after Simon Remus earlier in the night had scared him more than even the butchers who experimented on the other occupants of the cages.

"Who was that man? The red haired one?" Wren whispered. The lab was quiet, the scientists and doctors off somewhere else. Machines hummed and water dripped in the distance.

There was no answer for the longest time. It came just as he was about to fall asleep.

"Julian, Clan Leader of Birch Grove, the Mad Dog of New York City. Far worse than Roman McLennan could ever aspire."

THE HUMAN DOCTOR was dirty, incredibly pale, and the exact same man who tried to capture Ghost what felt like a lifetime ago back in Canada. Ghost lifted his lip and snarled, making the human doctor flinch and jump on the stool.

Since the root cellar was too small for the interrogation, Kane and

Caius decided to drag the human upstairs and into Andromeda's office. It was large enough to fit most of them, with the remainder of Kane's tactical team listening out in the hallway, the office doors remaining open.

Kane and Caius stood behind the desk, Andromeda in her seat, flanked by the two alphas. Ghost sat in a chair next to the desk, Kane within arm's reach. Burke stood guard behind the human where he sat on his school in the center of the room. Michael was near the door, a very nervous looking Gabe standing next to him. Night had fallen and Baxter was almost back to normal, or what Ghost assumed was normal. The visiting clan leaders had all parted. Only Caius remained, but Red Fern was part of his territory so his presence was common.

"Is this him?" Caius said addressing Ghost. He nodded, confirming that it was indeed the same human who attacked him along with Simon Remus weeks ago. The human doctor gave a pathetic whimper, his terror stinking up the room.

"Roman McLennan is dead." Kane stated, and the doctor somehow grew even paler. "He confessed his crimes before his death. He said that you had been sent along on the raid to garner DNA samples from my mate. Somehow, I don't see Simon Remus putting you in harm's way unless he was ready to write you off. No matter what he may have told you about why you were included in the attack on the Park, he no longer has use for you. As far as Simon Remus is concerned, you're already dead."

Kane left his place behind the desk and prowled toward the doctor. He stopped a few feet away and gave a sharp smile, full of teeth and menace. "Tell me your name."

"Harmon," the human whispered, breathing shaky. He coughed, and spoke up. "Dr. Mitchell Harmon, M.D, Ph.D. I work for...errmm, I used to work for Remus Acquisitions."

"Doing what?" Kane asked casually. Dr. Harmon hesitated, and Kane chuckled, a dark, rich sound that thrilled Ghost but terrified the human. "Don't bother trying to lie or hold back. I can smell the first and force the rest."

"I thought...I thought alpha mental abilities didn't work on humans," Dr. Harmon said, licking his lips, nervous.

Kane leaned down a bit, and whispered, "I don't need to use my gifts to make you talk."

The doctor squeaked and jerked on the stool. The human reminded Ghost of a rabbit, all quivering nerves and frantic heartbeat. Sweat poured down the man's face and darkened his already dirty clothing.

"I ran one of the labs for Remus Acquisitions. It was my job to identify the gene sequences that gave werewolves their powers. Simon Remus has investors from several shadow organizations and a few governments around the world, including the United States."

Ghost wasn't too sure what any of that meant, but the shock, anger, and intense protectiveness he felt along the bond with Kane told him that it was bad.

"What is Simon Remus's goal?" Kane asked. "Does he want our gifts?"

"One of his goals is to give human soldiers werewolf abilities," Dr. Harmon said, shaking. "Things like increased strength and speed, the ability to force compliance, and total obedience."

"You mean the Voice."

The doctor gave a shaky nod. "The alpha ability to completely control another werewolf, yes. He wants a way to make it work on humans."

"And just how successful were you?" Kane asked. He never once raised his voice or physically touched the human, but every word, expression, movement was predatory and had the human focused on him like a mouse cornered by a fox. Or in this case, a wolf.

"We haven't managed yet to combine human and werewolf DNA in adult subjects. Adult humans' bodies reject the retrovirus we used to deliver werewolf DNA into human DNA. Even with antirejection treatments and medications, the process has a 100% failure rate. So, we attempted to take a different route. We tried to make hybrids."

"It is a common belief that our species cannot interbreed. Wolfkin have taken human lovers before, and there has never been offspring, even when pairs have tried," Caius interrupted. The human jumped again on the stool, eyes darting between the two alphas. "Of course, such attempts were considered taboo. Having a human lover is one thing, but integrating them into our society as mates has always been heavily discouraged, sometimes with lethal results. Can we breed? Have pairs just never been given sufficient time to try?"

"Humans and werewolves cannot breed naturally. Our DNA is separated by too many different chromosomal pairs. We've tried different techniques including via IVF, but it hasn't been successful. Only one attempt at cross-breeding a human and werewolf has managed to survive. But the specimen only reached viability and survived because all the werewolf traits were suppressed completely. It's werewolf DNA is regressive and totally useless. Since that is the opposite of what Remus wished, attempting to replicate that lone success was never tried again in the same manner."

A whisper broke through the startled silence after the doctor's reply. Ghost sat up straighter and leaned forward, eyes locked on the human doctor. His movement drew the human's attention, and Ghost spoke. "There is a human/wolfkin hybrid? A living person you made in a lab? Is he or she still alive?"

"The specimen was alive the last I checked on it, a few days before you captured me. I don't know if it still alive now—Remus was extremely disappointed in it, and only my insistence that it could still be useful kept it alive all these years." The doctor was terrified, yet Ghost was thrown by the casual indifference of the doctor's attitude when discussing the person he made in a lab.

Ghost stood and took a few steps to stand over the doctor, forcing him to tilt his head back and look up at Ghost. "Is it a male or female, and how old is this poor soul?" Ghost growled softly, and he knew his wilder side was glowing bright when silver light reflected off the doctor's wide eyes.

"He… He is eighteen years old now. He was the lone success in a long line of failures. He was alive the last time I saw him. Remus may have already ordered his death. I don't know if it…he is still alive now, it's been weeks." Dr. Harmon was breathing fast and erratic. Terror made his sweat stink even more, and Ghost had to restrain the urge to strike the human down. He didn't understand what IVF meant or any of the other technical terms that the doctor used, but from the emotional reactions he was sensing from Kane, it was all horrific.

"We will deal with the hybrid later," Caius interrupted again. Ghost took the hint and backed away before he did something rash. His Goddess was still whispering quietly to him, and he knew that his part in all this had something to do with the poor creature created by the monster masquerading as a man. Caius stood, drawing everyone's attention. He addressed the human, his tone dark and just as threatening as Kane's.

"The wolves that Remus has now. Why did he keep them? What does he want with them?"

No one looked at Gabe where he stood in the doorway. Ghost knew that Caius referred to Gabe's family. Half of his family including his father and his uncles were still missing.

"Roman identifies…or he did, since he's dead now…specific families with a predominant strain for alphas with what you call the Voice. The wolves Remus kept were all especially dominant and showed a predisposition to having some form of the Voice. They were not near their clan leader and operated independently in that area of Worcester. Made them easier to take." Gabe shifted on his feet, and Michael put a calming hand on his shoulder, keeping him still. The doctor gulped, but continued. "Part of the payment for Roman's participation was that he wanted stronger alpha abilities, including the Voice. He called one of those abilities the 'gift of command' and said only the strongest alphas had it in abundance. We even spent a great deal of time looking for werewolves he called Speakers, but Remus was never able to find any in a vulnerable enough position to capture. Many of them were too strong to attempt to take without being noticed, or were in too close proximity to clan leaders to capture."

Dr. Harmon seemed to be alternating between absolute terror and a remote sense of scientific curiosity. He apparently had no trouble disclosing the atrocities that Roman and Remus planned to commit in the pursuit of power. It was as if the human doctor was proud of what he was a part of and what he had done, and was only concerned with surviving the immediate moment. Ghost was inclined to believe that the human was only that in flesh and form and there was nothing humane in his soul whatsoever.

"Has there been any success in taking gifts from one wolf and giving them to another?" Kane addressed the doctor, voice sharp.

"No, not yet. Against all scientific processes and logic, I have been unsuccessful in giving shamanic gifts to alphas or increasing an alpha's own gifts. I would say the process has been cursed if I believed in that superstitious nonsense." The doctor sneered, tugging on his dirty shirt sleeves. An angry murmur whispered in Ghost's mind, and he realized that the failures Remus and Harmon encountered might not have been due to faulty science but the interference of the Great Mother. "In repeated attempts to see what genes could be turned off or activated, cloning has been tried on several different wolves and family lines with predominant traits that Remus and Roman wanted. Repeated failures in this avenue of thought were not enough to deter Remus in his plans—Remus wanted shamanic powers and longevity for himself. Roman wanted stronger alpha abilities. And the government investors wanted super soldiers."

"You're cloning wolfkin?" Kane demanded, infuriated and incredulous.

"I managed to begin the gestation process on a clone before I left and you captured me," Dr. Harmon said carefully, and he held his hands up, palms out. "It could be dead by now, like every other attempt I've made."

"By the Goddess," Burke swore softly, shaking his head. Ghost echoed that sentiment.

"How did we never notice these machinations with the human governments? Don't we have established contacts to prevent just the sort of thing?" Kane addressed Caius, crossing his arms over his chest and glaring. Caius quirked an eyebrow at his heir's attitude but did not address it.

"We do and that's a matter for another time. Right now, we need to stop Remus. We need to free the wolves that he has and destroy everything. All his labs need to be burned to the ground and all his information destroyed. This cannot continue. This must be stopped, and stopped with such finality that any attempts to do this again will be over before they start. A message must be sent to human governments that we will not stand idly by while our people are killed and experimented upon." Caius declared, voice rising enough that everyone, even those in the hall, could not mistake his determination.

Caius opened a drawer in the desk, pulling out a notepad and pen. He strode over to the doctor, who shrank back, cowering on the stool. "Look at me, human."

Caius' growl was deep and threatening and the human was incapable of disobeying. He lifted his eyes to Caius, who held out the paper and pen. "Write down every single lab you have ever been to. Every single building, warehouse, home, apartment, parking lot! I do not care what these places are or why you were there, but everything that has a connection to my people, to Simon Remus, that you have been to or even suspect of existing, you will disclose it. Do this, and you live another day."

The doctor took the pad and pen with cautious motions and a short nod. "OK…yes."

"Kane, with me," Caius ordered, and Kane nodded. "Burke, don't take your eyes off him."

Kane followed Caius as he left Andromeda's study. Burke loomed over the human, and Ghost shot out into the hall after his mate and his grandfather. Those in the hall either scattered or moved to the side, letting the clan leader and heir pass. Ghost dodged around wolfkin, dogging Kane's heels into the living room.

Caius went to the fireplace, staring down at the flames. Ghost took a seat on the couch not far from where Kane stood, arms crossed, his mate watching Caius.

"Simon Remus is far more widely known than his brother ever was," Caius said, rubbing his chin before turning his back to the low flames in the hearth. Caius paused for a second when he saw Ghost, then with a tiny, wry smile, continued, addressing Kane. "We were able to kill and dispose of Sebastien Remus easily. Fifteen years have nearly passed since then, with social media and technology making it harder for a rich man to disappear without a reaction. Simon is a popular man in Augusta. He dies, it will get attention."

"We can stage his death like we did his brother's," Kane mused, eyes distant as if remembering. This was new to Ghost—he was aware that the first Remus brother was dead and that Caius killed him, but he didn't know any details. "A car accident is the easiest."

"When we find him—and we will—save him for me," Caius said, and an icy chill ran down Ghost's back. "That bastard has to pay for what he's done."

"Yes, Sir," Kane agreed.

This was a new dynamic Ghost wasn't accustomed to. Seeing his mate defer to another was…odd. The wilder part of Ghost knew Kane and Caius were alphas, dominant—they were in charge. Yet that sense also told him that Kane was…more. Caius was formidable, and if Kane wasn't in the room, he would be the strongest, most dominant wolfkin Ghost had ever come across. Kane was stronger, more powerful than Caius. His presence took up more room, more of the focus and awareness of the wolfkin around them. And yet Kane made no move to depose Caius and take over Black Pine. He knew that such ambition was not in Kane's nature—he had no desire for authority and rank. It was only through Kane's reluctance to lead that Caius remained clan leader.

There was a soft cough, and they all turned to the wolfkin standing hesitantly in the doorway. Michael held the notepad, and entered the living room a few paces, holding it out to Kane.

"The human doctor finished the list. Andromeda was…offended by the stench, so she ordered Speaker Burke to have the human cleaned up. Burke is taking care of that now. He's under sufficient guard—Burke and the young alpha named Gabe have it in hand," Michael said, rubbing his palms down his thighs as he spoke.

Kane took the list and went to Caius, the two alphas reading through the list, which looked to be a few pages long. Ghost patted the couch next to him, and Michael gave a start but walked over. He sat, hesitant, and Ghost grabbed his elbow and tugged him down onto the cushion next to his. Michael kept one eye on Kane, as if expecting a negative reaction from the alpha. Ghost rolled his eyes, a response he'd picked up from the youngsters in Andromeda's family pack. All Kane did was offer a sharp glance to the older shaman and went back to his discussion with Caius.

Ghost leaned on Michael's shoulder and he waited, watching his mate and his grandfather as they discussed options for searching the locations on the doctor's list. The alphas were quiet, sentences half-formed—they were speaking to each other mind to mind, as much as they were with words, and Ghost was sure they hadn't even noticed.

"There's over thirty locations on this list. Half of them are at science labs on college campuses here in Maine and in Massachusetts. Many of these places are in Augusta and Boston. Colleges are still in session; spring break isn't until the second week of March. If we're going to search these locations, we need to choose a time when there aren't as many humans around. Spring break is in two weeks," Kane said aloud. "I can send scouts to each of these locations, but I'll need more Black Pine wolves and a base closer to many of these locations. Red Fern is not trained or equipped to handle surveillance or investigating."

"Back to Augusta?" Caius mused, eyes distant. Kane nodded, and Caius took the notepad, ripping off the top few pages and folding the list into his pocket. "Very well. We're going home. Organize your team. We leave for Augusta in the morning."

Caius strode from the living room, and Ghost heard him call Andromeda's name.

"Home?" Ghost asked, quiet, feeling suddenly worried. Kane came to stand over him where he sat beside Michael, and held out a hand, helping him to his feet and into his arms.

"Yes, home." Kane leaned down, kissing him, a chaste press of lips that made him sigh and lean on his broad chest.

"I..." Ghost nuzzled into Kane's chest, breathing in a deep lungful of his alpha's scent. It reassured him, settled his nerves. "I only know this place as home."

"It'll be alright," Kane whispered, hugging him. Ghost hoped Kane was right. He'd already lost one home with Cat and Glen.... "Wait! What about my humans?"

He tilted his head back enough to see Kane's face. Kane was startled by his outburst, and Ghost could see and feel his mate thinking hard. "Let's go see them now, little wolf."

17

GOODBYE

"Ghost? Sweetheart, what's wrong?" Cat asked after she shut the door behind them, gesturing for them to take a seat.

The cabin smelled like soap and freshly-showered humans, his humans, and Ghost breathed in deep, appreciating the scents that once meant home to him. Cat's red hair was damp and piled high on her head, and she looked worried for him despite her disheveled appearance.

"I am fine," Ghost said with a smile. "Where's Glen?"

"Getting dressed," Cat replied. "He'll be out in a minute."

The silence that followed was awkward. He assumed that was what this sensation was—he didn't usually care or notice when things got uncomfortable, but then, this was Cat. The closest person to a mother he'd known for the last fifteen years. Ghost fidgeted and looked to his mate to take over. Kane gave him a fond smile and led him over to the couch, pulling him down to take a seat next him. Cat followed, her green eyes darting between Ghost and Kane, as if she didn't quite believe that everything was okay. Ghost found himself torn between his eagerness to take the next step towards finding justice for his people and his desire to stay in Baxter with his family, both human and wolf.

The bedroom door opened and Glen came out, hair still dripping, wetting the collar of his gray T-shirt. He saw them sitting on the couch and smiled wide. "Hey, good to see you both! Anything exciting happen since we saw Andromeda toss Julian out on his ass?"

Ghost had no idea what to say, opening his mouth but then closing it with a snap. He was too jumbled, too indecisive about what he wanted to do anything except sit there and frantically try to figure out how he was going to manage to say goodbye to the two people who raised him. Kane sensed his trouble, a large warm hand coming to rest on his shoulder. The reassuring weight settled some of his nerves, and Ghost took in a long, deep breath, trying to calm the rest.

"Sophia and Gerald have left Black Pine, and have joined Red Wraith." Both Glen and Cat looked alarmed, and Kane shook his head with a smile. "No, it's nothing bad. Royrick offered for them both as mates— and they accepted. Gerald needs a new start, someplace where he will never be known as *only* Caius's son, and Sophia has loved Royrick for a long time. They worked out their issues; I can see all three of them being very happy."

Cat sat on the coffee table, hands in her lap, while Glen came around and sat in a rickety wicker chair that creaked under his weight. Cat was curious, Ghost could tell by the gleam in her eyes and the way she leaned forward just the slightest amount. "Are triads common in your culture? Does it happen often? Have you come across many? Does it always happen so fast? Will the two of you want a third?"

"Cat! Boundaries, remember? Take a breath and pick one question," Glen said with a chuckle.

Kane didn't seem to mind at all. He wrapped an arm around Ghost, drawing him closer to his side. He put his head down on Kane's shoulder, relaxing completely.

"Threesomes are common in casual arrangements. As something more formal like a mating, usually it's an alpha with two beta females, each serving as alpha mate. Such arrangements are rare, and in some places, are frowned upon, but since Royrick is a clan leader, any blowback he might get will be minimal. Red Wraith is one of the more progressive clans in the Northeast," Kane explained. "Things might be tense, especially since Gerald is male and Sophia has a well-known history with Royrick, but Royrick and Sophia are both strong enough to mitigate any issues. I think they'll be happy after a brief adjustment period."

"But so fast?" Cat asked, head tilting to the side.

"Not fast for us, not really. Our people tend to know whether we're going to be compatible quickly—and the older we are when we mate, the better the matches. Sophia and Royrick have known each other for a long time, and Gerald fits them both. All three are a few hundred years or older. It's a good match."

Cat's hands twitched, like she wanted to take notes. Glen frowned at Kane, and looked at Ghost. He could almost read his human alpha's mind. "Kane and I are soulbonded—there will never be a need or room for a third. Their triad is a matter of choice—they have chosen to be together in such a way. Our pairing is Goddess-forged, and entirely different."

"You didn't have a choice? I thought wolfkin just moved fast compared to humans." Glen frowned even harder, narrowing his eyes at Kane. His human alpha was no match for Kane, and seeing Glen get worked up made Ghost feel better about his choices. Glen would always be family. No matter where they were.

"I would have chosen this mating with Kane," Ghost said, leaning forward, meeting Glen's concerned gaze and holding it. "I love him. I've always loved him. Even when I forgot who I was, the impression Kane had made on me remained from our brief meeting when I was a cub. A soulbond is a blessing, not a trap."

"Is that how you feel?" Glen demanded of Kane. "Would you have chosen Ghost if given the choice?"

"Yes," Kane answered, without hesitation and with enough force Glen sat back in his seat, blinking. "I never could let go of the belief that Ghost was alive. He may have been a cub when last we met, but he left a lasting and permanent impression on my heart. Finding him now, a grown wolf, has been the greatest joy and gift I could ever receive, and I will be thankful forever that our Goddess joined us. I love him. She can bind us together, but She cannot create love. We came to love each other on our own."

"Why would your Goddess join you?" Cat asked, confused. "If you were going to fall in love anyway, why do the soulbond thing?"

"I don't know." Kane answered. Ghost looked up at his mate. "She has a plan. She never does anything without purpose. Maybe She knew we would need the protection of the soulbond to see us through. I am grateful for it—I don't know if I would have the courage to claim Ghost as mine without it. Not if it meant his life would be in danger."

"You would have," Ghost murmured. "No one is braver than you. I might have needed to nudge you along if we didn't have the soulbond, but us loving each other is as inevitable as the sunrise."

Kane pressed a kiss to his forehead, and Ghost heard Cat give a happy sigh. Glen interrupted them with a discreet cough. They gave him their attention, and Glen shifted in the chair.

"I know you two survived the Tribunal and the clans acknowledged the soulbond, but that doesn't erase the tension I sensed in those alphas before they left. I get that the shamans endorsed your union, and the tribunal accepted it, but that isn't going to change what seems, to me, to be thousands of years' worth of animosity and cultural programming that cast such unions as sacrilegious and against the law. Are you going to be in danger if you leave Caius' territory? Are those alphas going to go home to their clans, and tell their people what happened, and then you'll have to keep defending yourselves over and over?"

"If the shamans weren't privy to the truth, I would say you have cause to be concerned, Glen." Kane nodded to the human. "But the shamans who were here do know the truth, and despite their personal feelings, their calling will prevent them from lying or misleading their clans. Rumors and ill feelings will still happen, but the shamans can curtail the worst of it. We will be in more danger from those wolfkin who don't yet know about us—though considering the nature of our people, nothing of this magnitude will remain secret for long. We all live long lives, and the older clan members know many wolves on almost every continent. I bet by the end of the week, most clans across the world will have heard some portion of what transpired here. By this summer's gathering, almost every wolfkin will know."

Glen nodded, face clearing, his frown turning thoughtful. Cat leaned over and patted his knee, and he gave her a small smile. Cat sat back up, and turned back to Ghost and Kane. "So, what prompted your visit?"

Kane rubbed a warm hand along his bicep, and Ghost sighed. He looked to Cat first, her bright smile and wild curls, then to Glen, his solid presence and absolute personal strength as reassuring as ever. "We're leaving Baxter in the morning." He just blurted it out, unable to think of another way to say it. Kane chuckled, an indulgent sound that made his face grow warm.

"Leaving? Who's leaving?" Cat asked.

"All of us. Well, the Black Pine wolfkin. I guess that's me, too," Ghost explained, frowning. He hadn't really thought about it much—he had trouble seeing past his nose too many times. A wolf focused on the present, rarely concerned for the future. He was indeed a Black Pine wolfkin—Red Fern and Baxter were not his home. Nor was the wolf sanctuary in Canada, despite his years spent there. "We questioned the human doctor, and we have leads on the missing wolfkin. Caius, and Kane," he looked up to his mate, who gave him a small nod, "decided it was best we go to Augusta, to Black Pine's home territory. That's where Remus is—that's where we're likely to find our missing wolves. We need to end this."

He could see when the truth of what he was getting at sunk in. Cat's eyes filled with tears, and Glen's expression went blank, but his white knuckles clutching the armrests of his chair gave him away.

"You're still my family. My packmates. I love you," Ghost whispered, playing with Kane's fingers, trying not to give into the tears that threatened to spill from his eyes. He looked away, blinking fast.

A slim, delicate hand covered one of his, holding tight. Cat smiled at him, despite her own damp eyes. "Sweetie, a lot has changed in the last few weeks. Our lives are different now. But one thing that'll never change is how we feel about you. You're part of our family. We love you, too."

Glen gave him a nod, his eyes damp. Ghost clutched Cat's hand in both of his, holding tightly as he could without damaging her. "I don't think you can come with us," Ghost said, hesitant. He knew the answer before he even looked to Kane with hope in his eyes.

"They are most welcome here in Baxter, but in Augusta, at the clan house, is another matter. We need to be focused on hunting Remus and our lost wolfkin—they might be safe, but they would be just as likely to cause upheaval with their mere presence. Caius maintains firm control over those who live in the clan house, but that doesn't mean Cat and Glen would find the same welcome there that they have here."

"That's okay—we know how rare it is for humans to be this involved in your people's lives," Cat murmured, and Ghost nodded, agreeing. It was unusual, even he knew that.

"Do we stay here, or go home to New Brunswick?" Glen spoke up, rubbing a hand over his eyes in quick, short movements. "I've got an email inbox full of reports for wolves—the normal kind—needing rescue, and a few from the police back home, wondering where we are. I told some of our friends that we had a family emergency here in the States, and that the wolves we had at the sanctuary were sent to other facilities before we left. I don't know if they bought it or not, and I need to give some people more definitive answers before this goes on any longer."

"There is no longer any reason for Remus to go after you," Kane said. "You may be in danger still, but I don't think Remus will risk himself or anymore of his people by going after you again. Losing Roman and his rogue wolves must have depleted the ranks to some degree. I think it's safe for you to go back to your home. Maybe we can discuss it with Andromeda, see if we can spare some wolfkin to go back with you, provide protection until Remus is taken out."

"Could we stay here?" Cat asked, looking back and forth between Ghost and Glen. "I would love to learn more about your people, and if we can reassure the people back home in New Brunswick that we're fine, I think we'd be okay here, right?"

"We can ask Andromeda," Kane started to say, and Cat got up like she would charge up the mountainside and corner the Red Fern clan leader that very minute.

"Hold on," Ghost said, turning his focus inward before reaching out with his mind. He was no alpha or Speaker, but it was only a matter of a few minutes walking distance between this cabin and Andromeda's.

Finding her was easy—she shined the brightest amongst the stars in the heavens that swirled within his mind. A white-gold star that burned with an intensity that was no easier to look upon now than it had been the first time. She could sense him as he did her—and when he reached out, she caught him, her mind opening to him like a flower, petals sharp and icy.

Shaman.

Her consciousness was vast, and he realized with a sense of awe that she hid herself away from everyone, perhaps even from her children. Her mind felt different than Burke's—she wasn't a Speaker. The female alpha was a mystery in all things, maybe even to Caius.

He found his words and tried not to have them quaver. *May my humans remain while we go south? They would go home, but I would feel better if they had protection. May they stay here, safe in Baxter, or return to their home over the border, with Red Fern's protection?*

She mused, white and gold light spinning slowly, somehow peaceful despite the power that sang quietly along the link between their minds.

They may remain. I would rather they stay where I can see them. Your humans are pack now.

It took him a moment, but he was able to whisper his sincere thanks, pulling his mind back when she released him.

Ghost blinked, dragging in a deep breath. Cat and Glen were both watching him with expression varying between confusion and concern. He smiled wide, relieved.

"Andromeda said you can stay. That you're pack now—and I think she meant more than just your connection to me. She claimed you both."

18

BLACK PINE CLAN

Cat hugged him long and hard. She pulled back and held him by his upper arms, while she looked him over head to toe, as if memorizing everything about him. Glen gently disengaged his mate, and gave him a hug of his own, lifting Ghost off his feet. Glen set him down, and ran a large hand over his hair and down his neck to the shoulder. Ghost had a feeling that his human alpha had no idea that he had scent marked him like any wolfkin alpha would. Ghost smiled, doing his best not to let his tears fall. This goodbye was not for forever—he would see them again, Goddess willing.

"Be careful," Cat said with a sniffle. "Stop that awful man and then come back and tell us all about it. And if you need us, make sure you call. I gave your handsome mate our numbers. At least this time you have fingers now and you know better than to eat the smartphone."

Ghost winced as the memories came back, a rueful smile lifting his lips. While a wolf, he had found smartphones to be crunchy and entertaining to gnaw upon. Thinking back, he'd destroyed a quite a few.

Glen chuckled. "We're going to miss you—and you'll always know where we are. Home doesn't have to be a place. Home can be the people who love you the most."

"I understand. Stay in one piece. Defeat the bad guy. Don't eat the smartphone." His recitation got him another smile from Cat and a laugh from Glen. He would miss his humans, but there was no safer place in the whole world than under Andromeda's watchful eyes. They would be well, and all he had to do was keep himself and everyone else alive.

"It's time, little wolf," Kane murmured, taking his elbow and gently nudging him toward the black SUVs laden down with gear and Black Pine wolves.

"Take care of him," Glen reiterated again, something he'd already said multiple times that morning as they loaded up the vehicles. Kane, to his credit, only nodded respectfully to the demand from the human alpha.

Glen wrapped an arm over Cat's shoulder, holding her close as Ghost and Kane headed to the SUVs. Andromeda and her family stood on the porch, their goodbyes given over an early breakfast. The female clan leader gently reminded him that they lived for a very long time, and no goodbye was meant to be forever. He would return to Red Fern. Sooner or later, all wolves crossed paths.

Gabe jumped into the front passenger seat while Burke got behind the wheel. Kane held open the door to the rear passenger seats, letting Ghost get in first. Kane hopped in behind him, shutting the door with a solid thud. Ghost watched with interest as Burke and Gabe clicked their seatbelts into place. He looked for his and tried to decipher how it fit together.

Big hands took over the task, Kane buckling him in before tending to his own seatbelt. Ghost shifted on the seat, unaccustomed to being secured in place. He'd ridden in plenty of vehicles growing up at the sanctuary—he just had four paws and stretched out on the backseat.

He could see through the front window, and saw Caius get into the SUV in front of theirs, a blonde wolf hopping in the backseat. "Who's the Red Fern wolf?"

Kane spared the other SUV a quick glance. "That's Marjorie. Andromeda put her forward as a temporary First Beta replacement for Sophia. If she fits in and does well, she'll become a Black Pine wolf."

"Oh." Ghost shrugged. It seemed very...human of them all.

The human doctor was bustled into the rear of Caius' vehicle, hands bound and legs hobbled. Two Red Fern wolfkin all but tossed the human into the back of the SUV, securing him in place before slamming the door shut. Ghost frowned, not wanting to be anywhere near that miserable excuse for a human, but he could understand the practicality of it. Getting information out of him would be easier if he was present in Augusta instead of hours away in Baxter.

"We all set?" Burke asked, looking back over his shoulder.

"Wait!" Ghost leaned forward as far as the belt allowed, and patted at Kane's arm to get him to reopen the door. Michael hurried down the path, a backpack slung over his shoulder and a blush on his cheeks. He scrambled into their SUV, ducking down as he worked his way to the last bench seat all the way in the back. "Sorry! I'm ready now."

Kane grumbled, but he shut the door without a word. Ghost gave Michael a sympathetic glance before he nudged his mate with a frown. Burke and Gabe wisely said nothing, the Speaker grinning wide at Kane before turning back around and starting the vehicle. "Homeward bound we go."

Three SUVs started, theirs in the middle, with Caius leading the way and the rest of the Black Pine wolves in the rear. Ice crunched underneath tires as the large vehicles pulled away one by one. Ghost peered over his shoulder, looking back at the cabin where so much of his life changed. He got a quick glance of Cat and Glen, and Andromeda on her front porch, before the pines blocked his view.

THE DRIVE WASN'T too long, just under three hours. Ghost spent the drive curled into Kane's side, his mate's arm draped over him protectively. Gabe and Burke chatted back and forth, talking about Gabe's aborted college career, Kane occasionally sharing a comment. Michael read a book, though somehow that made Ghost feel ill just thinking about it. He barely recalled how to read, but the thought of doing so while the SUV rumbled along the highway left his stomach feeling odd and his head swam. Ghost dropped his head down on Kane's shoulder, and Kane hugged him tighter.

"Try closing your eyes, little wolf," Kane murmured. "First time in a car in your human form probably isn't helping the nausea."

Ghost nodded, closing his eyes, letting out a long sigh.

"He okay?" Burke asked.

"Car sick," Kane replied, and Burke made a sympathetic hum.

"Want to stop? There's a rest area a few miles ahead."

"I'll be okay," Ghost sighed. His head lolled when the SUV hit a bump, and he groaned. A part of him felt like he was about to fall over, despite being firmly seated and held against Kane.

"Stop at the rest area, Burke," Kane ordered, putting a hand on Ghost's head and holding him tighter. His stomach flipped, and Ghost whined, feeling as pathetic as he sounded. "Tell Caius we're taking a break."

"Wait," Michael said, and there was a warm, light touch to his shoulder. "I'm not much of a healer, but I can…" Soft warmth spread from where his fingers touched the back of his shoulder, and Ghost could feel a lessening of the nasty sensation that ate at his stomach and head. He felt grounded, more secure, and didn't feel like he was about to fall anymore. Ghost went limp, whimpering with relief. "There you are," Michael murmured, pulling away his hand. "Better?"

"Thank you," Ghost whispered, and yawned, cuddling closer to his mate.

"So, not stopping?" Burke sounded amused, a chuckle in his voice, and Kane gave a soft growl, which only made Burke chuckle more.

"Just get us home," Kane growled quietly, and Burke laughed. Ghost smiled, and fell asleep.

GHOST WASN'T SURE what he expected, but the huge stone and wood mansion surrounded by a wide lawn and high trees wasn't it. Three stories tall, with arching gables and numerous chimneys, huge windows that caught the light, and iron torches that stood tall on either side of the pathway that led to the double front doors. A paved and plowed driveway split, one route going to the front of the huge mansion where it circled a large, dormant fountain, the other swinging around the back where a long, multi-bay garage waited. The doors opened at some hidden signal, and the SUVs all pulled into spots that must be designated. The engines cut out as the automatic garage doors began to close, shutting out the winter air. It was just after lunch, and he should be hungry, but nerves ate at his stomach. His nap left him refreshed, but he woke with minimal time to prepare mentally for the arrival at the seat of Black Pine Clan.

Kane helped him down from the vehicle, Michael squeezing out with his bag. Gabe exited the SUV and glued himself to Ghost's side, the young alpha looking as nervous as Ghost suddenly felt. Ghost grabbed Gabe's hand and held it tight, earning him a small smile from his friend.

Caius and his entourage disappeared through a wide door that presumably led into the rest of the mansion. Marjorie held the human prisoner by his arm and marched him inside after the clan leader. The rest of the tactical team were organizing their gear and luggage, Burke and Kane each hefting two large duffel bags apiece.

"Follow me," Kane said with a tilt of his head. Burke went ahead, then Kane, with Gabe and Ghost on Kane's heels, Michael bringing up the rear.

The door into the house opened to a wide hallway, arches on each side. They followed Burke and Kane, the two alphas marching ahead down the hall without deviating. Their footsteps echoed, the noise of excited wolves speaking loudly in the garage following them down the hall. Burke bumped the door at the end of the hallway open with his shoulder, holding it open to the side with his foot to let them pass.

They were in a large, high foyer. Stone and wood made up the walls, the floor a patchwork of tile and hardwood. On each side was a fireplace, and in the rear of the room was a tall staircase that curved off to the left and right with a stain-glass window on the first landing that cast muted colors across the floor and walls.

Kane dropped his bags in the center of the space, Burke doing the same. Betas came out from almost nowhere, picking up the bags with bowed heads and quiet feet, disappearing as quickly as they appeared. Gabe gave him a confused glance and raised brow, Ghost echoing the sentiment.

"How many wolfkin live in this place?" Gabe whispered, leaning down a bit. Ghost shrugged, eyes wide as he tried to take it all in. Above them and on each side of the large foyer were balconies, and assorted wolfkin were gathering, curious and talking excitedly to each other as they examined the newcomers and returning clanmates.

The remainder of the tactical team came out from the hallway, and greetings came from those assembled on the balconies. Wolfkin came down the stairs in pairs and alone, greeting friends and clanmates among the returning wolves. They all nodded to Kane and said a short greeting before heading to their loved ones and friends. Ghost could feel curious eyes resting over him and Gabe, and every time he made eye contact with a strange wolf they looked away quickly. Some few gave him a respectful nod in greeting before looking away.

"Wolfkin in the higher rankings, perhaps?" Ghost murmured to Gabe, since no one was close enough to hear him. A small crowd was growing around Burke and Kane, wolfkin darting in to get a quick smile from the Heir and Speaker, a couple words before slipping away.

Michael was known to a few, the shaman nodding to quiet hellos and greetings, but none came close to the three of them, the buffer between them and the Black Pine wolfkin somehow impenetrable.

Ghost breathed in, his senses assaulted by the intense multitude of individual wolfkin. It smelled like fur, blood, sweat, a spicy twinge of excitement and…home. He did it again, and held it in his chest, his nerves buzzing. He might not remember this place, but his senses did—he had been here before, when he was Luca.

He could hear the thud of running feet, high pitched giggles and excited yips. Warm hands lifting him in the air, a kind voice chiding him with a rueful laugh. He swallowed, all but able to taste the cookies and hot chocolate he ate at a large, dark wooden table in a long, stone and steel kitchen. A tall wolfkin male with a wide smile and bright eyes sat across from him at the table, laughing. His heart raced and his body thrummed—he knew that laugh.

"Little wolf?" Ghost blinked, clearing away the memories. Kane was smiling down at him, his head tilted inquisitively to the side, long dark hair falling over one shoulder. "Ghost?"

"I was…I'm fine," Ghost whispered, dragging in a fresh breath, clearing away the clinging memories. "I saw…I remember my father."

Kane's expression softened, and a big hand lifted to gently brush across his cheek. "Josiah and Marla brought you and your littermates here often when you were little. Marla lived here before she mated Josiah."

Ghost shook, and blinked hard. Gabe tightened his grip on his hand, his friend's concern a balm to his nerves. The foyer was rapidly emptying, Burke and Michael were gone, and the balconies above them were empty as well. "Where did everyone go?"

"I sent them off when your scent changed," Kane explained, eyes darting to Gabe quickly before returning to Ghost. "You wouldn't let go of Gabe."

Ghost released Gabe, stretching his stiff hand and giving Gabe an apologetic glance. "Sorry, I lost myself for a bit."

"I know how that feels," Gabe murmured, ducking his head. "I understand. It's okay."

"Let me show you where the bedrooms are," Kane gestured, pulling Ghost under his arm and nodding Gabe towards the staircase.

The stairs were carpeted, their footsteps muffled as they ascended. The stained glass window rose high over their heads when they reached the first landing, and Ghost could see the dark green of pine boughs and the dark forms of wolves running before he had to look away to take the staircase on the left.

"How big is this place?" Gabe asked, nerves making his voice a bit thin.

"I'm not sure," Kane answered, taking them to the second floor. The landing opened on the right while the stairs continued upwards to the left. They came out to a hallway that branched out in three directions; straight ahead, to the left and the right. "There's just over thirty wolfkin here in the mansion. All single wolves or cub-less mated pairs. When they have cubs, Caius has property with land and sufficient housing for them to go. He doesn't do this for all the Black Pine wolves, as there are a few thousand of us, but anyone he invites to live in the clan house with him eventually takes him up on the offer for their own place if they mate. Caius owns over two dozen properties in Augusta and surrounding suburbs. For Black Pine wolves who don't live here, he has housing assistance programs if they need it. Most of the younger wolves take him up on the help."

"Is this where Claire and Roman lived?" Gabe interrupted. His face was pale, jaw tense.

Kane paused, and turned to Gabe. "They used to, yes. But I called ahead, and had the rooms stripped and all their belongings trashed once they were searched for evidence. Anything of note was taken to Caius' study and the rest was burned. There is no trace of them left in this house."

Gabe grumbled, angry, but he nodded that he heard Kane, and after a tense moment, Kane lead them deeper into the mansion. They took the hallway that went straight, their footsteps now loud on the dark wooden floors. The walls were stone and dark, nearly black, and the floors were just as dark, polished to a high sheen so that their reflections were blurry as they walked.

Ghost was curious, the doors they passed were all shut, and there were no windows. The hallway appeared to run down the center of this side of the building. Eventually they came to the end, the hallway opening to a sitting area beneath tall windows, and a smaller, less grand staircase that went up and down. He couldn't smell that many other wolfkin, though he caught traces of Burke and Kane, their scents faded, and a hint of Sophia.

Kane pointed to the left, and there was a door set in the recessed wall of the sitting area. A gold plaque was engraved with Burke's name. "That's Burke's suite, obviously. Mine is here," and Kane pointed directly across the space to another door, the plaque this time engraved with a symbol of a tall pine tree, the metal blackened for the branches. "That is my suite. These stairs lead to the lower ranked rooms upstairs, and the side exit for this wing of the mansion. Directly up those stairs is an empty suite that used to be Sophia's. Gabe, that'll be your space. Michael will be housed directly across the hall from you. Your suite is right above mine on this side of the hall."

Burke's door opened, and the Speaker stepped out. He was wearing different clothes, and smelled like he just took a shower. "I'll show Gabe his room. I already got Michael sorted out. The betas readied the rooms before we arrived." Burke nudged Gabe toward the stairs, and the two alphas went up, Gabe sending Ghost a small smile and a tiny wave before he went around the bend in the landing.

Kane opened the door to his suite, holding the door for Ghost to go in before him. Ghost ran his fingers over the engraved plaque on the door before stepping past his mate and into a wide room with tall windows that overlooked a snowy field of trees and hedges. The room had its own fireplace, several places to sit, and a small kitchenette in the corner. Two doors off to his right were cracked open enough for him to see a large bathroom and the corner of a canopied bed.

Kane shut the door. "This has been my suite since I moved here as a teenager. It had remained vacant since Caius built the mansion a few lifetimes ago. I updated it, added in high-speed internet, the kitchenette, and there is a television in the bedroom."

Ghost inhaled, enjoying the heady scent of his mate that permeated the space. Curious, he headed for the bedroom, opening the door completely. There was a large bed next to a window overlooking the same view as the main room. The bed had posts that ran up from each corner and a canopy above the bed with deep red velvet curtains tied off to each post. It looked like the curtains could be drawn around the bed to block out sunlight. Part of him wanted to jump into bed immediately, but it was the middle of the day and he was starving.

"Do you like it, little wolf? We can stay here as long as you like, or I can begin looking for our own place nearby." Kane sounded nervous, and Ghost turned back to his mate. Kane stood in the doorway, hands in his pocket, his expression hopeful and guarded at the same time.

"My life has changed a lot in the last weeks, but one thing hasn't changed. I want to stay with you, and it doesn't matter where that is, as long as we are together." Ghost went to his mate, and slipped his arms around Kane's waist, snuggling in close. Kane hugged him back, one arm around his shoulders, his free hand running through Ghost's hair. The kiss landed on the top of his head, and Ghost hugged Kane tighter.

KANE SHUT THE door after thanking the beta who brought up his grocery order. He stocked his small fridge in the kitchenette corner of his living room, listening to Ghost putter about in the bedroom. Ghost had no belongings aside from the donated clothing from River while they were at Red Fern. He could hear Ghost rummaging through his closet, then footsteps as his mate went to investigate the bathroom. The bathroom could be reached through either the bedroom or main room. Kane rarely had anyone visit him in his rooms, aside from Sophia and Burke, over the years. Caius never came to his rooms— he always went to the clan leader.

Ghost came out of the bathroom to see what he was doing. "Do you eat in here or is there a room where everyone eats together? This place is a lot bigger than Andromeda's cabin."

"I usually eat here or across the hall in Burke's room with him. A couple of times a week I will be in the dining hall with the rest of the wolfkin who live here in the mansion. Though I don't think we're going to have many sit-down dinners until Remus is stopped and the missing wolves are found."

Ghost opened the fridge, poking about the contents. He closed the door after a moment and sighed, fidgeting. "What's the matter, little wolf? You hardly held still since we got here."

"I feel out of place. I can remember some things about this huge den, but it's small flashes. Nothing more solid than impressions of sound and scents. I can see my mother bringing us here and my father standing over us laughing and talking. But nothing solid. I can't remember the words or anything he said. I feel like I know this place," Ghost said, waving a hand to indicate he meant the entire house and not the suite in which they stood. "You have closets full of personal belongings. Memories and items, you hold value for. I have nothing but fragmented memories and borrowed clothing."

"You are not lacking. Your worth, your importance, none of that depends on what you have or don't have. None of that depends on what you can or cannot remember. You have never cared about material possessions before— don't start caring about that now. Don't think you have to change who you are just feel like you belong here."

"I just feel... Unsettled. Nervous. I know I shouldn't. I am a shaman. Our Goddess looks out for me, and you look out for me. But a part of me that always felt lost and wanted to come home is now realizing that everything I wanted to come home to is gone. I feel more like Luca now than I ever have, and Ghost is slipping away."

Kane hugged Ghost to him. Ghost clung, pressing his face into Kane's chest. "Whether you are Luca or Ghost or you choose a new name, none of that will change how I feel about you. Your family may not be the way it was before you got lost, but I am here. You came back to me. And I am never going to let you go."

"Promise?" Ghost whispered, fingers digging into Kane's back.

"I promise, little wolf."

THAT EVENING CAIUS summoned Kane to his study. Ghost refused to stay behind and followed his mate as Kane took him towards a new section of the large mansion. They passed a couple wolves on their way there, and Ghost smiled nervously at the strangers as they continued. The wolves they did meet backed out of Kane's way and gave him a nod of respect as they passed. Black Pine appeared to be far more formal than Red Fern's relaxed atmosphere. Or maybe it had something to do with the fact that Kane was heir here in Black Pine, and was just another wolf when compared to Andromeda. Maybe this was the way that their people functioned everywhere, and he was just too young when he got lost to realize how things worked.

He didn't know if he liked it or not.

Kane ushered him into a large room. It was long, with a fireplace on either side of the room. Each was big enough that he could probably walk into the fireplaces and not hit his head. Small fires burned in both, giving off enough warmth to keep the room comfortable. Bookshelves covered free wall space and portraits of forest scenes and what looked like Caius and other wolfkin Ghost couldn't identify, wearing old-fashioned garments. Kane led him down the center of the room to a large desk, behind which Caius sat. Burke was already present, his arms crossed and his usually easy-going demeanor dampened. He stood off to the side, there was an awkwardness about the Speaker that made Ghost curious.

Caius gestured to a few seats on the other side of the desk and Kane sat. Ghost took one look at the seat next to his mate and passed by it in favor of exploring, ignored his grandfather's unspoken request to sit. He heard Caius sigh in exasperation and his mate chuckle.

"Still a wild thing," Caius murmured, but Ghost couldn't hear any censure or reprimand. Ghost shrugged and wandered around the space next to his grandfather's desk. Shelves held mementos and small knickknacks, everything from a bare human skull with a large crack in the cranium, to what looked like daggers made of stone. There were books and maps and black and white photographs framed in brass. The room smelled heavily of his grandfather, a few stray wolfkin he could not name, and leather and smoke. He took a deep breath, held it for a long minute, and let it out slowly. He knew this place. Aside from memories of the kitchen and dining room, he had the strongest feeling that he knew this room best.

"Did the human doctor give up any more information on the drive down?" Kane asked, leaning back in his chair.

"No," Caius growled, exasperated with the human. "We have the list still, and I have sent scouts in pairs to those locations here in the city. One of the locations was conveniently destroyed in a reported gas leak a few weeks ago. I think that was where they were last. No sign of where they went after that site was scrubbed."

"Anything in Roman's old room?" Kane asked, and this time there was a note of hesitancy. Caius worked his jaw, and Burke looked even more nervous, but Caius leaned forward and opened a drawer.

"Most of his belongings were removed when I had him banished from Black Pine. Everything he didn't take with him was put in storage until he could have it forwarded to his new address. The betas scoured the boxes and found nothing of importance aside from a few trinkets and some papers." He pulled out a thin folder and a small box, pushing the items across the desk to Kane.

"Bank accounts?" Burke asked suddenly, while Kane picked through the small box. "Remus must have been paying him something. I don't see Roman participating all these years without compensation. Even with the promise of more power, I just don't see it."

Kane tossed the small box onto the desk, having given up on the contents. "I think tracing the money might lead us directly to Remus, but I don't see how it'll lead us to our missing wolves. What about Roman's car? The GPS in it might have some answers."

"His car is missing. The GPS in it was disabled. I reported it missing to the authorities. Thankfully it was in my name, otherwise I would have to explain to the humans why I was searching for my son's missing car and not my son." Caius stopped, face darkening. Wood creaked, and the armrest under one of his hands groaned in complaint as he tightened his grip.

"I sent for the paperwork from our usual forger. As far as the human world is concerned, Roman died in a car accident, and was cremated," Kane said quietly, and after a short pause, Caius nodded in acknowledgment.

"The scouts I sent out will begin reporting back as soon as they learn anything. Until then, we wait." Caius made a short, abrupt gesture, and both Burke and Kane nodded respectfully. Kane stood and Burke went to his side, both alphas radiating low-key tension.

Kane held out his hand to Ghost, who, after a long look at his grandfather, slowly made his way past the big desk. He stopped though, his attention caught on a picture. It was the only one on the desk.

Ghost picked it up, cradling it in his hands. A female wolfkin smiled back at him, dressed in clothing from an era decades' past.

"Your mother," Caius rumbled. "You...favor her strongly."

Even with the few glimpses of himself in mirrors since regaining his human form, Ghost had to agree with his grandfather. He did indeed look like his mother. He ran a fingertip over the line of her jaw, taking in her sparkling eyes and long, thick hair. He gently put the picture down, angling it so his grandfather could see it better. He gave Caius a small smile, and took Kane's hand.

They left, walking down the long length of the room, and Burke held the door open so he and Kane could pass. He sent a glance back over his shoulder, to see Caius staring at the picture of Marla McLennan, eyes dark, grief radiating from every line of his body.

19

THE WINTER MEADOW

Ghost whimpered, arching his back and lifting his ass. Kane growled, nipping at his shoulder as his big mate moved on top of him. Ghost sighed in relief when Kane's thick cock slid deep inside, stretching him, the warmed lube helping his body adjust. It stung and burned and felt amazing, every slow, deep stroke of his alpha's cock leaving him breathless.

The curtains were pulled tightly around the bed, blocking out the rising sun and leaving them cocooned in their soft, warm den. He woke in time for Kane to plunder his lips in a demanding kiss, and desire took over.

Kane bit the back of his neck, holding him still, hands around his hips, changing the angle at which he thrust. Ghost sobbed at each plunge into his core, reveling in Kane's weight and the undulating motion of his hips. He gripped the sheets below him, muffling his needy cries as Kane's teeth sunk deeper, his thrusts growing more urgent.

Kane released his shoulder and licked at his ear. "You feel so good, little wolf," Kane whispered, making Ghost cry out in intense pleasure, stroking deep with small half-thrusts, never withdrawing completely before pushing back inside. His body rocked back and forth, his knees spread and hips lifted just enough for the head of his cock to rub over sheets, teasing him, making him want to push down to get more but also lift up to take more from his mate.

"Please...more." Ghost turned his head to the side, accepting Kane's kiss before another stroke made him cry out again, this time louder. He arched his spine, pushing up as best he could, desperate to get closer to his mate.

Claws sprang from fingertips and cloth shredded, Ghost's fingers tearing into the bedding. Kane growled, a deep rumble of satisfaction that made Ghost whine loudly in answering need. Pinpricks of pain came from his hips, his mate's wilder nature rising to the surface to match his own. One stroke after another fell upon an aching, sensitive spot deep inside, and Ghost howled as he came, his release shooting across the bed and over his abdomen.

Kane wrapped his arms under and around Ghost's torso, teeth clamping down on the back of his neck as he came with a deep, full-body shudder. Hips plastered to his ass, Ghost accepted everything his mate had to give him, enjoying the wet heat that filled him.

Ghost fell limp in his mate's arms, Kane's weight pushing him down. He could hear and feel the racing of Kane's heart, sweat slicking the space between them. His stomach smeared the evidence of his pleasure across the bedding, but Ghost didn't mind. He enjoyed the scent, and it mixed with that of his mate's.

Kane rolled to his back, pulling Ghost with him, his head coming to rest on his mate's shoulder. He snuggled, pressing his nose to sweat-damp skin and breathing in the intoxicating scent. Kane chuckled, sounding less winded, fingers combing through his hair. "I love you."

Ghost opened his eyes, smiling up at Kane who looked back at him with such affection it made his chest ache. "I love you, too."

Kane smiled wide, pulling at Ghost until he lay spread out over Kane's torso. He pushed his head under Kane's chin and relaxed, all but melting into his embrace.

LUNCH TOOK THE place of breakfast by the time they managed to stumble from Kane's rooms. Ghost trailed after his more than patient mate, his curiosity rising now that his nerves were settled. Kane was explaining how to find his way through the mansion, Ghost trying his best to follow along, but he got lost after a few turns and figured he would just use his nose if he needed to find his way back to the suite and he wasn't with Kane. He doubted he would be far from Kane regardless—after the last few weeks, he flat-out refused to think about being parted from his mate. He had trouble believing sometimes that Kane escaped the Tribunal with barely a scratch. Any wounds he took in the impromptu battle with Heromindes healed within hours of the fight.

"Here is the dining room," Kane said, opening one tall wooden door. Ghost peered around the doorframe, and took in the long room. It had one wall of tall windows that overlooked a snow-laden expanse, and was full of tables big enough for a dozen wolfkin apiece. He couldn't count high enough to determine how many tables there were, but he figured the room could hold a couple hundred wolfkin at capacity.

There were wolfkin already seated, eating and talking in small groups and pairs. Swinging doors on the far side of the dining room opened up into what he could guess to be the kitchen, enticing smells making him step around the door and into the room. His stomach growled and Kane put a hand on his shoulder, guiding him away from the door.

"Hungry?" Kane teased, and Ghost huffed out a short laugh.

"I was ambushed this morning and now I'm starving," Ghost teased. Kane gave him a swift, bruising kiss before leading him around tables, heading for one that sat beneath the windows. Kane ushered him into a seat, and Ghost looked around, slightly confused when Kane sat beside him. "Food?"

The tables were bare, not even silverware or napkins were on them. Kane gave him a smile and gestured to a lean beta female who was standing beside the kitchen doors. She darted through the nearest door, returning moments later with two more betas, the three of them carrying platters of steaming food and drinks. Ghost sat back, giving the betas room to put their burden of thick beef stew and warm cider down in front of him, a basket of fresh hot bread and sweet butter rounding off the offerings. Cutlery, napkins, and spare plates found places around them, and Ghost was momentarily baffled by the efficiency. Kane murmured a thank you, Ghost giving the betas a startled smile in thanks before they left as quickly as they came.

"What is the word that humans use? Servants?" Ghost asked, reaching for the bread and tearing off a piece.

Kane took a sip of his hot cider before addressing the topic. "Caius is old. Old enough to have servants back in the Old World. He's ruled here since the Great Exodus, over 200 years ago. Many of the betas who live here in the mansion are just as old, if not older. They run things as they always have. Sophia tried to change things not long after I moved to the mansion, before she became First Beta. The other betas, both male and female, were happy with the way things were run so she backed down. No one is forced to serve—Caius has always been clear about that. Here betas without mates or powerful family packs can stay and be safe, a roof over their heads and a place to sleep at night. In return, the betas run the household."

"So, they are not servants?"

"Would Andromeda call her children servants?" Kane retorted, and Ghost snapped his mouth shut and frowned. Andromeda had many children, and even more great and great-great-grandchildren, and they acted as the betas here did, just less formally. For the entire time Ghost was in Baxter, not once had he seen Andromeda order about or mistreat any of her family or pack. He didn't think Caius would either, but what he was experiencing in the last day or so was different than he was used too. He sighed, thinking that his experience was truly limited, and he might do better thinking before assuming.

A warm breeze caressed his cheek gently, ruffling the napkin beside his plate, and he sighed, reaching for his food before he stuck his foot in his mouth again.

"I guess...I just see more of humanity in the clans than I expected," Ghost mused, attacking his beef stew, digging out a chunk of meat with his fingers as he spoke. "This reminds me strongly of this TV show Cat used to watch about nobles and servants. I just...assumed."

"It's okay, little wolf. Believe me when I say that no one is here doing something they don't want. With our noses, it would be hard to miss or ignore another wolf's misery. I wouldn't ignore such a sorry state, nor would Caius. The exception is personal relationships, and we only intervene if we suspect abuse. Caius is more remote than Andromeda, but he does look after his people."

Ghost nodded, and Kane rubbed a big hand down his shoulder and back before returning to eating. Ghost devoured his stew completely before he remembered to use his spoon and fork, and he licked off his fingers in appreciation. A new bowl found its way in front of him, a sneaky beta swiping his empty bowl and even giving him a new mug of cider. A wink and a cocky smile told him that he hadn't been all that quiet, and Ghost found himself in the odd position of being embarrassed.

"Eat up, little wolf." Kane chuckled, and Ghost nudged him with his elbow. He remembered to use his spoon this time, and ate a bit slower.

A familiar wolfkin drew his eye to the door. Burke smiled as he was greeted by several wolfkin present, and he stopped to talk with a few before making his way over to their table. Burke sat across from them, getting the same treatment from the ever-watchful betas. He thanked them and dug in, devouring his fresh bread in two bites.

"Any news from the scouts Caius sent out?" Kane asked, and Burke shrugged as he swallowed.

"I'm keeping tabs on them," Burke said, tapping his temple with a long finger, "But so far they've found nothing. No clues at the warehouse destroyed by the gas leak, either. Caius sent out five pairs, and they've managed to explore over half the Augusta sites on the list. No scent markers, no mental contact."

"The human slavers we rescued Gabe from used silver to dampen the wolves' mental voices," Kane said, pushing his empty bowl away. "We can't guarantee that the scouts can hear them if the missing wolves are there."

Burke frowned, but nodded in agreement. "That's why the scouts are going by scent. They aren't moving on from a location until it's been thoroughly searched. The places with humans present are taking longer. We don't need the police involved."

"Can't you hear them?" Ghost asked, and Burke gave him a startled glance.

"If I knew who I was listening for, yes," Burke said slowly, fidgeting with a fork. "If I open my mind, I can hear every wolfkin within a few hundred square miles, maybe more. The problem is, there are different clans and packs within that radius. I can't just blunder into the clan and pack mental links without causing mayhem. I need to be invited into a mental link, the framework that each alpha or clan leader holds. I can burst my way in, but that'll cause significant trouble—well, more like utter diplomatic chaos. And since I don't know the wolves still missing, I can't search for their individual minds. And if they are drugged with silver like we suspect, then the likelihood of even a Speaker reaching them is almost nonexistent. That's why we're doing this the old-fashioned way—with our noses."

"How does it work?" Ghost asked, leaning forward.

"How does what work?" Burke replied, confused.

"The gift of command. I know clan leaders and heirs and Speakers all have it to some degree, but I don't know the details."

"There's different types of mental links we create among our people," Burke said. "Some are clan links, mental connections a clan leader maintains with the clan he or she leads. Those are born through repeated mental contact and familiarity. Friends develop similar links over years, even if they are in separate clans. Depending on the strength of the clan leader involved, he can either maintain a subconscious link without active contact with a few wolves or up to a hundred different minds. Some clan leaders and pack alphas can only reach a few minds, and rely on Speakers to keep tabs on the clan."

"Like you," Ghost said. Burke nodded.

"Yes. Black Pine is a bit different, though. Caius has a moderate range with his gift of command—I just make things easier on him. When Kane becomes clan leader, I'd be more of a help to him than I am to Caius. I just make things easier, more efficient."

"Are there other types of mental links?"

"There are. There's blood—minds joined by family connections. Caius and Kane are cousins, though very distant, and they have a faint blood bond made deeper by the clan bonds and the bond they share as Leader and Heir. There's mating links," Burke said, winking at Ghost. "Both regular matings and soulbonds have the mental connection. A soulbond, from what I can tell just by looking at the two of you, is on a deeper and more steady level than a normal mate link."

"Blood, clan, and mate."

"Yup."

"Can Gabe search for his family? How strong is his gift of command?" Ghost asked, and Burke blinked at him in surprise before the Speaker turned to Kane.

"He'd have the same issues with the silver poisoning, but he might recognize their minds far faster than I would," Burke said to Kane. "The cub is a greater alpha. It's worth a try."

"I'll run it by Caius, see if we can get Gabe out on one of the scouting teams if they don't have any luck," Kane replied, brow furrowed. "He's still fragile after what happened, and he has minimal control over the

Voice. I think he needs to be a last resort."

Ghost sat back in his seat, fiddling with his spoon. Something was off. He felt like he was missing something, but he didn't know enough about his people to even guess what it might be.

THE DAY WENT by slowly, too slow for Ghost's peace of mind. He languished on a soft leather couch in Caius' study, his grandfather, Kane, and Burke talking with Gabe by the huge desk. Their discussion was on the merits of Gabe joining the search teams, and Gabe was getting a crash course on keeping control of the Voice.

"If you get worked up while searching with the scouts, you can end up unleashing your gift on them and endangering everyone," Caius warned Gabe, who bit his lip, nodding once, reluctant. "Emotions make it harder to control. You can hurt wolves around you if you don't know what you're doing. You saw Roan at the Tribunal. The Voice is dangerous."

Gabe paled, and nodded quickly, eyes wide. Ghost sympathized with his friend, but he had no clue how the Voice worked either, and his input would merely distract Gabe.

He looked out the window nearest the couch, from his angle able to see the clear dark blue of the evening sky. Twilight was still swift this time of year, though the days were getting longer, the sun slowly melting away the snow. Spring was coming.

The couch beneath him was soft, warm. The room smelled like family and mate and pack. The mansion still didn't feel like home, but the familiarity was increasing. He caught hints of memories as he walked along hallways, passing doors that led to rooms that looked different but felt familiar. Kane said that he once lived with his immediate family in a place not far from the mansion, but somehow, he thought they spent more time here than they did in the home he couldn't even recall.

He rolled onto his side, nose pressed to the cushion. He was tired. Waiting was exhausting.

WIND PULLED AT his hair, tangling it in front of his eyes. He pushed it back, the vista in front of him strange yet familiar.

The wide, flat tree stump was the same, the snow around it patchy instead of a solid blanket of white. Green grass and small, colorful flowers shyly peeked out between patches of ice. There was a path beneath his feet, alternating between bare, damp earth and thin layers of snow.

Spring was encroaching on the winter meadow, the air was less biting, softer. It was still cold, but it didn't touch him—he was aware of the chill yet untouched.

There was a lone track of footprints in the path before him; large wolf tracks that changed every few steps into bare human prints and then back to wolf. He tilted his head, listening, but heard nothing but the wind and the rustle of branches above him. He followed the path, taking care not to step on the tracks. It led him to the center of the meadow; he sat on the stump, drawing his knees up to his chest and wrapping his arms around them.

The sky above was a field of brilliant light, more stars than a mortal could count in a lifetime sparkling and shining down. The horizon glowed gold and orange, and he could not tell if it was dawn or sunset. Considering where he was, it might well be both at once.

A whimper nearby was a surprise—a gray wolf stood not far from him. Larger than him by half, this wolf was every shade of gray, from dusky charcoal to misty tones just shy of white, eyes that glowed silver and reflected the light of the heavens. His coloration made him fade in and out, Ghost's mortal eyes somehow insufficient to see the wolf in all his glory.

"Hello," Ghost said, curious. He held out his hand, palm up, and the great head dipped to sniff his fingers. A warm tongue darted out, licking his hand, and Ghost laughed. He scratched the big gray wolf behind his ears and down his back, the wolf dancing on happy paws at the attention. He almost got knocked off the stump when the wolf sat in front of him, and Ghost crossed his legs and let the big beast rest his head in his lap.

He tugged gently on one big, pointed ear, and his heart ached sharply for a second. The wolf rolled an exasperated eye up at him, giving a great sigh of fondness. Shiny eyes closed as he continued scratching and petting.

"He was most impatient," a voice chided fondly from over his shoulder. "I bid him wait, but this one always took his own path."

She came from around the stump and sat beside him, the wide surface more than enough room to hold them both. She smiled at the wolf at Ghost's feet, shaking Her head with a chuckle. "You two are so similar. Stubborn and bold."

A silver eye cracked open in a brief wink before closing again, happy rumbles coming from a deep chest as Ghost kept up the scratches, fingers digging through thick, soft fur.

"Why am I here?" Ghost asked, meeting Her endless gaze directly. The infinite lived in Her eyes, a celestial vista that matched the one that spun above their heads.

"You tell me," She retorted with a quirk to Her lips. A white fang flashed at him when She grinned wider. "My shamans find their way here on their own—I haven't called a wolf across the winter meadow unless it was his or her time."

"Why didn't you stop Roman and Remus?" Ghost asked, blurting out the first thing that came to mind. "You're present among us—your people have been killed and hunted and tortured."

She nodded, not denying it. "I am present. I am there in every drop of blood spilled, every breath to pass across the lips of the dying. I am in every heart that fails to beat and every song that lifts in mourning for the fallen."

He frowned, and She chuckled. "Not the answer you wanted?"

"No."

The gray wolf rumbled affectionately, and Ghost went back to petting him.

"You want to know why I didn't intercede directly," She clarified, and Ghost nodded. "You think I haven't?"

His confusion must have shown. The gray wolf stretched his muzzle out and nudged Her knee with his nose. She laughed, shaking Her head. "Very well. So impatient."

A warm wind cut through the meadow, lifting black strands of Her hair back from Her face and shoulders. "I hear the prayers of those suffering. Those that yet live still have hope. A hope that will not be in vain if all happens as it should."

"Do all deities speak in riddles?" Ghost asked with a frown.

"My kin are not as concerned with mortals as I am," She replied. "My penchant for interference has drawn their ire and scorn many times. But that is not why you are here. Do you remember what I told you the last time you were here?"

"That all I need to do was ask for help, and you would answer." Ghost said quickly, recalling the last time he spoke to Her. "Help us now. Please."

She leaned in, and rested Her head on his shoulder, a hand resting on the wolf's head. "I have given you all that you need to save those missing and stop what is coming. Open your eyes, your heart, see past your limitations. Each one of you is part of something bigger. Wolves work best as a pack—a lone wolf rarely succeeds."

He thought about what She said, mind whirring. "What is coming?"

"If Remus is not stopped in time, I fear the days of my wolves are numbered. He has what he needs already to start in motion the end of the wolfkin, though he does not know it."

"I must tell Kane," Ghost said, fear jumping in his heart. "I need to get back."

"Time does not pass here, my shaman," She comforted, and he settled. "You'll wake in your mate's arms soon enough."

He sat back, and tipped his head to the sky. Stars winked and shined across the heavens, a field of unending possibilities. He could make out the hint of wolves running across the sky, a phenomenon Kane called constellations.

"We are wolves," he murmured, and the gray wolf rumbled in agreement. "We work best together. I have what I need already."

She hummed in agreement. "That you do, shaman."

Ghost reexamined his past choices, the times he heard Her speaking to him, to others in his presence. "Gabe, Michael, Caius. Burke and Kane and myself. Pieces of my pack. Parts of a whole."

She nodded, and he kept going, encouraged. "Gabe is related to the wolves still missing. Blood ties. Burke has the range. I can see their soulstars, even with their minds dulled by silver. I am soulbond to Kane, and he can use my Spiritsight. Michael has the training I lack, and can see soulstars as well. He can stop any wolfkin's gifts in its tracks, so he can stop Gabe if he loses control. Gabe and Burke have the connections and the range and Kane can share my Spiritsight with Burke! We can find them!"

The gray wolf danced away from Ghost as he stood in excitement, turning to face his Goddess, a wide smile breaking across his face. She tilted her head to the side and curled Her long legs up underneath Her on the stump. "Is that all? Think."

"Caius." She nodded, and the gray wolf whined, a low, sad sound that tore at his heart. "But why Caius? He is clan leader of Black Pine, and the wolves missing are Ashland. He has no connection to them. What is his purpose?"

"His purpose is that he must go with you all when you track down Remus. He must be present. Do not let him stay behind while he sends his Heir, as has been his habit the last fifteen years. He has embraced his grief at last, and grows stronger within the pain he endures. He must go with you and Kane."

"Why?"

She stood, moving to his side. She took his hands in Hers and met him eye to eye. Constellations flared and danced in their depths, and he breathed in, scenting flowers and blood and heat. "Three souls will need you when you find the missing wolves. Tragedy and a missed chance will destroy Caius and prevent a brighter future from unfolding if he remains behind. Do you remember what the human doctor told Kane?"

"He made a hybrid, and did something called cloning." Ghost replied. She nodded, Her grip on his hands tightening, urgency in Her words.

"A wolf born not by my grace but the impertinence of man slumbers not far from the lost wolf. I would claim them both and call them home to the clans, but time is essential. The pack you have chosen must come together and find them all. Stopping Remus is only part of a greater whole."

"What?" Ghost shook his head, his heart aching. Doubts crept into his mind, but he banished them as fast as they appeared. Now was not a time or place for doubts.

"A lost wolf, and wolf who slumbers, and your grandfather, will all die, and soon. If Remus learns what he has, the lost wolf will die before he bows to Remus' will. All wolfkin will face exposure and war with humanity as Remus gives into rage and hunts our people openly. If you can make it in time but go without Caius, you can still stop Remus, but the sleeping wolf and Caius will die. What you bring back with you will break Caius past saving, because he will be too late when he learns the truth. If Caius goes with you, tragedy can turn to hope and all might be saved. You have what you need to save everyone, and stop Remus."

"I don't know if Caius can survive anymore loss." Ghost spoke quietly, the gray wolf's ears drooping and his tail ducking between his legs. "Always duty before all else—and that left him cold and remote. Duty before all else has led to death and grief at every turn. Sending Kane in his stead will be his move because that is dutiful—the clan leader remains with the clan while the heir executes his will. And he will die for that choice."

"Yes."

So many futures, so many things that could go wrong. The thought of Caius dying, after losing so much, his life nothing but cold duty, grief, and pain, weighed on him the most. The gray wolf whined again, and Ghost looked down at him, sighing. Silver eyes pleaded with him to believe, to understand. He tugged again on an ear, and the gray wolf dropped his jaw in a wolfish grin, ears perking up and tail flagging with joy and hope.

"You said hope for a better future?" He asked, wondering. "What do you mean?"

"Find the missing wolves. Save the three who need you the most— the lost wolf, the one who slumbers, and your grandfather." She looked down at the gray wolf, who with an oddly human gesture, nodded back at Her, once, firm. She turned back to Ghost. "Sacrifice, duty, redemption. It all comes down to one thing in the very end. Love. It can heal wounds, soothe scars, repair broken lives, and even right a wrong choice made for the right reasons in the depths of history. If you succeed, a wolf's willing sacrifice from long ago will be rewarded, and the clans will have new hope to guide them forward. All choices have led to this point, this place, and the choices you have now. I have done what I can to rearrange the pieces, to return my children to the right path. All that is needed now is for you to begin."

"I will do my best," he said, taking a deep breath.

She leaned in and pressed a kiss to his cheek. Pulling back, She smiled, a hint of fangs flashing in Her grin. "Your best has always been enough, my shaman."

She backed away, and with a bright flash, She stood before him as a wolf, grander than his mind could comprehend. A flicker of light and She was gone, bounding into the sky with a great leap.

The gray wolf danced across the field, his coat shining under the starlight. Ghost gave in and chased the wolf, laughing as he ducked and wove around his legs, out of reach of his hands. The winter meadow began fade, darkening around the edges, but the gray wolf ran without hesitation, melding with the shadows perfectly, his eyes glowing in the night.

20

CONSTELLATIONS

GHOST SAT UP, BREATHING HARD, THE COOL WINTER MEADOW GIVING way to a warm bed and a slumbering mate. It was fully night, the curtains around the bed tied off, a clear night sky shining full of stars visible through the windows.

Constellations. The gray wolf. His Goddess.

"Kane! Wake up!" Ghost shouted, tumbling from bed, tripping over the long hem of a pair of sweats slightly too big for him. He yanked the waistband up and dashed for the door, shouting over his shoulder. "Kane! I know how to find the missing wolves!"

"What?" Kane sat upright, pushing tangled hair back from his eyes. "Ghost? What's wrong?"

Ghost threw open the bedroom door and ran into the main room. "I know how we can find the missing Ashland wolves!"

Kane's confused shout chased after him as he tore out into the main hallway and across the hall, banging on Burke's door. "Burke! Wake up! Hurry!" He slapped the door hard a few times, and heard Burke's startled exclamation from within. The door opened just as he was about to bang again, and Burke stared at him, wide-eyed.

"What's going on?"

"C'mon!" Ghost grabbed Burke's wrist and yanked, Burke's shocked state the only reason he could move the bigger alpha at all. Kane came out of their suite, wearing a concerned expression and a pair of low-hanging sleep pants. "Kane, hurry! We need Gabe!"

"Ghost! Slow down! What's going on? Burke?" Kane asked, and Burke shook his head in confusion.

Ghost tugged on Burke one more time before letting go and leaping for the stairs, dodging Kane's outstretched hand. He took the stairs by three, following his nose to the rooms where Gabe slept. He reached the top of the stairs, the heavy footsteps of the two alphas right behind him.

He found Gabe's room, the plaque still bearing Sophia's name, and burst through the door. Gabe must have heard him coming, as the young alpha stumbled out of his bedroom, half-asleep and confused. Ghost ran to Gabe and grabbed his hands, tugging him further into the main room.

"What…what's going on?" Gabe blinked, clearing away the sleep from his eyes as Kane and Burke burst into the room behind Ghost.

"I know how we can find your family," Ghost said, breathing fast from his rush up the stairs. Gabe's mouth dropped open and Burke and Kane went quiet. "We can end this tonight."

"How?" Gabe burst out.

"Your blood bond to your family. Burke's mental range. Kane can access my Spiritsight. The four of us, a constellation of minds and gifts. We can do this."

BURKE SAT NEXT to Kane, Gabe next to Ghost, and Michael paced behind them, his reflection blurring over the top of the glass coffee table around which the four wolfkin sat.

"Do you understand what's about to happen?" Caius murmured to Michael, who stopped his pacing and shrugged. Michael moved over to Caius where he leaned on his desk, and crossed his arms, eyeing the four wolfkin who sat quietly, hands joined together.

His grandson had come charging into the study not long ago, dragging behind him a sleepy shaman and three very excited alphas.

"Kane can access Ghost's Spiritsight, which is the strongest manifestation of the gift I've seen since…" Michael gave him a nervous glance, but Caius knew who he meant. "Since Gray Shadow." Michael coughed, and continued. "Apparently, Kane shared it once with Burke. With Burke's range as a Speaker, and combining the gift of command with Spiritsight, they can bypass the silver poisoning preventing us from reaching out to the missing wolves directly on a mental level. Gabe knows his family on a spiritual level, not just a mental one, and hopefully will be able to pinpoint which soulstars are theirs and not regular wolfkin."

"Why didn't we think of combining shaman and alpha like this before?" Caius breathed out, rubbing at his face. It was rhetorical, and Michael didn't answer. They both knew why. Alphas didn't intrude on shamanic matters and shamans kept to their duties and rarely involved themselves in matters considered to be the purview of the alphas. Eons of tradition handicapped them. "Or even asking shamans with Spiritsight to search? The lot of you would have done so tirelessly."

"We didn't think of it, either," Michael replied, shame darkening his cheeks. "Not a lot of us have Spiritsight as powerful as your grandson's, though, and we don't use it in such an active manner. But we would have, if we'd thought to try."

"Hindsight is pointless now," Caius said, and Michael nodded. "Is it working?"

Michael's eyes went distant, and after a moment, he nodded slowly. "Something is happening for certain."

KANE OPENED HIS connection to his mate, and the rush of awareness that met his mind almost broke him out of the mind link with Burke. The Speaker's mind adroitly caught his, and the links steadied, growing more vibrant. Gabe's awareness hovered just out of reach, but Burke gently reached out, and drew the young alpha into the meld. Kane was connected to Burke and Ghost, and Burke held the meld between Ghost and Gabe and himself. From Ghost came the Spiritsight, and Kane embraced the gift as it changed his perception. Where before he saw only the glow of minds, there was a new layer, and the whole world exploded with colors and vibrancy.

The mansion was aglow, dozens of wolfkin soulstars burning with a kaleidoscope of colors, a rainbow of reds and blues and gentle yellows. Caius was a storm of dark red and smoke gray, and Kane knew him instantly despite never having seen this level of the other wolfkin before. He saw Burke and Gabe, and recognized them instantly as well—his soul knew them. Despite having limited mental contact with Gabe and none with Michael, his ability to recognize them transcended into this plane, this level of reality. It was as if scent, hearing, taste, and touch all became one and there was light deep within everything that lived.

Ghost shined the brightest. Silver-white lighted that glittered and spun, a fiery inferno of brilliant energy that did not consume as it touched, but fed power into him. Ghost's light traveled to his star, and from Kane into Burke and Gabe. He could feel the tension and alarm from the other two alphas as they experienced the full effect of Ghost's Spiritsight. Burke's brief exposure to it the day after Ghost returned wasn't enough to prepare him for the unrestrained power of Ghost's gift.

Easy—don't fight it, Kane soothed. *It's just Ghost.* Gabe, oddly enough, settled down first. Kane could sense that Gabe trusted Ghost completely—there was a bond between the two younger wolves, it was similar to the one between Kane and Burke. Burke was hesitant, but soon the Speaker's mind and emotions evened out, once again perfectly calm and in control. *Burke. See how far you can reach.*

Burke's range was immense. There was a reason Burke was courted by clan leaders every gathering. His skill and talent and power was singular, even among Speakers. And when he unraveled his gift of command to its full measure, the world opened around them further. The earth fell away beneath their feet and reality around them was shadow and shifting light.

There was nothing holding Burke back except his willpower.

It was dark, shadows for walls and roof, translucent darkness for form and shape. The earth below the mansion slumbered, a soft green awaiting spring. The forest around the mansion glowed green as well, with tiny flares of light for living creatures. A few wolfkin patrolled the grounds, betas who glowed rich dandelion yellows and soft, gentle purples and blues.

Kane could feel Ghost's elation, and Burke's quiet surprise. Gabe was all eagerness and impatience, his mind tugging at Burke's, trying to get him to move out further. When Burke let go, and his awareness spiraled out, Kane felt as if he were flying and falling at once.

The melding settled, grew more concrete, and Kane absorbed the connections from Burke, leaving the Speaker free to cast his mind further into the night, Kane anchoring them all.

GHOST CHASED AFTER Burke through fields of starlight, Kane anchoring him. Gabe followed the same line to the Speaker as Ghost. Burke's mind, his reach, was impossible to measure. They went up and out, somehow still in the mansion, but Burke's mind spread out, and each new wolfkin mind flared when Burke used the Spiritsight that was communicated via Kane's bond with Ghost. He fed as much of his ability through Kane as he could—this had to work.

Weeks of captivity—the missing wolfkin would be weak, their minds dulled by silver. As would their stars—but that was why they had Gabe. His kinship would help the three of them determine if they had found the right wolves.

Trees blurred into buildings. Paths in the forests became sidewalks. Fireflies of small beasts in the woods became the muted colors of humans, arrayed in soft palettes in large groupings.

Augusta. The city shone to Ghost's mental gaze as a nebula of spinning stars. Colors of every shade, the humans did not shine like wolfkin within his perception, making it easy to see the smaller starbursts of wolfkin amidst the human population.

There were family packs, easy to determine by the red stars of alphas the soft glow of betas. Burke dismissed those minds as quickly as they made contact; Ghost could sense Burke's realization of their identities each time. Gabe's awareness hovered with Ghost, the young alpha impatient. He dismissed stars as swiftly as Burke did minds, increasing Ghost's confidence that they would succeed eventually. All they had to do was keep looking.

Through it all, Kane bore the brunt of their connections—he gave them all an anchor from which to cast off from. His mate took the mental strain in stride, his strength immense. His gift of command was nothing compared to Burke's, but Kane could handle a melding of four minds while channeling Ghost's Spiritsight. The flow from Kane was smooth and uninterrupted.

Suburbs fell away as Burke combed through a few hundred wolfkin. Perception narrowed. Burke guided them down among ethereal shells of tall buildings full of muted light. Apartment buildings and hotels flashed by as humans were dismissed in great swathes. The speed of Burke's mind was staggering—all Ghost had to do was make sure Kane got complete access to his Spiritsight, and Burke adapted to it quickly.

The passage of time was different. Odd. He couldn't tell how long it had already taken, nor how much longer it would be before they found something. The only measure of time he had was Gabe's growing impatience.

I can't sense them! Gabe's strained mental voice whispered along the meld.

This will work, Ghost whispered back.

Burke kept on, swiftly dismissing each section of the city. Eventually they came to a heavily populated cluster of buildings. It was odd—to Ghost, at least. It did not look like the apartment buildings, but close. *What is this place?*

University of Maine, Augusta campus. Kane replied, his voice echoing along the meld. *Humans send their younglings to school and they live on top of each other each semester. Those are the dorms. We have a few wolfkin younglings enrolled, and some out-clan younglings here, too.*

Even as Kane spoke, Burke found and dismissed the mentioned wolfkin younglings, nestled in their dorm rooms or in buildings, one of which Ghost guessed to be a library, from the shadows of countless bookshelves and tables laden with stressed students studying through the night or sleeping on their notes. Gabe's impatience grew, and the young alpha pushed and prodded, desperation beginning to stain the red-blue of his star.

Ghost sent a wave of wordless reassurance to Gabe, hoping that the young alpha would calm himself. Michael was watching them from outside the meld—if Gabe lost control, Ghost and Kane would be safe, but Burke was susceptible to the Voice, and Gabe might cause the Speaker inadvertent harm in his impatience. Gabe settled, but Ghost doubted it would be for long.

Burke led them past the dorms, down grassy flat spaces and parking lots. Humans still dotted the landscape, and Burke headed for a bright swath in the distance, most likely more suburbs where humans slept in neat rows of houses. Ghost followed behind the Speaker, Gabe alongside, the young alpha despondent.

A building on either side of a narrow street and empty parking lots signaled the end of campus before a long strip of narrow wooded lots that abutted a large subdivision of human homes. Dull stars of humans were spattered about, and the building on the left had a couple dozen dull stars grouped fairly close together...in a sublevel.

The other floors of the building were empty—only the tiny flares of rodents and birds nesting. Nothing sentient moved around at all on the ground levels or higher. Only the basement level that ran the length and breadth of the building. It was only two stories tall, the ground floor space cordoned off into separate rooms along a central corridor.

Ghost stopped, and sent his awareness closer. The spectral shadows outlining a flat, pocked surface of an empty parking lot sprang up around him, and Ghost moved closer, Gabe trailing along behind him. Burke went past, but stopped when he noticed Ghost wasn't moving.

Human stars were similar to wolfkin soulstars, but the burned in softer, muted hues, and did not have the same size or intensity. The lights were more varied in colors, too, humans' spirits sometimes a myriad of mixed hues instead of a couple primary shades like wolfkin. These human stars were odd, half of them moving in pairs, a quarter stationary in one section, and the rest not too far from the stationary stars, they were moving about, but not much.

Ghost went closer, his spirit and awareness gaining a better perception of his surroundings. He peered downwards once he got to the outside wall of the building, and he would have gasped if he were more corporeal. *Gabe.*

Gabe came closer at his name. Ghost tugged on the alpha, and he poured more of his Spiritsight into the meld. Kane sensed his rising suspicion, and Burke hurried back.

As more of Ghost entered the meld, the stars bloomed in greater details, their colors became more distinct. The few in the common area near the wall below them glowed with dulled reds and blue, and the insidious veins of tarnished silver snaked amongst the stars. One near the end was a gentle, soft blue, almost that of a summer sky without a cloud to be seen, and it was near the red and blue stars. The only difference was that there was no silver stain poisoning this star, and it was almost human but for the vibrancy and the way the light of the soulstar moved.

Gabe halted, froze, his thoughts and emotions churning. His attention sharpened and Burke pushed at the same time.

Wolfkin soulstars tainted by silver poisoning. Gabe's epiphany rolled through the meld just behind Ghost's realization.

It's them. Dear Goddess, it's them. My father! My uncles! Ghost, it's my family! Gabe's mental voice was ragged with elation and disbelief.

Burke's awareness became stronger, more present, and pushed harder, reaching out for the soulstars. No returned contact, but Burke was able to reach out and get very close. Ghost sensed the dulled and painful rhythm of wolfkin minds, and as the seconds whirled past, Ghost knew it to be true.

We found them.

21

BEFORE THE BATTLE

GABE, FOR LACK OF A BETTER WORD, LOST CONTROL. GHOST TRIED TO calm his friend, but the young alpha was overwrought by emotions, pain and fear and desperation coiling together with relief and sharp elation.

We can't do anything here, not like this. Let's get back to our bodies and start planning our next move, Kane whispered.

No! I'm not leaving them! Gabe cried.

Michael! Burke called out, the Speaker's voice a layered echo of sound, reaching out past the meld and contacting the shaman back at the mansion.

Gabe's mind became chaotic, the red and blue being swallowed by darkness, the Voice unravelling as Gabe fought back. Just as Ghost began to worry for Burke, Gabe's mind dropped from the meld, his spirit disappearing. Burke settled, and Ghost would have breathed out in relief if he was in his body. Michael's brief mental touch a moment later told them that he'd used his gift to nullify Gabe's ability and broken him free from the meld.

Kane's awareness and Burke's came to surround Ghost, the new shape of their meld adapting quickly. *Burke, can you hear them?*

Nothing concrete. The silver poisoning is severe. They are dying, though, I can tell that much. The damage to their systems is extensive.

I can see the damage, too. But for the mind, there, Ghost drew their attention to the soft blue soulstar that hummed gently beside the tainted stars. *The mind and soul of whoever that is—he is untouched by the silver poisoning. I would say *human, but the soulstar is too similar to wolfkin. Can you hear him?** Ghost asked.

Burke was quiet, but Ghost could sense the Speaker pushing his awareness toward the sky blue star. *I can, but I don't know if he can respond. It's as if he's a youngling who hasn't found his wolf yet.*

*The hybrid?** Ghost asked, and both Burke and Kane reacted with surprise.

*Maybe,** Burke replied, his awareness quieting, as if he were trying to come to terms with the reality of the unknown creature's existence. *Might just be a young wolfkin who hasn't found his wolf yet, but then he would still be able to hear me. A youngster may not be able to answer, but he would hear me. I don't think he can hear me, though.*

*We will know soon enough,** Kane responded, interrupting them. *Burke, how many wolfkin?*

The count matches those still missing from Gabe's family. I think we can assume the missing wolves are all accounted for—and if the strange one is not the hybrid, we have a youngling that hasn't been reported as missing yet.

*Let's get a firm count. Note locations, patterns. We will come back tomorrow and free them,** Kane said. Both Kane and Burke began counting the humans, and Ghost returned his attention to the sky blue soulstar.

He was certain it was the hybrid. Still alive, and untouched by silver poisoning. Ghost drew closer, curious.

Walls were nothing, lines of shadow and light that he walked through with ease. Cages in two lines filled a corner of the basement. Muted stars glimmered, Gabe's family suffering under the imprisonment and the silver drugs. Ghost wished he could help, but he was on the far side of the city…he had no body, no hands to lay upon their bodies.

A whisper. He startled, and turned. The sky-blue star morphed into a humanoid shape. He approached the cage, and knelt. A young man, about Ghost's age, slumped against the back corner, shivering. He was thin, the cold of the late winter night wracking his frame, even in the basement of the odd building.

Eyes opened, locked on his. Ghost startled again, awed. The young man…this hybrid…looked like Marla. Like Ghost's mother. It was there in the eyes. The shape of his jaw. There was no color to this world aside from the stars that shined within the living, so he could not tell what color the hybrid's hair was, but the part was familiar, the thick waves and the way it fell across his brow. He was reminded strongly of the portrait that sat on Caius' desk. Ghost's awareness shivered, and the hybrid's eyes narrowed, and he frowned. Could he see Ghost? He was curious, and shifted, the narrowed eyes tracking him, the young man's confused expression changing to one of certainty. The hybrid may not know who or what was watching him, but he knew something was.

Ghost knew that look, that emotion. Perfect certainty. Like Marla the hybrid may be, but his expression was all Caius. Ghost quaked. Alarm skittered across his mind. How? How could the hybrid look like Marla, like Caius? When did Remus get access to his mother's or his grandfather's blood, this thing Harmon called DNA? Ghost knew his mother fell in the ambush, the massacre Roman orchestrated with the late Remus brother.

Roman.

Ghost would have sat on his haunches if he was more than thought and energy. Roman. Of course. Roman, son to Caius and brother to Marla. Worked with the Remus brothers for twenty years. His own testimony before his death told Ghost that Roman participated in the sexual assaults and experiments on wolfkin. Roman revealed during his questioning that he gave his seed to the cause, and this youngling might well be the result.

You may not hear me, cousin, but you will be safe, and soon. I swear to you. He might not be able to hear Ghost, but he tried anyway, pushing outward with determination, with conviction. The youngling in the cage jolted, eyes searching, but unable to see Ghost.

The youngling in the cage sensed something, but Ghost could not tell if his words made it through.

Little wolf, Kane whispered. *We must get back, tell Caius everything. We need rest before we can return and free them.*

Coming, Ghost murmured. He backed away with reluctance, his cousin's form blurring, returning to shadow and star.

He was about to return to his mate when something pulled at his mind. A whisper, and he turned, looking to the corner of the room. A curtain hung, haphazard, figures moving behind it.

Humans.

Ghost approached with caution, though he knew the humans would not be able to tell Ghost was there. Humans were blind to the soul, the spirit world. He got to the edge of the curtain, and peeked, curious and nervous at once.

Humans sat at a couple tables and computers, talking to each other, their stars muted yellows with dull brown lines snaking through them. His lip would have curled if he was wolf—these were rotten souls, as rotted as Roman's rogue wolves who attacked Ghost in Baxter weeks before. Evil corrupted both their species.

There was a long table, a single occupant stretched out. Ghost hovered, curious. The body glowed with a dull light, the flesh alive. It was living…but…there was no soul.

A soulless wolf lay upon the table, hooked to wires and tubes. A heart still beat, lungs filled and released air, but there was no consciousness within, no soul, no spirit.

Horror filled his mind, and Ghost froze, stilled by terror and an utter sense of despair. A sheet covered most of the poor creature, disguising its features, tape over eyes and a tube stuck down its throat. Kept alive by mankind's machines.

The wolf who slumbers. She would call it home, but how? It was empty, flesh without spirit.

Ghost! Kane called again, urgent.

Ghost spun away. He pushed his awareness towards his mate, letting Kane and Burke pull him back to themselves, the meld retreating. Burke pulled back on his awareness and Ghost diminished the Spiritsight, and the shadow world fell into darkness.

He thought of his body, sitting beside the coffee table in his grandfather's study. The warmth from his mate's body sitting next to his, the way his scent filled his senses and gave him comfort.

He opened his eyes on a gasp, blinking, tears running down his cheeks. Burke was coughing, Gabe holding him up. Kane slumped, catching himself with one arm before he fell to the floor.

"Are you well?" Michael asked, leaning over him. Ghost nodded, coughing a few times.

"We're okay," Ghost breathed out. Exhaustion hit him, and he swayed. "We found them."

"So Gabe said," Caius replied, standing over him. "He came back frantic. What can you tell me?"

"We found the missing wolfkin, Sir. Almost two dozen humans, half of which I would think are well armed guards." Kane explained, and

Burke nodded.

"I found three more wolfkin nearby, a block or so away from the building. I was able to break through their mental walls—they are surviving members of Roman's rogue wolves." Burke slowly stood, Gabe helping him. "Based on the structure and location, I can tell you it's part of the old campus grounds of the university. That used to be the old storage facility for the Science Department back when I was a student there."

Kane crawled over to Ghost, who gladly let his mate pull him onto his lap. Ghost sagged, utterly spent. Kane kissed his hair and then looked back to Burke. "Have you been in that building before? Do you know the layout?"

Burke was going to answer but he staggered, Gabe having to catch the bigger alpha, both of them nearly falling to the floor. Caius shooed Gabe away and lifted Burke one-handed back to his feet, keeping a grip on his upper arm. "The four of you are about to pass out. You all managed a feat of magic I did not think possible. I'll alert the scouts to the building and have them set up a perimeter. Get some sleep, and we'll discuss our plans this afternoon. We go in tonight and I need my Heir and Speaker functional."

"Yes, sir," Kane said, and Ghost let sleep take him when Kane got to his feet, holding Ghost securely in his arms.

THEY ALL SLEPT for hours, waking in the late afternoon. Ghost found himself alone in bed, a brief mind touch enough to tell him his mate was with his tactical team in Caius' study. A tense atmosphere hummed through the mansion, and Ghost felt like he was on edge himself, ready for something to happen.

He showered, and thinking of the night's activities, actually managed to put on a normal enough outfit. A couple bags of clothing with store tags still attached appeared in the room while they were sleeping, likely from a helpful beta. Boots, dark jeans, and a dark sweater was all he could tolerate, and he grew out his claws long enough to slice the sweater's collar, loosening it around his neck. He still disliked wearing shirts, but walking around the city at night without a shirt in winter would draw more attention than he wanted.

Ghost left the suite and headed for his grandfather's study. A few wolves were about, and they paused and stepped to the side, eyeing him with something akin to awe, their eyes wide and their hearts thumping harder when they saw him. No one said anything, and Ghost was too impatient to think about why they would react in such a way.

The scent of deer made him perk up, all but jogging when he slipped inside the partially open door of the study. Kane's tactical team lined up along the walls and near the rear of the room, some nodding to him as he entered. He smiled, but hurried forward, stomach growling as he narrowed in on the platters of warm food on the coffee table. Slabs of seared venison and oven-baked potatoes made his mouth water, and he only ended up using a plate because Burke shoved one into his hands, laden with food.

Kane was in the middle of what seemed like a briefing, reminding Ghost of all the human police shows he used to watch with Cat every night on television.

"The scouts report that there's been no activity. No shift change. Wherever the humans are sleeping it has to be in the building somewhere. It's been almost twelve hours since we discovered their location. They may do twenty-four hour shifts, so when we go in tonight, we may or may not run into a shift change." Kane was standing next to a large flat screen TV on a stand with wheels, and a small remote he was using to switch between pictures of an abandoned building with signs around it with red lettering. "We aren't going to take the chance that Remus will notice the scouts and move the Ashland wolves. We go in tonight. Live ammo. Kill the guards. Doctors or scientists ..."

"No," Ghost said, dropping a piece of meat before he bit into it. "Those men, the scientists—their souls are rotted through. They know too much and have committed horrible acts against our people. Sparing them will only give them a chance to harm us again or share what they know with more humans. Kill them all."

Heads turned in his direction, mouths gaped, shocked breaths held. Kane gazed back at him, steady. "Are you sure, little wolf?"

An angry whisper muttered from the corners of the room, behind Ghost's ear. He nodded. "She wishes this to end. All the humans who participated in this nightmare must die."

Ghost remembered what the Great Mother told him in the winter meadow. That Remus already had what he needed to destroy the wolfkin. Remus and the human monsters all had to die.

"Do as he said," Caius ordered calmly from his seat at the desk. "Remus dies as well."

"We don't know if he's there," Burke spoke up, looking between Kane and Caius. "The scouts can't tell the identities of anyone in the building. They only got as close as they did without being spotted because they were only taking pictures. Any closer for scents and they will give themselves away."

"We plan as if he were so we don't lose him in the chaos. If he's not there after this op is done, we find him another day." Kane said, and growls echoed around the room. Everyone wanted this over with.

"Normally I would do this sort of thing with just my team, but the building is too large and we don't know when or if more humans will arrive once this starts, so I'm calling in everyone with combat experience. My team is trained in firearms and modern tech, but we'll take anyone from the clan who's fought before in a structured way. Even if the last time in battle was with a shield and sword. Send volunteers to Burke. We leave tonight at 9pm. Breach at midnight. Be ready to move earlier if the scouts report back that the Ashland wolves are being moved. Eat, check weapons, rest, and wait for my order. Dismissed."

The tactical team nodded to Kane and Caius as they left the study in pairs or groups to prepare. Ghost happily sat on the leather couch, gnawing at a venison steak he held in his hand. Once the crowd left, he saw Michael near the opposite wall and Gabe was standing next to him, looking exhausted. "Did either of you sleep?"

Gabe shook his head. "Not much, not really. I can't stop thinking about my father and my uncles."

"I called Heromindes earlier, but it went to voicemail. I left a message." Caius said quietly, and Gabe gave the clan leader a wan smile.

"His pride was deeply bruised by the events of the Tribunal," Gabe dared, and Caius actually cracked a smile.

"Don't worry about Hero," Caius said. "Leave that to me."

"I don't understand," Ghost said around a chunk of meat. Kane chuckled and hit a button on the remote, powering off the TV.

"Gabe would like to stay in Black Pine," Kane explained. "Caius already said he could once this is over."

"You don't want to go back with your family?" Ghost asked, taking a bite out of a loaded potato.

Gabe shrugged, and looked down. Michael put a hand on his shoulder and rubbed, the young alpha drooping. "C'mon, cub. Let's both get some rest while we can."

Michael led Gabe from the room. Burke followed, closing the door behind him as he went.

Ghost ate, ravenous. Kane gave him an indulgent smile and replaced his empty plate with a full one, and a tall glass of water. A quick kiss from his mate, and Ghost went back to eating.

Caius was still at his desk, and Ghost sneaked a peek. His grandfather stared at Marla's picture, his expression empty, but his eyes were dark. Little of the wolf showed beneath Caius' steely exterior, and Ghost thought back to what he had seen in the night while their spirits traveled.

The youngling, the hybrid who shared a strong resemblance to his family. The soulless wolf who slumbered, the body nothing but flesh and artificial life, a shell.

"Grandpa Caius," Ghost said, putting his now empty plate beside him on the couch, clutching his water glass. Kane looked up from his own meal, casting an inquisitive glance between Ghost and Caius.

Caius blinked, and looked away from his daughter's portrait. He quirked a brow at Ghost, who smiled wide. "You need to come with us."

His brow furrowed. "What do you mean? Kane has this well in hand. This is what he does."

Kane sat up, as if to object. Ghost flicked his eyes to Kane for a heartbeat, silently begging him to have patience. Kane sat back, and picked at the food on his plate.

Ghost stood, handing his glass to Kane as he passed his mate. Kane was worried, but stayed quiet, trusting Ghost.

He walked to the desk, and went around to the side. He looked at the portrait of his mother. A woman he could barely remember. Long hair, the same color his was now, and a soft voice full of laughter. And not much else. He ran a finger along the top of the picture, the brass frame cool under his touch. "You must come. If not for the wolves still missing, but for a chance to end this all."

He glanced at Caius, who sat back in his chair, looking back up at him with a contemplative expression. "Is this my grandson telling me I need to come, or the shaman?"

Ghost smiled. "Both."

"Remus may not even be there. It's likely he won't be there at all. This truly ends when he is dead and the data he's collected over the years is destroyed as well."

Ghost nodded. He remembered the winter meadow, and the shadow wolf who danced over the thawing earth. Three lives depended on Ghost. One of which was as stubborn as he was. "Remus will be there tonight."

He wasn't sure, and She wasn't speaking to him, but he thought of all the paths taken that led them to this moment. Fate and destiny and the potential for ruin hovered, waiting for a choice to be made.

Caius was no fool, but then Ghost didn't think it of him. Caius huffed, as wolf-like a sound as any alpha could make in his human form, and looked over at Kane. "Your mate wishes me to come with you and your team tonight. Where can an old warrior be used? Shall I submit my name to our Speaker?"

Kane stood, curiosity in every line, but he approached the desk, eyeing Ghost before nodding to his clan leader. "I've learned to not argue with Ghost. Sometimes it is best to just go with it. And I would not call you old, Sir."

Caius laughed. Ghost blinked, then smiled wide, as Kane looked on in shock. "You'll not be going alone. I'm coming too."

Caius laughed harder at the rueful grimace on Kane's face. Ghost winked, laughing himself when Kane glowered, his own lips twitching.

THE TRIP ACROSS town was uneventful. The distance they traversed the night before in their spirit trip was somehow quicker, but Ghost felt nothing but an anxious sense of impatience. Black SUVs cut through the evening traffic, he was too on edge to get car sick again. Caius and Gabe were in the vehicle in front, Kane in the middle with Ghost, Michael, and Burke. Three more vehicles trailed behind, Kane's tactical team in full gear along with six more wolfkin betas with previous combat experience. Ghost was pleased and surprised that four of the six were female betas, strapped with what looked to him to be daggers, a short sword, and another beta wielding two black guns in thigh holsters and a shotgun in a sling at her back.

A cool touch preceded Caius' mental voice, shivering along bonds that until now had lain quiet. Ghost was experiencing the pack bonds, it awakened inside him in a way that told him better than words that he was home, where he was meant to be. *Kane has lead. Speaker Burke will coordinate as per usual.* Somehow Ghost knew that Caius was speaking to all the wolves involved in the rescue. There was an echo effect, and he could feel the hint of other minds within the pack bonds.

Ghost could feel Kane's pleased surprise along their mate bond, his alpha showing no outward sign he was affected by his clan leader's words. *Stick to the plan. My team has point. Speaker Burke with Shamans Ghost and Michael in Beta Team. Clan Leader Caius has the support team at the perimeter. Scouts are waiting. No sign of activity. Once the building is secure and the threats neutralized, switch to triage response. Guard the shamans while they attend to the hostages.*

A chorus of agreement came back, and the pack bonds lessened but did not disappear. Burke was not driving, he sat in the front passenger seat, his eyes wide and open, yet distant, his mind most likely in communication with the scout teams Caius had sent to watch the building after their discovery.

A warm, strong hand curled around the back of his neck. Ghost turned into his mate, absorbing his heat and love. Kane was worried, he could feel it, but Ghost was not. This was the end. And the beginning. All they needed to do was their best, and the Goddess and Fate would solve the rest. He had faith.

Be careful, little wolf, Kane whispered to him alone. *I love you.*

I love you, my alpha, Ghost said, looking up into Kane's dark eyes, seeing and feeling that love as it reverberated through their bond, unending.

He cuddled into Kane as best he could, considering his mate was covered in a strange assortment of black gear. A thick vest covered his chest and back, he wore heavy boots and black, rough pants that had a multitude of pockets. A long sleeve dark shirt was under the vest, and there were buckles and straps attached everywhere for weapons. Kane had a shotgun at his feet, and two pistols attached to his thighs in black holsters. Ghost sniffed, hating the scent of the oils used on the weapons, and Kane chuckled.

What if you needed to Change? Ghost asked, perplexed. Kane smiled, but shifted on the seat, pointing to a seam that ran the length of the vest. A similar seam ran down the outside of the pants as well.

If I need to Change, the vest breaks apart at the sides where the velcro is, and the pants do too. The holsters are break away as well. My gear is broken in, and I've practiced Changing in them until it's as easy as breathing. Same for the rest of my tactical team. The boots are the easiest. I just pull my feet out.

Ghost huffed, frowning, but he accepted the answer for what it was—reassurance from his mate. He was wearing all dark clothing himself, and despite Kane's offer before they left, he wasn't going to wear one of the bulky vests.

They reached the building sooner than Ghost was prepared for, the SUVs taking narrow, empty back streets with the lights off. The convoy came to a halt two blocks away, in an alley that was full of shadows. The vehicles were all but swallowed by the darkness. They carefully exited, slowly shutting the doors with caution so there were no echoes. Ghost went to Burke, Michael on his heels. Ghost had no idea what to really expect or how to contribute except to follow orders until the humans were neutralized. This was Kane's purview—what his mate trained for, spent the last fifteen years doing.

Kane, with thought and sharp, efficient motions, broke them into three teams. Caius would hold the perimeter and guard their backs, in case reinforcements arrived or Remus or the rogues made an appearance. The three rogue wolves had yet to appear, though Burke was able to confirm they were in a smaller building close enough to hear the disruption once they made entry in the storage facility. Kane would lead his team on entry, neutralizing all humans as they went. Ghost sniffed, thinking it was an odd word to use for hunting and killing, but Kane was in something Burke said was commando mode, and Ghost went along with it. Burke would lead a secondary team with Ghost, Michael, Gabe and two of the beta volunteers.

Burke knelt at his feet, and Ghost took the Speaker's clothing as he handed it over, putting it in a bag that Gabe held open. Gabe slung the bag over his shoulder once Burke was naked, and soon a large, chocolate brown wolf shook out his fur, ears flapping against his skull as he settled into his wilder form. Golden eyes flickered, and Burke gave a wolfish grin, tail wagging.

We go in quiet. No talking unless it's an emergency. Once the all clear is given vocal communications may resume. Kane said, and pointed at Burke, who gave a human nod in answer to Kane's query of readiness. *All teams ready. Approach.*

Kane took off, a silent predator in the night, even carrying weapons and wearing human gear. His team followed, and Ghost patiently waited for Burke to signal when to follow. They jogged down the alley, the stink of refuse and exhaust mixed with damp earth a noxious combination that Ghost was glad he did not need to deal with daily.

They followed the first team, not a word spoken. The thrum of heartbeats was the loudest noise they made, and Ghost grinned. It felt like hunting, despite the urban location and their human forms. Burke preferred to be in his wilder form when he was acting as Speaker, something about how he was better able to focus. The rest of them were in their human forms, and it made sense. Any humans who saw a pack of huge wolves running through a college campus would likely call the police.

The building from their spirit trip came into view, and they all halted in the shadow of the building across the narrow street from where the missing Ashland wolfkin were being held. Figures appeared from the dark—in pairs, wolves who slunk with liquid grace to where Kane stood waiting for them. The scouts. There were five of them, dark browns and grays, eyes glimmering with low intensity, they crowded around Kane in a tight semicircle.

Ghost sensed a murmur in the pack bonds, but nothing he could determine clearly. He waited beside Burke, kneeling in the alpha's shadow as they waited.

KANE GESTURED TO the scouts, who left as silently as they appeared. They would hold the outer perimeter and be the first to sound the alarm if reinforcements arrived once they breached.

Burke, Caius. He called, and they sent echoes back along the bonds. *There has been no movement. The scouts are returning to their positions. We move once everyone is in place.*

Silent confirmation from them both, and Kane moved to the corner of the building. There was an empty and treeless lane that separated the two buildings, the one they needed to breach with a wide, empty lot in front of it. The sky was cloudy, but with frequent breaks as the wind moved the clouds above, letting in random moonlight that raced across the ground before breaking apart. Shadows moved with the wind, the soft howling and the inconstant light would be a help—humans, even experienced combatants, were less equipped to handle the fluctuating conditions than the wolfkin.

Kane stood, turned, and pointed to Caius, his clan leader decked out in Kane's spare gear, holding a shotgun with ease. Caius had fought in both the Revolutionary War and the Civil War, since human conflict never stayed within species' bounds Black Pine and her vassal clans were threatened time and again by war. Caius took off, running with his perimeter team to set up along the far side of the building and the rear. He would meet up with the scouts guarding the back and arrange cover. They were out of sight within moments, and Kane waited, patient.

Kane got what he was waiting for, the scouts sending their readiness. Kane opened the pack links, and let Burke take the burden from him. The shift in control was enough to signal the rest of the wolfkin, and Kane took off, his strike team following without hesitation at his back.

Across the road, the shadows from the clouds high above covered their approach. Kane and his strike team headed for the front entrance— this building had only three ways in—the front entrance lobby, a rear service entrance for trailers, and a fire door on the far side. Caius' team would set up around the exterior, and would take down any humans who used the two other doors to escape. The rest of the scouts and the volunteers would hold the front once Kane breached. Burke and the shamans would wait in the lobby as Kane's team cleared the top two floors and then swept back down the staircases to the sublevels behind the abandoned security desk in the lobby.

Two wolfkin on either side covered the doors as Kane kicked them in, glass shattering, the metal frame flying off the hinges and crashing into the wall. Kane went in, shotgun to his shoulder, covering high, the rest of his team flowing in behind him, taking the corners of the lobby. A shadow moved next to the staircase access, and Kane pulled the trigger. A spray of blood painted the wall as the human guard fell to the floor.

Kane pointed two fingers at the door and two of his team went to check the human and cover the door. His shot likely alerted the rest of the humans to their presence.

Burke's team came in, the Speaker keeping his larger body between the shamans and the rest of the building. Ghost and Michael knelt, making themselves small as possible, while Gabe huddled behind them. Kane took one last look at his mate before he led half of his team up the stairs. The other half would clear the ground floor while Burke's team would hold the lobby.

There were limited rooms on the second floor. Room after room was empty, not even furniture remaining in the abandoned spaces. The air was dusty and stale with old traces of human scent. It was likely the human guards only came up here on rare occasions to secure the area. They checked everywhere leaving no closet or bathroom unsearched. In less than two minutes Kane led his team back downstairs to the ground floor. The rest of his team came back within seconds, wordlessly confirming that the above-ground levels were empty but for the guard Kane had already shot.

They regrouped at the stairway access, and Kane nodded to the two wolves he left at the door, the dead human already moved to the side and searched. Kane could hear movement past the door leading to the basement level, and it was likely the humans were expecting them to come through any moment. Kane grabbed a flash bang grenade from the satchel hanging off his hip, pulled the pin, and at a short nod from him one of the wolves opened the door a few inches and Kane tossed the grenade down the stairs. The door was pulled shut immediately, and there was a muffled explosion a second later.

Another nod and the door was flung open, and Kane covered high as another of his team covered low, both aiming down the staircase. Two shots later, and two humans collapsed at the base of the stairs. Kane's first shot took off the head of one and his second took out the other, who clutched at his leg.

Without hesitation Kane led the way down the staircase. Kane went to the human shot in the leg, cracking open his skull with a single kick abruptly ending his cries of pain.

The stairs turned at the bottom, opening into a complicated warren of support beams, crumbling, concrete walls and clearly excavated open spaces full of equipment.

Alpha team converge, all engage. Complicated terrain. Mind for friendly fire. Volunteers shift, go wolfkin for assault. Two humans down at the base of the stairs. Kane pointed left and right, splitting his team, and took the hall straight ahead.

GHOST HEARD THE muted thumps of shots through the floor, the door held open by one of the tactical team members. Burke stood, great head swiveling, ears twitching, hypervigilant as they waited for the all clear to come from below. Michael and Gabe crouched behind Burke, eyes wide, Gabe exuding a mix of fear and impatience. Michael appeared calm and ready, despite the danger of their situation and the nightmare into which they were walking.

The rogues are approaching, Caius said along the pack lines, and Burke growled, Ghost turning in his crouch as he peered back out at the parking lot. The clouds were moving again, the lot a stretch of deeper blackness in the night, and saw no sign of Caius and his team or the approaching rogues. Burke nudged his hip with his muzzle, and Ghost paid attention to what was going on below them. Caius could handle the three rogues.

THEY CAME IN wolf form, a foolish action to take, even in the dead of night in winter. Humans might prefer the indoors in the cold weather, but they were in a populated area, a thriving campus center not too far away. Any shots fired outside might be heard, and the police called. They would settle for tooth and claw.

Caius snorted in disdain, creeping along the corner of the building, the scent of dirty, poorly-fed, alcohol-stinking wolves scrambled over the pavement. He could smell old traces of them on the fire door at the side of the building, and when he had tried it earlier, a single claw under the metal's edge proved the locking mechanism was broken, the door held itself shut only by weight. The rogues weren't quiet—he and the team under his command heard them coming, claws loud on rough pavement as they came closer.

Caius and two of his betas crouched by the corner, as the three rogues, fur rough and unkempt, tumbled from the shadows and went to the door. He wondered how they would open the door with fully wolf paws, when one of the rogues sat back on his haunches and began to Change, the process rough and sluggish.

Caius leapt, snarling as he took the distance in less than a second, his betas right behind him. He landed on the rogue who was caught mid-shift, Caius' own claws out, fangs lowered, and he ripped out the rogue's throat before they even hit the ground. Hot blood sprayed, the rogue's eyes wide in fear and shock, and Caius grabbed his skull and twisted. He dropped the body at his feet, and spun towards the other rogues.

His two betas, both wolves in their wilder forms, had one rogue cornered against the building. Caius leapt again, clawed hand out, and he grabbed the hind paw of the third rogue as he attempted to flee. A sharp yank and the leg broke at the hip, the rogue screaming. Caius pulled the wolf back to him, claws sinking into fur and flesh, and with a negligent flick, broke the struggling wolf's neck. He tossed aside the rogue's corpse, and turned back to the remaining wolf.

His betas lunged forward together, and the rogue found himself buried under the two females, throat and chest ripped open. He died within moments, the females backing away, shaking their heads to lose the taste of his foul blood on their tongues. Caius smiled down at his wolves, proud and pleased, and they danced happily with wide, sharp grins when he petted them gently on their heads.

Caius reached out for Burke. *The three rogues are dead.* Caius smiled, lifting his face to the wind, blood and death heavy in the air. He growled, a smooth purr that expelled some of the tension he had been carrying for far too long. Burke responded with subdued acknowledgment, and Caius tilted his head.

The rumbled of engines. He moved to the corner of the building at the front, and looked carefully out toward the front lot. Headlights glanced off the ground, highlighting potholes and dead grass in cracks. A dark SUV and a limo were about two hundred yards out, and Caius grinned.

A limo and escort car are coming from the west, Caius told Burke, the Speaker's surprise echoing back.

*They will likely be armed. Any confrontation outside will run the risk of *drawing the human authorities.**

Get the shamans out of the line of fire. Let them into the lobby. We'll trap them inside between us.

Like herding frantic deer into the rest of the wolf pack, the humans would die. Caius called in the rest of the perimeter team, and split them between his side of the building and the far side. His eyes could pick up the soft pops of gunfire in the sublevel, telling him Kane was still encountering the humans within.

The two approaching cars parked side by side in front of the building, engines ticking. Guards exited the vehicles, human men in dark suits with the soft stink of gunmetal broadcasting to anyone with a nose that they were armed.

It took everything Caius had not to leap out from hiding and eviscerate Simon Remus when the human bastard got out of the limo. He paused, and backed away from the door, another man exiting behind him.

Rage and disbelief battled for supremacy. It took him a moment to regain his equilibrium, but then all he could feel was cold, icy purpose. He reached out to Burke, sensing Kane was still too busy neutralizing threats in the basement to respond.

*Burke,** he said, pausing before continuing. Burke waited, the Speaker's mind processing everything else happening in the background. **Julian is with Remus.**

Hostage? Burke asked, disbelief clouding his mental voice.

Julian tugged on his suit jacket, smoothing down his tie. His red hair appeared black in the night, but the smirk on his face was unchanged and he walked beside Remus without issue. *No. He's here willingly. I think we have another traitor.*

I don't understand, Burke replied, the Speaker at a loss.

He's always been a mad dog—betraying his own kind wouldn't be out of the realms of the possible, Caius explained. *Never mind the why of it—alert Kane when you can. Trap remains the same. I'll take care of Julian.*

Caius carefully sat, and began stripping down. He would confront Julian as a wolf, and tear him and Remus apart.

22

SHAMAN'S WRATH

JULIAN? THE BIRCH GROVE CLAN LEADER? MICHAEL ASKED, sounding just as shocked as Burke. All four of them backed away, Gabe and Michael going up the stairs to the second floor, Ghost and Burke behind the corner of the lobby that led to a supply closet and a pair of bathrooms.

Ghost wasn't surprised at all. Julian's presence was unexpected, but Ghost had faith in his mate, clan mates, and Goddess. Ghost crouched down, behind Burke's bulky wolf-form, even though Ghost was more likely to be able to stop any bullets shot in their direction.

Any response from Kane? Ghost asked, keeping his mental voice small in case Julian could intrude on their conversation. Ghost had no knowledge of Julian's skills or strength, aside from the fact he had to have enough personal power to become a clan leader. He could feel Kane's herculean focus on his task in the back on his mind, and didn't want to risk distracting Kane by trying to speak to him.

He's taken out most of the humans, the guards are going down easy. He's almost done. I'd prefer we wait for him to finish before Remus and Julian got in here but we're out of time, Burke said at the same moment Ghost heard the overloud noises of humans walking across the tiled floor in the lobby.

The scent of sweat, humans, and guns swept in ahead of the group surrounding Remus and Julian. It was seconds after they came inside when a low, rumbling growl came from the lobby, and Ghost heard the familiar sound of the Birch Grove clan leader's voice. "I smell Black Pine bitches. Did you set me up?"

"Wait? What?" Ghost assumed it was Remus, the voice familiar to him. He flashed back to the sanctuary in New Brunswick, an armed human aiming a gun at his head. Ghost bared his teeth in a silent snarl, and he wanted nothing more than to finish what he started all those weeks ago. Remus needed to die.

"Move! We aren't alone in here!" Julian ordered, and the confused exclamations of the human guards were exactly what they needed.

Snarls and shouts came next, and Burke charged around the corner, Ghost on his heels. Humans raised their weapons at them, but Ghost shouted, hands coming up in a mirror response, a wall of searing heat bursting ahead of him in a wave. Metal grew red-hot, tiles blackened, and clothing smoked. The humans dropped their weapons and scrambled away, coming up short as wolves came in from the front of the building, Caius in his huge wolf-form leading the charge. Burke slammed into two humans, bowling them over, and Ghost jumped. He went high, dissipating the heat wave as he cleared the human guards and landed on Remus.

Snarls, shouts, the hot taste of blood on the air combined into chaos. Ghost rode Remus to the floor, the human screaming beneath him. Ghost landed with his boots on the bigger man's chest, his clawed hands encircling Remus' neck. Remus was a big man, easily a third bigger than Ghost, but human strength against wolfkin, there was no match. Ghost snarled as he tightened his fingers, ducking his head as Remus landed blows to his shoulders and skull, trying to knock him off.

A clawed hand latched onto the back of his neck, inch-long claws digging into the sides of his neck. Ghost was yanked backwards, and his hands were pulled from Remus' neck. He fought, shouting, claws out and fangs dropped. His magic discharged and snapped, sparks flying, landing on the suited arms trying to restrain him. Rough curses came from the wolfkin male that pulled him back and then down, pushing him to the floor.

"Kane's wild little bitch," Julian grinned at him, his eyes glowing, red hair a mess, fangs dropping. Ghost slammed his hands, electricity arcing from his fingers, into the sides of Julian's head, who shouted in pain and anger. Ghost pulled his arms back, building a new charge, determined to get Julian off him.

Julian gripped Ghost's shoulders, lifting him up, and before Ghost could attack again, Julian slammed him back down, the back of Ghost's head slapping on the hard tile floor.

His vision blurred, pain lancing down his spine, and Julian did it again, slamming him down too fast for him to stop it, to get free. Everything went dark.

His feet catching on the side of the hallway woke him. Pain radiated out from his right arm, held over him.

He was being dragged, and fast. A clawed hand was around his bicep, his face inches from the rough, wet concrete floor. And Kane was shouting in his head.

Ghost!

My alpha, he managed to whisper back, blood dripping in his eyes from his hair. He couldn't move, not yet, his body still limp and his head aching horribly.

Where are you? Are you hurt? Is he there? Kane demanded, concern, love, and anger coming across their bond.

He is here, oh mighty heir of Black Pine, Julian's mental voice intruded on their link, and Ghost gasped, the sensation of having a greater alpha bursting into a private mind link painful and disruptive, scattering his thoughts. *I have your wild little bitch. Not much of a shaman, is he? His blood tastes like prey.*

Kane's presence in the back of his mind was a seething, red and black storm of rage. Ghost moaned, and tried to twist free from Julian's iron grip on his arm, but his head ached too much, his limbs refusing to cooperate. Julian chuckled, unhinged and carefree. There was malice and something dark, dangerous in the sound, and a pool of icy fear settled in Ghost's belly.

Julian dropped him. Ghost rolled to his side, face wet from the damp floor, and he blinked. He wasn't alone.

Simon Remus groaned, eyes fluttering. A bruise was forming along his left cheekbone and down his jaw. Ghost snarled, lips pulling back as his own fangs came out. His whole body hurt, and his thoughts were still muddled, but he was healing fast. Remus was a few feet away from him and Ghost wanted to end it.

"Now you two little bitches wait right here for me," Julian stood over them, removing his suit jacket and tossing it aside. "I'm going to tear out Kane's throat and then force Caius to eat it before I snap his neck. Or maybe I'll feed Kane bits of Caius before I kill him."

Ghost tried to get up, but Julian kicked him in the side, a wet snap coming from his ribs. Ghost fell back to the floor, curling into a ball. Julian sneered down at him and then checked on Remus. The human seemed to be struggling with regaining consciousness.

Ghost whined in pain, shivering, and Julian huffed in satisfaction before leaving.

Kane.

Ghost! You're in pain. Are you okay? What did he do?

Knocked me out for a while. I think I have a broken rib. He's coming for you and Caius.

Anger was Kane's response, a deadly wave of it that erupted along the link between them. *I'm with Caius and Burke. Michael and Gabe are upstairs, tending some of our wolves who got shot. Can you sneak away? Is he still there?*

Ghost bit his lip to keep from crying out, and turned his head. He looked past Remus' limp form and blinked, then again. *Kane. I'm with the missing Ashland wolves.*

Cages were arranged in two rows, and Ghost gingerly moved one of his arms out and beneath him, and lifted himself just far enough to see better. Kane responded almost immediately, his mate's mind cooler, more focused, the anger controlled. *Is Julian there? Can you free them?*

Ghost opened his mind fully to his mate, letting Kane see through his eyes. A battered and thin wolfkin male in the closest cage was staring back at Ghost with absolute shock, and the man's resemblance to Gabe was immediate and striking. Ghost sat up more, his mind clearing, the injury on the back of his head healing. Kane took in the odd room through Ghost's eyes; the shrouded machines near the rear, the cages, and Julian's absence. *Ghost, we're coming to you. Stay safe. Some of the guards who came with Remus and Julian are between us and your position. It's likely you're on the far side of the sublevel. Protect yourself until we can get there.*

Remus is unconscious. Ghost looked back to the human still passed out beside him. Julian must have struck the human too hard, the bruise on his face was now a deep purplish blue. If Remus were awake, Ghost had no trouble with snapping his neck. Remus was a monster. Without conscience or compassion, Remus cared only for profit and himself. And yet Ghost hesitated. The human was literally helpless, injured, unaware of the danger he was in and that his death was imminent.

Ghost relaxed, his fangs pulling back, his claws ceased and his anger left him. Simon Remus' fate belonged to those he wronged the most, and that was not Ghost.

He could sense Kane as his mate dropped his combat gear and began Changing into his wilder form. *Do what you must to save yourself and the Ashland wolves. If you cannot end him, Caius will do so once we get there.*

Ghost wrapped an arm around his ribs and carefully stood, wavering before he found his balance. *Stop the rest of the humans. Julian is insane and coming for you. I'll be fine.*

A roar echoed through the sublevel, long and deep. A challenge, full of madness and fury. Ghost got a glimpse of a red and black wolf the size of a brown bear charging at his mate, before Kane dropped the more intimate connection and his focus shifted to fighting with fang and claw. Ghost withdrew, his faith in his mate absolute.

"Youngling?" A thin whisper drew his attention, and Ghost smiled when he met the now lucid gaze of the nearest wolfkin. "You must leave if you can, it's not safe. Please, go, before you end up in a cage too!"

Ghost slowly stood, breathing deep, and felt his ribs snap back into place. He was healing, and he wasn't leaving without everyone. He stepped over Remus, the human unresponsive, and went to the closest cage. "I'm not leaving. She wouldn't have gone through all the trouble to get me here and then be happy that I left."

He knelt, avoiding the silver bars, and examined the lock. It was a simple one, nothing more than an embedded square that needed a key to insert, but the fact the entire structure was covered in silver meant touching it to open it was impossible.

He had never needed to touch a lock to open it.

Ghost stared at the lock, and with a tiny push of mental effort, it snapped open. Ghost lifted a hand, and with his mind, pulled the door open wide. The wolfkin inside the cage began to cry, tears streaking down his dirty, thin face. "Shaman."

Ghost nodded, and with another mental nudge, the shackles holding the wolfkin fell away. Ghost reached out, and took the prisoner's hands, and pulled him from the silver cage, gently lowering him to the floor. "Stay right here. Watch for humans or the red-haired wolf, yell if you see anyone coming. I need to free the others."

"Thank you," the other wolfkin whispered, gratitude in every deep line of misery carved in his face. "I will."

Ghost smiled, and moved on to the next cage.

BURKE DODGED A bullet, the impact in the wall right over his head. He crouched, peeking around the corner, and leapt when he saw the human reloading. He died with a strangled scream, and Burke dropped the body before following Ghost's scent deeper into the building.

Julian had grabbed Ghost and Remus, and then barreled through his human guards without concern nor care for anyone but himself. The unexpected maneuver had gone unanswered as the humans began firing indiscriminately. Whatever Ghost did to the weapons to make the humans drop them hadn't extended to the guards in the back, and they were still armed.

Several wolfkin were shot, but the guards were defeated, with a spattering running down the stairs after Julian. Burke thought that was utterly stupid of them, but then fear and desperation made humans do stupid things every day. Michael stayed behind, using his limited healing ability to stop the worst of the injuries, and Gabe's gift of the Voice was too dangerous to let the young alpha go anywhere without Michael, so he stayed behind as well. Caius and Burke raced ahead, meeting up with Kane in the sublevel, only to have a few remaining guards begin to fire from cover.

Julian's arrival meant they had to split up, and Burke went to find Ghost. Julian was huge—a black and red monstrosity that fought without forethought or reason, a truly mad animal. Kane and Caius would usually fight in tandem, but the confusing jumbled maze of half-walls and corridors meant the fighting was in close quarters, both Caius and Kane were too big to take Julian on simultaneously. Burke left reluctantly, but knowing Ghost was alone with Remus made up his mind for him.

No one else fired at him, so he ran, nose down, backtracking Julian, the clan leader's scent overlaid with Ghost's. He cleared a corner, and he wanted to howl in joy when he found Ghost. Remus was unconscious, he was tempted to end the human, but Ghost and the Ashland wolves needed him more in that moment than Remus needed to die.

The small shaman was freeing the Ashland wolves, all of them weak, malnourished, and suffering from silver poisoning. Ghost was helping a tall wolfkin male from one of the far cages, the man stuck in between human and his wilder form, the silver poisoning destroying his ability to fix himself. Burke paused, and focused, needing hands to help Ghost. He stood, his Change moving swift and sure, adrenaline forcing it along faster than usual.

"Do you need help?" Burke asked, and Ghost smiled at him, his silver eyes full of something Burke was surprised to see might be satisfaction.

"There's one more cage. I already opened it and took off the shackles. Be careful with the youngling—he's not what you think he is," Ghost said, helping the warped wolfkin male to his family, the half-dozen of them huddling together, hugging and crying quietly.

Burke ducked around Ghost and his burden, and saw the remaining captive. He was small and thin, and he was sprawled on his face, halfway out of his cage. He was thin and skin was blue-cast, and he shook with the cold. Burke knelt, and gently turned the youngling over. He stilled for a moment, wondering why he smelled a human, but the small figure in his arms cried softly in pain, and Burke clutched him to his chest. "Shhh, you'll be alright now. I won't hurt you."

Burke fell back on his ass when the young man opened his eyes. Crystalline, brilliant, the color of a midsummer sky at noon, his eyes were beautiful, and yet their perfection was nothing compared to the wavering, shy smile that graced the youngling's mouth. The most beautiful smile Burke had ever seen lifted lush, soft pink lips, and the precious being in his arms spoke softly, as if he were seconds from sleep. "I'm cold," he whispered, and Burke curled around the younger man, hoping some of his own body heat would help.

He cradled the young man closer, holding him tightly, pressing their naked forms together. Burke never felt the cold, not really, and right now he felt like he was sunning himself on a tropical beach, he was so warm. Everywhere they touched, Burke burned, but it was without pain. The youngling whimpered, and greedily snuggled with him, pressing his cold nose to Burke's throat, arms wrapping around his neck. Burke hugged him back, and he'd never felt such a desire to never let go again.

"What's your name, youngling?" Burke whispered, dipping his head, breathing in a lovely, alluring scent. Sweet and clean, despite the grime of captivity and dirty hair.

"Wren Harmon," the youngling replied, voice still a meager whisper.

"Hello, Wren. My name is Burke," he said gently in return. The last name was a problem for another time.

He had no idea how, or why, but he was certain. He might have needed Sophia to point out the obvious to him weeks ago regarding Ghost and Kane and their soulbond, but he needed no help now. After weeks of seeing the bond between his best friend and the young shaman, he could recognize one when it smacked him in the face. Or the soul, even.

The youngling in his arms who appeared to be human, bore the last name of a mad scientist, and smelled like heaven on earth, was his soulbonded mate.

GHOST HELPED THE warped alpha to his brothers, the family similarity obvious. He checked, and there were no approaching enemies, but the sounds of a fierce fight echoed through the sublevel. Remus was still unmoving, clearly injured more severely than Ghost had assumed. Humans were fragile.

"Thank you," the alpha said, grabbing Ghost's wrist when he pulled away. "I thought we were going to die here."

"You're welcome." Ghost said quietly, and patted his hand. "Let me go check on the youngling."

"He's…" the alpha paused, his strength intermittent. Ghost would need to heal them all, and soon, or the rescue would be for naught as the silver killed them from within. "The youngling is not human. He's something they called a hybrid. I don't understand how, but the humans made him."

"I know," Ghost replied, trying to reassure. "He is safe. I will not let anyone harm him. I swear." The alpha nodded, releasing his wrist, accepting him at his word. Ghost was grateful that the automatic trust wolfkin had in shamans was helping them accept his help despite his age. He caught the Suarez family alphas casting startled glances in his direction was he opened their cages. His age never bothered Ghost, but then he forgot it was important to humans and wolfkin alike. To both species, he was barely older than a cub.

Burke was cradling the youngling in his arms, and the youngling was gazing up at Burke like the Speaker was the most marvelous thing he'd ever seen. Ghost titled his head, and on a wild guess, shifted into his Spiritsight.

The sky-blue soulstar of the youngling mingled with the darker reddish hues of Burke's soulstar. The thinnest of bonds, but it grew stronger with every beat of their hearts. Ghost chuckled, and dropped the Spiritsight. He knelt beside the pair, and they youngling nervously huddled against Burke, watching Ghost with wary, frightened blue eyes. He gently brushed dirty hair back from the youngling's face. He saw again the resemblance to his mother's portrait. Ghost smiled at the person who looked enough like him to be his brother, but likely was born from the forced union of Roman's seed and an unfortunate human female.

"He's cold," Burke said, without looking away from his mate's face. "Ghost, we need to get him out of here. He's human, you can't heal him. Wren needs human medicine."

His cousin's name was Wren. A shy forest bird with a beautiful song. It fit, somehow. And their Goddess called this one her lost wolf. Ghost was sure his magic would work on the youngling.

"He's the hybrid, Burke." The Speaker finally tore his gaze away, and Ghost nodded when he saw Burke's eyes go from dark brown to liquid gold. "Wren is your soulbonded mate, and he isn't entirely human. His soul is wolfkin. Hold him close. I'll heal everyone once the fighting is over."

Burke nodded, his eyes wide, but his jaw set with determination and he somehow managed to get an even tighter, more protective grip on the small creature in his arms. The youngling was smaller than Ghost, though they were of the same age. Not so much a youngling, then, and Ghost gave his cousin a soft smile before standing.

His mate still fought Julian, Caius at his side, the two greater alphas trading off against the mad wolf. Ghost would go and help, but he refused to leave the Ashland wolves and Wren alone with only Burke to protect them. Burke was formidable, but his mate lay sick and injured in his arms and he was unlikely to let go in case of danger. Ghost didn't blame Burke at all—if it were Kane lying naked and emaciated on the cold concrete floor, Ghost wouldn't leave his side either. Kane and Caius were handling Julian well enough, and hopefully this would be over, and soon. He spared a quick glance; Remus was still unmoving.

The plastic curtain was pulled halfway, and Ghost knew what he would see. He pulled it back, got a handful, then yanked it free from its moorings in the ceiling. It fell, metal clasps pinging in the shadows, and Ghost got a clear view.

The slumbering wolf lay quiet, soulless still, and only the low, soft beat of a heart told Ghost that the body lived. His entire being rebelled at the abomination the human wrought—they corrupted the divine gift of the wolfkin Goddess and tried to craft themselves a wolf of their own.

Save him, so that you may save Caius.

Her words found him as if She stood at his shoulder, and Ghost's heart raced. He took another step, then one more, and reached out. Machines beeped and chimed, a steady, soft rhythm, one that spoke of death gathering in the corners, the shadows deepening. His fingers touched the white sheet that covered most of the soulless wolf, and he pulled, careful, and it fell away.

Gray fur. Soft and thick beneath his fingers. A sob burst free, and tears ran down his cheeks, scalding hot. He dashed them away, and with shaking fingers, plucked the wires and sticky pads from the shaved pieces of skin along the wolf's side. He did not understand what cloning truly was, nor how the science worked, but the mad impossibility staring back at him was irrefutable proof cloning worked.

Gray Shadow.

His grandfather, dead all these long years, stolen from his peaceful afterlife and made flesh again. Ghost leaned over the slumbering wolf, and buried his face in the thick fur along the wolf's shoulders. Somehow, the scent was the same. Memories came rushing back, and Ghost was once again a small cub cowering behind the great gray wolf that towered over him, between Ghost and a human man with a shotgun. He could feel the river, the current horrific, smothering him, battering him against rocks and trees, his lungs burning as he drowned.

An image of an astral wolf guiding him through his first Change, saving his life and ending Gray Shadow's. He clung to the sleeping form that lay on the cold, steel table, and wept now as he could not then.

My shaman. Do not grieve. Save him.

"How?" Ghost whispered, choking on tears. She did not answer, but a gasp from not far away drew his attention.

A human man in a white coat stood shaking in the corner, the plastic sheeting falling to the ground revealing his hiding place. He was kneeling behind a desk, and he had a gun in his trembling hand.

Ghost breathed in, cursing himself mentally for not paying better attention. The scent of the wolf was strong, and carried human scent markers as well. Including the human who cowered not far away, staring at Ghost like he was monster.

"Stay...stay away from me! I'll shoot!" The human cried out, standing, edging his way. Ghost moved, placing himself between the human and the slumbering form of his grandfather. Ghost snarled quietly, and sucked in another breath. He smelled blood, sweat, and fear. The human gulped, hand shaking even more. "I won't shoot if you let me go."

"Ghost?" Burke called, worried. "What's going on?"

"Burke, stay with Wren." Ghost ordered, and when the human glanced over toward Burke, Ghost flicked his fingers and sent the gun flying from the human's grasp and into the shadows. The human shrieked, and Ghost snarled at him again, claws pricking each fingertip as they grew.

"What are you?!" The human cried, knocking into a table covered in metal instruments. They were bloodied, and stunk of terror and pain.

"Shaman," Ghost said past his fangs as they dropped. The human screamed, but there was no mercy in Ghost then, not after everything. He lifted his hand, and sent the human flying backwards across the lab. He smashed into the far wall, bones shattering, and fell to the floor in a limp jumble of limbs.

Dead.

"Ghost!" Burke's shout made him jump, and Ghost spun, just in time to see Simon Remus getting to his feet. He pressed hand to his head, the other reaching under his suit coat and pulling a gun.

Ghost ran, leaping over Burke and Wren, and he sprinted around the Suarez wolves. He barreled into Remus before the human even managed to lift the weapon and aim. They tumbled across the wet floor, and Ghost managed to knock the gun to the floor. He slashed at Remus, who shouted in pain, but managed to get an arm up and swung at Ghost, punching him across his jaw. Ghost stumbled, and he crouched, eyes narrowed at the man who was responsible for so much death and suffering. Remus cast about, looking for an escape, but Ghost darted between Remus and the doorway.

Remus swore at him, but brought his hands up, fists ready to strike at Ghost again. Ghost did not know how to fight like a human, with hands and feet. He knew tooth and claw, though, and Changed so fast in a flurry of silver-white energy that he was leaping at Remus before his clothing hit the floor.

He landed on Remus, sending them to the ground, and Ghost tore at his arm. Remus screamed and pummeled him with his free hand, striking at Ghost's head and back. He shook his head, worrying at the limb like he would a rabbit, and blood spurted over his tongue. He did it again, and bone broke.

Remus rolled, and managed to fling Ghost off him. Ghost was readying to leap again when the concrete wall beside them collapsed with a deafening roar. Dust and debris flew, and Ghost scrambled to avoid the bigger sections of the wall as it fell. Remus ducked to the side, and Ghost lost sight of him in the chaos.

A large red and black wolf rolled past Ghost, regaining all fours as Kane and Caius boiled into the room through the fresh hole in the wall. Julian was a mess of bites and claw slashes, blood dripping from jaws and his sides. Ghost howled, and leapt at the clan leader, landing on the much larger alpha's side, claws digging in. He bit the back of Julian's neck as Kane charged into him from the front.

Julian was three times Ghost's size, and Ghost's jaws were too small to break past the thick muscles of the alpha's neck and slice the arteries. Kane's momentum knocked Ghost off Julian, the two alphas rolling over the floor, snapping and snarling furiously. Caius ran after them, and just as Julian and Kane broke apart, Caius took the lead in the attack, harrying Julian back across the room.

Kane ran to Ghost, nosing him gently. Ghost was sore, but he got back to his feet, and he nudged at his mate. They needed to end this, and now.

A movement to the side made them both look—Remus had the gun. He pointed it at Kane, who covered most of Ghost. Kane roared in challenge, and Remus fired.

It felt like time stopped, his heart lurching in his chest, the bullet meant to shatter his mate's skull screaming across the short distance between them. Ghost tried to raise a shield, as he had when the bomb exploded at their cabin weeks ago, but Remus and Kane were too close and the bullet was moving too fast. He had no warning. She had warned him with whispers before the bomb blew—here, not even his Goddess could be heard over the chaos in the lab.

A dark blur slammed into them, knocking them both off their feet and to the side. Kane regained his feet in seconds and leapt, landing on Remus. Blood sprayed, Remus dying instantly as Kane bore him to the ground.

Ghost struggled to his feet in time to see Julian run from the room. Shouts and gunfire came from the hall, and screaming. The wolfkin teams were trying to stop the mad wolf from escaping, but it didn't sound like they were succeeding.

He was about to follow, but he stopped. He had to, his feet were unable to move.

Caius lay not far away.

Still, quiet.

Blood dripped from his thick, dark fur, and puddled on the floor.

Ghost regained his human form quickly, instantaneous. He ran to Caius, hands searching desperately for the wound than was making his grandfather bleed out. Ghost was crying. He was kneeling naked in his grandfather's blood as he lay dying. A warm hand landed on the back of his neck, and Ghost shook off his fear and reached for his magic.

Caius was damaged by teeth, claws, the bullet, and bruises that littered his body. Caius' heart was strong, and Ghost called to his light. Pushing it from his center into the wounds that covered most of Caius. He found the bullet, and used his mind to yank the offending silver from the flesh beneath. Caius jerked, his whole body reacting, and Ghost went faster. He chased the silver remnants away, and closed the wounds.

Ghost fell back, and Kane caught him in his arms.

"Will he live?" Kane asked, covered in blood and gore and looking wondrous.

"He should," Ghost gasped out, wrapping his arms around Kane's neck. "He took the bullet meant for you."

"He did," Kane agreed quietly, and ducked his head, pressing their foreheads together. "He could have stopped Julian, but he saved me instead."

They stood quietly for a moment, and it took the sound of many running sets of feet to break them apart.

The Black Pine wolves ran into the lab, some of them still in their human forms, most of them wolves. Gabe was at their center, Michael beside him. Gabe smiled at them, relieved, then a shout from the Suarez wolves drew his attention.

"Father!" Gabe screamed, and ran for the alpha warped between his two forms. "Father!"

Gabe launched himself at his family, who caught him eagerly, gathering around the young alpha.

They watched, and Ghost was gently lowered to his feet, though he refused to let go of his mate. Burke and Wren still huddled together not far past the family reunion, both smiling.

Michael approached, nervous. "Kane."

"Julian got away, didn't he?" Kane said, without recrimination. Michael blanched, and nodded.

"He may not last long. We shot him several times before he got past us, and he was already wounded. Two of your wolves went after him. You should hear back from them soon."

"We lose any of our own?" Kane asked.

Michael shook his head. "No. We have some silver poisoning, but with Ghost's help, they should be fine. Your wolves found several human scientists hiding nearby. They're dead now. All human guards are dead, too."

Kane lifted his head, and spoke loudly enough for all to hear. "Send wolves for the SUVs. Burke, contact the mansion and have the betas send more cars. Assist the wounded upstairs. We're going home."

23

LOVE, LIKE THE SOUL, NEVER DIES

Ghost nodded to the Suarez wolves as they thanked him profusely, the Black Pine wolves helping them out of the lab. He would heal them all once they were back at the mansion. Burke carried Wren, the small hybrid wrapped in jackets donated by the strike team, swaddled until not even his head was showing, but for his brilliant eyes. Several Black Pine wolves grabbed computers, notepads, and hard drives, smashing everything else. Remus' body was searched, his personal items removed from his body, the same with all the humans. IDs were left behind, but anything electronic or capable of carrying information was stripped away.

A few Black Pine wolfkin came back from the vehicles with white bottles full of accelerant, and they doused every corpse, and the cages, and the instruments. Kane said that anything that could hold DNA or organic traces would be destroyed.

"Ghost? We need to leave. I have charges we can detonate once the building is swept again." Kane spoke quietly from behind him.

"I need you to carry him to the SUV," Ghost said, and Kane looked confused until Ghost nodded at the slumbering wolf. Everyone had been either helped or carried out of the labs but for the clone, still attached to the thing Kane called a respirator.

"Little wolf," Kane began, perhaps to talk him out of it.

"She wants us to save him," Ghost interrupted. "She would call him home."

"It's an empty shell, love," Kane replied. "An empty shell without a soul or mind or spirit—it's not alive, not like you and me. Machines are breathing for it. Mercy would be to unplug it, and let it die before we burn this building to the ground. Maybe calling him home is letting it die in peace."

"If we save him, we save Caius." Ghost argued, and went to the machine that breathed air into the wolf's lungs.

"Caius is still unconscious, and I am thankful for it. If he saw this... this abomination, it would destroy him, not save him. Caius will survive his injuries, and he's been coming out of his grief. Gray Shadow is dead, and gone. Little wolf, let him go. This isn't your grandfather."

"I already smell like Gray Shadow, Kane. Wren bears my mother's features, and is likely my cousin through Roman's seed. How do you think Caius is going to react when he learns he has a new grandson who's half human, looks like his dead daughter, and his other grandson smells like the wolf he loved above all others and should be dead and burned? Do I then lie to him, despite the fact he can smell the truth and sense my lie? Or maybe tell him that there was a clone of his great love, and we let it burn with the building? Imagine if he had stayed behind. You would be dead from a gunshot wound to the head, and Burke would be left to defend Wren, trying to explain why I went feral and ran away after you died, and why he didn't save Gray Shadow. Caius would snap for certain, likely kill Burke and anyone else strong enough to stand up to him, and then go berserk until the humans gunned him down."

"Ghost." Kane sounded sad, but not as certain as before. "This may drive Caius insane if we take it back with us."

"I will not lose Caius. I will not." Ghost declared. "He won't survive this unless he has a reason to. The clone's scent is everywhere. I recognized it immediately, and Caius will too. If he learns about this clone the wrong way, he will break. This sleeping wolf will give him a reason to stay, to hold onto his sanity."

Kane appeared pained, his hair a mess, bruises on his face and neck standing out stark on his exhausted frame. His mate shrugged, at a loss, and Ghost couldn't blame him at all.

Ghost sighed, stroking the soft fur below the wolf's eye. He pried gently at a piece of tape that held the lid closed, and when it came away, a hint of light glinted. Silver eyes. Same as his. He looked back at his mate.

"Do you trust me?"

Kane opened his mouth, then snapped it shut, shoulders drooping. "I do, little wolf. I fear this will end badly, though."

"I promise that everything will be okay."

Ghost picked at the tape that held the tube in the wolf's mouth, and carefully pulled it free. Kane moved closer, as if afraid something might happen, hands up to yank Ghost away. The tube came out next, and Ghost hoped the wolf would keep breathing. It was close, but the body continued to draw air into its lungs. "Can it breathe without help?" Kane asked quietly, face pale, obviously disturbed by the clone.

Ghost put his hand on the side of the wolf's body, and the ribs rose and fell with a slow, shallow rhythm. "He can, but we need to move quickly. Don't put him in with Caius—just you, me, and this wolf."

Kane reached down, and with slow, careful motions, picked up the gray wolf. Kane grimaced, disturbed, but he cradled the wolf carefully to his chest. "I'll come back and set the charges once you're in the SUV with the wolf."

Ghost said nothing. They wouldn't need explosives.

He followed his mate and the sorrowful burden in his arms. They left the sublevel, bodies strewn about. Some torn apart by tooth and claw, others shot with cold efficiency. Blood and fur and gore riddled the stairs. In the lobby, more bodies. None wolfkin—their people made it through with injuries Ghost could heal easily once they were home.

Burke met them outside. The humans' vehicles had been searched, the contents removed for information, the keys in the ignitions. GPS systems were downloaded for more information on unknown locations, and from what Ghost overheard, it was likely they got something helpful.

The Speaker helped Kane put the wolf in the back of the front vehicle. Everyone was already situated, the wounded carted off to the mansion. The only cars remaining were Burke's, with Wren in the front seat, the engine and heat on. Ghost nodded to his cousin, who gave him a shy smile in return.

Kane carefully shut the rear hatch. Burke spoke quietly, handing Kane a satchel that Ghost's nose told him was full of the compounds Kane called explosives. "Caius is still unconscious. He's in the back of my SUV. I'm going to head back."

"Put Caius in his study," Ghost spoke up, both alphas looking to him.

"I'll heal the Suarez wolves and our wounded first. Caius should wake up by the time I'm done."

Burke nodded, and clapped Kane on the shoulder before heading for his vehicle. Burke drove away, and left Kane and Ghost and their sleeping passenger.

"We won't need those," Ghost said, at the same time confirming the building was still empty with his Spiritsight. He turned to face the front, and when he could say that only the dead remained, sent out his will.

As he lit the flames for Roman's pyre, here he lit a spark deep in the building, feeding it until the accelerants caught. The bodies lit first, flames reaching for the walls, the ceilings. An orange glow flicked within the building, and Ghost spread the fire, feeding it will his will and magic.

He let go once the flames fed themselves, the sublevel engulfed.

A warm chuckle broke his concentration, and Kane wrapped an arm around his shoulders. A soft kiss pressed to his temple, and Ghost smiled, leaning into his mate. "Glorious, little wolf. Simply glorious."

Ghost tipped his head back, accepting the kiss that fell softly on his lips. The fire rose, the heat and smoke reaching them in the parking lot. Kane pulled back, and said, "Time to go home."

GHOST ARCHED HIS back, lifting his hands to the ceiling. His muscles ached from the strain of the last few hours, but he was fine. A bit tired, but nothing he couldn't handle. He dropped his arms and backed away from the bed.

Enrique Suarez lay gasping on the bed in the guest quarters, Gabe holding his hand. Enrique was the last healed, insisting that his brothers and family be seen to first. Gabe crawled into the bed, and curled against his father, crying quietly. His father held him close, once again free from silver poisoning and back in his wholly human form.

Ghost slipped away, shutting the door behind him. His mate waited for him in the hall, an anxious expression on his face and worry in his eyes. Kane hugged him close, and Ghost leaned on his mate, breathing in his alpha's heady scent. Kane had taken a shower, washing away blood and gore, relaxed in a pair of sweats and a thin tee.

"I called Ashland, told them we recovered the last of their missing wolves. I spoke to the First Beta, since Heromindes didn't answer his personal number. The beta sounded happy, at least. They should call back tomorrow, presumably after they've talked to Heromindes." Kane said, rubbing Ghost's back.

"Is Heromindes avoiding you specifically or everyone?" Ghost asked, curious. He could understand why Heromindes would want to avoid speaking to Kane, though the alpha was a clan leader, and surely had experience dealing with uncomfortable situations.

"Hero's dishonorable actions during the end of the Tribunal have become public knowledge. I wouldn't be surprised if Hero is dealing with Challenges for clan leader of Ashland. He's got a mess to deal with at home. Talking to me is likely last on his list of things he wants to do," Kane answered, and Ghost thought his mate did an admirable job of sounding unphased by it all.

"I'm glad the Suarez wolves are finally going home to their families. And maybe Heromindes needs to lose his position as clan leader. He lost his honor, and needs to pay for his actions. Ashland needs a stronger wolf to lead them than Heromindes," Ghost said. He took in a deep, cleansing breath, then exhaled, soaking in Kane's strength, his warmth. He paused, thinking, worried he might be missing something in the chaos of the last couple of days. "The other places on the human's list, have they been checked?"

He could feel Kane smiling against his hair. "I have Black Pine wolves scouting each location to make sure there's no more surprises. So far there's been nothing. Each place has either never been used by Remus, or scrubbed before they were abandoned. The wolves I have going through the GPS hard drives and the information from the lab say they've found addresses for likely lab sites, and I will send scouts there as well."

"I hope there's nothing to find," Ghost sighed.

"Me, too." Kane sounded as unwilling to think about what was coming as he was, but the sleeping wolf downstairs wasn't going away.

"Is Caius still out?" Ghost finally asked, gathering the resolve for what was next.

"He is, though Michael says he should be awake soon."

Ghost groaned, but pulled away from his mate. "Almost time."

Kane wore an expression that told Ghost exactly how reluctant he was for the upcoming revelation.

The mansion was quiet, but for the large dining room downstairs. Ghost could sense the party was in full swing. Remus was dead, Julian chased off, and the missing wolves were finally home. For many, the nightmare was over. Only a handful of wolfkin knew about the clone's identity—and they weren't talking. Wren was secure in Burke's suit, the Speaker standing guard over his sleeping mate. Wren had fallen asleep after a pair of betas helped him shower, tucked him into borrowed clothing and into bed, then some food. Burke was unmoving from the chair beside the bed, eyes locked on the young hybrid, as if afraid Wren would disappear with the dawn.

They made it to Caius' study, and Ghost went in first. Michael looked up from his vigil, Caius still in his wilder form, lying on a thick rug before one of the fire places. Ghost went to his grandfather, reaching out with his senses to confirm that Caius was healed, and finding his way back.

"I don't know how he's going to react," Michael said, tears in his eyes, voice thick. The clone lay not far away at all, sharing the same rug, firelight casting a soft glow over the spectacular pattern of grays in every hue imaginable. "The clone is...it's dying. This is cruelty."

Ghost sat between the two wolves, and smiled to himself. Gray Shadow had been the wolf who sought him out in the winter meadow. As a wolf, a form Ghost had trouble seeing in its full splendor under the stars. If Gray Shadow had appeared as a man, Ghost would not have been in any state to listen to his Goddess. Even in death, Gray Shadow was wise.

"Everything will be okay, I promise," Ghost whispered, and put one hand on the clone's side.

Kane moved around the rug, and sat on the opposite side of Caius. Ready to grab the clan leader if things went badly. "I don't understand what you mean to have happen, little wolf. You can't put a soul in a body...can you?"

Ghost smiled over his shoulder at his mate. "I can't, no. But then I won't be the one doing it."

Caius stirred, and Kane jumped. He got to his knees, hands hovering over the dark wolf, but all Caius did was groan, and begin to shift back into his human form. It took him longer than it should have, the gunshot wound taxing him on top of his injuries from the brawl with Julian.

Caius rolled to his back, throwing an arm over his eyes. "I'm alive, then? Could I not be put in my bed? Why the floor?" His voice trailed off, his entire body tensing. He took a deep breath, nostrils flaring as he scented.

Caius dropped his arm, staring up at the ceiling. His dark eyes glowed, full of pain and misery. "I must be dead. I died."

Kane shifted, hesitant, but his movement drew Caius' eye, and the clan leader's face warped into a rictus of pain. "No. Tell me, please, that I am dead, that I am in the forests of our ancestors, and he waits to welcome me home."

Michael gasped, slapping a hand over his mouth, and the shaman bowed over his knees. Ghost hurt, too, but he had faith. She would not instigate this horrible situation without something good coming of it.

Caius sat up, Kane moving with him, his mate holding his hands away from Caius by a few inches, as if afraid Caius would snap and try to kill them all. He might.

Caius had yet to turn his head and look at the wolf he scented. Just as Ghost had known instantly who the sleeping wolf was cloned from, so did Caius. Impossible to forget. Ghost gently petted the sleeping wolf, his breathing shallow, heartbeat weak.

"Caius," Ghost said softly, gentle. "Look at him."

Caius shook his head. His whole body shook, his golden complexion pallid, eyes watery and glowing with distress. Ghost sighed, and moved fast, grabbing Caius' closest hand and bringing it to rest on the sleeping wolf's head.

Caius' reaction was instant. Kane jumped when Caius leaned forward, wrapping both his arms around Caius' torso and keeping him from getting closer. Kane strained, muscles bulging, and Caius half-shifted. He roared, mouth wide, a sound of such horror and grief it shook the floor and walls, the windows creaking. Silence fell over the mansion, as if the building itself were frozen by the torment in that cry.

Ghost didn't flinch when Caius strained against Kane's grip and came closer. His grandfather was inches from the sleeping wolf, eyes locked on the familiar patterns of marvelous grays, the common coloration rendered impossibly beautiful by nature and chance. Caius shook his head, as if in denial, and the hand on the wolf's head sank deeper into thick fur, tender and unsure.

Ghost didn't know what to do, but he knew who did. "Goddess, help us now. Call your wolf home," he whispered.

Caius collapsed, face buried in soft fur, and he cried, quiet sobs into the wolf's neck. Michael could not take anymore, and jumped to his feet, bolting from the room. Kane let go, releasing Caius, sitting behind the other alpha with a hand upon his back, Kane's head bowed.

She did not come with a whisper, or softly spoken words. Movement from a dark corner on the far side of the room drew Ghost's gaze, and She stepped forward just enough for the firelight to line the side of Her face. She gave him a small, mischievous smile, and movement at Her side turned from shadow to wolf. Silver eyes glowed in the dark, winking like stars overhead on a cold winter night.

The gray wolf from the winter meadow loped silently from Her side, paws without sound on the wood floors, crossing the large room far faster than he should have been able to. As he came, his form blurred, shifting patterns of light and shadow, silver-white particles enveloping his body until he was ephemeral energy. He stopped at the sleeping wolf's shoulder, and slowly lowered his head, nose to nose...with himself.

The body absorbed the wolf made of light, silver-white particles flying gently, burrowing under the thick fur, flashing within flesh and bone, until the light-wolf was gone, and the body had taken it all inside.

The familiar and heart-breaking scent of Gray Shadow grew richer, warmer, a hint of pine and fire. Life. The weak heartbeat strengthened, grew more pronounced, and shallow breaths became deeper, longer.

Ghost backed away slowly, and could see a long, bushy tail twitch. Paws flexed, the dreamer chasing after prey, and a deep, long sigh, full of fond exasperation made Ghost smile even as tears ran down his cheeks.

Kane jolted, lifting his head, to stare in disbelief at the sleeping wolf, no doubt sensing what Ghost could. He did not need to invoke his Spiritsight, it came on its own—the soulstar within Caius, fierce red and smoke gray, reached out as if seeking something it had lost, and the silver-white star within the sleeping wolf, so like Ghost's own, answered in kind.

Two halves became one. A sundered soul found its way home.

Gray Shadow inhaled, ears twitching, nose scenting. His tail thumped the floor, once, twice. Caius shuddered. He quieted, and his hands clenched in Shadow's fur, as if afraid to let go.

Ghost carefully stood, and backed away, motioning for Kane to follow. His mate stood, eyes wide, and came to Ghost, grabbing his hand and clutching it tightly. Ghost backed away, guiding Kane with him, and they went to the doorway. Ghost stopped in the door, Kane shocked enough to let Ghost maneuver him so they could both watch.

Caius sat up, face wet from tears. Gray Shadow stretched, claws to tail, groaning as if awakening from a long, wonderful nap. He lifted his head, shaking it, ears flapping against his head, before looking up at Caius.

"Shadow. *Mo ghra*," Caius whispered. "Am I dreaming?"

Ghost grabbed at Kane in excitement, barely holding back his shout when Gray Shadow slowly sat up. Light enveloped him, and much like Ghost learned to Change as a cub, Shadow Changed in a flurry of light. Where Ghost was silver-white, Shadow was smoke gray with swift flares of red.

The soulbond was set. Immutable and perfect.

And so was the man who emerged from the light.

Gray Shadow grinned up at Caius, the same smile Ghost remembered from his past. The vague hints of age were gone, the man sitting now on the rug appearing only a few years older than Ghost. Caius inhaled sharply, hands lifting, to gently cradle Shadow's face with awe and reverence.

"It's me, *mo ghra*. I'm home," Shadow answered. His hands came up, gripping Caius' wrists, holding the alpha to him. "I've missed you."

Whatever Shadow might have said next went unspoken. Caius kissed him, pulling Shadow to him, and Shadow answered in kind, crawling into Caius' lap. The kiss was deep and almost frantic, and Ghost grew red in the face, looking away.

She was gone, nothing in the corner now but empty shadows.

Ghost grinned, and tugged on his shocked mate. He pulled the door to the study shut. He tapped the lock, and it set from the outside, insuring the occupants some privacy.

He turned, and somehow seeing the whole of Black Pine crammed into the hallway didn't surprise him. Expressions ranged from absolute shock, like Kane, to confusion with Michael, and only Burke grinned as widely as Ghost.

"It's late. Why are we all in the hallway?" Ghost chided with a wide grin, waving his hands at the clan. "Neither of them will be out of there for several hours—I think we can all get some sleep."

EPILOGUE

"YOU WANT ME TO WHAT?" KANE ASKED, AGHAST.

Caius smiled at him, wide and cheerful. "I'm stepping down as Clan Leader. It's your turn."

Caius looked exhausted, but somehow cheerful. It might have something to do with the shaman who sat on the nearby couch, watching every move Caius made with a fond, mysterious smile and joy in his eyes. Caius gave off a heady combination of scents, from the sweetness of happiness to the cloying aroma of exhaustion. Caius smiled at Kane's loss of words, and Kane had trouble even remembering the last time he saw Caius smile. He couldn't. "My time as clan leader is over," Caius continued, and Kane tried to find a coherent response.

"I…" Never in his forty-four years did he ever expect to hear Caius say those words. He fully expected to have to one day kill Caius to take Black Pine, and since there had yet to be moment that pushed him to that point, Kane had expected to remain Heir his entire life.

"I think you should," Ghost said to him from the other side of Caius' desk, the little shaman poking about as usual. "Grandpa Caius and Grandpa Shadow have been through a lot. One of the reasons everything got so messed up was because Grandpa Caius was a Clan Leader and didn't know how to stop being one. Letting go of the position and giving it to you now that Grandpa Shadow is back is a great idea."

"Yes, thank you, cub," Caius said with a straight face, though his lips twitched. Shadow laughed from his seat on the nearby couch, the shaman so like Ghost they could have been brothers. It was less in their appearance and more in their behaviors. "Though I think 'through a lot' is a mild understatement."

Ghost snorted out a laugh. He came over to the desk and swiped Marla's portrait before running over to his other grandfather and sitting beside Shadow. Gray Shadow lifted an arm and embraced his grandson, their heads pressed together as they looked at the picture of Ghost's mother.

Kane returned his attention to Caius, still shocked. "Me, Clan Leader of Black Pine."

Caius nodded. "You're more than qualified. Why else were you my Heir all these years? I have every reason now to abdicate, and you have every reason to take the role. It's been your destiny for over half your life. It's time."

"But what about…"

"What about Wren?" Caius interrupted, one brow raised. Kane nodded. "Well, according to both our mates," Caius smiled at that last word. "There is a solution to Wren's predicament. I say let the shamans settle the issue with the youngling. We need not make public the origin of his birth if the shamans can help him find his wolf. Dr. Harmon is Wren's adopted father—and I did promise to spare his life for another day or so for his help. Now that Wren is here, I am going to let you and the youngling decide what to do with the human."

Kane frowned at that, but Caius had a point. Wren was fragile and weak, and though he claimed no affection for the man who'd made him, Kane wouldn't kill the boy's only parent without talking to Wren first. Caius continued, interrupting Kane's thoughts. "And Birch Grove and Ashland are both in our debt—the Suarez wolves are safe and on their way home to Worcester soon, and Julian's treachery and dishonor has been made known. I expect him to be challenged for the rank of clan leader any day now. I doubt his successor will spare him."

Kane nodded, agreeing. Birch Grove was in a riotous place right now—Julian held control only by his teeth, and packs and lesser clans were breaking off in droves by the day. Julian was still wounded, shot with silver and injuries from the fight with Kane and Caius. Unless Julian was deposed, Birch Grove may not last much longer. Ashland was indeed in Black Pine's debt—Enrique Suarez, Gabe's father and Heromindes' favorite cousin, was quite vocal and adamant in his praise for Black Pine, and especially Kane and Ghost. Heromindes did not want strife in his clan nor his family, so his animosity towards Kane and Black Pine was lessening a bit. The likelihood of a blood feud was growing more remote. Heromindes held onto Ashland Clan by a slim margin, and had defeated a pair of Challenges to keep his position.

The scouts Kane sent out to check the remainder of Dr. Harmon's list reported back that the locations held nothing living. The first few were empty, but he was awakened by Burke in the early morning hours with reports of new discoveries. Plenty of the locations appeared to be information caches, holding servers and file cabinets full of data. Any place that once held people or active employees appeared to be abandoned in a hurry; word must have spread somehow of Remus' downfall. No signs of more wolfkin prisoners, though, and Kane took that to heart.

Kane, since Caius and Shadow were not to be disturbed, had ordered everything to be broken down and brought back to the mansion, where it would all be sorted and searched. Anyone discovered, be it human governments or private citizens, who might have been in league with Remus would eventually feel their wrath.

A knock at the door interrupted them. "Enter," Caius called, and Gabe stuck his head in around the door.

"Gabe! How's your family doing? Are they ready to go home?" Ghost called from his seat. Gabe came in slowly, shutting the door behind him, and he had some trouble taking his eyes off Gray Shadow. The shaman gave the young alpha a kind smile.

"Um," Gabe stuttered, but he gathered his courage and came deeper into the room. "I was wondering if the offer to remain in Black Pine was still open?"

"It is," Caius replied, and Gabe all but drooped with relief. "Though that's not up to me anymore."

Caius nodded at Kane, and Gabe's face lit up in a wide smile. He all but ran to Kane, stopping a foot away and vibrating with happiness. "That's wonderful news, Alpha Kane! Congratulations! You'll make a wonderful clan leader, I know it."

Kane looked in askance at Caius, but the other alpha shrugged and walked away, joining Gray Shadow on the couch. Ghost got up to make room, and the two mates curled into each other, as if they were the only two wolfkin left in the world, for all the attention they paid anyone else.

"I," Kane coughed, and tried again. "You're family, now, Gabe. You'll always have a home here."

Ghost barreled into Gabe, hugging his best friend ecstatically. Kane frowned, and shot Caius a dark look. "You already abdicated, didn't you?"

Caius drew back from kissing Shadow, and smirked at Kane. "I sent all the First Betas and Heirs that act as point of contact for the clans around the world an email last night. I said you were the new Clan Leader of Black Pine, and I was retiring to enjoy life with my new mate. There's an entire inbox of well wishes if you want to get started."

Ghost and Gabe descended on him, and pulled him from the study. They chattered on about Gabe learning to control his gift of the Voice, and the problem with Wren. The small hybrid was weak, though he was recovering from his ordeal, albeit slowly. Burke's careful and devoted attendance upon his mate was the stuff of romantic poems, according to the gossip from the betas.

Kane let himself be dragged into the dining room. He was drawn from his chaotic thoughts by a heavy, expectant silence in the large room, and looked up to see the entire clan gathered. Even cubs were in attendance, pulled from school and university. Black Pine was thousands strong, and while they all couldn't fit in the dining room, a few hundred were crammed inside.

Gabe darted out of the way, sitting with Burke and young Wren, who leaned on Burke for support. Burke smiled and gave Kane a nod, and he warmed at the implicit love and support he could feel from his best friend.

Ghost took his hand, gifting him with a brilliant smile full of love before turning to the assembled wolves. Ghost lifted their joined hands, and shouted.

"Wolves of Black Pine, I give you your new Clan Leader, Alpha Kane!"

The cheers rose in a deafening crescendo, and Kane pulled Ghost into his arms, kissing his mate.

The Wolfkin Saga will continue.

CHARACTER LIST

Characters from The Wolfkin Saga Books #1 & #2

An "Old World wolf" is a wolfkin born before the Great Exodus to North America.

In no order, whatsoever. Contains massive spoilers, so read the books first!

Caius McLennan—Clan Leader of Black Pine, greater alpha, grandfather of Ghost, Old World wolf, age unknown, but several centuries at a minimum

Ghost/Luca—Shaman, soulbonded mate to Kane, grandson of Gray Shadow and Caius, 19 years old

Kane—Greater alpha, gifted with the Voice, Heir of Black Pine, 44 yrs old

Burke—Black Pine Speaker, greater alpha, third ranked wolfkin in Black Pine, 49 yrs old

Sophia—Black Pine First Beta, Old World wolf, over 400 years old, becomes Alpha Mate to Royrick alongside Gerald

Andromeda—clan leader of Red Fern, female alpha; Old World wolf, older sister of Shaman River, theorized to be the oldest living being on the planet

River—Shaman, Red Fern and Black Pine, last child of Stormcloud, youngest sibling to Andromeda, Old World wolf

Gerald McLennan—youngest living child of Caius McLennan; lesser alpha, Black Pine wolfkin, 225 years old, becomes Alpha Mate to Royrick along with Sophia

Roman McLennan—second to youngest living child of Caius, great traitor of the clans, mass murderer, killed by Heromindes during the Tribunal in Bk #2, 250 years old

Gray Shadow—Greatest Shaman of the clans, Black Pine, former lover of Caius, grandfather to Ghost, dies in Book #1, returns to the living in Book #2. Becomes Caius McLennan's mate. Several centuries old, exact age unknown. Old World wolf.

Helen—Andromeda's great grandchild, whom Andromeda named after Helen of Troy. Teenager, though not yet an adult by wolfkin standards. Only recently found her wolf.

Marjorie—Andromeda's daughter, nominated to replace Sophia as Black Pine First Beta.

Claire—Andromeda's daughter. Traitor, occasional lover of Roman McLennan. Was banished after receiving 100 lashes with a silver-laced whip as punishment for her crimes.

Simon Remus—Human businessman, runs Remus Acquisitions, responsible for kidnapping, experimentation, and murder of hundreds of wolfkin. Took over after his older brother took the fall for the Baxter Ambush that killed Gray Shadow, and was killed by Caius. Simon dies at the end of Book #2, Kane kills him.

Dr. Mitchell Harmon—Human scientist, works for Remus. Created Wren in a lab, adopted Wren after the boy showed no wolfkin traits. Engineered a soulless clone of Gray Shadow. Captured by Kane at the end of Book #1. Still held captive at the end of Book #2.

Julian Richards—Clan Leader of Birch Grove, Mad Dog of New York City, greater alpha. Joined human society as a business mogul, humans unaware. Psychopath. Sat on the Tribunal. Andromeda kicks him out of Baxter when he becomes violent.

Mercuriel—Clan Leader of Dread Claw. Greater alpha. Phenomenally strong. Tribunal member, Old World wolf.

Heromindes—Clan Leader of Ashland. Greater alpha. Charges Kane with illegal use of the Voice and levies claims of blasphemy against Kane as well.

Royrick—Clan Leader of Red Wraith. Greater alpha. Former lover of Sophia. Tribunal member. Manages to woo Sophia into taking him back, and claims Gerald as a mate as well.

Dr. Walsh—Human scientist who takes over after Dr. Harmon was taken captive by Kane. Killed during the rescue by Ghost.

Wren Harmon—Wolfkin/human hybrid. Sick, weak, and suffering from chronic illness. Adopted by Dr. Harmon after Wren failed to present wolfkin traits. Only successful attempt to combine species. All wolfkin traits are suppressed, though Ghost can see his soulstar, and claims it is not human. Immune to silver. Ghost believes Wren to be the biological child of Roman McLennan. Becomes Burke's soulbonded mate at the end of Book #2.

Josiah—Wolfkin beta, former First Beta of Black Pine. Went feral and disappeared after the death of his children and soulbonded mate, Marla. Son of Gray Shadow.

Marla McLennan—Black Pine beta, only daughter of Caius McLennan, soulbonded mate to Josiah and mother of Ghost. Died in the same ambush that killed her cubs and Gray Shadow.

Gabriel Suarez—Greater alpha of Ashland, Heromindes' cousin. Captured by Roman and experimented upon by humans, then sold to underground sex slave traffickers. His father Enrique Suarez and his uncles remain captives of Remus. Gabe's trauma spurs his gift of the Voice into manifesting. He has no control over the ability. Becomes Ghost's best friend.

Enrique Suarez—Father of Gabriel, greater alpha of Ashland. One of the captured wolfkin held by Remus in the labs.

Catherine (Cat) Medeiros—biologist and conservationist, wolf specialist. Raises Ghost after finding him as a wolf cub, mistakes him for a feral wolf. Runs a wolf sanctuary in New Brunswick.

Glen Mitchell—Human. Wildlife photographer, specializes in large predators. Runs the wolf sanctuary with Cat. Ghost calls Glen "his human alpha." Raises Ghost with Cat.

Sebastien Remus—Human, first began hunting and capturing wolfkin for experiments. Simon, his younger brother, arranged for Roman to have him killed so Simon could take over Remus Acquisitions. Dies in Book #1.

Sarah Suarez—Gabriel's little sister, abused by the same humans that hurt her older brother. Ghost heals her and her family in Book #1.

ALSO BY SHEENA JOLIE

The Wolfkin Saga

Wolves of Black Pine
Wolf of the Northern Star

Beacon Hill Sorcerer Series*

(as SJ Himes)
The Necromancer's Dance
The Necromancer's Dilemma
The Necromancer's Reckoning
A History of Trouble (collection)
Mastering the Flames
Love Spring Eternal
Blood Omen
The Necromancer's War

Werewolves of Boston[*]

Wolfsbane

Realms of Love

The Solstice Prince
The River Prince

Scales of Honor

Knight's Fire

Standalone Titles

Saving Silas
Treasured

(*An *Infinite Arcana* title)

ABOUT SHEENA

Sheena Jolie (they/them) resides in MidCoast Maine, close enough to the beach to be enchanted by the views and annoyed by seagulls at the same time. They live with Wolf and Silfur, two cats who love them but hate each other.

Sheena writes urban, epic, and sci-fi fantasy romances with an emphasis on plot and character development. Almost all of their characters are LGBTQ+...and that is very much intentional.

To keep current on what Sheena is working on
and where to find them, visit their website:

www.sjhimes.com

SPECIAL THANKS TO PATRONS

Valerie Oakley
Giacinta Hooker
Kayla Betts
Ange Capra
Janessa Edwards
Stephanie Diaz
Daniel Attaway
Cheryl Russell
Kaci Bowen
Lisa Johnson
Karla Monahan
Kirsten Ozimek
Hillary Schommer
Grace Long Pope